A Few Brave Men

a novel

by John R. Taylor

and Earl W. Green

iPicturebooks
Habent Sua Fata Libelli

iPicturebooks
1230 Park Avenue
New York, New York 10128
Tel: 212-427-7139
bricktower@aol.com • www.BrickTowerPress.com

Library of Congress Cataloging-in-Publication Data

John R. Taylor
Earl W. Green
A Few Brave Men
ISBN-13: 978-1-87696-337-8, Trade Paper

Library of Congress Control Number: 2011927491
Fiction/Suspense, Adult/General
Aviation History/Adventure

Based on the original screenplay “The La May Story” by Earl W. Green

First Trade Paper Edition

May 2011

A Few Brave Men

a novel

Book I

The Cold Winds of War

by John R. Taylor

and Earl W. Green

ACKNOWLEDGEMENTS

This novel has been a labor of love for the late great Earl Green and for me. The Second World War period of America's history made the research very challenging. The best part of the research was the time spent meeting with the late General Curtis E. Lemay. His story and place in American history is inspiring, to say the least. A close second is my time discussing the flight characteristics of the B-25, B-17 and B-29 with an aviator extraordinaire, Ronnie Gardener. He is an exceptional aviator who is qualified in all of the old World War II aircraft as well numerous modern day jet aircraft. Today, he is retired from a lifetime career of flying. Now, he donates his spare time to furthering aviation history and conducting flight demonstrations of old Warbirds at air shows across the country. He works tirelessly with The Cavanaugh Flight Museum in Addison, Texas to insure that the legacy of aviation continues. His input to this book was invaluable.

I would be completely amiss if I did not thank Jim Cavanaugh for his philanthropy in the field of aviation history. He personally funds the acquisition, restoration and demonstration of this country's greatest Warbirds. The Cavanaugh Flight Museum is a non-profit 501(c)(3) educational organization devoted to promoting aviation studies and to perpetuating America's aviation heritage. Thanks to Jim Cavanaugh, the museum fulfills its mission through the preservation of vintage aircraft and by collecting materials related to the history of aviation. If you have a spare dollar or two send it to this magnificent museum. (www.cavanaughflightmuseum.com). It deserves your support. Thanks Jim. Your efforts are greatly appreciated. Your generosity will sustain the history of aviation for generations to come.

My thanks also go to Scott and Jim Darnell who have been of incredible assistance in the cover art and the publishing of this book. Lastly my thanks go to Garrett Glover whose editing and creative critique has been fantastic. Now that the book is completed I don't have to grimace when I see his name on Caller ID.

Thanks Earl....we did it.

DEDICATION

It is the purpose of this book to tell a story about military heroes from the era of the Second World War. America was at its finest during the Second World War. Everyone of age rolled up their sleeves and did their part for the war effort. It's no wonder that today we proudly refer to that period as the "Greatest Generation. "

My father was a WWII veteran who explained that "Heroes" and "Great Men" are titles that we often bestowed upon special people. I also remember the words of Fleet Admiral William F. "Bull" Halsey, Jr. who said during the battle for Guadalcanal in 1942, "***There are no great men. There are only great challenges that ordinary men are forced by circumstances to meet.*** " These are powerful words and reflect the situation that each of our special people encountered in their individual heroic efforts. But it's hard for me to not to think of "Heroes" when given the contributions by military and civilian heroes like Omar Bradley, George Marshall, Chester Nimitz, George Patton, Chesty Puller, Jimmy Doolittle and Curtis Lemay. Each of these men to mention a very few came to the aid of this country in its time of need. There are countless stories about these and many other American heroes that should be mentioned and remembered by all Americans. However, in this book, I chose to focus on Curtis Lemay. While this is a novel it does tells many stories of real people who distinguished themselves and fictitious characters that are composites of real people who did great things. It also reflects the historical events in the development of Strategic Bombardment, the development of the B-29 and the events associated with the air war in Europe and over Japan.

Curtis Emerson Lemay stands out in my mind as his contributions to this country spanned five decades. He distinguished himself in the early years of World War II in the development of strategic daylight bombing in B-17's over Europe. Later he took a hastily developed and badly flawed B-29 bomber and developed it into a viable and potent weapon system flying against Japan from bases in China and the Marianas. His individual efforts in Europe and in the Pacific directly led to the end of World War II in both theaters.

After World War II, he recognized the growing nuclear threat to the United States posed by the Soviet Union. He took the remnants of the old B-29 fleet and developed a potent deterrent in the creation of the Air Force Strategic Air Command (SAC). Lemay's philosophy in the development of this mighty air operation was "Peace through Strength." SAC continued to be a major deterrent to foreign aggression into the 1990's. Today a modernized version of SAC still maintains the vigil against aggression through the use of bombers, intercontinental ballistic missiles, and sophisticated 21st century high-tech weapons. This is the legacy of Curtis Lemay. Admiral Halsey may be right about there not being any great men. However, I'm compelled to revere General Curtis Lemay as a Hero as well as a great man. It's with pride that I dedicate this book to General Curtis Emerson Lemay.

PROLOGUE

A FUNNY THING HAPPENED TO ME ON THE WAY TO WAR.

Major John C. Kennedy and a stocky First Lieutenant stood on the tarmac of Brooks Field in Texas watching the repeated flawless landings of a North American O-47 observation plane. After a full stop landing, the plane taxied over to the two officers and turned off the engine. The pilot, Samuel Barton Coltrane, an athletic built black haired Second Lieutenant, approached the two men and saluted. "Pardon me, Major," he said with true military protocol, "have you given any thought to my request for reassignment to bombers?"

The major looked into the hazel eyes of the nearly six foot aviator. "Bart, you really want to go from this agile 180 miles an hour observation aircraft to that lumbering LB5 Keystone bomber?" You know that damned thing is like flying an outhouse at a max speed of 95 miles an hour.

"Yes Sir, I do. When the war comes, that monster and the new B-17 will be in the thick of things. That's where the action will be and that's where I want to be."

The First Lieutenant took the stubby unlit cigar out of his mouth and said "So you think a lot of the role bombers will play in combat."

Before Bart Coltrane could reply, Major Kennedy interrupted, "Bart, let me introduce you to Lieutenant Curt Lemay. Curt is here to get a checkout in the O-47 before he goes to the Second Bomber Group."

Kennedy resumed, "Lemay here is a great pilot and an even better navigator but has the control touch of a gorilla when it comes to the O-19. Think you could help him?" Then, before Coltrane could reply, he added "Make you a deal. If you can get that control grip problem resolved, I'll get you transferred to bombers."

"Deal!" exclaimed Bart, who was more commonly referred to by his peers as Black Bart. "Lieutenant Lemay gave me ten minutes for a pit stop and to get my training aid and we'll go make smooth holes in the sky."

Bart took off at a run to the operations office latrine and came back on a slow trot to his aircraft. A couple of minutes later, he went to the two aviators and said, "Sir, we're ready when you're, this shouldn't take more than an hour."

Lemay looked at Major Kennedy without expression or comment and started walking to the observation plane. As he got in, Coltrane came up to him and took away the flight gloves normally used by Army Air Force pilots. This didn't faze Lemay until he started to reach for the control stick, his hand stopped when he saw that it had been wrapped with Texas barbed wire. "What the hell is this, Lieutenant?" Lemay said in a loud and gruff voice.

"Sir, that's my control touch training aid and every time you squeeze or jerk the control stick, you're going to know it," Coltrane said with a positive tone. It won't hurt if you're gentle, Sir."

The aircraft took off and flew a series of maneuvers, turns and normal combat tactics before returning to the airfield. After five touch and go landings and takeoffs that got better with each succeeding attempt, the plane turned off the runway and went back to the waiting Major Kennedy. Coltrane and Lemay went over to Kennedy. Lemay had a slightly blood-soaked rag in his right hand.

Kennedy looked at Lemay and asked, "Was that you or Bart making those landings?"

Bart interjected "Those were all his landings, Sir."

Lemay took the cigar out of his mouth and said, "If the 7th Bomb Group doesn't have a position for him, I'll find one for him in the 2nd Bomb Group. He knows his aircraft and can fly it very well. He sure taught me a lot in a short period. Thanks to both of you for helping me on this transition. I'll be headed for home base." He saluted the Major then extended his left hand to shake Bart's. "Thanks, I mean it, if you want to fly for me in the 2nd Bomb Group, let me know." He turned and started walking away.

Bart and Major Kennedy stood there watching the departing Lemay. Kennedy then commented, "There's a man that will someday make aviation history."

Bart turned to Kennedy and said, "Not before his hand heals."

CHAPTER 1

The Boeing 299 prototype touched down at Wright Field in Dayton, Ohio on the evening of October 20, 1935, its touchdown less than perfect due to the stiff crosswind. It taxied to the parking area. Edward Wells and Claremont Egtvedt, both wearing civilian clothing, anxiously stood near an old Army Air Force aircraft parked near the end of the ramp on the airfield. They had been observing the wobbly landing of the new bomber but were impressed with its size as it taxied to the ramp. A 1935 Ford pickup was parked a few feet away from them.

Edward Wells glanced at his watch, and then back at the approaching B-17.

"We flew two thousand miles in nine hours!" Wells exclaimed. "Not bad!"

Egtvedt shook his head in amazed agreement.

The 299 pulled into the parking area and turned broadside to Wells and Egtvedt. The pilot, Leslie Tower, ran the engines up, cut the switches, looked out the cockpit window and waved at Wells and Egtvedt. The four crew members, Tower, Wait, Benton and Iago, emerged from the cockpit one by one and dropped to the concrete ramp below where they were greeted by Wells and Egtvedt.

"Welcome to Wright Field," Wells said.

"Where's all the Army brass?" Tower asked.

"You're two hours ahead of your ETA, Les," Wells said. "They're still over at the Officers' Club."

Wells and Egtvedt shook hands with the crewmen, all of them

obviously jubilant over the success of the flight.

"You've designed one hell of an airplane, Ed!"

Edward Wells grinned. "Any problems coming out?"

"Hell, no!" Tower said. "We stayed on automatic pilot almost from the time we cleared Seattle."

"What about fuel consumption, Les?" Egtvedt asked. "How did that go?"

"I'd say there's about an hour's reserve left in the tank."

Egtvedt continue. "You cruised at twelve thousand?"

"That's right, Clair," Tower said, pulling his leather flying helmet off.

Wells shook his head in amazement. "If my calculations are correct that's two-hundred thirty-seven miles per hour average…"

"Amazing," Egtvedt said. "Well, better get our debriefing over with. Major Hill's going to start wringing 'er out early in the morning."

A gust of wind moved the horizontal elevator on the fortress attracting Wells' attention. "The elevator locking pins, they aren't in the locked position."

Louis Wait, the co-pilot said, "I'll get 'em, Les." Wait went back to the cockpit hatch and climbed inside.

Wells turned to Tower. "Be sure you brief Major Hill on those locking pins. They're a …new innovation. They must be released before takeoff."

Tower nodded. "I guess we need some kind of "preflight check list pasted up in the cockpit somewhere. Too many damned things to remember."

"Yeah," Wells said, as he looked at the aircraft looking for any abnormality.

Egtvedt began to walk towards the Ford pickup and the others followed him. Wells and Tower brought up the rear.

"Rumors are going around that Congress has already authorized production for a hundred eighty five ships, Les," Wells paused. "That's, if we get through these final evaluations. I guess half the brass from the Pentagon will be down here observing 'em."

"Relax, Ed." Tower said. He gestured back towards the prototype "She's already exceeded every damned spec in the book."

"Yes, I know. The whole theory of strategic bombardment, though;

it's still unacceptable to a lot of people in Washington. Failure in any segment of these evaluation trials could spell disaster." Wells paused unconsciously in thought then continued walking. "It would be a costly failure, Les…for Boeing…and the Air Corps."

They arrived at the pickup where Louis Wait rejoined them in a trot.

Wells grinned. "Sorry about the transportation, gentlemen. The Air Corps people had a couple of staff cars set aside for personal comfort but you got here too early."

"Too bad! One of those times where the bird was too early to get the worm!"

"You better stick to running Boeing aircraft, Clair. I don't think you'd make it as a standup comic," Leslie Tower said as they climbed into the pickup and drove away.

It was shortly after nine the next morning as the Boeing 299 prototype B-17 prepared to take off with a military crew as a part of its acceptance by the military. Major Ployer Hill sat in the pilot's seat with Lieutenant Donald Putt in the co-pilot's position and Les Tower standing between them. They all gazed intently as the instrument panel before them.

"Left magneto," Major Hill said, switching.

"Right magneto," Lieutenant Putt said, and did the same.

Then Major Hill glanced at Les Tower and Tower nodded.

"Looks okay, Major."

Major Hill continued to do a check on the aircraft. "Gyro's?" He asked.

"Gyro's set, Sir," Lieutenant Putt said.

"Generators?"

"All on, Sir."

Major Hill then spoke into the intercom. "Intercom check."

Everyone then turned to look at Benton. "Benton here," He said.

A moment later they spotted Iago standing by the rear fuselage and he and Major Hill looked at each other and nodded, then Major Hill picked up the microphone.

"Boeing two-nine-nine to Wright Tower. Ready to go when cleared,"

Major Hill said.

"Boeing two-nine-nine, this is Wright Tower; the field has been cleared of all traffic," The tower operator said. "Cleared for takeoff."

The engines of the Boeing 299 began to run up for takeoff and then the giant ship started to move slowly down the runway. The co-pilot, Lieutenant Putt, noticed that the elevators were in the parked position, but said nothing.

The, press, including one network radio reporter, were standing on a press platform, all wearing binoculars suspended from neck straps. Some of the reporters were peering at the 299 in the distance.

"And it's an auspicious day for the U.S. Army Air Corps here at Wright Field, Ladies and Gentlemen," the radio reporter said. *"In just a matter of moments, Major Ployer B. Hill and Lieutenant Donald Putt from the Air Corps test center will begin the final performance evaluation of the largest land plane ever built in the United States...a veritable 'Flying Fortress'...weighing in at fifteen tons!"*

The radio reporter looked around at the large group of military officials and congressional types standing in the foreground. He could see the 299 in the distance, now in takeoff position at the end of the runway. Wells and Egtvedt stood near a mobile radio van with a speaker mounted on top to allow those assembled to hear all radio communications with the 299.

"Ranking military officials from the Pentagon along with key members of the Congressional Military appropriations committee are on hand to observe... and there she goes!"

The 299's engines came up full and the aircraft began its takeoff roll. The announcer could barely control his excitement.

"I've covered a lot of events, folks, but never anything quite like this! What a sight! A beautifully streamlined, gleaming giant of a plane rolling down the runway."

Everyone watched as the 299 prototype gained momentum, and the roar of the engines was deafening. The aircrafts tail lifted from the runway as the flow of air lifted it just prior to lifting off into flight.

Lieutenant Putt, Les Tower and Major Hill were all deep in concentration as the aircraft hurtled down the runway. Major Hill moved his right hand from the throttle console and began to apply back pressure to the control yoke as Lieutenant Putt followed through on the throttles with his own left hand.

Then a bewildered expression crossed Major Hill's features as he applied back pressure on the unmoving control yoke.

"What the hell!" Major Hill said.

"Damn!" Les Tower said. He reached frantically for the elevator release lever. "The elevators are still locked!"

"Reduce power," Major Hill said. "I'm going to let 'er back down."

The left wing of the prototype began to drop dangerously as the co-pilot attempted the power reduction.

"The wing, Major!" Lieutenant Putt said.

Major Hill struggled to counter control against the torque that was pulling the left wing down. "Reduce the power, damn it!"

Lieutenant Putt's attempts to throttle back were momentarily hindered by Tower's attempts to move the locking pin lever at the base of the throttle console so the controls would work.

The 299 arched towards the runway, its left wing dragging only a few feet off the ground. The cockpit crew stared out the windscreen in shock as the prototype begins careening, its left wing dragging only a few feet from the ground.

"Look out!" Major Hill said as he stared at the approaching ground in shock "Ahh, Shit!"

Hill, Tower and Putt braced for the impact. Major Hill, his face frozen in fear stared straight ahead. The aircraft hit the ground with a thud and with the second impact the Prototype skidded wildly before coming to rest. For the crowd of military and congressional observers, the noise was loud and terrifying, but not as terrifying as the eerie silence that followed the crash. Dust made it almost impossible to see the aircraft from the reviewing stand.

The prototype fuselage was separated and gaping just left of the trailing edge of the wings; the left wing itself was demolished. Then with a flash there was a fire. The fire raced inboard along the left wing from the ruptured fuel tanks to the main fuselage.

The radio reporter was momentarily speechless and horrified at what he was seeing.

"My God!" the reporter said. *"It just crashed!! The 299…it's…it's on fire, ladies and gentlemen!"*

The military and congressional observers continued to stare in stunned silence at the 299 while Egtvedt and Wells race toward one of the staff cars parked by the press platform. The wail of sirens could be heard in the distance.

Fire was billowing up on the far side of the wreckage. Lieutenant Putt lifted himself out through the right cockpit window. Dazed, his clothing smoking from the intense heat, he staggered along the separated right wing and dropped to the ground. Half crawling, half walking, he dragged himself away from the wreckage.

. Benton and Iago emerged from the hatch near the tail assembly and staggered away from the wreckage, obviously in shock. The terrified expression on their faces was one of shock and awe.

The first ambulance arrived on the scene, accompanied by two staff cars -- one filled with Army officers, the other carrying Wells and Egrvedt. The siren on the ambulance was still on, causing an air of panic.

Two young lieutenants jumped from the staff car, running. One of them, Lieutenant Giovanni, ran up the right wing to peer inside the cockpit. The other, Lieutenant John Harmon and the other occupants of the two cars, directed their attention to Putt, Iago and Benton.

Lieutenant Giovanni pulled the unconscious Les Tower up from the cockpit and out through the cockpit window. Tower's clothing was also smoking from the intense heat in the cockpit.

Lieutenant Giovanni dragged the lifeless Tower to the end of the wing where ambulance personnel took over and started emergency treatment.

Giovanni grabbed a blanket from one of the stretchers, threw it over his head, raced back along the wing and entered the wreckage through the gaping break in the fuselage. He worked his way forward through the dense smoke and heat to the cockpit area. He unstrapped the unconscious Major Hill and attempted to lift him from the seat. Major Hill's boot, which was caught in the mangled rudder pedal assembly made it impossible to get him out. Giovanni took a pen knife from his pocket and cuts the boot free. Then he started lifting him out of the seat and through the cockpit window. An Army officer pulled Major Hill free and dragged him along the wing as Lieutenant Giovanni crawled through the window, badly burned.

Base fire fighting units continued arriving on the scene, the fireman beginning to work on the blaze on the opposite side of the wreckage. The wails of sirens started to diminish as the ambulances began departing the scene with the injured. The silence was a welcome relief to those around the burning aircraft.

The military and congressional people began to gather near the press platform area in stunned silence. Some began to walk to the parked automobiles.

The radio reporter turned to a broadcast engineer on the ground by a mobile broadcast van.

The radio reporter gestured in the direction of the departing observers. "Rig a hand mike…down there…on the double!"

"You got it!" The van technician said.

A senator and a brigadier general entered one of the several Army staff cars parked near the press platform. The radio reporter approached them.

"Senator Clay?"

The Senator paused, looking towards the radio reporter as he walked towards him, microphone in hand. He thought this would be a great political opportunity to drive another nail in the coffin of the Air Corps plans for the future.

"Senator, would you comment on the…uh…situation here?"

"I'd be glad to share my views with your listeners, young man," the Senator said.

The radio reporter looked toward the van for and signaled for a break in the network broadcast. The broadcast engineer replied by giving a thumbs up signal.

He paused, his fingers pressing his earphones closer as he waited intently, while looking towards the radio reporter.

"Stand by." The broadcast engineer raised his hand for the "you're on" signal.

The radio reporter waited momentarily, and then nodded to his cue.

"Ladies and Gentlemen, we've been standing by here at Wright Field to bring you the latest developments on the tragic crash of the Boeing 299. I have Senator Titus Clay, a ranking member of the military appropriations committee here with me now." The radio reporter turned to the Senator. "Senator, it's been a tragic day for the Air Corps…a day that will have far reaching affects no doubt. But perhaps the most unfortunate of all is that this airplane has come close to fulfilling the Air Corps long struggle to achieve strategic air power capability."

"Do you feel, Senator, that the Congress will go on with its plan to order several hundred production models of the 299, assuming, of course, that the cause of the accident can be isolated…and corrected?"

"For years, officers of the Army Air Corps have shoved the so-called 'Mitchell-Douhet' theory of strategic air supremacy down the throats of anyone who would take the time to listen," Senator Clay said. "Frankly, I've always found it hard to believe that this great nation would even accept a theory that embraces the indiscriminate bombardment of helpless civilian population from thin air. Strategic bombardment is an intrinsically unacceptable and unworkable theory."

The Senator dramatically gestured towards the 299 crash site and said in a condescending tone, "There's a wrecked airplane out there…people critically injured…millions of dollars down the drain! How many more lives must be sacrificed at Billy Mitchell's altar of strategic bombardment before the country rises up in collective protest?"

The Senator's remarks were incredible to the radio reporter. "What about our own hemispheric defense, Senator?" He asked.

The Senator was pleased the reporter has taken his bait. "Battleships! Battleships are our first line of defense against any enemy who would dare approach this nation on sea lanes lying on either side of the continent."

The radio reporter, realizing that he had been "used" attempted to reintroduce a remnant of objective debate.

"But…uh…would you preclude the possibility of an enemy

establishing airfields in this hemisphere and flying his own heavy bombers over our country? Isn't a part of the Air Corps' objective to develop an offensive capability against that kind of enemy presence?"

"What enemy? What bombers?" Senator Clay asked. "You see, even you've succumbed to General Mitchell's techniques of fear! Just who is this obscure enemy with sufficient air power to blow up Pearl Harbor out there in the Hawaiian Islands as the General has so dramatically theorized from time to time…or to bomb New York City, San Francisco…or London?"

"Thank you, Senator, thank you," the radio reporter said.

The embattled radio reporter turned to the Brigadier General who stood looking quietly at the ground during the preceding interview.

The radio reporter "General…"

The General raised his hand in a gesture of refusal. "Sorry."

As the Senator and the General entered the military staff vehicle driven by an Army Air Corps sergeant, the reporter recounted the events of the crash, then indicated a cut to the broadcast engineer.

The Senator's car began to pull away from the scene and the radio reporter gazed after it.

Wells and Egtvedt stood about fifty feet from the prototype, listening to the crackle of cooling metal while gazing at the demolished Boeing prototype. Wells shook his head as he stared at the smoking ruins in disbelief, "Who could have guessed this would happen?" he asked.

CHAPTER 2

A late model Auburn sports coupe sped along the roadway that wound through the scenic Hawaiian country side lying between the precipitous North Shore of Oahu and the island interior. A young Lieutenant named Curtis Lemay was behind the wheel of the vehicle enjoying the island's beauty. He glanced at his wrist watch, then turned the radio on and scanned the sunny sky ahead.

"… And that's the early morning news from around the islands. The weather forecast calls for clear skies, growing partly cloudy by mid-afternoon."

"A late news bulletin…."

Lemay reached to turn the radio to another station, but paused as his attention was arrested by the continuing broadcast.

"...Major Ployer B. Hill, the Army Air Corps test pilot injured in an Army bomber crash on the mainland, is dead," the radio announcer said. "Leslie Tower, the Boeing test pilot who was on board the ill-fated flight, remains in critical condition."

Lemay stared straight ahead as the broadcast continued.

"Elsewhere in the world, Italian Premier Benito Mussolini's invasion force continues its sweep into Ethiopia, supported by the powerful Italian air force. Sources close to the British Government say it was Mussolini's massive air build up in North Africa that prompted Prime Minister Baldwin to move the British fleet to Malta. Before this strategic move, it had been deployed off North Africa as a deterrent to the invasion."

Lemay snapped the radio off and pulled the sports coupe into the entrance gate of Wheeler Field. The guard saluted him and Lieutenant Lemay returned the military courtesy.

The guard waved Lemay through. "Good morning, Lieutenant Lemay," he said.

Lemay drove through the gate and looked for a moment at the identification near the gate that read: *Wheeler Army Air Field, Scoffield Barracks, Oahu, Hawaii.*

Lemay entered a military class room building and walked brusquely along the hallway, carrying a briefcase in one hand and a wooden carrying case that held a bubble sextant in the other.

He paused before one of the classrooms, deposited the sextant case on the floor as he opened the door, then retrieved the cases and entered the room. The printed identification on the door read: *Navigation Instruction, Lt. Curtis E. Lemay, Lt. John W. Egan.*

Lemay put the sextant case on a work table near the instructor's desk of the white walled military class room. He went to the rear of the room where a row of steel lockers stood, and laid the briefcase on a nearby student desk which had seen better days.

Lieutenant Lemay began to change into a standard aviator flight suit as Lieutenant Egan entered the room. Lemay was about to say something when Egan blurted out, "Good morning, Curt. Hear about the 299?"

Lemay glanced at Egan and continued to change. "Yeah, on the way in here."

"What about Senator Clay's remarks?' Egan asked in a very cynical tone.

"No. What did *he* say?"

Egan spoke slowly in a pontifical tone for dramatic effect. "How many more lives must we sacrifice at Billy Mitchell's altar of strategic air power before this great nation rises up in protest?"

Lemay frowned. "Sounds like William Jennings Bryan! But then… I've never found Senator Clay original in anything he says."

Egan sat down on a desk top near Lemay's locker, looking at him waiting for him to continue.

"He's going to fight the 299 procurement program…tooth and nail! Before he's through, he'll have the whole damned country believing anything with more than two engines can't be managed by the Air Corps pilots, and he's going to use the 299 accident to prove it."

"The son of a bitch will do it on the basis of one flight!" Lemay said. We've cracked up other airplanes! That's why we've a test program."

"Tell that to congress," Egan said. "You know, it isn't just the Air Corps's doctrine of strategic bombardment he's out to destroy…he's after the total and final repudiation of General Mitchell along with it. That has become a personal thing with those people up there on the Hill."

Lemay glanced at Egan, smiled and then continued to change. Lemay was silent for a few seconds in thought, then continued.

"We aren't going to win wars with just fighter planes, John… as much we like to fly them. They just don't have the destructive power. That has to come from heavy bombers. Damn sure not the ones we've now. But the ones we'll build in the future."

Lemay closed the locker door and turned again to Egan. "The 299 was the first step in that direction. If this country is to have a military deterrence we must have the 299 and a lot of them."

"I don't think we'll lose the 299…in spite of Senator Clay! The Strategic potential was already established before the accident."

Lemay secured the briefcase from the desk top and turned to exit the classroom. Egan grinned and shook his head.

"What's the matter?" Lemay asked.

"Nothing really," Egan said. It's…it's just that you've been in fighters since we got our wings out at Kelly, but…you…you talk like a bombardment group commander."

Lemay only grinned, and then headed toward the class room door. Egan got off from the desk top went to the instructor's desk at the front of the class room.

"You're damned persuasive too, you know." Egan said as he began to open his own briefcase and remove folded charts and military pamphlets. "Otherwise, I'd never have been coaxed into helping you pass navigation qualifications in that lousy one hour a week course we took under Gatty." He glanced at Lemay. "I didn't realize how little he actually taught us about celestial navigation."

Lemay looked away momentarily in serious thought. "Old Harold Gatty reminded me of Pee Wee Wheeler. First cadet instructor I drew out of March Field who taught by generalization and ignored specific altogether! I damn near washed out of my check ride because of him. He never got around to telling me the specifics about power settings at higher altitudes…about what makes the difference between turning into a dead engine on approach for landing or going straight in!"

"That was him, alright," Egan said. "Navigated Old Wiley Post around the world, but when it came to communicating his technique in a class room, he was lost!" He paused "No wonder I haven't been to bed before two A.M. in so long I've forgotten what it's like…and I still don't have a comfortable feel for that damned bubble sextant." Egan gestured towards the wooden box on the work table…solving celestial triangles in an acceptable time frame…or…my ability to teach the technique."

"We're beginning to make progress," Lemay said. "I've got a dead reckoning exercise set up this morning." He grinned. "…out to Niihau Island. You're cleared to fly the same exercise tomorrow with your half of the class."

Egan smiled. "You got permission! That's great! Any problems with the old man?"

"He just couldn't figure out how we'd find our way back." Lemay closed his eyes. "Funny thing…it made me feel good to know I could do something he couldn't do."

"Don't get lost out there," Egan said. "I'd be pretty embarrassed if the Navy had to fish you out of the drink!"

"Probably make us swim home! But I'll tell you one thing: we're going to learn enough about navigation ourselves to tell the Navy to go to hell. We'll be able to find our own way around the globe."

Egan watched as Lemay walked away, then shook his head and continued unloading his briefcase.

A twin engine consolidated PBY amphibian with Army Air Corps markings began to lift off the runway at Wheeler Army Airfield. The airplane gained altitude and its landing gear retracted into the fuselage.

Lemay, in the left seat of the cockpit, settled the aircraft on a predetermined heading and stared out at the early morning beauty of the island. He then turned to the Second Lieutenant navigation student flying co-pilot.

"Stay on a heading of two-seven-zero…five thousand feet…a hundred twenty-five knots."

"Two-seven-zero, five-thousand and one-two-five knots," the Second Lieutenant repeated.

"I'll set up the problem and then relieve you so you can participate in the exercise," Lemay said.

The student nodded. "Right, Sir."

Lemay released the controls to the student, eased out of the seat and moved down into the bay area of the aircraft. He entered the bay area of the PBY where he found five Army Air Corps officer navigation students at a special table prepared for aerial navigation exercises, three on each side of the bay area. Lemay looked at the large navigational chart on the bulkhead adjacent to the cockpit area. The officers each had charts laid out before them on their work areas, along with various navigational instruments. A special drift sight and compass pedestal stood to the left and adjacent to the forward bulkhead.

Lemay pointed to Niihau Island on the navigation chart and the five Air Corps officers began to work out their dead reckoning problems that would produce a heading for Niihau Island. When they were finished, the students gathered jubilantly at a side blister of the PBY and congratulated each other profusely. Lemay, returned to the PBY cockpit looked out at Niihau. He smiled and was pleased with his student navigators' progress.

CHAPTER 3

Lieutenant Colonel Robert H. Olds walked briskly along the hallway of the Administration Building at Langley Field in Virginia. Olds, a tall, well-built officer, wore the wings of the Army Air Corps pilot. Three rows of service ribbons stretched across the left breast of his uniform jacket under the Air Corps wings insignia. He carried an old government issue briefcase in his left hand. Olds turned into a doorway where the words *General Headquarters Air Force* were written in gold lettering on the door panel.

Lieutenant Colonel Olds entered the cold and impersonal office as the Staff Sergeant looked up from his desk.

"Colonel Olds, the General wants you to go right in, Sir," said the old Sergeant whose weathered and lightly scarred face told of decades of military service.

"Thank you, Sergeant."

Olds walked to the door leading into the GHQ Chief of Staff inner offices. General Andrews rose from his paper covered desk, and shook hands warmly with Colonel Olds.

"Bob, glad you could make it up here this morning," General Andrews said.

"General Andrews," Colonel Olds said.

General Andrews motioned for Colonel Olds towards one of the two large, leather covered chairs that sat a few feet in front of the desk, on either side of the large, mahogany coffee table. He went back behind his desk and pressed an intercom button there.

"See that we're not disturbed, Sergeant," General Andrews said.

"Yes, Sir."

General Andrews casually leaned far back against his chair. "Well, Bob, about got your feet grounded out there on the Second Bombardment?"

Colonel Olds nodded. "I'm working on it. We're still trying to get over the excitement of our first B-17, General. I flew it in from Seattle yesterday"

"Yes, I know." The General dropped his gaze for a moment. "We consider the Second Bombardment critical to the Air Corps future right now, Bob. That's why you're there, you know."

"Well, I hope I don't let you down, General."

"I may not have done you any favors," General Andrews said. "You're going to find yourself right in the middle of the perennial strategic air power versus battleships debate, you know."

Colonel Olds smiled. "We're already involved in that argument, Sir." Olds paused for a moment to collect his thoughts. *'Air Power is as vital a requirement to the military efficiency of a great nation as land and sea power, and there's no hope for victory in war for a nation in which it's lacking.'* Those are your own words, General. They've become our articles of faith!"

General Andrews stood up and walked over to his desk and picked up a sheet of paper then strolled back to his desk chair, and sat down, almost wearily. "I'm an old horse cavalryman. I spent the first twelve years in the cavalry after I graduated from the 'Point'." The General continued. "Technology, range and surface weaponry, all that made the horse cavalry obsolete, a military anachronism." The General smiled. "Oh, we loved the cavalry, make no mistake about it." He looked at Colonel Olds. "Some of those older generals fought like hell to preserve it as a serious fighting element of the Army…knowing it had become militarily useless. That type of myopic thinking prevails today within the Navy and the old mossy back government bureaucrats."

"Oh well, the cavalry was a gallant way of life," Colonel Olds said.

"Perhaps…but the point I'm making is this." General Andrews leaned forward slightly and made a fist. "The fallacies of this argument for military status quo today are far less obvious than were the fallacies of those old general's arguments to keep the horse cavalry alive." He thought for a moment. "They're complex…subtle." He looked at Colonel Olds. …but no less in error."

The General got up from his desk, and walked to a large wall map of the world. A long narrow credenza table stood against the wall, below the map. It had a half dozen family photos set in an irregular configuration on one side and the General's hat and gloves were on the other side.

"Within a couple of years, bombers now being developed in Europe will have a sufficient operating range to strike our vital industrial triangle." He traced out the triangle with his forefinger, Bangor, Maine the apex, Chicago on one base leg, and Norfolk, Virginia, on the other. "Just as Mitchell had prophesied years ago. They'll only need a suitable string of operating bases… generally obtainable." General Andrews pointed to Norway, Iceland and Greenland. "Neither battleships nor land forces could prevent such an attack."

"We've lived with that nightmare for a long time now, General," Colonel Olds said. "The question is whether we can convince the disbelievers before it's hammered home by a sudden and devastating attack."

General Andrews looked at the single sheet document in his hand and handed Olds the sheet.

"That's how the War Department General Staff planned to spend our military budget this year," The General pointed to the document. "These figures haven't been made public yet."

Colonel Olds pondered the sheet for a few moments. "Looks like it might be mostly surface vessels!"

"From what we can gather, that's the trend…for years to come," General Andrews said.

Colonel Olds frowned deeply "I don't see any strategic capability."

"Nothing! Only support type aircraft."

General Andrews sat down in a chair across the coffee table from where Colonel Olds was sitting, leaned slightly forward and his voice assumed a firm tone of quiet urgency.

"If they're wrong, Bob, in the broad conception of national defense, then I think the first step toward defending our country in the future is to make the error apparent. Now prove it to the congress and to the American people."

"And how would we go about doing this, General?'

General Andrews leaned back in his chair and crossed his legs. "We've been working on a series of…uh exercises up here, specifically designed to draw public attention to the strategic capability of the Boeing B-17's, the necessity for strategic air power…more B-17's…and even development of designs for even longer range heavy bombers." General Andrews ginned "Propaganda stunts, right?" He grew serious. "At least a part of our success is in the exercises that would be contingent upon second ability to navigate over long stretches of ocean or unfamiliar terrain."

"I believe we could handle that General Andrews, in fact I'm sure of it."

"I believe you've a Lieutenant Lemay in your outfit now, I personally approved his request for transfer to bombardment several months ago," the General said.

"Yes Sir. He was in operations at the squadron level when I took command. I've just brought him up to the group."

"Then you're already aware of his background in navigation?"

"Oh yes, quite." Colonel Olds said.

General Andrews began to contemplate his fingers by tapping them together. "The Navy is holding a fleet maneuver exercise off the west coast in August." He looked up at Olds. "You should have received most of your B-17's by then and had time to fully train your people."

Colonel Olds nodded "That's right, Sir."

"I've talked to the Chief of Naval Operations about our participating, jointly, in those exercises. The plan is to bomb one of the battleships, possibly the Utah."

Colonel Olds grinned broadly. "And what was the CNO's response?"

"He's stalling. But I've predicated the request on paragraph four "C" of the Joint Actions of the Army and Navy Manual. I don't think he can refuse," The General leaned forward using his hands to emphasize his words. "In the meantime I want you to start training programs designed to sharpen the skills of your pilots, navigators and bombardiers."

General Andrews got up from his chair and Olds did the same.

"I want the group brought up to its maximum efficiency. Bob, we're going to show Congress and the American people that battleships are too vulnerable to air power to continue as America's first line of defense."

Colonel Olds was still grinning. "That puts a pretty big carrot out in front of my men, General Andrews."

General Andrews clasped Olds' shoulder momentarily as they walked toward the door.

"There are risks involved, you know…to your career…and…to mine."

They reached the door.

"The opponents of Air Power in the War Department won't give up without a fight. If you succeed in the fleet exercises you'll become number one on their enemies list."

"Well…the only thing that could keep me out of this, General, would be a court-martial."

They shook hands.

Olds exited and General Andrews gazed after him, realizing that his selection of Olds gave Air Power a real chance to succeed. Andrews turned back to his desk and started to draft a letter to the CNO.

CHAPTER 4

It was a partly cloudy morning in August 1937 when Lieutenant Colonel Olds' three B-17's pulled up to park at Oakland Airfield. The pilots carefully applied the brakes as their noses came even with each other. The engines ran up, and then the switches were cut. Several Army mechanics approached the fortresses with wheel chocks. The group engineering officer stood waiting expectantly as the crew members began dropping from the nose hatches of the aircraft. Lieutenant Colonel Olds approached the engineering officer, followed by three officers. Among the crew members was Lieutenant Curtis Lemay.

"You got here earlier than we expected," the engineer officer said.

"How long to gas up and get our bombs loaded?" Colonel Olds asked.

"Maybe an hour, Sir," replied the engineer.

Colonel Olds turned to a very young looking crew member. "Lieutenant, you look like you're the low man on the totem pole so you stay on the radio."

The rest of the crew members from the three ships had gathered around. Colonel Olds looked at them and nodded. "The rest of you grab breakfast." He looked at his watch "I want everybody back here at ten o'clock and somebody relieve the Lieutenant so he can eat. I'm going to check in with the Navy."

Colonel Olds walked away and the crew members began to walk towards the mess hall for breakfast. A gas truck started to refuel the aircraft as several mechanics pushed a cart loaded with practice bombs. Lieutenant Kilpatrick, the bombardier, and Lieutenant Lemay, the navigator, passed and looked at the type of bombs on the cart, both perplexed. Lieutenant Kilpatrick turned to a Corporal, one of the men pushing the cart.

"Where the hell did you get those?"

The Corporal stopped in his tracks. "Navy sent them over, Sir!"

"The Navy?" Where are the practice bombs we sent out?" Lieutenant Kilpatrick asked.

The Corporal shrugged. "We were told that we got to use these, Sir."

Lieutenant Kilpatrick shook his head in disbelief as the mechanic moved away with the bomb cart. He and Lemay followed the other crew members headed for a quick breakfast.

Lieutenant Lemay gazed up at the overcast sky. "We'll be lucky if we've a five hundred foot ceiling out there."

A crew member entered the aircraft through the fuselage hatch that led to the radio operations area. He was carrying a paper coffee cup and three sugar coated donuts, which he gave to the Lieutenant left to monitor the radio

"Colonel Olds wants you down there."

The Lieutenant took the coffee and stood up to leave. "Thanks."

The six crew members assembled in front of the lead B-17 as the Lieutenant joined them, sipping his coffee.

"Gentlemen, I just want to remind you how important our mission here is." He looked at each crew member. "You all know your jobs."

"What about those bombs the Navy sent over?" Lieutenant Kilpatrick asked.

"What about them?"

"Well, they've a different trajectory than the type we've been using in practice."

Colonel Olds grinned. "Well, Kilpatrick, the Navy holds all the cards in this game. However…" He looked at the overcast sky. "Maybe we'll be too close to miss!"

The crew members laughed.

"Here's the plan," Colonel Olds said. "Sometime this morning, before the exercise begins at twelve noon, the Navy will radio the fleet location, probably heading and speed, to us here. We'll take off immediately." Colonel Olds turned to Lemay. "Lieutenant Lemay will calculate our heading to intercept the fleet, probably three or four hundred miles out."

"What about formations, radio frequencies and search patterns?" Lemay asked.

"They'll all be exactly as rehearsed and as briefed this morning in Phoenix," Colonel Olds said. "The Battleship Utah is our target. It'll be flying the international preparatory pennant as a means of positive identification. It's been especially rigged for this exercise. Personnel will have been notified of our approach and will have taken appropriate cover."

The crew members began to smile

"*Do not bomb any other vessels in the fleet,*" Colonel Olds said.

A Navy Lieutenant came to stand beside him and Colonel Olds gestured to him.

"Lieutenant Moorehead, on loan from the Navy, will be on my ship to assist with identification. I want every man in his aircraft ready for immediate takeoff the minute we receive the fleet location. The exercise begins as twelve noon today and ends at twelve noon tomorrow."

The crew members listened closely to Colonel Olds' words and their facial expression registered their reactions.

"If we fail to locate the Utah, and successfully bomb in that time frame, we'll have forfeited the exercise." Olds frowned. "Needless to say, that would be a severe disappointment to me…and to General Andrews." He looked at his watch. "My time is…five minutes past the hour of ten. Good hunting, gentlemen."

The crew moved out to their ships. Lemay settled down at the navigator's table and began to arrange the instruments for ready use. The clock on the navigator's panel read ten minutes past ten. When the clock read twelve noon, Colonel Olds put his arm out the window and tapped the side glass, impatiently. The pilot's head was resting against the back rest, his eyes closed. Olds pulled the side glass closed and turned to the co-pilot.

"Let's get airborne," Colonel Olds said. "We can get the radio message on the way out."

"Stand by to start engines," the co-pilot said.

The engines of the three aircraft began to fire to life, belching smoke and flame, roaring to life. Lemay's head emerged into the cockpit.

"What's the heading, Colonel?' Lemay asked.

"West," Colonel Olds said.

The lead B-17 lifted off with the other two B-17's following close by. Lemay studied his navigation chart and looked at the course steered by the squadron of B-17's, turned here and there in various heading that extended out from the takeoff point altogether, and obvious dead reckoning plot problem.

The co-pilot pointed to his right. "There's a hole over there."

Colonel Olds nodded "Yeah, a sucker hole if I ever saw one. I guess that's our only way down, so we're the suckers today."

Olds' B-17 turned towards the hole in the cloud layer and the Colonel looked out the window and at the large hole in the cloud layer and saw the ocean far below. He turned to the co-pilot but did not speak. He adjusted his turn and rate of descent to stay in the open air of the hole. He didn't want to lose sight of the sea below. That would be a sure way to get disorientated and possibly crash into the sea. He was almost down to 500 feet when he heard the radio crackle to life. The radio operator quickly scrawled the Morse code message which read as follows: *Flagship One from Navy station six-five, fleet position to follow,"* The radio operator flipped a switch "They're transmitting fleet position now, Colonel."

He glanced at his watch. "I got it," Colonel Olds said. He glanced at his co-pilot. "Four hours late!"

After Lieutenant Lemay finished his calculations, he spoke over the intercom. "Our heading will be two-one-zero degrees, thirty minutes. Execute turn to that heading in one minute, Colonel Olds."

"Flag sprout, this is Flagship One." Colonel Olds said. "Come left to a heading of two-one-zero degrees, thirty minutes. Stand by…execute turn!"

The B-17 moved away in a sweeping turn.

"Lemay, how far to the target?" Colonel Olds asked.

"About one hundred seventy-five miles, Sir."

"How much daylight left when we get there?"

Lemay spoke into the intercom. "Less than an hour."

The sun began to descend into the heavy cloud layer stretched out toward the distant horizon giving off a red and yellow hue. The sound of the B-17's engine filled the sky. Colonel Olds' eyes searched the horizon, and then he spoke into the intercom.

"Flag Sprout…this is Flagship One. We're going to have to look down there. Hold your altitude until we break out."

The front section of Olds' B-17 began to plow through the cloud layer. The distant gray cloud layer was ragged and uneven about three to five hundred feet over the ocean surface. The B-17 emerged, eerily through the bottom of the cloud layer and the dark white capped ocean was visible below. Colonel Olds watched as the clouds began to disappear and then he spoke into the intercom again.

"Flag Sprout, this is Flagship One. Come on down…EASY! You only have four hundred feet to play with down here."

In the navigator's compartment of Colonel Olds' B-17, Lieutenant Lemay continued to plot the heading, the dead reckoning plot looking like a jig saw puzzle. The clock read seventeen forty hours. Twenty minutes later, Lemay noted that the clock now read eighteen hundred hours. The time went by quickly as he made more navigational computations.

Anger began to show on Colonel Olds' face as he gazed out the cockpit, ahead and to the side.

"Where are they, Lemay?" Olds asked sarcastically.

Lemay worriedly rechecked his dead reckoning line "We ought to be right over them."

Colonel Olds raised his voice. "There's nothing down there but white caps, Lieutenant!"

Lemay was determined to remain in control of his emotions. "We can set up a search square. We've got a half an hour of daylight left."

"Set it up!"

On the flight deck of the B-17 off the right wing of the lead B-17, both pilots scanned the ocean surface intently. The pilot gazed out at the ocean which stretched out cold and gray below, white caps breaking across its surface in turbulent troughs.

In Colonel Olds' B-17, he scanned the surface below and Lemay leaned back from his chart, glanced at his watch, then out at the gathering dusk.

"We'd better break off, Colonel," Lemay said. "It's getting too dark."

Olds spoke wearily into the microphone. "What's the heading back to Oakland, Lemay?"

"Zero-nine-six degrees, thirty two minutes forty seconds," Lemay said.

Colonel Olds spoke again, his voice filled with disappointment. "Flagship One, break off. Turn zero-nine-six degrees, form up on me…going home."

Lemay took out the bubble sextant and stood it up to take a celestial reading. At that moment Colonel Olds entered the compartment. Lemay knew how disappointed the Colonel was and understood how he felt and would be patient with him.

"Lemay, why didn't we find the fleet?"

Lemay turned to Olds, the sextant still in his hand. "Well, they weren't where they said they'd be, Colonel. I'm going to double check our position. But, if I was right…the course I gave you…we should be seeing the lights of San Francisco any minute now."

Lemay pointed to that position on the chart with his forefinger, indicating San Francisco. Colonel Olds looked him in the eye.

"You better be right, Lieutenant."

Olds left the Navigator's compartment while Lemay continued with his celestial shots. When Olds entered the cockpit he found the co-pilot pointing off to his right at San Francisco and the California coastline ahead and below.

"San Francisco," the co-pilot said.

Colonel Olds smiled broadly. The co-pilot, having been instructed by San Francisco approach, control to proceed to Sacramento, glanced at Olds, who still had a big smile on his face.

Early morning sunlight was starting to light up the airfield in

Sacramento. The crew members were spread out on the concrete floor, of the hanger, sleeping on blankets and life jackets. Colonel Olds entered the hangar, found Lemay and roused him with his foot. Lemay rose up sleepily.

"How about breakfast, Lieutenant?"

Lemay shook his head to clear the sleep away and stifled a yawn as he stood up. They began to walk away.

"You were right, you know," Colonel Olds said.

Lemay looked at Olds, a grin playing at his lips.

"I've been up all night talking to Navy people," Olds said. "The position they gave us was one degree off. That put us sixty miles from the position they gave us." Olds clapped Lemay on the shoulder in a gesture of trust. "We're going to resume the exercise. We've got until noon today."

Later that morning the cumulus clouds filled the blue sky above Oakland Airfield. The engines of six B-17's, flying in formation, roared loudly as they flew out over the ocean which was now far below them. In Olds' aircraft, the radio operator's voice came over the intercom.

"…Stand by for fleet position." The radio operator said.

Lieutenant Lemay, inside the navigator's compartment was once again plotting the course. He leaned forward, intent on completing the task at hand. A few moments later, he walked into the cockpit.

"Colonel, we can't reach their position before twelve o'clock. Noon! Too far…"

Colonel Olds groaned. "Damn!" He paused for a moment. "We'll try anyway." He began to transmit over the radio. "Flag Sprout, Flagship One. Form up abreast…fifteen hundred yard separation… five hundred feet altitude."

As the hour of noon approached Colonel Olds spoke to the pilots over the radio. "Keep your eyes peeled," he said.

The B-17's, six abreast, raced across the ocean. In the bombardier's compartment of Olds' B-17, Lieutenant Kilpatrick pointed excitedly out the window.

"There they're!"

Colonel Olds glanced at his watch and kept grinning. "Five minutes to twelve." He looked out at the fleet steaming leisurely below.

"Which one's the Utah?" Lieutenant Kilpatrick asked the Navy lieutenant who was crouched beside him looking out the greenhouse.

"Can't make it out," The Navy lieutenant said.

Lieutenant Kilpatrick beamed. "Ya gotta do better than that, Mister!" He adjusted his bomb sight. "Something down there's about to get hit!"

Lemay, who has come up to the front of the cockpit, began to gaze through his binoculars. He pointed to one of the ships below.

"There it's!"

"Let's go!" Colonel Olds said "Single file!"

The bomb bay doors opened, and the bombs began to fall away.

Both pilots began to yell "Bullseye!" at the same time.

Several sailors were sitting casually on the deck, gazing upward at the oncoming B-17's. Suddenly, a dummy bomb struck the deck nearby, showering rumble everywhere. The sailors literally dove for cover.

One sailor looked up at the sky. "What the hell!! What do you bastards think you're doing?!"

The ship's general quarter's siren shrieked "General Quarters, General Quarters!"

Olds' B-17 turned after the bomb run while the second B-17 released its bomb on the Utah.

Colonel Olds peered down at the Utah. "Look at them run for cover. They damned sure weren't expecting us."

At the Admiral's bridge, the Admiral was looking towards the Utah when a junior officer approached him.

"Sir, you want me to call off the exercise?" The junior officer asked. They've won, Sir! And…they're reporting some damage over there on the Utah."

The Admiral stood up and remained silent. His facial featured seemed carved in stone.

Colonel Olds entered the navigator's compartment and found Lemay and Kilpatrick grinning and laughing, much in the same way he was doing.

"Well, Lemay…"

Lemay interrupted "Remember I told you we couldn't get there in time?"

"Yeah," Colonel Olds said.

Lemay pointed to his chart. "They weren't where they were supposed to be.

Olds glanced at the chart and then at Lemay, puzzled "Well?"

"The position they radioed us was one degree off," Lemay said.

"If you're right, Lemay, they were giving us bad information intentionally! We stumbled on them by sheer accident!"

Lemay nodded as he turned to the chart. "Our heading to March Field will be zero-nine-six degrees based on my dead reckoning calculations here." He tapped the chart with his divider. "If I'm right, we'll pass twenty-one miles north of Point Conception when we hit landfall about sixty-two minutes from now, and that will prove my point,"

Olds nodded and then left. A moment later he entered the cockpit and got into the co-pilot's seat. He glanced at the compass as he did and saw that the compass heading read, zero-nine-six degrees. Colonel Olds spoke into the microphone.

"Pilot to radioman: inform March Field mission successful. Tell 'em to notify General Andrews. Mission was successful."

Colonel Olds turned and looked back at Lemay who was now standing behind the pilot looking out the cockpit window into the distance. "Okay, Lemay, I assume you'll want to quietly add some key people for future expansion."

"Yes, Sir, I feel that we'll need key people on board if we've to expand rapidly due to the war in Europe," Lemay said dryly.

"What war in Europe?" Olds said mockingly. "Okay, I agree. Get me your list of the four and only four people. I know that you want Bart Coltrane. I don't know anything at all about this Coltrane fella. Who is he?"

"He's a true believer, Sir. He believes in strategic bombing and the value of Army aviation. He's an excellent pilot and he knows aviation engineering from the landing gear to the rudder top," Lemay said with a slight excitement in his voice.

Olds looked at Lemay and knew that Coltrane must be an exceptional officer to get that type of endorsement from Lemay. Then he looked back out the front of the B-17 and spotted March Field. He reduced the power setting and started the descent to land.

General Andrews, the March Field Commandant, Lieutenant Colonel "Hap" Arnold and an aide, were seated in the Control Tower, obviously awaiting word from Colonel Olds. The tower radio man transcribed an incoming Morse code message, finished, walked to General Andrews and handed him the message. General Andrews read the tersely worded statement and his features broke into a broad smile as he handed the message to Colonel Arnold.

Colonel Olds and the co-pilot searched the horizon ahead for first sight of landfall. The co-pilot pointed to his right.

"There's Point Conception," the co-pilot said.

"How far?" Colonel Olds asked.

"About twenty miles I'd say."

"That proved it," Colonel Olds said. "They never intended for us to find that damned fleet."

"Hell of a way to run an exercise," the co-pilot said "We're supposed to be testing our national defense systems."

Olds nodded equally as disgruntled as the co-pilot. "General Andrews was right. Battleships are as obsolete as the horse cavalry."

The co-pilot glanced at Olds, puzzled by his remark.

"They're going to fight like hell to keep battleships as our first line of defense. It doesn't matter a damn that they're totally vulnerable to air power." He gazed ahead, deep in thought. "And as long as they've got a stranglehold on the War Department, it's going to be damned hard to change that."

The co-pilot looked at Olds, then he turned away, pondering the words he'd just heard.

The three B-17's landed at March Field and Colonel Olds dropped from the lead ship and walked to where General Andrews stood waiting for him.

"Well done, Bob," General Andrews said.

Other members of the crew gathered around, laughing and talking.

"You should have seen those sea jocks dive for cover," one crewman said.

"Yeah," another said.

"All six of our ships scored hits," Lieutenant Kilpatrick said. "We could've sunk the whole fleet."

Colonel Olds began to walk off to one side and General Andrews followed him.

"I've got a call in to the San Francisco *Examiner*. They're going to break the story in the evening edition."

Even as the General spoke, he saw a junior staff officer walking towards him, his face a study in disappointment.

"What's wrong, Lieutenant?" General Andrews asked.

"The story, Sir…it was killed."

The General threw his arms up in disgust. "Why?"

"War Department request," the lieutenant said. "A matter of national security."

The crew began to cross toward General Andrews and Colonel Olds, each of them sensing that something had gone wrong.

CHAPTER 5

There were three loud knocks on a second floor Sunnymeade, California door. Then two knocks. The door was opened impatiently by the anxious visitor, who entered the typically appointed bachelor apartment of James Barton Coltrane, better known as Bart or Black Bart, depending on your level of friendship with him.

"Bart, Bart, you son-of-a-bitch, wake up, it's almost eight o'clock and you've orders," said Tom Dillon, a fellow pilot with the 7th Bombardment Group stationed at March Field, California. "Wake up. You've transfer orders," Dillon said as he opened the bedroom door to find Coltrane in bed with a long-haired woman. The woman by this time had awoken and had pulled the sheets up to her eyes in fear and embarrassment.

Dillon started shaking Coltrane as he looked around at the three empty bottles of cheap champagne from a northern California vineyard.

"Dillon, I'm going to kill you if I can ever get out of this damned bed," Coltrane said in a mockingly angry voice. "Right now, that could take some time and a medic. My head is blowing up." Coltrane looked at his bed mate and asked "What kind of rotgut were we drinking? Forget it," he said as he turned his attention towards Dillon who had taken a couple of steps back as a precautionary measure, knowing of Coltrane's often belligerent attitude when awoken with a hangover. It was an event that had become a more frequent event in recent months. Coltrane was bored with the lack of emphasis being put on war training. He had found temporary relief in the volume of booze that he consumed and the never-ending quest for sexual conquests.

Coltrane, now sitting bare-assed on the side of the bed with his feet on the floor and his head in his hands, asked "Now what is this shit about transfer orders?"

"You're being transferred to the Second Bomb Group. That guy Lemay got you transferred to his B-17 Squadron."

Coltrane's head snapped up despite pain and almost said something, but didn't.

He looked over at the gorgeous blonde who was silently observing the whole event. He then turned back to Dillon.

"Pardon my manners, Amy this is Tom Dillon my…."

"It's Ann," the blonde said, interrupting.

"Oh yeah, Ann. It was a rough night and you damned near killed me," he said, as he turned his head towards her and smiled, saying "Thanks, you made life worth living!"

She smiled and pulled the sheet down to her shoulders, no longer trying to hide her embarrassment. In a soft sexy voice she asked, "Do I get another chance at giving you a heart attack?"

Coltrane laid back over on her hugging her and biting her ear.

"Excuse me," Dillon said loudly, "I'm still here and you've to report to Colonel Olds at 1300 today."

Ignoring Dillon, Coltrane asked "Okay, when does your husband fly off into the wild blue yonder again?" Quickly looking at Dillon, "He's a pilot with Western Airlines."

He's on the Friday afternoon flight to San Francisco-Salt Lake and back on Sunday," she said.

"Perfect," Coltrane said. "Same barstool at 7:30 Friday?"

"Absolutely, better take your vitamins," as she resumed her sexy voice while rubbing her hand on the inside of Coltrane's thigh. "I'll do my best to do you in next time."

"Okay, okay, Bart. I've done my job to let you know. Here are the orders, you're on your own," a frustrated Dillon said, throwing the orders on the bed as he left the room.

Precisely at 1300 hours, Bart Coltrane entered the office of Colonel Olds. He advised the Master Sergeant of his name and instructions to report to Colonel Olds. The tough looking NCO knocked twice on the door and went in. Moments later, he came out, leaving the door open.

The Colonel will see you now, Sir," barked the Sergeant.

Coltrane marched into the office and stopped less than two feet from the desk and saluted. "Sir, Captain James Barton Coltrane reports as ordered, Sir."

"At ease, Captain" said the Colonel as he got up and extended his hand. "Welcome to the Second Bomb Group. Have a seat," he said, pointing to a chair just to the right of the desk. He then noticed Captain Lemay setting in the other chair. "I understand that you already know Curt Lemay."

"Yes, Sir," stated Coltrane.

Good, you'll get your B-17 transition from him and become his co-pilot for now," the Colonel said in a matter-of-fact tone. "Curt tells me that you share the same two fundamental beliefs that we do. First, you believe in the bomber as a strategic weapon of the future and second, the world will once again be at war. I assume that you expect that the United States will be drawn into the fight."

"Yes, Sir, if Britain is attacked, we'll have no choice but to come to her assistance," responded Coltrane.

Olds nodded and then walked over to a wall map of the world and pointed to March Field. "Currently, we've six B-17's at March Field. More will be arriving soon. We must take what we've and accomplish a long list of tasks. Mission deployment plan, tactics, operating procedures, maintenance procedures, crew training, war preparations and, lastly, convince a 'battleship-minded Congress and Pentagon of the importance of strategic bombing in a new type of warfare. Europe will be won or lost in the air. Hitler has already proven his new emphasis on aviation in his attacks in Spain. Intelligence has been getting some very disturbing rumors on the size of the new Luftwaffe, especially in its bomber fleet. If the rumors are true, and Colonel Lindbergh does believe them, they've an air force over twenty times the size than we thought…and Hitler plans to use them in any invasion or assault as a front line force. Our little Army Air Corps is massively outnumbered and outgunned. We must prove that the Air Corps can be a major force in any future combat in Europe and that we must start building thousands of fighters and B-17s. What you and the others here in the Second Bomb Group have is the nucleus of that future force. Europe will depend upon our ability to support them with air power and, more importantly, the fate of the United States may also depend upon us," Olds said as he sat back down.

"You'll work for Curt but you'll also work with others on the staff in the development of tactics, operations and maintenance. I understand you're quite knowledgeable in aviation maintenance. That's a critical area for us," Olds said as he leaned forward. "Are you ready to take on this assignment?"

Sir, I have dreamed of this assignment. I'm ready, willing and able to do this job for you," Coltrane said in a confident tone as he stood up to salute.

"Carry on, Lieutenant," Olds said as he returned his salute.

Coltrane did a military about face to leave then paused long enough to say to Lemay, "Thanks, I owe you. How's your hand?" He smiled then left.

Lemay broke out laughing as he held up his right hand.

CHAPTER 6

General Frank Andrews was dynamic in his efforts to prove to the Congress, the Pentagon and American people that strategic bombardment was both effective and essential to America's homeland security. As if the twelve thousand mile, round trip flight of seven flying fortresses to Buenos Aires only last March wasn't enough, his GHQ people had pulled off still another feat - highlighting not only the awesome capability of the mighty flying fortress, but the skill of the GHQ navigators as well.

The flight to Argentina was made over land, where check points could be established for visual navigation. Hardly had the shouts of the welcoming throngs died away before General Andrews and Major Ira C. Eaker, Chief of the U.S. Army Air Corps Information Section, began planning an even more daring exercise.

As the cruise ship Rex approached the Eastern seaboard on its regular run from Naples to New York City, Andrews' flight of three B-17's found the tiny dot… seven-hundred miles at sea. Thus, the mighty B-17 flying fortress provided a striking example of mobility and range of modern aviation.

The Armed Forces were conducting war games off the New England coastline. Three B-17's approached the ocean liner, the Rex and flew directly over it. Several newsmen and cameramen were on board the B-17, recording the event.

One early morning in May 1938, General Malin Craig's staff car pulled up in front of a private entrance of the munitions building. The driver got out of the car, went around to the rear door and opened it for the General and his aide, a young Army Captain. The General and his aide walked to the entrance hurriedly and disappeared through the doorway. General Craig and his aide walked quickly across the foyer and then stopped at the reception desk where a staff sergeant was seated. He quickly stood up as the General approached.

"General Westover in?" General Craig snapped.

"Yes, Sir," The staff sergeant said.

General Craig walked away. "Thank you," he said over his shoulder.

The sergeant waited for a moment until the General and his aide had disappeared from sight and then he flipped an inter-office communication switch. He plopped down wearily in a chair and spoke into the intercom.

"The chief's on his way up." The sergeant said. "Thought you'd like to know."

"Thank you," the Air Corps sergeant said. Then he flipped a switch on the intercom console. "General Westover, General Craig is on his way up, Sir."

As the Sergeant closed the intercom circuit, General Craig and his aide burst into the reception area and merely glanced at the Sergeant who formally greeted the visitors as they strode up to his desk.

Startled, the Air Corps Sergeant rose to his feet. "General Craig, Sir!"

General Craig ignored the receptionist and entered the door leading into the U.S. Army Air Corps Chief of Staff's office. The General looked briefly at the lettering on the door: *Office of the Chief of the Air Corps Oscar M. Westover, Major General, USAAF.* General Craig and his aide entered the office. General Westover stared at them and did not move to greet them. General Craig peeled his gloves off, laid them on a small receiving table, along with his cap and his swagger stick. He walked briskly over to Westover. His aide remained in the background.

"Oscar, did you authorize Frank Andrews to carry out the Rex exercise?"

General Westover looked puzzled. "The plan was submitted to the General staff."

"Nobody on my staff authorized it!" General Craig said. "Nor did any of my ground commanders!"

"Frank considered the absence of any response from the staff as tacit approval, and there was a time limit involved, I believe," General Westover said.

General Craig sat down in a chair directly across from General Westover's desk and General Westover sat back down in his desk chair. General Craig lit a cigarette, shook the match flame out and dropped it in an ash tray by the chair.

General Craig gazed at General Westover through the smoke. "Were you aware those war games were designed to emphasize the President's naval appropriations bill… or did Andrews and Baker even stop to wonder why there was no U.S. fleet presence out there during the exercise?"

"They knew that, General Craig and the war games judges knew it too."

General Craig slapped the desk with the palm of his hand. "If there had been a fleet out there, it would have sunk the enemy long before he got close enough for those damned bombers to hit them!"

General Westover leaned forward and used his hands to emphasize his remarks. "General, most of the major powers of the world are building up their air power… actively developing a capability to do just what Frank and his people are demonstrating! The flight to South America; it proved the capability of the B-17 to reinforce the Panama Canal Zone in time of national emergency, flying there with heavy bomb load and returning nonstop."

General Craig sighed. "I know all of that, Oscar!"

"We've got thirteen long range bombers in our inventory. Unless someone dramatically demonstrates the urgent need for four hundred more, we're liable to find ourselves in serious trouble if we've to fight against an enemy that already has that level of strategic capability," General Westover said.

General Craig turned to his aide. "Ted, would you wait outside, please."

"Yes, Sir."

The aide left the room and General Craig stood up, went to the window and looked out onto the Potomac River and beyond. When he turned to look at General Westover, exhaustion was etched on his face.

"Look, Oscar…I…I don't want to fight any more political battles. I'm tired. Retirement's just a little over a year away…"

General Westover was standing next to General Craig, but did not look at him when he interrupted him.

"But General… the future security of the entire American hemisphere is at stake here! We can't afford to sit passively and let potential enemies develop an undeterred capability to destroy us from the air! Everybody over there on Capitol Hill knows that, even if they won't admit it. And they know that surface vessels are vulnerable to air attack. In the name of God, why are they so determined not to face the facts? Strategic air power is no longer a hypothesis, General, it's a reality."

General Craig glared at General Westover. "Damn it Oscar! I'm the Chief of Staff of the United States Army. The Air Corps is but a division of the Army, and GHQ Air Force is but a division of the Air Corps itself. It's a mandate, under the Baker Board, to operate under the jurisdiction of Army ground commanders in time of a national emergency.

General Craig took a deep breath.

"Now just who in the hell does Frank Andrews think he's… out there acting like he can win a war all by himself? And the son-of-a-bitch even had those airplanes stuffed with reporters and radio people!"

"There are political and military considerations that make the issue a stick of dynamite, and Andrews keeps trying to light the damned fuse. There are congressional elections in less than six months. The American people really don't want to get involved in another war. The politicians hear them and will act accordingly. The President will obviously run again in two years. He's torn between the cries for help from Europe and England, the apathy and disinterest on the part of the electorate, the normal fighting and grandstanding by Congress, and our own in-house fighting between the Army and the Navy. Both are fighting for more funding for their own conventional needs. The only thing that they do agree on is their hatred for the Air Corps. Regardless of the rather impressive recent events by the Air Corps, they've not changed and will not change the battleship defense strategy held by the senior generals and admirals. Hitler is making tanks and aircraft at an alarming rate. Nobody will officially acknowledge the potential regional danger posed by the German Luftwaffe, much less the danger posed to the United States," General Craig said pausing. Allowing the anger to leave his face, he lifted his cigarette and gazed out the window. Then he continued in a much softer voice, "I've given my… my word that Army planes will not participate in any activity in the future beyond a one hundred mile limit off our national shore lines."

"Impossible!" General Westover said. "How could you agree to such a thing?"

"It's none of your damn business, Oscar! Orders are orders! You'd better be damned sure they're carried out." General Craig picked up his cap, gloves and swagger stick. "Every Army ground commander and Navy admiral is after Frank Andrews' head… and… I'll tell you something else: the climate's not too promising for the Air Corps navigation programs either!"

General Craig placed his cap on his head and began putting on his gloves, glancing at Westover as he did.

"I want a public statement from Andrews indicating his acceptance of the basic military tenant and that the Army ground forces, together with the Navy, provide the primary capability of defending this country against any form of aggression. Understood?"

"I understand, General Craig… fully."

"Then see to it, Oscar."

"Yes, Sir!" General Westover said.

General Craig left the office and General Westover stared after him in angry frustration came over him as he considered the implications on the air development program.

In the smoke-filled press room of the Pentagon, several reporters were seated expectantly before a speaker's podium that bore the seal of the United

States Army. Presently, General Frank Andrews entered the room along with Major Baker. General Andrews unfolded a sheet of paper and placed it on the podium surface.

"Gentlemen, I have asked you over here this morning to read a prepared statement. I believe you understand that when I'm finished that it would be imprudent of me to respond to questions. And now the statement."

The reporters began to take notes.

General Andrews continued. "Notice has been taken of some press reports that there's a tendency to indicate the Army GHQ is planning to fight a war by itself! I would like to correct that impression." Sudden laughter broke out among the reporters. "We must realize that, in common with the mobilization of the Army Air Force in this area, the ground arms of the Army would also be assembling, prepared to take the major role in repelling the actual landing forces of an enemy. I therefore ask that you not accuse the GHQ Army Air Force of trying to 'win a war alone'. Thank you."

One reporter leaped to his feet. "General, does this mean the B-17 flying fortress is a dead duck?"

"No comment," General Andrews said.

"But General… you've proven the nation's critical need for the four engine, heavy bomber. Are you giving up the fight for future procurement?" asked a second reporter.

"No comment. I'm sorry, gentlemen," General Andrews said.

The reporters would not give up. "General, word has leaked out that the War Department has restricted all activities to a one hundred mile limit off our National shorelines…"

General Andrews smiled. "We… uh… plan additional 'good will' flights to South America designed to…to…strengthen hemispheric relations… friendships… but…we'll stay inland on those flights!"

The reporters laughed again and another one stood up, pen poised at his notepad. "General…"

General Andrews and Major Eaker began to walk out of the room and the reporters, knowing the press conference had ended before they wanted it to, did the same.

Major Ira C. Eaker strode rapidly down the hallway in the Munitions Building toward the door way leading to the USAAF Chief of Staff's outer office. The Sergeant's receptionist smiled at Eaker and then flipped a switch on the intercom. He informed General Westover that Major Eaker was there and was told to send him in. Eaker walked to the door that led to the inner offices. General Westover rose to his feet and shook Major Eaker's hand.

"Sit down, Major," General Westover said.

"Thank you, General."

General Westover leaned back in his chair. "I believe the President's going to dig down pretty deep to replace General Craig when he retires next year."

"It's a pretty good bet it's going to be General Marshall," Major Eaker said.

General Westover thought for a moment. "Marshall's a reasonable man… not encumbered by a lot of old line, surface defense dogma." He smiled. "General Andrews and Bob Olds have been after me to get Marshall in a B-17 since they heard about it." His smile broadened. "Well… we've got it all arranged. You're to pick Marshall up over at State in the morning."

General Westover handed Major Eaker a prepared brief sheet. Here are the critical points that we need to get across. We can't be seen as overselling him at this point, but he must see what bombers can become in the combined military arsenal. He's bright and open minded. Let him arrive at his own opinion."

"Take him out to Langley, Major. Stand by to help Andy and Bob in any way you can."

Major Eaker glanced at the brief sheet.

"Of course, Sir."

"I'd like to go myself, but I'm scheduled to inspect Lockheed's Burbank plant tomorrow afternoon with Major Wolfe. He's our factory rep out there," General Westover said.

The General flipped up a key on the desk intercom. "Ask the Assistant Chief to step in here, please."

"Yes, Sir."

"Hap's been working through Harry Hopkins trying to get some Air Corps requirements and capabilities before the President himself. It looks like we're never going to get anywhere through the War Department."

General Westover got up from his desk chair, walked slowly to the window and looked out on the scene beyond reflectively, his hands clasped together behind his back.

In a soft but firm voice, he continued, "Major, we *need* Marshall on our side in the worst way. The entire Air Corps mission needs a friendly voice on the War Department General Staff, particularly the heavy bomber program." He paused and then looked back at Eaker. "General Craig… he was in here the other day… a tired old man… sweating out retirement. He fought a lot of people for *his* Army: the Navy, politicians… public opinion. It wears a man down and speeches…." General Westover shut his eyes for a moment and sighed deeply. "You know, I'm scheduled to make speeches and inspection stops all the way to Burbank and a half dozen or more, I guess… just enough time in between to fly from one to the…"

At that moment, the door opened and General Arnold walked in, interrupting General Westover. Major Eaker rose from his chair and shook hands with General Arnold.

"Major, how are you?" General Arnold asked.

"The Major's taking Marshall to Langley tomorrow, Hap. I thought that you might want to brief him on what to emphasize."

General Arnold smiled at Major Eaker. "I don't think I can point out anything that the Major doesn't already know about our problems up here, General." He thought for a moment. "You helped Frank Andrews plan the Rex mission, Major. Brilliant piece of work….proved the strategic potential of the B-17 dramatically. But, the War Department General Staff, along with Malin Craig… they all raised hell like country gentlemen finding poachers in their game preserve. That reaction pretty well typifies our situation, I guess."

Major Eaker looked at both generals, and asked "What about the hundred mile limit? Ever cut an order to that effect?"

"Hell no!" General Westover said. "Nobody up there wants history to associate their names with something that stupid. It's merely a *verbal* directive… from the War Department General Staff, *collectively*! We aren't dealing with amateurs, you know. A bunch of old fools maybe, but not amateurs."

"And… as long as they control the purse strings," Major Eaker said. "The Air Corps procurement program will be spent for *support* type aircraft."

General Arnold leaned forward in his chair. "The B-17's has had only one predecessor of equal importance: the first military aircraft Orville and Wilbur Wright sold to the Army in 1908. We've simply got to have hundreds if not thousands of them!"

"If George Marshall is properly briefed, he could be highly instrumental in bringing that about," General Westover said.

General Westover went to a large wall map adjacent to his desk and pointed to Southeast. "With Japan's army occupying nearly half of the Chinese mainland in just a little over a year, her clear intention's to move on to the Dutch East Indies. Hitler is preparing to invade Czechoslovakia… perhaps all of Europe."

"The isolationist and pacifist influence in our foreign policy will eventually run its course," General Westover concluded and sat back down at his desk. "I believe the day is very near when we'll be forced to equip, train and fight a two front war with an Air Force that has not been dreamed of… all of that…*at the same time*! God help us when that time comes. Even if we could have started yesterday, already be years too late!" He extended his hand to Major Eaker "Well good luck out there tomorrow."

"Thank you, General."

General Westover started to sit down, but had an afterthought. He grinned wryly at the Major. "By the way, Major, see they don't fly out too far from the coast line."

Eaker stopped, hand on the door knob. He caught the General's innuendo and smiled. "Don't worry, Sir." He pondered what the General had said. "You're doing your own flying out to the coast, General?"

"My mechanic, Sergeant Hymen, is going out with me. Why do you ask?"

Major Eaker was reluctant to reveal his apprehension openly. "Well… I…I guess I was just hoping you'd be able to get some rest on the way out, General, that's all."

General Westover smiled. "I'll be all right, Major… just fine."

Major Eaker nodded, and then left the office with General Arnold. Westover gazed after both of them, began to smile when he thought of the conversation that had just taken place. After a moment, he began to look through a folder on his desk marked *Lockheed-Burbank Plant.'*

The next day Major Eaker and C.V. Barnes were seated in the cockpit of the aircraft of the Second Bombardment Group B-17 waiting to be airborne. The sound of the aircraft roared in their ears. Captain Lemay was sitting in the navigator's position discussing navigation technique to Brigadier General George C. Marshall, who was paying close attention to what he was saying. Colonel Olds and General Andrews were also listening to the conversation.

After Lemay finished telling him what he wanted to know, General Marshall moved to the front nose section of the aircraft with Lieutenant J.B. Montgomery who gave him a rundown on the new top secret Norden bomb sight. When he was finished, Montgomery grew intent on his bomb run. The bomb bay doors swung open and the bombs tumbled from the B-17. A mock up outline of a battleship on the bomb range come in to General Marshall's view as the bombs find their mark, and shattered the mock up. The B-17 completed a 180 degree turn back over the target. General Marshall looked down at the devastated mock up, smiled delightedly, and patted Montgomery on the back.

"Well done, Lieutenant Montgomery."

"Thank you, General Marshall."

Colonel Olds leaned into the cockpit and gave Haynes and Eaker a reassuring thumbs up gesture.

Later that afternoon, at the Burbank Lockheed runway in Burbank, California, Major K. B. Wolfe and three Lockheed executives gazed off in the distance at a small military plane as it approached the runway in the distance. General Westover was at the controls of the small aircraft and Sergeant Hymen in the rear seat…dozing. After a moment, General Westover shook his head as if to clear his thinking, his eyes revealing his physical exhaustion.

One of the Lockheed executives turned to Major Wolfe with concern on his face. "Major, I believe something's wrong up there. He's much too low."

Wolfe watched as the aircraft skimmed dangerously low over telephone and high voltage electric lines a mile or so from the end of the runway.

Major Wolfe raised his hands. "Up… pull up, General."

Suddenly the aircraft landing gear snapped a high line, followed by a sudden burst of electrical sparking, and then the aircraft exploded. Major Wolfe and the executives watched in horrified silence. Within seconds, sirens began to wail.

On Major Eaker's B-17, the radio operator pressed his earphones to his ears and began to write something on a small notepad. Then he went to the navigation section where he found General Andrews and General Marshall observing Lemay with his navigation work. The radio operator handed a folded note to General Andrews, who read it and then crushed it between his hands.

Marshall looked at Andrews questioningly.

"It's… Oscar Westover. He was killed a few minutes ago," Andrews replied softly.

Montgomery and Lemay looked at him with shocked expressions on their faces.

CHAPTER 7

A White House aide hurried along ornate hallway, and then turned into the doorway leading into the old Cabinet Room. He entered the room quietly and then stood waiting for a break in the discussion around the large conference table. The aide was annoyed by the repugnant odor of stale tobacco old smoke. President Roosevelt was seated at the head position with Secretary of State Cordell Hull and two aides to the right and Harry Hopkins on the President's left. Hopkins had been speaking when the aide entered the room.

"I respect Secretary Hull's opinion, Mr. President," Hopkins said. "But as Secretary of State, I'm concerned about the broader consequences that could arise from our failure to support further negotiations."

The aide approached the Secretary of State, leaning towards him and speaking softly.

"Excuse me, Mr. Secretary… its Ambassador Kennedy, he's on the line from London, Sir," The aide said.

The aide turned to a bank of telephones along the back wall, lifted a receiver from the hook. "You can take it right here, Sir."

Hull got up and went to the phone. "Hello, Joe?" He said. "Yeah, the President's here now." Hull paused and listened. "Well, we're trying to reach a decision on that matter right now, Joe."

Roosevelt spoke softly to Harry Hopkins. "I agree with Cordell, Harry. I believe the United States ought to evidence some final leadership in the matter. After all, England and France both have consistently sought our opinion ever since the crisis began."

Hull was still on the phone. "Right down the middle, eh?" He listened. "Lindbergh? When?"

Roosevelt paused, looked at Secretary Hull, and then turned back to Hopkins. "If war does break out I want it clear to the rest of the world that it was Hitler's…"

Harry Hopkins interrupted the President. "But, Mr. President! The American Press is already accusing both England and France of selling Czechoslovakia down the river. They're saying the Czechs are being raped! If you send still another last minute message urging the participants to further negotiations you're opening yourself to..."

"Damn!" Cordell Hull said, still on the phone. "All the frontiers? That serious, eh?"

"Harry, we can't sit by idly and let another World War engulf Europe and us without at least *trying* to do something to forestall it… anything," Roosevelt said. "I certainly don't agree with Chamberlain's course of action so far, but we're at the eleventh hour now!"

Cordell Hull ended the telephone conversation with Ambassador Joseph Kennedy. "All right, Joe. Yes, we'll keep working on it and, I'll be in touch tonight."

"Secretary Hull crossed back to the conference table and sat down.

"Mr. President, Ambassador Kennedy sends his regards."

"Joe's in a pretty tough position over there tonight!" the President said.

Secretary Hull nodded affirmatively. "Chamberlain and Deladaier both hope that you'll send one more message to Hitler… urge him to meet with them. The British Parliament is split right down the middle on Chamberlain's appeasement issue. If Hitler crosses the Czech border October first, Chamberlain's opposition wants an immediate declaration of war. I think Chamberlain will resign if there are any hostilities. I get the feeling that the real powers are waiting for the inevitable and will then bring Churchill in. They've already established wartime military and clandestine intelligence operations. J.P.C. Holland has a workable plan and will put it into operation."

"And Chamberlain's for peace at *any price!* You can bet on that," Roosevelt said.

"Seems that way, Mr. President," Hull said.

"What's Germany doing?" Roosevelt asked.

"'Joe said Hitler has got a massive troop concentration pulled up along the Czech border."

President Roosevelt slammed his palm down on the table. "Any fool can see Hitler's over-all master plan and it goes a great deal further than the Sudetenland! Germany's armed to the teeth!"

"Some of the top British politicians had Lindbergh in this morning who apprised them of the massive strength of Hitler's air arm," Hull said.

"What did he tell them?" FDR asked.

"That Hitler's Luftwaffe could defeat all of the air arms of Europe combined." Secretary Hull said.

"I'm sure Lindbergh made quite an impression on Chamberlain, if no one else," Roosevelt said. "However Hitler's air power seems to be what everybody is afraid of. Those claims by the French about the size of the German Air Force being ten times the size reported are true. They've a real threat on their hands. London itself could come under heavy German bombardment."

"France began evacuating all of the art objects from the Louvre this morning, getting them out from the threat of German bombs," Hull said. "England, France… the Czechs… they're in the process of full mobilization."

Roosevelt thought pensively for a moment. "Cord, I want you and Harry to go ahead with options two and three that you've outlined here." He pointed to brief sheets sitting on the table before him. "Tell Hitler he'll achieve a greater place in history by preventing a world war than he would by starting one. Urge him to abandon the October first ultimatum…and…instead… strive to reach a negotiated solution to the problem. We'll send it out to all the parties concerned tonight."

"Yes, Mr. President," Cordell Hull said.

"And Harry, I want you to set up a meeting tomorrow with the Secretaries of War, the Treasury, and the Navy," Roosevelt said. "I want to meet with Malin Craig, Admiral Stark and Hap Arnold too, and, of course, I want you there too, Harry…and Harry, get the President of Boeing on the phone for me, please."

Hopkins nodded. "Yes, Mr. President."

Two months later, in November 1938, Secretary of War Woodring and Assistant Secretary of War Johnson entered the old musty smelling Cabinet room and took their places at the large conference table, briefcases in hand.

Secretary of the Navy Edison, Admiral Stark, the Secretary of the Treasury Morgenthau and Assistant Secretary Oliphant, General Craig, General Marshall, General Arnold, General Brett, Colonel Burns and Harry Hopkins were all sitting around the dark oak conference table, talking softly.

Even as Woodring and Johnson started to seat themselves, a side door at the opposite end of the room opened and a Presidential aide appeared.

"Gentlemen, the President," an aide said.

The conferees stood as the President was wheeled in by Secret Service agent. The President moved into position at the head of the conference table and told everyone to sit down.

"Hap! Good to have you with us," The President said.

"Thank you, Mr. President," General Arnold said.

President Roosevelt grinned mischievously as he looked around the table. "We… uh… had a little bit of difficulty with Hap's appointment, you know." The group stared at the President as he continued. "The investigating committee received a report that Hap was frequently seen drunk and disorderly on the streets of Honolulu during a tour of duty out there several years ago. Of course, that was all pretty serious… then… the committee discovered that Hap had never been to Hawaii!"

Everyone began to laugh and the President turned to General Arnold.

"I didn't realize Air Corps leaders generated that kind of resentment, Hap. I thought that was reserved for Presidents."

"Yes, Sir, just wait until the next broadside is fired. They'll question who my parents really are and claim I'm a German double agent," Arnold said mockingly. The President laughed loudly.

The expression on the President's face became serious when he opened a folder on the conference table before him. Similar folders had previously been placed at each position around the table.

"Gentlemen, you've before you a report that deals with our industrial capacity to manufacture airplanes in large quantities," the President said.

Several of the conferees began to open their folders.

"The report was compiled secretly at my request by Harry Hopkins, General Westover before his death, and with the assistance of General Arnold, of course."

President Roosevelt looked around the table "The devastating effect of the German Luftwaffe bombers has played a major role in the recent appeasement policies of France and England, and this has led to certain inescapable conclusions. We need airplanes…*now*! And…lots of them!"

Secretary Woodring frowned. "Mr. President, the war department has already submitted the plans for the expansion of our ground forces… and air forces for the years 1939-1940. I believe we've recommended the procurement of… uh…" Woodring opened a report he'd brought with him and searched for the right page. "One hundred seven aircraft are projected for Air Corps expansion during the next two years." The General Staff is in agreement with that number of new aircraft."

Roosevelt visibly showed anger as he said "Secretary Woodring, a new regiment of field artillery… or a new barracks at an Army post in Wyoming… that's not going to scare Hitler one damned bit! Only *airplanes* will do that! And… the hundred seven airplanes of various types that you've included in your expansion plan would be tragically inadequate! We need modern long range bombers like the B-17 and in large numbers."

"Surely, you don't feel that our Army and Navy are incapable of defending the country, Sir?" Woodring countered.

"Not at all, Malin," President Roosevelt said. "I'm saying that airplanes are the only implements of war that will have an influence on Hitler's *future* plans."

"What type of Air Corps capability are you talking about, Mr. President?" Admiral Stark asked.

"I'm talking about air power generally, Admiral Stark. Aviation… developed to its maximum potential as a means of waging war! Protecting our hemispheric shorelines! Depriving the enemy of his industrial capacity!

Destroying his *will* to make war! And…supporting our surface defenses."

General Craig frowned. "But Mr. President! Those objectives are already clearly defined in the missions of the Army ground forces."

"I know that, Malin. But Hitler's Luftwaffe has clearly shown in Spain and in Eastern Europe that aviation will pay a major role in this war. In short, your battle plans need to be updated."

Admiral Stark said, "The Navy has traditionally been our first line of defense, Mr. President, particularly the defense of our shorelines. That's our mission, Sir."

"We must begin to rethink those previously defined missions, gentlemen," President Roosevelt said. He indicated the folder by tapping his finger on it. "This report will immediately be updated. The Army ground forces have their area of war time responsibilities and combat mission. This mission statement clearly outlines the individual missions of our military services. It served us well in the Great War."

He again indicated the folder. This report immediately establishes an Air Corps of seven-thousand five-hundred air craft… with a production of ten-to-twenty-thousand additional planes a year to follow."

"The Congress… the American people will never buy that, Mr. President," Secretary Morgenthau said.

"Gentlemen, I well realize all of the implications involved and the attitude of the American people themselves. But we're faced with the gravest crisis in history. I'm convinced now that we should've begun expanding our Air Corps years ago. I… I can only pray, as the rest of you should, that we're not too late." He opened the report folder. "Now let's get to the report itself and see if we can develop a new strategy to defend the U.S. and god forbid, engage in a war in Europe."

General Arnold and General Brett walked out of the old Cabinet room, briefcases in their hands and smiling broadly. They had only moved a short distance down when General Marshall emerged from the old conference room. He caught up with them as they passed into a spacious hallway.

"Well, the Air Corps finally got its Magna Carta," General Marshall said.

"Thanks to you and Mr. Hopkins," General Arnold said.

"No, General not entirely," General Marshall said. "The Army Tactical School… Billy Mitchell… Oscar Westover… you… Andrews and his Second Bombardment people…all of you made the evidence of our tragic position undeniable."

"Wish General Mitchell could have been here this afternoon," General Arnold said.

General Marshall nodded at General Arnold. "Well we've won a battle, but not the war. I'll need all the data on the B-17 procurement schedules. What the President said in there will be construed by the War Department general staff to mean medium bombers, *not four engine heavy bombers. Air power* may have been saved today…but the battle of *strategic* air power is still to be fought."

"I'll get our people on it right away," General Arnold said.

General Craig and Colonel Burns left the old cabinet room and began to walk towards General Arnold. General Craig was smiling broadly as he extended his hand to General Arnold.

"Hap, I'll be over to see you in the morning. I have some questions about the report." He thought for a moment. "Our…defense emphasis is shifting…and that's hard for me to accept. But I just want you to know that I'm with you."

The two men shook hands and General Arnold said: "Thank you, Sir."

General Arnold and General Brett watched as General Craig, General Marshall and Colonel Burns walked away.

With the telephone receiver to his ear, the sergeant receptionist at the office of the Chief of the Air Corps office flipped a switch on the intercom.

"General Arnold, the radio room is on the line, Sir," The sergeant said. "They've got a radio message coming in from the Queen Elizabeth. She's docking in New York in a few hours."

General Arnold was working at his desk and lifted the telephone receiver from its cradle. "General Arnold here." He listened for a moment. "Lindbergh! Tomorrow?" He paused for a moment. "Well, I don't know. Mrs. Arnold and I, we're leaving for West Point tonight. We're going to the Army-Navy game. Look… tell him we'll be at the Thayer Hotel up there. It's a good place to meet. Private… no reporters. Maybe he'll want to see the game too."

The huge passenger ship docked at the New York waterfront pier and people began to disembark. Crowds of relatives, and friends waited anxiously, happily at the foot of the gang plank. Among those who started down the gang plank were Charles and Anne Lindbergh who were met by several reporters as they stepped onto the pier.

"Colonel Lindbergh… Colonel Lindbergh!" shouted one reporter.

Lindbergh frowned, unhappy with the reporter and the crowd that had begun to gather around him and his wife.

"Why do you think Air Marshall Goering gave you such a complete look at the Luftwaffe?"

"Look, gentlemen, I've just finished a two hour press conference on board the ship there. Why didn't you fellows attend that?"

The reporters completely disregarded Lindbergh's position and continued to clamor over the crowd noise with their questions. Every few minutes a photographer's flash bulbs popped.

"Do you think your report to the British Parliament was responsible for Chamberlain's giving in to Hitler at Munich?" another reporter asked.

"As I told your colleagues earlier, I only told the British what I had seen in Germany," Lindbergh said.

The first reporter asked: "Colonel, do you really think Hitler could whip England and the United States?"

"They're presently superior in air power," Lindbergh said.

"You were treated pretty royally by the Germans over there. They even decorated you, didn't they?" A third reporter asked.

"I'd rather not respond to that," Lindbergh said.

"Are you returning to the U.S. to live, or just to visit?"

"We've come home to stay," Lindbergh said with a tone of disgust at the implications of the question.

"Have you and Mrs. Lindbergh gotten over the kidnap-murder of your son, Colonel?' The reporter glared at Lindbergh. "Is that why you've come home?"

Suddenly, Lindbergh, repulsed by the line of questioning, pushed his way through the crowd, propelling his wife, Anne, ahead of him.

In the poorly illuminated main dining room of the Thayer Hotel in West Point, New York, a waiter dressed in a white waistcoat and a black bow tie brought coffee to a table where Charles Lindbergh and General and Mrs. Arnold were seated. The waiter refilled their coffee cups and walked away. The dining room was empty, having been cleared in deference to the meeting taking place there.

"Well…I…guess that's about it," Lindbergh said thoughtfully. "I'll submit a comprehensive report just as soon as I can get my notes in order."

"I'd appreciate it," General Arnold said. He paused. "I find it difficult to believe that Germany could have amassed such airpower without U.S. and British Intelligence knowledge of it."

"They'll continue to use the Luftwaffe as a black mail capability," Lindbergh said. "Of course, I was selected for their premier unveiling because they felt the world would listen to what I had to say about air power... no matter whose it was."

"I spoke with General Craig before I left Washington, yesterday afternoon, Colonel Lindbergh," General Arnold said. "He's appointed a board to develop a five year plan for the Air Corps. It'll be headed by General Kilner. He'd like to have you serve on it."

Well…I…suppose I'll do what I can, General," Lindbergh said.

Thanks, your input will be of significant value to our development of both fighters and bombers in a battleship mentality. I think you can see our future involvement over there as well as I can. We must develop our aviation capability as quickly as possible. Even with that sense of urgency, it may be far too short of the level required for our initial entrance into hostilities."

Lindbergh looked at Arnold and smiled, "I'm relieved that you can understand my deep concern. You're right. It will not be enough when the first American shot is fired. That shot will be fired far sooner than you or even Roosevelt think."

"How long do we've?" asked Arnold.

Lindbergh sat quietly for a moment then replied, "We'll need to help the British within six months. We'll become involved directly within two years at most."

Arnold had a cold sick feeling at the ominous words of this aviation hero.

CHAPTER 8

A newsboy riding a bicycle approached the Lemay residence at Langley Field and tossed the morning newspaper against the door. Helen Lemay opened the door and retrieved the paper and a bottle of milk before softly closing the door behind her. She unrolled the newspaper and gazed at the headlines. *Hitler Invades Poland.* Underneath that in smaller, but still bold column headline: *General George Catelet Marshall succeeds Malin Craig.*

Helen walked from the door into the dinette area where Curt Lemay and Janie were sitting at the table eating breakfast.

Lemay playfully fed Janie some baby food which she promptly spit out playfully.

Helen passed the newspaper to Lemay as she sat down at the table.

"What does it all mean, Curt?" She asked

Lemay glanced at the newspaper. "That we're in a helluva lot of trouble!"

"At least they had the good sense to appoint George Marshall to succeed General Craig," Helen said

"Thanks to that old fuddy-duddy, Craig, and the others up there on general staff like him. We're four or five years away from an adequate air force … and the damned War started yesterday!"

"You shouldn't speak so gruffly around Janie, darling," Helen said.

Lemay gazed at Janie and then smiled at her. "Guess I shouldn't at that."

Lemay folded his napkin, placed it in his plate, brushed Janie's cheek with a kiss, and then kissed Helen tenderly. He went to a coat rack by the front entrance, put his garrison cap on, then, waved goodbye to Helen and Janie.

Helen rose, went to the kitchen window, looked out at Lemay as he started the family car, began backing out of the driveway, then caught sight of Helen gazing out at him, and blew her a kiss.

Helen gazed after Lemay pensively.

When Lemay got to the flight line, there was a lot of unscheduled activity. The news from Europe had made everyone very conscious of what could happen here and its effect on their lives. They had been training for this situation but in training it was always just an exercise. It was just play and not the real thing. Before today, when they were finished they went home and had supper and sat down in an easy chair and listened to Amos and Andy and the Great Gildersleeve on the radio while drinking a beer. This changes things for everyone. In a war people die, especially if they're not properly trained as a combat unit. Now, they eagerly looked forward to training and what it could do to keep them alive when the U.S. ultimately got into the war.

Lemay saw Bart Coltrane looking at the left main landing gear of a B-17.

"What's the problem, Bart?" asked Lemay.

"Bart Coltrane pulled his head out from the wheel well and put on his hat. "I've noticed that the hydraulic line seems to become badly chaffed and eventually fails after three or four hundred hours of flight. I got the boys in maintenance to put high pressure connectors on the ends of a grease gun hose. I just installed it in this plane to see if giving it an additional four inches, so it could go further back in the wheel well during flight, would stop the problem. I just don't think the boys at Boeing had enough time to detect this problem. I put a new standard equipment hose on the other side so we had a good comparison."

Lemay took off his hat and stuck his head in the wheel well to see the unauthorized installation. He noted the path and projected movement of the new test hose. He came out and looked at Coltrane.

"While you're right about the problem and this is unauthorized," Lemay said, then looked up at it again. "Okay, write a memo to me covering your thoughts and anticipated results. We'll call this a 'field test.' "

"I think you've a good idea and a practical solution. Keep it up. This is what we need to really make this bird ready for combat," Lemay said as he walked away.

CHAPTER 9

On a street in downtown Seattle, a well dressed man stopped at a newsstand and bought a copy of the Wall Street *Journal.* He quickly read the headlines, then folded the paper under his arm and paid the newsboy. Then he opened the newspaper again and read the headline.

"Kilner-Lindbergh Report Submitted to Congress"

At the main Boeing-Aircraft factory in Seattle, Ed Wells and P.G. Johnson, the President of Boeing Aircraft, stood talking in front of partially complete mock-up of a primitive B-29 concept.

Johnson looked up at the forward section of the mock-up. "It'd be a beautiful airplane Ed… even if it had nothing else going for it."

"I… I just hope we're not wasting our money," Ed Wells said. "Well, the Kilner-Lindbergh report's going to carry some weight, P. G. Our sources at Material Command reinforce that opinion."

Johnson was suddenly exasperated. "They're under the same damned pressures from the War Department everybody else is under!"

"Look, Ed… Louis Johnson's still holding firm on the $195,000 price tag for the B-17. He knows we'll lose money at that price."

"I'm sure he's under pressure to hold the budget down," Ed Wells said.

"Budget hell!" Johnson exclaimed. "He's being pressured to hold that price simply because the War Department General Staff think we'll cancel the whole damned program! That would divert more budget monies to the development of battleships and tanks! Those self serving bastards are only concerned with their own turf and perceived importance."

Johnson paused, trying to control his temper. "Believe me, I'm tempted. They've only ordered thirty-five B-17s anyway… and they want the "add-on" option extended through April, 1940. What the hell do they think we're - a charitable organization?"

"Well… with world events developing as they're, a long range super bomber might very well become critical to our national defense, especially if England and France fall to Hitler."

Johnson gazed at the mock up. "You foresee any problems?"

"Power plants! Nothing available right now that will develop the required horse power." Ed Wells said.

"Well …?" Johnson asked.

"The Wright people, they're developing a twin radial…the R3350. The problem is delivering it in time."

"Go ahead with your plans and research Ed," Johnson said. "As President of the Company, I can authorize it. "I'll square it with the board of directors somehow. Maybe they'll realize somebody's got to look out for the country even if the Pentagon warriors won't."

Wells gazed after Johnson as he walked away. A technician walked up and gave a blueprint to Wells, pointing to a questionable area on the print.

Wells turned his attention to the print, shaking his head as he listened.

CHAPTER 10

Two well-dressed middle-aged gentlemen got out of a government sedan at the historic Reform Club situated in the Pall Mall suburb of London. They're met by a tall, slim man of the same age who extended his hand in welcome. "Welcome back to the Reform Club, Winston," said the man as he walked into the main salon on the first floor.

Churchill looked around the stately appointed paintings and historical plaques decorating the walls briefly and said "It's the same bloody place it was in 1913 when I resigned. Some things just don't change. Now where are we going to meet, Holland?"

"I have arranged for us to use the Library. I have asked that we not be disturbed," J.P.C. Holland said in a dry matter-of-fact tone. They walked past the gentlemen reading the *Times* and sipping cognac in the reading room as they entered a large room with beautiful cherry wood paneling surrounding walls of books, paintings and other important documents encased in ornate picture frames. Churchill took a seat at the end of a long mahogany table with twelve Louis XIV chairs around the table.

"Okay, where are we with our as yet unapproved clandestine intelligence service?" Churchill asked.

"A quick question, Winston. Has the King and opposition party in Parliament set a date for you to become the Prime Minister?" asked Holland.

The future British Prime Minister leaned back lighting his cigar and looked at the group seated around the table. "Yes, we're looking at mid-May. His Majesty feels that the appropriate political posture and maneuvering can be done by then. Chamberlin's peace at any cost has not been a success to say the least. His agreement with Mr. Hitler isn't worthy of paper for the crapper. In the meantime, he fully expects this group to develop a viable and operational clandestine intelligence service. We should be able to officially authorize it in the House of Commons and House of Lords in late June or early July. The political problems should be resolved by then. Until then, we must proceed without legal authorization and completely hush hush. We must not be exposed as it would embarrass the King and cause a great deal of political problems here and abroad. Yes, his majesty has given us clear direction, but it must be done totally behind the veil of secrecy. Maintaining secrecy may be a challenge to you chaps given my official mission orders to Dalton was simply, "Set Europe ablaze." If I know Dalton, he'll do just that.

"Grubbins," said Churchill, 'How is Dalton doing across the Channel?'"

"Sir, it's difficult to find capable people in the countries who we can rely on. They often don't have a clue on how to organize the locals and maintain secrecy. The Gestapo is finding and interrogating them as fast as they get started. Supply is another problem along with communications. We've developed a radio called a Type 'A' Mark III transceiver to send in with our people or get into the hands of resistance leaders who have some basic knowledge of how the radio works. We must send more of our people in to train and organize them. We're identifying, recruiting and training agents to insert but it's a slow process. This is a far bigger challenge than we originally projected. Supply and resupply is another big problem. We've set up a unit down at Tangmere flying Lysanders. They're great for this type of mission, but they're limited on range and payload. It can only carry one passenger and about 250 kilos of supplies. We've some excellent covert operations in the early stages or organization in Norway, Denmark, Spain, Holland and France. We just can't service them by air due to the short range of the Lysander, even if they fly out of the new base being built at Tempsford. We tried using Whitney bombers with unsatisfactory results. They've the range and payload capability but are extremely vulnerable to anti aircraft fire. So far we've lost four out of five missions. We really need a medium range aircraft that can fly at very low altitude and has the maneuverability and fire power to take on the Luftwaffe fighters."

Churchill turned his head back to the map slowly smoking his cigar. He remained silent for almost a minute contemplating the situation. "What is Dalton's position on the aviation requirement and his ability to develop the required number of agents capable of working behind the lines?"

"Let's first cover the recruiting and training," said Grubbins. "We've found that it's extremely important that selected agents be very knowledgeable on the specific area being assigned to or risk being arrested by the Gestapo. They must already speak the specific language of the area. Book or school language education will not really work. Dalton is encouraged by the number of qualified volunteers. He's begun to acquire the needed training facilities."

"Most of our facilities are being requisitioned in the Milton Keynes area. Chicheley Hall has recently opened and training commenced. Poundon House is due to be operational in sixty days. There are a large number of volunteers in the respective countries that we can use if we can extract them by air. The Lysander is the only aircraft that can work for us as long as it isn't further than 400 air miles away. Dalton has learned of a possible aircraft that's being developed in the United States that could solve the problem for us."

"What would that aircraft be?" Churchill asked as he watched his cigar smoke drift toward the ceiling.

"The U.S. has a plane being built known as the NA-62. It's still classified as secret, but we got word about it from the U.S. Air Attaché in London. They're going to give it a designation of B-25. It's maneuverable, good firepower, has a 1,350 mile range with a payload of 3,000 pounds. It's perfect for low altitude resupply missions. Do you think we could get the Yanks to lend us one or two?" Grubbins asked in conclusion.

Churchill pointed his cigar at Grubbins and said in contemplation of the many ramifications of the issue, "That will be a real sticky one for sure. I'll make a call to Harry Hopkins and see what can be worked out. There's a lot of political opposition to any transfer of any equipment, services or personnel to us. We're working on an idea that would allow them to "Lend" or "Lease" certain items, but that's months away from being a reality. Until then, we just have to ask for training personnel with associated equipment. We might get lucky and get one or two of the aircraft with experienced crews. Tell Dalton to be ready to go over to Washington in a couple of weeks. Is there anything else?" If not, I'll leave you gentlemen to your cloaks and daggers."

In a committee room located in the Senate Building in Washington D.C., Senator Clay was sitting behind a curved panel type conference table, flanked by three Senate colleagues on each side along with various aides. General Arnold, General Brett and their aides are seated before the panel, with the usual spectators and news people seen in the in attendance.

Senator Clay, who had been talking, now lifted a thickly bound report from the table before him.

"General Arnold, I have here a preliminary report issued by the Kilner-Lindberg Board that was recently submitted to the War Department. Now… my question is: just *who* are we going to fight with all of this super air power?"

"Well, Senator, it seems to me that the report is quite clear on that matter. Germany used 600 aircraft to flatten Madrid and Durango in 1937. Mussolini's air power allowed him to occupy Ethiopia. Hitler's Luftwaffe brought about the Munich appeasement!" General Arnold said. "Today, England and France are at war with those same belligerents…and if they should fail to overcome them, well then…."

Senator Clay interrupted. "Why even Colonel Charles Lindbergh, one of your own kind, doesn't seem to feel that we've an enemy to worry about… as long as we don't go looking for one!" The Senator reached for another sheet from the table. "Allow me to quote Colonel Lindbergh: 'Let us not delude ourselves, if we enter the quarrels of Europe during War, we must stay in there in time of peace as well. If we enter fighting for democracy abroad, we may end by losing it at home. What more could we ask than the Atlantic Ocean on the east, the Pacific on the west? An ocean is a formidable barrier, even for modern aircraft.' Senator Clay looked disdainfully at General Arnold. "So…I ask you, General Arnold, who is this invincible enemy you speak of so ominously?"

General Arnold stared in dumbfounded incredibility at the Senator.

"Well…?"

Arnold found the words he wanted to use in tell this pompous bastard, but he decided to refrain and use a more polite choice of words. "Senator, every day the newspapers radio news and dispatches from the governments of Europe report the exploits of the German Army and Luftwaffe. It's only a matter of time before we're forced by circumstances and honorable obligation to England to provide assistance. The enemy threat is clear to most Americans. I don't see how you could fail to see the obvious."

A very embarrassed Senator Clay slammed his gavel down and announced "Committee adjourned," He left the room red faced and angry. General Arnold stood up and smiled. He knew that he would pay dearly for those choice words. But to see that asshole lose his composure was worth the price.

CHAPTER 11

The weather was clear but unusually humid for August 1940 when Colonel Olds walked up to Captain Lemay at the March Field Transit Terminal. Lemay stiffened up to attention and saluted Olds and asked, "What's this all about, Sir?"

Curt, I don't have a clue." I got a call from General Andrews who said to meet these VIPs and give them our full and absolute cooperation. They're here at the specific direction of the President."

"Wow, that's real horsepower," he said expressing his being impressed with the situation. That must be their C-47 landing on three two."

The C-47 transport pulled up in front of the transmit terminal and shut down the engines. The door opened and General Andrew's aide-de-camp deplaned ahead of three men in civilian clothes and General Andrews being the last off. The delegation came over to Colonel Olds and Lemay.

General Andrews returned Olds and Lemay's salutes and introduced the civilians. "Colonel Olds, this is Mr. Roberts, the Deputy Under-Secretary of State, and this, gentlemen, is Major Sir Hugh Dalton and Squadron Leader Howarth, our special visitors who have the full backing of the President. Major Dalton works as a special representative of the British government. He needs some highly specialized personnel of ours for an extremely important mission. Squadron Leader Howarth is our liaison to the RAF Special Operations Executive and will be training our people for a special mission. Let's go find a place we can talk besides this hot ramp.

"This way, Sir," Olds said pointing to the two staff cars standing by.

Ten minutes later they were in a conference room at the base headquarters building. After all were seated and the door closed with a guard posted outside, General Andrews continued. 'Major Dalton and I are looking for an experienced and exceptional bomber pilot who has a keen understanding of aircraft tactical operations. He must have the intelligence and leadership to be a project manager now and a squadron leader in combat later.

"Our second requirement is for a highly skilled navigator that has the ability to fly long over water missions," he said looking directly at Olds.

Third is for a crew chief that's an exceptional aircraft maintenance man. This man should know all aspects of aircraft operations and maintenance. Plus be able to work independently in a clandestine environment.

Four is two junior maintenance personnel that have at least three years in either military or civilian aircraft maintenance.

Fifth is a co-pilot that has above average potential and won't freeze upon in a combat situation.

"Now Colonel Olds, who do you know and recommend for this mission?" the General said with confidence.

Lemay raised his hand and asked, "Sir, you didn't mention a bombardier."

"None necessary, Curt," Andrews replied.

Olds and Lemay turned to each other and discussed various names for about 30 seconds then turned back to Andrews.

"Sir," Olds said, "Captain Lemay has some names for your consideration."

"Question, Sir," Lemay asked, "can I assume that the crew will be working with a new aircraft at the factory level and taking it to a combat situation?"

A big smile came over Major Dalton's face and he said "That's correct."

"That narrows the possibilities to a very few. Sir, we would recommend the following," Lemay said taking a breath.

"Pilot – Captain Bart Coltrane

"Navigator – Lieutenant Kelly Sharp

"Co-pilot – Lieutenant Robby West

"Crew Chief – SFC Rupert Royston

"Chief Mechanic – Sergeant Jack Martin

"A&P Mechanic – Corporal Andy Lightfoot

"These are the very best men we've at March that meet your requirements," Lemay finished."

"Colonel Olds, have these men in this briefing room at 1330 hours today," the General commanded as he turned away from Olds and left the room.

Lemay and Olds stood to attention as the General and Major Dalton left. "That just gives us forty-five minutes to round them up," said Olds. "If you can get the pilot and navigator, I'll get the others here, okay?"

Lemay nodded and left the room in an almost run.

Captain Coltrane came into a small conference room at base headquarters and saw that there were five others already there. He knew all of them even if most were from other units. As he entered, everyone looked at him and silently asked the question, "Why am I here?"

Coltrane looked around at the stares and said, "I haven't a clue." He sat down as everyone smiled at the comment. Coltrane thought to himself , "It's never good to be in a room of excellent people without knowing why you were there."

Just then the door opened and Colonel Olds came in and called the room to attention. Then he was followed by General Andrews and a bunch of men in civilian clothes.

Seeing a four-star General, everyone became nervous and weak in the knees.

"At ease, gentlemen, take your seats," commanded the General.

Colonel Olds stood at the end of the table next to the blackboard. He lifted a clipboard and looked at the paper on it then looked up. He started a roll call of sorts. "Captain Coltrane, please stand. General, this is Captain Bart Coltrane who is an excellent pilot and navigator. He's experienced in aviation and maintenance. Okay, Bart, sit down." "Lieutenant Kelly Sharp" he said, as Sharp stood without being told, "is an outstanding navigator. He flew for Pan Am on the Miami to Buenos Aires-Rio run." Olds nodded and Sharp sat down. He continued, "Sergeant First Class Rupert Royston, a 1922 British immigrant who worked for North American Aviation and Boeing before joining the Army Air Corps in 1933. He knows every nut, bolt and rivet in our bomber aircraft. Sit, please. Next is Sergeant Jack Martin, who worked in the Curtis Wright Engine Plant prior to the service. Our other aircraft mechanic is Corporal Andy Lightfoot, who was an assembly line worker at Douglas Aircraft before enlisting."

Robby West looked around to see why he had not been introduced. This attracted Olds attention who smiled and said, "lastly, General, we've Second Lieutenant Robby West, the selected co-pilot who has volunteered."

West blurted out, "Volunteered?" Everyone laughed.

Olds continued, "Just pulling your leg, Robby." Lieutenant West is considered by his commander to be an exceptional aviator dispute his youth and experience. General Andrews, these are the best we've here at March Field." Then he sat down next to Coltrane.

General Andrews moved forward to where Olds had been standing and put his hat on the table. He looked at the six men at the table silently then said, "Gentlemen, from this point on everything said in this room is classified top secret. He paused, then continued, "The two gentlemen at the end of the table are special visitors from England who have a special situation that required some support from us. The President has sent them here for us to provide a solution to their problem. It will require volunteers who are willing and capable of undertaking a very difficult and extremely dangerous mission in Europe. If you volunteer, you'll be reassigned overseas and will be working with our dearest allies in their struggle against the Axis Power. Again, I must warn you that the mission is extremely dangerous, but of utmost importance. If anyone wants to volunteer, remain seated. Those of you who are not interested, may now leave. Remember, you're not to divulge anything said in this room should you not volunteer. Anyone care to leave? Silence came over the room. Nobody moved or even looked around.

Andrews looked over at Dalton and smiled. "Very good! Now let me introduce our visitors," the General said with a calm air and easy demeanor.

"The gentlemen in the corner is Mr. Roberts who is the Deputy Undersecretary of State here as the personal representative of President Roosevelt. The gentleman at the end of the table is Major Hugh Dalton, who is a special representative of General Sir J.P.C. Holland, head of Section D, Sabotage and Subversion Section, of the British Special Intelligence Service. Across from him is Squadron Leader Horwarth, who is the British Liaison to this mission from the RAF Special Operations Executive, or better known as the SOE. His section flies a Lysander over hostile territory supplying resistance fighters and deploying British agents. He'll be assisting in the modifications of your aircraft for the mission. Later he'll train you in the type of flying to be performed out of England. He'll also teach you the important policies and procedures for flying in and out of England. When you and your plane are ready, you'll deploy to England. Once there, you'll conduct highly sensitive clandestine flights into occupied Europe in support of resistance movements operating throughout the area of conflict. You'll report directly to Major Dalton who directs their entire operation. Captain Coltrane is the project manager for the aircraft development portion of the U.S. side and is Squadron Commander of the unit. Bart, your squadron consists of one aircraft…for now, with others on the way.

Mr. Roberts from the State Department has some information. "Mr. Roberts," the General said as he sat down and the bureaucrat came forward.

"Afternoon gentlemen," Roberts said in a soft voice. Coltrane could see this was another limp wristed bureaucrat who was as worthless as teats on a bore hog. He took an immediate dislike towards him.

As you know, the United States isn't at war and is maintaining a position of neutrality at this time. Officially, you're members of the U.S. Army Training Command in England to train British pilots on the characteristics and deployment of U.S. aircraft in reconnaissance and maritime search and recovery missions. This is your cover story for everyone on both sides of the Atlantic. Unless told otherwise by Major Dalton, you must assume that nobody has been cleared or has a need to know. This program and your operations are classified top secret sensitive information. Very few people in State, War, Army Air Corps and the White House know of the mission.

"The President has decided to show his appreciation for accepting this important and dangerous mission by promoting each of you one rank. That will help as you'll need the extra money living on the British economy instead of a military base. Since you'll be living near the remote base or in London, you'll be given an additional allowance. You'll be paid a $10 per day food allowance and housing allowance. Officers living in London next to the headquarters will also get a $15 per month train and taxi allowance. This is to cover your travels back and forth from the headquarters and the remote airfield. Lastly, your mail will be sent through a special Armed Forced Postal Office in Washington. You'll write your mail and put it into another envelope and send it to the APO where it will be mailed from there. Mail will show a Washington address instead of a British posting. This is an important security matter. You're to tell your family and friends that you're training pilots at various bases in the U.S. and Canada so you don't have a permanent assignment station. That will discourage the desire for people to come see you. For all intensive purposes, you're to disappear here in the states. Are there any questions?"

Major Dalton stood up and went over to the map. "Gentlemen let me extend my congratulations to you on your courage to volunteer and your new promotions. You'll certainly earn them and quickly. As you know, we're in a nasty conflict in Europe. Mr. Hitler attacked Poland last October and is gobbling up all of Western Europe in his so-called Blitzkrieg. Currently, we're engaged in what the press has called 'The Battle of Britain,' and so it's. Our chaps are fighting off the bloody Bosch aircraft by day and night and I might say in a bloody good fashion.

"Mr. Hitler has encountered a very nasty problem. It seems that the residents of those countries that he's occupied have some basic objection to his plans. They either are trying to form, or are in the process of forming, local resistance groups to fight the Bosch in guerilla operations. They also gather critical intelligence for us which is critical to the war effort.

"Since the outbreak of hostilities in October, we've been trying to make contact with these resistance groups and others within Europe that will fight the Germans once they've completed their land grab. Communication is difficult at best. Knowing who will fight and who will report the resistance group activities to the Gestapo is even more difficult. We've sent in a half dozen agents who all have been killed or captured within a fortnight. We learned a lot from their sacrifices and have changed our tactics and procedures. We're getting footholds in France, Spain, Holland, Netherlands, Denmark, Belgium and Norway. And yes, we even have a couple of resources in Germany and Italy. All of these are in the very early stages of development and training. Most of the people are just farmers, shop keepers and the average bloke. They don't know a bloody thing about sabotage, intelligence gathering and resistance operations. We're helping by providing agents who will train them and supplies. So far, we've organized the main air operations out of Tangmere, a coastal airfield south of London. That's where Squadron Leader Howarth has been operating. Recently, we started construction of a new base near Tempsford just north of London where we're going to hide your flight operations. Squadron Commander Howarth and his men have been unofficially flying over our newly trained agents and supplies to the resistance groups in a Lysander at night. The Lysander is a weird looking bird but is truly ideal for its covert mission. It's a single pilot aircraft that can carry a rear gunner or a passenger. But not both! It can carry about a thousand pounds of cargo or a passenger/cargo combination. It's a very rugged aircraft that can land on rough terrain. It can land in 320 meters and take off in 250 meters. Its range is only 600 miles. It's two Browning 303 machine guns fitted into its wheel spats. Not much protection and they're fixed so the pilot has to make himself vulnerable to even take a shot at the bloody bastards. Frequently, we've made small drops of supplies only to have our Lysander and the resistance fighters on the ground be ambushed by the Gestapo or Abwehr. The Lysander can do little to fight off the Germans until the supplies are collected or the escape of the fighters. It's a very sticky situation that must be changed.

"They're also subject to German fighters. So far, we've been lucky on that point as the Germans don't fly very much at night when we do. We've tried to use Wellington and Whitley bombers to increase the size of our supply payload as well as range, but that was disastrous. They're big, slow and easy targets for both anti aircraft and fighters. They've no maneuverability and cannot fly as low as the Lysander or low enough to avoid the Flak.

Coltrane raised his hand and said without being recognized, "Sir, the B-17 would have the same limitations. The Whitley is a good aircraft too but both would be sitting ducks."

"You're absolutely correct, Major, Coltrane" said Squadron Command Colin Howarth. "But the B-25 does not."

"B-25!" exclaimed Coltrane. "That bird is just now in test flight. No telling when and if it will be certified and accepted by the Army Air Corps, Sir."

Dalton took the conversation back to himself, "The B-25 made it's first test flight forty days ago. The subsequent test flights showed no problems. The U.S. government has made an initial order and the British government has ordered one with an option on three others. North American Aviation has been directed to start immediate production of the bomber. The jig for aircraft 40-007BX was laid down yesterday. That will be your bird." It's one of the very first production models."

Everyone in the room was stunned.

"Shall we continue?" Dalton asked.

"Sir," asked Kelly Sharp, a B-25 is a bomber but there's no bombardier in the room."

"Very good point, Captain Sharp and I shall explain in a moment," Dalton said as he took a sip from a glass of water. Then he looked over at General Andrews and continued. "You won't be dropping bombs. You'll drop people and supplies. Occasionally, you'll pick up passengers in the occupied territory and nip on back to London.

"Be patient and all of the pieces will fall into place," Dalton said. He took a breath then continued.

"This Operation is named 'Black Bart.' No, Major Coltrane, it's not after you. It's named after a British Pirate John Bartholomew Roberts of Pembrokeshire, Wales. During the golden age of piracy, he was the most successful. He captured over 470 vessels before he was killed in battle in 1722. It's hoped that you'll be our "pirate" and steal success from the Germans. You're to make very low level flights deep into occupied territory and drop off thousands of pounds of supplies, agents, communicate with the underground resistance fighters, perhaps "pick up a few for debriefing in London. If necessary, provide fire support so they can get the supplies and escape. Your B-25 will be modified especially for this purpose. Since it's cargo and personnel that will be delivered, there's no need for a bombardier. High speed low level flying is the order of the day, gentlemen."

"Anyone getting weak in the knees or want out?" asked General Andrews. There was no reply. The general smiled and set back down.

Dalton continued, "Black Bart Missions are high priority as the resistance units rely solely on our shipments to be able to conduct operations against the Germans. We must drop in our agents as well as extract them. There are very few places that you can land a B-25 in enemy territory, so I wouldn't expect that to be a big item."

"As I mentioned earlier you'll be based at Tempsford, about sixty miles north of London. The base is still under construction. Currently, we only have one operational runway with the second to be finished within a few months. There will be a third scheduled to be completed by February, 1942, weather permitting. Come December of next year, we'll be putting some Wellingtons from Bassingbourn there as well. Wing Commander P.C. Pickard is also deploying a special mission squadron there in the spring. The navigational radios and tower are up and operational. Secretly, we've been flying a few of our SOE Lysander's out of there to take some of the load off Tangmere. As you may guess, the facilities are limited. We have a large tent erected to put your bird out of the elements. Hangar space is full and we don't want general knowledge of your operations known, even to our own personnel. My experience tells me that after a few missions, the Germans will put a very high price on your heads and for information on you and your whereabouts. One lone B-25 will undoubtedly attract a lot of attention anyway, but let's not expose the mission any more than necessary.

"For the enlisted crew, we've a nice three-bedroom cottage for you in Tempsford. Yes, we're trying to reduce your exposure to the other crews. We don't want to put you on the spot having to lie to them as to what you do. Most are a part of the Lysander operation but still don't have the need to know. Many are support personnel and other RAF personnel don't know and cannot be told. The Germans have operatives in England and would not hesitate to kill you or destroy your plane.

"The cottage for the enlisted personnel is very cozy. You've a house lady that will come by every weekday morning to put out a breakfast, do your laundry and keep the place tidy. If you want her to cook for you too, you'll need to take up a fee with her. Your hanger, or should I say, tent, is within a brisk walk of your cottage, but we'll have a Lorry for you as well. Tempsford has several good places to eat and get a pint of ale. I recommend The Anchor and The Wheatshief. You can eat at the enlisted mess hall as usual. You're work will be generally during the daylight as missions flown across the Channel are usually at night. You maintain and repair the bird during the day.

"Our operation is being reorganized as we speak. The new designation is the Special Operations Executive (SOE). I'm Sir Hugh Dalton and I'm the new Minister of Economic Warfare. Under the main organization known as the Special Operations Executive (SOE) headquartered at 64 Baker Street. Sir Frank Nelson is going to be in that position. You're a part of Section D which handles sabotage and its support. Section D is commanded by Major Lawrence Grand. Our Section D operations as well as yours will be office in the headquarters area at Dorsett Square. You'll have an operations room on the fourth floor. It's a four meter by twelve meter room that has a small desk for Major Coltrane along with four high security filing cabinets on two walls you'll find detailed aviation maps of Europe and the Scandinavian countries. There are two plain blackboards and a scheduling blackboard. In the middle of the room there's a one meter by four meter conference table and eight chairs. This is where you'll be working when not flying a mission. I would expect an average of four to five missions per week, depending on weather. Plan by day, fly by night. You can sleep on the train from London to Tempsford. You'll be supported by an able bunch of chaps from the Military Intelligence Research Branch (MI-6). They'll provide you the intelligence, order of battle and mission coordination needed to fly your mission. We've made arrangements for you to rent hotel rooms in the Montrague Mansions area, a short walk from the office. If you find something you like better in the area, feel free to move. You're paying for the accommodations out of your housing allowance. Any questions so far?" Major Dalton said.

"I'm sure that your mind is full and spinning around with all of this.

Not to worry, there's more. Starting at 0800 hours tomorrow, you'll report to Squadron Leader Colin Howarth who will start the task of going over the type of flying and operations that we…you'll be doing. Based upon these tactics and mission details, you can start thinking of how your B-25 should be configured. Obviously, you won't need bomb racks for example. Day after tomorrow, you'll proceed to the North American Plant in Inglewood where your bird is being built. You'll meet up with Arthur Bede who is your factory representative. He'll be the one you work with on changes and modifications.

This bird has one purpose and that's the direct support and supply of the resistance underground in Europe. Make the bird fit the mission. It's what gets you there and back alive. Now is the time to build it up your way. Listen to Colin Howarth. He's flown dozens of missions over there in the Lysander and knows what he's talking about.

"Mechanics," Dalton said in a commanding voice, "you're to be at the factory watching and learning everything you can about the bird. Every rivet, nut and wire. If you see any modification that can help performance or improve maintenance, now is the time to say something. You'll be working in a cold damp tent, so you need to make maintenance and battle repairs easy and efficient.

"Once the bird is completed and North American signs it over to the U.S. government, you'll be transitioned by the contractor into the bird. After you're qualified, Colin will move all of you to Tacoma Field. I guess they've renamed it to McCord Field outside Tacoma, Washington. There Colin will give you an accelerated training course on SOE flying procedures and mission tactics. McCord is much like England and you can fly low level over the Pacific on navigation exercises. You'll be trained in short field take off and landings, cargo drops, and low level flying in mountains. I'll try to give you some tips on flying in bad weather and many other procedures that we've learned the hard way. Usually that means at the loss of someone's life. Last chance to ask questions," he said in completion.

Coltrane stood up and asked, "Sir, our code name is Black Bart, but what is our priority code for parts, supplies and services?"

General Andrews stoop up. "Thank you, Major Dalton for that

excellent briefing." Turning to Coltrane he responded, "It's Silver Fox." Both terms are to be treated as 'Top Secret' 'Need to Know' only. "If there are no questions, I must depart for Washington. Good luck, gentlemen," he said as he left the room.

The two car caravan arrived at the main gate to the North American Aviation Plant in Inglewood three minutes early for its 0800 hours meeting with Arthur Bede. The recent government orders for more aircraft and the fear that the U.S. could be drug into another war had the pace around the plant considerably more animated than it was a year ago. There were lots of new faces, all of which had a look of professional purpose. The security guard checked the ID of all eight of the occupants against the authorized visitor list. He motioned for his supervisor to come over. He showed him the annotation beside their names. He nodded and lowered his head so he could talk to Major Coltrane. "Sir, I'm to take you over to the security office to get you security passes then to the conference room. Please follow me."

It was almost 0900 hours by the time the group got over to the assigned room where a balding man in his early forties was waiting with a middle-aged assistant.

"Good morning gentlemen, please take your seats so we can get started. I'm Arthur Bede, your factory rep for this project. Today I would like to introduce you to the B-25 serial number 40-007BX, which is configured for Special Operations in England. First let me show you some film of recent flight test of our pride and joy," he said with the pride of a new father at a maternity ward.

The assistant in the back turned down the lights and started the projector. The black and white film showed the B-25 taxiing out for takeoff then leaping into the air like it was under great power. It showed several different airborne maneuvers including slow flight with landing gear and flaps extended. Coltrane was impressed. It then made a short field approach and landing. Then it took off again and performed several high speed low altitude turns and maneuvers in the hills east of Los Angeles. The film suddenly ended and the lights came on.

Bede moved back to the front of the room. "I believe that this aircraft will do the job described in the letter from the White House."

Major Dalton looked over to Colin Howard as if asking the question. Howarth smiled and nodded back. He then looked at Coltrane and asked, "Can you fly this speedster?"

"Sir," answered Coltrane, "I'd pay a month's pay to just kiss its tires." That's one hell of an aircraft and it can do the job that you described." Then he joined the group in a little laugh.

"Okay then," Dalton said to Bede, "Tell us all about the B-25."

The better of three hours was spent by Arthur Bede showing various slides of the various systems of the plane and endless performance charts. When the engine, fuel, electrical and hydraulic systems were on the screen, the three mechanics came out of their seats talking among themselves as well as asking Bede endless questions. Bede was excited about the high level of interest in his and North Americans new creation. Bede had to call a halt to the questions for the lunch break.

After lunch, Bede had representatives from the plant who specialized in the engine and other critical areas of the aircraft present to go deeper into the details. The pilots and Howarth talked with design and performance engineers and the prototype test pilot. Five o'clock came quickly. It was agreed that the Black Bart maintenance team would come back tomorrow to work with the respective specialist on the aircraft systems and engines. The pilots would work back at March on tactics and objectives of the mission with Dalton and Howarth. They would return day after tomorrow to discuss suggested changes and modifications.

The drive back was one of elated chatter like that between kids in a candy store. They had seen a new and dynamic aircraft that they would get to fly. The ominous aspect of deadly combat wasn't even considered except as a non-emotional fact to be incorporated into the plane configuration and operation. The staff car somehow found its way to the March Field Officers' Club bar, where the conversation about what they had been changed to life and housing in London. Naturally, Coltrane asked about the women.

The next morning everyone showed up early for the meeting. Major Dalton started the meeting by letting Colin Howarth go into great detail of the type of mission they would be flying. A great deal was spent on routes usually flown, low level tactics, weather problems, navigation procedures and problems and of course the enemy anti aircraft and fighter hazards. His vivid and detailed description and personal experience in the Lysander was chilling to everyone. This brought about discussion on the aircraft configuration and equipment.

Bart looked over at Dalton, “Sir, did you get confirmation that we can get the new Wright-2600-13 instead of the dash nine engines?” he asked. Dalton nodded in the affirmative. Great, that gives us a little more useable power.”

Kelly Sharp looked at the blueprints of the plane lying on the table. “I'd like to get a Plexiglas sighting blister for celestial star shootings.”

Dalton made a note and then asked what was next.

“We really need that entire package of deicing boots. We'll be dealing with a lot of icing over there,” Coltrane said. I'm thinking that with the existing de-icing system that they're offering, we have two pneumatic air sources. The conventional one proposed looks good, but I think that we should ask for a booster that can deliver an additional amount of heated air to the boots in really bad ice. I know there's a heat limitation on the rubber, but if we could have the ability to temporarily heat them up for five or so minutes during heavy icing, it could make a big difference.”

Once again, Dalton wrote notes.

“Mr. Bede, you show a cover around the bomb bay. We do not want that option. We must have full access to the bomb bay from front and back. Any problem with that, Sir?”

“None,” Bede said as he took notes. “It will take a little engineering to do but it can be done.”

Kelly Sharp was next to the talk about the navigation and radio equipment being installed. “I suggest that they wire the bird for both the GEE and LORAN-A navigation system. I know neither is available today, but will be within a year, and that will greatly expand our capabilities in bad weather,” Sharp said in a questioning tone.

Robby West agreed and the point noted by Dalton.

Coltrane asked Colin about armament. "Sir, if we're flying at low altitude over the Krauts, we really don't need a tail gunner or a bottom turret. All of that's useless weight to us at that altitude."

"Agreed," chimed in West and Sharp. 'What about a top turret with two fifty cals in the back?' asked West. "If we get jumped by fighters we would need that. Granted, it can't shoot downward, but the only thing lower than us would be our buttons. So rear coverage from a top turret is all we need besides the eight fifty calibers in front and side."

Coltrane shrugged his head and shoulders and said, "Very true, but that turret cuts our speed by thirty knots. That could be the difference if we were trying to outrun or out maneuver the fighters. So we cut out the turret"

Sharp lifted his hand without thinking and added, "What if we went with only the two side waist guns. If we get jumped, we can use them and pray we can out run them. The weight savings is considerable."

"You've a good idea, Kelly, Coltrane said, "That's the way we go."

Coltrane nodded in agreement and looked at Dalton who started writing.

"What about the bomb bay configurations," asked West. "We need to replace the bomb racks with something that's more consistent with our type of cargo."

Colin added, "Yes, he's right. We could put the individual release hooks that we're putting into the heavy bombers. We could then hang the equipment pods vertically with the chute going on the end of the pod. Leave enough line on the ripcord to allow the pod to clear by two meters or so then pull the chute. That type of release could allow us to drop from a really low altitude."

"Sounds great to me," Bart said as he looked at the others.

"The only other thing that I can think of is instrument panel configuration and instruments. I can see that we'll be flying a lot on the gauges," Coltrane said, looking at West. "What have you got drawn up, Robby? I saw you making diagrams earlier."

"Given the amount of anticipated weather or instrument flying, I suggest that we outfit the bird with dual instruments. In combat one side could be shot up and if we only had one set, we could be sure out of luck in the clouds. Think about this configuration. We first put all engine and monitoring gauges in the middle so we both can monitor them. On each side we've an independent Radio Magnetic Indicator top front with the clock and gyro compass on either side. Below that we've a 4-inch attitude indicator, airspeed and altimeter on either side. Below the altimeter, we've the turn and bank indicator and climb and descent indicator. Leave the autopilot in the center with the engine instruments.

"That would give us both a navigation radio to monitor and cross-reference as well as full instrument panel."

"Wow", Coltrane said, "that would really be effective. Major Dalton, would you add that to your list?"

"I'll put it down, but we're running up a big bill. I'm not sure headquarters will like it, but they're not flying the bird, Dalton said. Is that all the changes?"

Everyone remained silent.

"Okay, then we'll leave for Inglewood at 0700 hours. I think we've accomplished a lot today. I suggest a gin and tonic," Dalton said, as he raised his hand as if it had a glass in it. "Meeting adjourned."

CHAPTER 12

Bart Coltrane looked out of the window of the train as it passed through the train station in Tucson, Arizona and noted the Christmas decorations. "Why wouldn't they've decorations up?" he thought, it's the 15th of December, 1940. Christmas is less than two weeks away. Christmas...I wonder how they celebrate Christmas in London. Well, I'm sure going to find out. I'll be there in a week.

Coltrane leaned back in the comfortable first class chair and thought about the past three months. They sure went by fast. There was the day-by-day oversight of the building and testing of the new B-25. Then there were the heart stopping training flights that Colin Howarth put them through in the mountains and valleys of Washington State and Canada. Then there were those grinding low altitude long-range over water flights to Anchorage. Those were killers. Twice his special heated deicing boot had come in handy. This was a real good bird in ice. Then there was the mobilization phase at March Field. They collected four spare engines, parts for another two engines, replacement parts for everything imaginable on the plane. Even two sets of spare tires. Short field operations were real hard on tires and brakes.

The shipping containers were sealed and delivered to the freight forwarding company that would ship the containers by train to port. There they took the risk of being sunk by German submarines in transit across the Atlantic to London. The process started on November 10th and 35 days later he had not been advised of any loss in transit. Maybe, just maybe, those loads got there on time and without being repositioned on the ocean floor. Tomorrow he and his crew would report in from the customary thirty-day leave prior to overseas deployment.

Bart enjoyed his leave back to Sweetwater, Texas as much as he could given the never ending thoughts about the missions over enemy territory that were ahead of him. It was great spending time with his parents. It was even better reviving his acquaintances with old girlfriends and other ladies of his checkered past. Now it's time to get some sleep. He would be in Los Angeles early in the morning and then it's back in the saddle.

When Bart signed in from furlough, he ran across Curt Lemay who had recently made Captain as well. "Hey, Curt, how are you doing? I thought that they would have you in jail for spreading the truth about Strategic Bombardment."

"Not yet, Bart, but they're waiting for the opportunity, "Lemay said. "Colonel Olds finally told me what you're doing overseas. That's going to be rough, damned rough. Be careful and use your head."

"I think we're well prepared for this. They gave us a great bird to fly and the Brits we're working for are solid as a rock. That's about all we can ask for," Coltrane said, trying not to sound melancholy. "You think you'll remain here or deploy to a forward area before the war starts?"

"Hawaii – real soon. That's all I know," Lemay replied. "I've got to go see the old man. Take care."

"Don't make him mad. We've a meeting with him this afternoon and we deploy in the morning," Bart added.

It was 1600 hours when Colonel Olds came into the conference room. "Welcome back to the working people," Olds joked as he went to the head of the table. "You've an incredible aircraft and an opportunity to really make a difference in the struggle over there. The people in these occupied countries want to fight for their country and they need your help to do that. You're the vanguard for the United States. We'll be entering the war in the not too distant future. I don't see any way of staying out. Have a safe trip and God speed." Olds shook everyone's hand as he left the room.

After the Colonel left, Bart told everyone to sit down. "Okay, has anyone failed to complete their overseas paperwork, last will and inoculations?" Everyone nodded in the affirmative. "Tomorrow's the day." We check out of the orderly room at 0700 hours. Load up and be ready to crank up at 0800 hours. We'll fly to Wright Patterson, refuel and stand by for some VIPs who want to look at the bird. It's got the imagination of some important people who support Strategic Bombardment.

"If we're off by 0800, we should be on the ground by 1900 hours. We should be finished with the VIPs by 2100, in bed by 2300 or so. We'll crank and depart by 0800 local. It's 1,269 miles to Goose Bay. If the winds hold, we'll be on the ground by 1800 plus or minus. You'll refuel, rest and stand by for a 0100 hours departure. That puts us into Reykjavík about 1030 hours. We need to refuel and take off within an hour if the weather is okay. We need to arrive in Prestwick prior to dark, so we don't scramble the RAF. We'll remain overnight and await squadron Leader Howarth's arrival. He's going to fly with us into the Tempsford, so we don't get lost, land on the wrong airfield or scare the cows. Then it's showtime! Any questions? Okay, see you at the bird in the morning."

"Hey, Bart," called out Kelly Sharp. "Want to grab a drink and supper at the club?"

"Maybe, let me make a quick call first," Bart said as he picked up a phone and dialed 9 for an off base phone line. He dialed a number from memory. The phone rang twice before it was answered by a female voice. "Afternoon, may I speak to Captain Andrews?"

"I'm sorry, he's out on a trip until tomorrow," she said.

Bart changed his voice back to normal and said, "Want to give a guy a heart attack?"

"Bart!" she screamed into the phone. "Yes, I would. When and where?"

Meet me at the Dew Drop in an hour. We can grab a couple of drinks first. I need liquid courage before taking you on."

"You clown. I'll grab a couple of things and head your way. I hope that you took your vitamins today, bye." She hung up quickly.

Bart hung up the phone and turned to Kelly, "Sorry, I have to meet a friend."

Kelly knew what that meant. The whore dog was on the prowl tonight.

The next morning the crew was anxious to get going. They had signed out then went to the bird and started a detailed preflight check about 0645 hours. They had finished when Major Coltrane arrived a little before 0800. He looked tired and sleepless. He threw his bag into the open bomb bay to Jack Martin who tied it down with the other bags. He then handed his flight bag with its charts, paperwork, E6B flight computer and other items used by seasoned pilots. Martin stepped across the open bomb bay and placed the flight bag in the pilot's seat.

Coltrane started a slow walk around the bird, carefully looking for anything out of the ordinary. Yank Royston came up to him quietly and stood by for any questions that the pilot might have about the plane. When he finished his pre-flight inspection, he looked at Royston and asked, "Ya got any problems?"

"No Sir, we're ready to go," Royston said proudly.

"Okay, let's go cheat death," Coltrane said as he climbed up the ladder into the aircraft.

Crank-up and pre-takeoff checks were completed and they were ready to start the adventure of a lifetime.

Coltrane called Royston over the interphone system, "Top, make one last check of that ferry tank. I'll leave the bomb bay open while you check it inside and out. That's one thing we don't need problems with in flight."

Royston looked at the connections, hoses leading over the auxiliary fuel connection point. Wires to the internal fuel pump were verified to be connected. There were no leaks visible. He climbed down the ladder and looked up inside the bomb bay and looked at the tank over one last time. No leaks or drips. He climbed back inside and put his headset back on.

"Crew Chief to Pilot. Ferry Tank secure and no leaks," he reported.

"Pilot to Crew, anybody got a problem or need to go to the bathroom before we depart?" Coltrane said jokingly. "Okay, let's get this show on the road."

He depressed the mike switch on the control yoke to activate the radio transmitter and in a calm professional voice said, "Tower, Black Bart 007, a single B-25, ready to depart when cleared."

"Roger, Black Bart, you're cleared for takeoff. Depart heading zero niner zero degrees until passing 4,000 then climb to one five thousand and cleared on course. Contact Los Angeles control after takeoff on one two zero decimal five. Altimeter setting two niner decimal three zero, wind zero four zero degrees at one zero. Have a safe flight."

"Roger, Black Bart on the go." Coltrane said as he advanced the two throttles to takeoff power and quickly placed both hands on the control yoke. The co-pilot Robby West put his hand on the throttles in case of emergency and started reading the increasing airspeed.

"Airspeed coming up," he said in a loud voice. He eased the right engine throttle back very slightly to insure the manifold pressure did not exceed the maximum limit which could cause one or more cylinders to blow up. He then started reading out the airspeed, "60 knots, 70 knots, 80 knots, 90 knots, 100 knots, 110 knots," Just then Coltrane eased back on the control yoke and the nose wheel came off the ground. Seconds later, the main landing gear lifted off and the bird was in flight. It continued to climb upward steadily.

"Gear up," commanded Coltrane as he turned to heading 090 degrees as directed by the tower. "Okay, pull up half the flaps and change my radio to 120.5."

"Gear up, flaps coming up and you're up LA control," West advised.

"Los Angeles control, Black Bart 007 is with you passing two thousand feet en route to one five thousand and on a direct 090 degree heading," Coltrane reported.

"Okay, flaps up and give me thirty-five inches and 2500 rpm," he told West.

West immediately reduce the throttles to adjust the engine manifold pressure to 35 inches of mercury and the prop pitch of the propellers to a speed of 2500 rpm.

"Black Bart 007, you're cleared on course, no reported traffic. Have a good flight," the Control Center directed the departing B-25.

"Roger, LA, good day," replied Coltrane. As he turned to a heading of seventy-five degrees as the aircraft continued to climb to its assigned cruising altitude of 15,000 feet.

As they passed above the mountains below, the air smoothed out and made the ride more enjoyable. As they passed through 10,000 feet, Coltrane ordered, "Passing 10,000, go on oxygen." Everyone put his oxygen mask on as they went about their duties or in the case of the crew chief and mechanics, laid down on anything soft that they could find and went to sleep. Kelly Sharp was busy marking their progress on his map. He got his E-6B flight computer out and dialed in some settings.

"If anyone is awake at the wheel, make your heading 072 degrees. We've a nice quartering tail wind," Sharp said, teasing the two pilots who were less than two feet away.

"Roger 072 it is," Coltrane said as he pushed the nose down and leveled off at 15,000 feet. He adjusted the throttles to thirty inches manifold pressure and 2000 rpm. As the aircraft adjusted its altitude and flight characteristics, Coltrane made slight adjustments to the trim tabs on the ailerons and two tail rudders. This smoothed the flight even further. He then turned his heading bug on his RMI indicator to 072 degrees. Once the plane had stabilized, he turned on the autopilot. The autopilot kept the plane heading 072 degrees and kept the wings level. Cruise flight conditions had been achieved. They were on their way to war.

After an hour and twenty seven minutes, Sharp said over the intercom, "That should be Williams, Arizona out your left side."

Both pilots looked out to see the town as if it had any relevance to the flight other than a known point en route.

Sharp added in a serious tone, "Come left to 070 degrees. That wind is shifting slightly to the north. We've a groundspeed of 219 knots. Not bad at this power setting." I estimate Wichita in about three hours twenty eight minutes. That will put us in Wright Pat twenty-eight minutes early if the winds don't go against us."

"Roger that," Bart said then looked at West and said, "I'm going to put it on autopilot." He then patted him on the head and said "You've it." West smiled and put his hands on the controls to show acceptance of the controls. The plane was already on the autopilot but Bart wanted to get up and stretch his legs and go to the rear for a piss call. As he got up, he went behind Sharp who was leaning over his navigation table making calculations.

It was almost 1830 when Sharp patted Bart on the shoulder and said "We're ten miles out, better contact approach control."

Bart nodded and grabbed the control yoke and triggered the radio transmitter. "Wright Pat approach control, Black Bart 007 is with you ten miles southwest at 15,000."

"Roger Black Bart, descend and maintain 5,000, expect runway twenty-four, wind 255 degrees at eight knots gusts to ten knots. Altimeter 29.08, visibility six miles, clear with a haze layer at 1,500 feet. Report five miles southwest."

"Roger. Black Bart is out of 15,000 for 5,000 will report five southwest. We have the numbers for weather," Coltrane said, "Okay, Robby take us to five."

Robby West hit the autopilot disconnect button and pushed the yoke slightly forward as he made a small reduction in power. The B-25 started to descend to its assigned altitude. Minutes later, West made a textbook landing.

"Great landing, Robby," Bart said as he requested taxi instructions to the transmit aircraft parking.

As they pulled up in front of the transit operations building, three staff cars pulled up. Bart observed what seemed to be a dozen senior officers and civilians get out of the car and start looking and pointing at the new B-25. He unstrapped and got up to go report to the VIPs while West shut down the engines.

The visitors were impressed with the new bomber. They asked where it would be assigned and Bart could only tell them that he was flying tests. He couldn't say his real assignment with the British. They didn't stay as long as he had anticipated. He and the tired crew were grateful. They made their post flight checks and servicing prior to heading for transit quarters.

The next morning, the flight departed on time and the 1,263 nautical mile flight to Goose Bay was very uneventful and routine if not boring. That changed when they got on the ground in Goose Bay only to find that the arctic storm in northern Greenland was moving southward and could affect the alternate airfield located in the far southern end of Greenland.

Coltrane was not initially concerned as they had no plans to land there except if their primary landing field in Iceland became below approach minimums. He decided to remain overnight (RON) and see what the weather was in the morning. If the storm didn't move south and affect their route of flight to Reykjavík, Iceland, he would take off. If it did, he would wait a couple of days and let it blow through. Now it was time to find the Officers' Club and a couple of stiff drinks and supper before getting some sleep.

The next morning Bart, West and Sharp went into the Goose Bay operations office. They went into the weather office to get the weather along the planned route which took them over Narssarssuag, at the very southern end of Greenland, to their destination at Reykjavík, Iceland. The Army Air Force meteorologist informed them that the storm had not moved much overnight but the direction had shifted to a more southeasterly. They might not be able to get into the Greenland airfield, but Reykjavík should be no problem. The old Sergeant looked at the data and a report from a Greenland weather outpost at Dundas which had reported within the hour that the storm had started to move rapidly to the southeast. "You know, Captain, if they're correct, it could affect them along the route including Reykjavík, Sir," the Sergeant said to the duty weatherman.

"Sergeant, I doubt it. Those guys are more interested in their ice flow studies than the weather. They've been wrong before on those Arctic storms," the weatherman said with some doubt in his voice. He then went back over to Coltrane and put the weather map in front of him. "Here's what we have as of now. The storm should not affect you except over Greenland if you get going soon. We did have a report from some ice flow scientist who inputs weather twice daily that the storm was moving to the southeast. I just don't see any problem getting to Reykjavík. If you do have a problem, you don't have an alternate and you can't come back here. We're forecast to go below minimums here by late today. It's your call."

Coltrane turned to Sharp, "What do you think?"

"Well, we barely have enough fuel to go on to Scotland if these guys are wrong. It would be real tight."

Coltrane turned back to the weatherman and asked "You did say we should have no problem to Reykjavík if we go now?"

"That's my read of the tea leaves, Major!"

"Okay, we'll go right away and get ahead of the bugger." Bart said with some reservation.

"Okay, let's crank!"

Three and a half hours later Black Bart 007 was flying between cloud layers southwest of Nanssarssuag, Greenland in very rough and turbulent air. The weatherman's prediction wasn't even close. They had a fifty-five knot quartering headwind that had slowed their progress and was eating up their fuel. It was rough, but Coltrane and the older crewmen had seen worse. But the conditions were getting worse. To make things worse, weather conditions at Goose Bay had deteriorated as forecast. They couldn't go back now. The wind should change to a more northwesterly direction soon he hoped. That would take it off his left quarter and more on the tail.

"Hey, Bart, could you go up to 20,000 and get above that cloud deck? I sure could use a good navigational fix before we get really in the soup."

"Yeah, but the winds are a lot stronger up there, so don't take long." Coltrane increased the power to be able to climb up through the clouds above. It took about eleven minutes to get through the deck at 21,500 feet.

"Okay, Kelly, make it quick. We've lost a bunch of ground speed in this wind," lamented Bart.

Kelly Sharp quickly got his sextant into the plastic bubble above the cockpit and looked for navigational information from the stars and sun.

A few minutes later Kelly said, "I got it, take her down. "Give me a minute to get our position."

Coltrane pushed the nose over and went down quickly back to 15,000 feet. Suddenly he heard voice traffic over the frequency that Narssarssuag used. He grabbed the control yoke tightly and pressed the radio transmit button.

"Narssarssuag, this is Black Bart 007 with you at 15,000 feet to the southwest en route Reykjavík." He said, "What's your weather?"

"Roger, Black Bart. We've 200 feet overcast, two miles visibility, wind 305 at forty gusting to fifty-five. Last report from Reykjavík was 22,000 overcast, 14,000 overcast, 5,500 feet broken visibility six miles, and wind 280 degrees at twenty, gusts to twenty-five. Weather is deteriorating. What is your estimated time of arrival at Reykjavík?"

Coltrane looked back at Sharp for the answer. Sharp said "Six hours seventeen minutes, based upon current winds. It was a little over five hours forty minutes if they move around to the tail."

"Looks like about six hours. What is the projected forecast for then?" Coltrane responded.

Black Bart, they're forecasting VFR conditions, but that storm is unpredictable," said the voice over the radio.

"Okay, we're continuing on as filed. Give us a call if the conditions change," a concerned Coltrane replied.

Black Bart 007 was slightly more than five hours from Reykjavík when he was finally able to reach Reykjavík on the radio. The wings were starting to get a thin coat of ice on them.

"Reykjavík, this is Black Bart 007. We're with you at 15,000 to the southwest. What is your current weather and your forecast for three hours from now?"

"Black Bart, our weather is deteriorating rapidly. We've less than 3 miles and blowing snow. Wind is 310 at forty-five gusts to fifty-five. Forecast is for instrument conditions and severe winter storm. The Arctic storm changed course and is expected to arrive here within two to three hours. Recommend that you proceed to alternate."

"Reykjavík, our alternate is below minimums and not useable. Stand by," a very troubled Coltrane said as he turned to Sharp.

"Kelly, can we make Scotland given the distance and the fuel used so far?"

"This isn't good, Bart, let me check," Sharp replied. After a long four minutes, he responded. "Bart, the changing winds may save us, but we'll be on fumes. Our fuel consumption going against the wind has screwed us. By turning to 115 degrees, the wind will be more on our tail and that might be just enough to get us to dry land. We'll be in a lot of bad weather. I expect a lot of icing most of the way," he said with a deep tone of concern.

"Thanks, Kelly", Bart said. "Reykjavík, Black Bart is turning to

Scotland direct, climbing to 21,000 feet," Coltrane announced as he pushed the throttles forward and made a climbing right turn to 115 degrees." Robby, make sure that you get every drop transferred out of the ferry tank. We're going to need it."

Black Bart 007 had leveled off at 21,000 feet. The instruments indicated that the fuel flow rate had declined slightly. He could feel the change in wind by the way the aircraft flew. He knew that he had made the right decision. Coltrane set the power settings for the maximum cruise efficiency. He was grateful to the fuel ferry tank in the bomb bay. Without it, they might get to try out that life raft in the back compartment.

"Hey, Bart, there seems to be something wrong with my airspeed indicator. It seems to be showing only sixty knots airspeed. Why?" asked Robby West.

"Shit!" exclaimed Coltrane, we're taking on ice."

He looked out his window into the gray sky at the wing and engine. His heart sank when he saw a heavy build-up of ice that had collected on the leading edge of the wing, engine, and propeller. He immediately reached over and turned on the co-pilot pitot tube heater, increased the carburetor heat, and the other de-icing equipment. Coltrane chided himself for not checking to see that Bobby had turned on his pitot heat when they ran into the first rain shower. Dumb mistake but not unusual for a young pilot like Bobby, but it was unforgiveable for him to overlook the switch. He saw that the ice was collecting faster than the deicing boots could handle. He knew that he had to turn on the extra heat position that he had put on at the factory. This might be enough to buy them time to get to a warmer altitude where the deice equipment could handle the problem. He pushed the nose over and hit the radio transmit button. "Reykjavík control, Black Bart is out at 21,000 descending to 10,000. We've some heavy icing at 21,000 feet." There was no reply. They were out of range so there was nobody that could advise other aircraft of their position and altitude. There's probably nobody stupid enough to be flying in this shit anyway," he thought. "Better safe than sorry." He turned his radio to the international distress frequency 121.5Mhz and transmitted, "Any aircraft this frequency, this is Black Bart 007 calling in the blind. Black Bart encountered heavy ice at 21,000 feet and is now descending to 10,000 southeast of Reykjavík en route Prestwick, over." There was no reply. He was comforted in knowing that there was nobody out there to run into. Unfortunately, there was nobody to report their going down in the Atlantic if their luck turned bad.

He could not see through the forward cockpit windshield due to the ice buildup. He put the windshield heat on then turned on the wipers.

He looked out again as he passed through 15,000 feet. It was getting better. He had to turn the de-icing boots back to normal or risk burning up a boot or seal that attached the boot to the wing. Coltrane just hoped that normal heat would be sufficient.

"My airspeed indicator is back to normal," West reported. Bart nodded and smiled slightly, knowing that Robby was embarrassed over his mistake.

He leveled the aircraft at 10,000 feet and reset the power settings to the best cruise setting possible. He decided that 1,740 rpm at 25.4 inches of manifold pressure would be best at this altitude and weight. He adjusted the heading bug to 115 degrees and turned on the autopilot. He lowered his sweaty hands, wiping them on the legs of his flight suit. "They were okay for now," he thought.

"Kelly, we're stable. Work up a position and fuel report," he said with authority.

"Roger, Sir," he said, understanding the seriousness of Bart's tone.

"Major, we're 593 miles from Prestwick and 334 miles to dry land. Our ground speed at this altitude is 222 knots. Time to Prestwick is 2 hours 37 minutes. If the winds remain steady and we can stay at this altitude, our fuel burn is 98 gallons per hour and we've 288 gallons of useable fuel, Sir," reported Kelly Sharp. "In short, keep this altitude, no significant wind change and we'll make Prestwick with about twenty-five gallons in the tank."

"Right," he said. "I'm not certain we can keep this altitude due to ice. I'll do my best. Start thinking about a suggested lower altitude based upon winds. Also, keep your eye on that line of islands on the west side of Scotland, just in case we've to go down before Prestwick."

"Robby, you watch the gauges and fly for a while. I need a breather. Do we've any coffee left?" Coltrane asked.

"Roger that, Major," Sergeant Royston said as he handed him a thermos and a white porcelain cup.

Coltrane got up from his seat and hunched over behind Kelly looking at his map and calculations. The rough and turbulent air made it hard to hold on and see the data.

"We'll be over dry land in an hour and thirty-four minutes," Kelly said without being asked. He had already learned how Coltrane thought.

"Thanks, that isn't too bad if..."

"Major," yelled West, "we're building up ice again."

Bart quickly got back into his seat and strapped on his parachute and safety belt unconsciously as he looked out of the windows on each side to get a clear picture of the situation. It wasn't good.

"Okay, Kelly, can you live with 8,000?" he asked as he indicated to Robby to let the plane down to 8,000 feet. West nosed the bird down without making a power change. It took very little time to get to the new altitude.

"We'll be chewing up some of that twenty-five gallon reserve, but we can still make it...barely," Sharp said with concern in his voice.

Bart looked at the windshield and then at the wings to see the ice buildup. It was holding at this altitude mainly because the precipitation had decreased more than the slight increase of outside air temperature. He reached up and turned up the heat level in the boots to the maximum level. He noticed a quick response and turned it back off for fear of damage to the boots. "Maybe this altitude will work out," he thought. He then looked over at the ratio transmitter controls and cranked in the coastal defense approach frequency that he had been given. They were six or eight hours ahead of schedule. He got his code book out as well. Satisfied that he had what he needed, he made the call. It was almost immediately returned. It wasn't very clear due to distance and weather conditions. Coltrane gave the proper identification code and authentications required. It was too bad that the new British Identification Friend or Foe (IFF) device had not been installed. That would happen at Tempsford. He could see the needle on the radio direction finder move from pointing off to the right to almost straight ahead. "Kelly was on course," he thought.

He looked at the clock on the instrument panel and saw that they had less than an hour to fly before landing.

"Prestwick Control, this is Black Bart 007 with you at 8,000 feet," Coltrane said, then waited for a reply.

Black Bart 007, descend to 4,000 feet. You should break out of the clouds at that altitude."

"Roger, Prestwick. Black Bart is out of eight for four thousand," he replied. Bart looked out west and pointed down. He lowered the nose to descend. They broke out of the overcast slightly below 4,800 feet. "The countryside was beautiful. It must be Arron Island to the west of Prestwick," he thought.

"Pilot to crew, prepare for landing!

"The Yanks have arrived!"

"So have the Brits," Royston said in response. "Look at your starboard wing. That's a RAF Hurricane."

"We've got one on our port too," Andy Lightfoot said as he looked out the left side window where a machine gun normally would be mounted in combat.

Coltrane said, "Looks like an RAF Identification sortie to make sure we're not bearing a Swastika."

"American Bomber, follow me to Prestwick" came the voice over the radio.

"Roger, take the lead. Black Bart 007 will follow. Be advised we're fuel critical," Coltrane advised.

"Roger on fuel state. Turn to a heading of 095. Prestwick is eight nautical miles. Descend to 1,500 feet. Tune in tower 119.5. Good day, mate," said the RAF pilot as he dramatically increased his speed and broke off contact.

"Prestwick Tower, Black Bart 007 is with you descending to 1,500 feet seven miles west. Request landing instructions."

"Black Bart, Prestwick Tower, enter a left downwind for runway 31, winds 330 at twenty, altimeter setting 29.05. You're number one for landing, understand fuel critical, you're cleared to land," came the metallic voice over the radio.

Coltrane started through the pre-landing checks then said, "Let me have ten degrees of flaps." Bart reached up and advanced the mixture controls, went to full prop pitch, and slowed the bomber to 120 knots. Okay, give me the gear and flaps and check turbochargers."

Robby West's hands flew across the instrument panel, complying with the pilot's commands. "Gear down and locked and the turbochargers are low and locked," he reported.

The plane made minor course connections on final approach to properly link up with the runway center line and the affects of the twenty knot wind on its right front. As it crossed the runway threshold, Black Bart gently touched down in Scotland.

"Black Bart 007, turn left on the taxiway and follow the "Follow Me" Lorrie to parking," ordered the control tower. "Welcome to Scotland."

"Roger, we're damned glad to be here," quipped Coltrane.

The aircraft came to a stop in front of a small transit aircraft terminal. Two men in civilian topcoats and hats left the building and headed towards Black Bart.

"Okay, let's shut her down and wrap it up. We'll do dailies and services in the morning," Coltrane said as he pulled the mixture controls to the rear stops stopping the engines. He flipped off the ignition and battery switch and the aircraft became almost silent. With only the sound of the gyro compass slowly spinning down.

Bart immediately recognized Major Dalton and Squadron Leader Howarth.

Dalton extended his hand and said, "I take it your flight didn't go as planned."

"Not exactly, Sir. We got caught up in some fast moving weather storm. Had to bypass both Greenland and Iceland," Coltrane reported. "Bad winds and heavy ice really tested the old bird."

"So I understand from Reykjavík Control. They really didn't expect that you could make it in the bloody bad weather. May I offer you and your crew a stiff drink, you've certainly earned it," Dalton said in classic British humor.

An hour later in a small private dining room at a popular restaurant near the airport, the crew was starting the second round of drinks. The crew described the hair-raising trip across the Atlantic. The waiter came in with a third round ordered by Major Dalton along with a menu. After ordering, Dalton nodded to Howarth who went to the door and closed it and stationed himself outside so nobody could enter or eavesdrop on the Major's briefing of the crew on their schedule for the following three days.

"Gentlemen, you'll stand down for today and tomorrow for crew rest. Then on the 21st we'll fly down to Croydon Airfield, which is near downtown London. Howarth will fly co-pilot to help you get there without being shot down. A B-25 is an unknown to our blokes. There you'll present yourself and aircraft to a number of the General Staff and other dignitaries. Then you'll fly to Tempsford, just north of London. Your crew will take occupancy of their cottage. The B-25 will immediately go inside the temporary hangar for your operation. In this case your temporary hangar is two large tents put together. Temporary probably means until after the war. Once everything is sorted out and the three officers will depart by train for London. There you'll check into the quarters at Montague Mansions. You'll start detailed briefings on the 22 and 23 December at SOE Headquarters at 84 Baker Street. You will have an office to work up missions there. All covert operations are planned there. On the morning of 24 December you'll take the 0510 train to Tempsford. The crew will be ready to fly at 0900.

"Squadron Leader Howarth will fly with you and give you an orientation on the local area, then take you across the channel and give you a familiarization on the coast and routes back to Tempsford and Tangmere. All SOE resistance ops go out of those two airfields. Depending on fuel and weather you'll fly north to RAF Sumpsford in the Shetland Islands. We normally go in and out of Norway from there. After that you'll return to Tempsford. Keep your aircraft in the hangar unless you're going on a mission. We want to keep your base a secret as long as we can. You'll then stand down until the 27th. Starting 27 December 1940, you'll no longer be in the organization category and will become a part of Section D. That's Major Lawrence Grand's command. He'll be directing your missions. Good chap Grand, you'll like him. You'll fly a short mission into France on the 28th after planning and preparations on the 27th. After that, we'll be working on the planning of many missions and probably some that may come up in urgency. Any questions?" Major Dalton asked. "No questions, then will someone collect Howarth. Good luck and good hunting."

CHAPTER 13

Kelly Sharp said over the interphone to anyone who was listening at 0405 hours, "When the Major said our first mission would be on the 28th, he failed to say it would be in the middle of the night."

Colin Howarth who was flying in the co-pilot seat retorted, "I say, you'll find that it's much safer to fly at night. Today, we're giving it a go in the early dawn so you can get a good feel for the countryside and the bloody Germans. I bloody well think that we can give them a little surprise on this one. They really don't know much about you yet. I'm sure their Intel people know about you, but they don't know what you're doing over here with us. That will change in about an hour. Captain Sharp, can you give us a time on this leg to Tangmere?"

"Sir, we'll be over Tangmere in eight minutes. Then we turn to a heading of 070 degrees for the channel crossing to the river delta area just south of Le Crotoy, Sir," came the confident voice of the navigator.

"Bloody good. Now after you leave Tangmere, you'll want to drop down to 500 feet for the crossing. It should be early dawn by the time we get over to France, so you should be able to see the Le Crotoy Delta," he said then continued, "Lieutenant West..." The usual co-pilot was sitting on the jump seat near the navigator. It's your job to keep a keen eye for check points and any fighters ahead of us. Sergeant Royston will watch for fighter coming from above and behind us once we're over the water or France you can expect fighters, flak and anti aircraft fire." Don't let it bother you or let it distract you from your assigned task."

Coltrane could see the first improvement in his ability to see things on the coastline ahead due to the dawn's early light. He hoped that the Germans were sleeping in, just like he wanted to do when they woke him up this morning. Sharp reported, "Coastline in two minutes."

Coltrane looked at the approaching coastline of France and mentally concurred. "Sharp was dead on with his navigation," he thought.

He resolved to find a better expression than "Dead on."

At 230 knots, the plane crossed the shoreline quickly. Sharp said "Course 135 degrees to Walrus."

He had no more said that when Coltrane saw several streams of tracers arching up ahead of them. "Shit, taking fire already."

Howarth smiled and said "This is nothing. It'll get much worse. Put it out of your mind. You might want to drop down to 200 feet to reduce the volume of fire." He looked over to Coltrane and smiled. "The lower you go the fewer of the buggers can get a shot at you."

Coltrane responded very quickly.

"Walrus in sixty seconds," Sharp reported. Howarth looked up and said, "I have it in sight, do you?"

Coltrane nodded as he gripped the control yoke more tightly. Fear was starting to have its effect on him.

Suddenly six or eight streams of tracers from machine guns started up at him. He could feel an occasional hit on the aircraft. Coltrane glanced at Howarth who looked like someone looking for flowers in the field.

"I say, you need to ignore the fire. You can't do much at this point. I have Walrus in sight. You'll be turning to 080 degrees then pop up to 1,000 feet and open your bomb bay as we planned. We kick out the first delivery pod on my command. Then we drop to 100 to 150 feet and turn to 062 degrees to overfly the clearing. Hopefully, the Gerries will be watching the first parachute and ignore us when we drop the real load in the clearing. Now don't get too crazy on me when we're up at 1,000 feet. They'll really be putting some fire power on us, he said in a calm voice.

Coltrane looked over at him and knew this man had seen much worse and lived to tell about it. "Bomb bay doors open," he ordered.

Sharp said that Walrus was ahead in ten seconds. Howard said "pull up now," and reached over and opened the bomb bay door himself. "Okay, release," then he pulled the release device that held the first supply pod from the bomb bay. Coltrane could feel the change in weight when the 300 pound dummy load went out. The sky was alive with tracers and puffs of black smoke just after a bright flash. Flak! Fear was starting to well up inside him again.

"Put it over and turn to 062 degrees. Stand by for second release," he said. "I have the forest and the clearing."

As he descended to 100 feet the flak stopped and the machine gun fire almost stopped. He spotted the clearing and adjusted his course so he would be directly over the center of the clearing.

"Stand by," Colin said. "Ready, release!"

The 1,200 pound load of weapons, ammo and explosives dropped out the bottom.

Coltrane felt the bomber to lift up suddenly as the supplies dropped out. The parachute immediately opened and slowed the pod down before it landed.

Sharp directed, "Turn to 120 degrees." Sharp felt the plane execute a hard right turn to the assigned course. He looked to the right to watch the bomb bay doors quickly shut. "Turn to 185 degrees in thirty seconds, stand by…turn." Again the plane turned to the right.

Howarth pointed out the front of the aircraft after closing the doors and said, "See that river up ahead?"

"I have it in sight," Coltrane said with a little more composure. The machine gun fire had decreased to just a few lines of tracers. Occasionally, he would feel two or three rounds hit the plane. Still dangerous, but not as bad as it had been.

"Okay, follow it to the channel. Stay low, very low. We'll go through a couple more bad areas". He could see the channel ahead about five miles. He also saw the tracers increase as well. He got the bomber down almost into the trees. The tracers nearly stopped. "The bastards couldn't get a shot at him at this altitude," Coltrane thought.

"Now, there you go, mate. Keep it low and stay alive," Howard said as if he were ordering a beer. "Sharp, how about a course back home?"

"Three miles offshore turn to 355 degrees," the navigator directed.

As Coltrane turned north, he climbed to 500 feet. He felt relieved. The hard part was over. They were safe and on their way home. Then he saw a black dot in the sky ahead of them starting down towards them.

"Shit," Coltrane said as he reported. "Bandit, 12 o'clock just above us. Coming down." He lowered the plane slightly to ensure that the enemy ME 109 couldn't go below him.

Howarth said nothing. He just looked at Bart and smiled slightly. He was evaluating the pilot and his actions in a one-on-one situation with the enemy.

Coltrane saw the ME 109 start to level off at the same or slightly higher altitude on a head on course. The 109 still had a little more altitude advantage as it approached at a combined speed of over 600 knots. Bart flipped the cover up that protected the button that fired the eight 50 caliber machine guns mounted in the nose and sides of the B-25. He slightly raised the nose and hit the fire switch. The impact of the eight streams of 50 caliber bullets tore the ME 109 into pieces. Fire consumed the falling pieces of the fighter.

"Nice shot, Bart," Howarth said. "Those 50s are impressive. Now be a good chap and take us home without any more excitement. You chaps are ready to go it on your own. Can I buy you a pint or a shot of whiskey when we get back to Tempsford?"

MSG Royston and his two mechanics walked around the B-25 looking at the bullet and flak holes without comment. After they finished the walk-around inspection, Royston looked at his two assistants and asked the question that everyone knew was coming, "How long will it take you to get it ready to go again?"

Jack Martin looked at him and said, "If the engines check out, you can have it back late tomorrow, maybe sooner, Sarge. They really didn't hit anything we can't fix quickly. There's a lot of patching and some minor damage, but that's it. You were damned lucky."

"Okay, I'll pass it on to Major Coltrane. I hope they don't have any mission planned for tonight or tomorrow," Royston said with resignation.

"Speak of the Devil," Lightfoot said as Coltrane and Sharp came out of the operations building with Howarth.

Coltrane walked up to the group and looked up at the obvious damage. "Let me guess, I get it back tomorrow," he said with a smile.

Royston nodded with a short, almost silent laugh, "We were lucky, this time."

Howarth looked at the damage as they walked around the aircraft. "I'll be surprised if you could get back up by day after tomorrow. We'll stand down for a couple of days. Let's go get a shower and head for the office. We've an After Action Report to complete. Then we've a talk with the boss to see what he's in mind for your next mission. Sergeant Royston, do you really think it will be ready for a mission tomorrow night?"

"Yes,Sir, it'll fly tomorrow night. Black Bart will be ready to go." He paused then asked Coltrane and Howarth, "Can we paint nose art on our bird like the other squadrons?"

"I see no reason not to," Howarth said as he looked at Coltrane.

Coltrane switched his look from Howarth to Royston, "What do you've in mind, Yank?"

"Just who we're Sir, Black Bart!" We'll put the original Black Bart pirate flag on the nose!

Coltrane smiled and nodded. "Okay with me."

The hour and a half train ride to London was occupied by sleep. The train had not left the Tempsford Station before all of the flight crew were asleep.

It was a little after two in the chilly and damp afternoon. The first thing on the agenda was to debrief the mission to the key staff. In the past, they would report the events of the flight to Major Lawrence Grand, the head of Section D. This time, Hugh Dalton, the new head of SOE came into the debriefing along with four others. Everyone quickly took their seats at the long conference table in the center of the new Black Bart operations office.

"Well, Major Coltrane, Black Bart's first mission was even better than I had hoped for. My personal congratulations, gentlemen. You delivered the delivery pods exactly on target, you shot down an ME-109, and you brought your crew and aircraft back alive and in flyable condition."

"Sir, I was nothing more than a bus driver on this mission. Squadron Leader Howarth directed every aspect of the mission and deserves the credit," Coltrane said.

Howarth leaned back in his chair and said, "Other than to spot the landing zone and say when to drop the pods, I did nothing. I certainly didn't have a thing to do with shooting down the ME-109. I didn't even see it until you called the bloody bugger out. Lieutenant West will be quite able to fill in my place in future missions. I can report that Black Bart is fully operational and ready for assignments," he said in a commanding tone.

"Very well, then, "Dalton said, then Black Bart will be operational effective immediately. Any questions for me?" he asked as he got up to leave. "Well, then, carry on."

Major Grand stood up and turned to the four new people seated at the end of the table. "Let me introduce the operations and intelligence team that you'll be working with. The big ugly gentleman at the end of the table is Lieutenant Colonel Julian 'Hak' Smythe. He's the man that coordinates all field operations. He spent two months in Norway, two months in Denmark and four months in Belgium making contact with potential resistance leaders. I might say he was right under Gerry's nose and lived to tell about it. He knows the ground operations side across the channel. Next to him is Captain Sanford Balfour, our Order of Battle specialist. He'll give you his best guess on enemy location, strength and anti aircraft positions. He works closely with the lady to his right, Major Annabel Beddows, who heads up our Intelligence Collection and Evaluation Section. Lastly, we've Lieutenant Commander Rupert Chapham who we stole from the Royal Navy. Rupert coordinates all air supply missions like yours. Essentially, he gets a request for supply or personnel drop from Hak. He reviews the available intelligence, actual mission requirements and priorities. Then he schedules the mission. He assigns it to either one of the Lysander Groups at either Tempsford or Tangmere and now Black Bart. Once tasked, you and your crew will get detailed enemy information from Major Beddows and Captain Balfour," he said in conclusion.

Bart nodded with a smile as each was introduced. He was especially taken with Beddows. He thought this raven-haired beauty was stunning. He looked for wedding rings on both hands, but didn't see any. This excited his salacious nature. His attention was broken by Lieutenant Girard.

"I understand that enemy battle damage has your aircraft non-op until late tomorrow." Rupert Chapham said. "Are you certain that it will be available for a mission tomorrow night?" he asked with an irritating air of superiority and contempt.

Bart knew that he wasn't going to like this son-of-a-bitch. "Not certain, but my crew chief believes it will be ready."

"Major, we don't deal in 'beliefs.' We deal in certainties and absolutes," Chapham retorted.

"Alright, Commander Chapham, I'll report when it's operational again. No matter what time it becomes operational." Bart said in a tone designed to stand his ground and not cower to this asshole. Bart knew that this war might have many combat fronts and this man might be one of them.

"Very well, you do that. I'll be interested in exactly when you do report operational. We shall see how good your Crew Chief estimate really is," Chapham said contemptuously.

Major Grand saw the level of conflict start to escalate and intervened." Well then, let's get down to mission details."

The debriefing took the better part of an hour. Being the first time to undergo this form of debriefing, the questions and answers were somewhat choppy at first. At the end, Chapham got up and left without comment or ceremony. The others left with polite farewells. Bart was still taken by Beddows, even though she was expressionless. "She was beautiful," he thought.

It was almost 1700 hours in the afternoon when they finished and were very tired and sleepy. They left the building and walked over to their quarters at Montrague Mansions. Bart went in to his room. It was frightfully small. He went to the bathroom to relieve himself. He became irritated when the old pull chain toilet wouldn't work. Frustrated and tired, he went back into the room and lay down. He went to sleep immediately with his clothes still on.

It was almost 2100 hours when a hard knock at the door woke Coltrane up from a deep sleep.

His room was dark and still somewhat unfamiliar despite living there for almost a weeks. He flipped the switch on the wall to turn on the overhead light. It promptly flashed and went out. "Damned light bulb," he said in a low, angry voice. He opened the door and found both Sharp and West standing in the hall in civilian clothes.

West said in a flippant voice," We're hungry. We flipped a coin and you lost. You're buying!"

Shaking the cobwebs out of his head, he smiled and replied, "Yeah, me too. Let me change clothes. I'll meet you downstairs in five minutes."

Bart got off the old elevator to join the other two standing near the door. Okay, where do you want to go?" Please, no damned fish and chips. I've had my fill of that shit. I need a real steak or at least something different."

"Yeah," West said. "We asked one of the Lysander pilots who just came through here what was available in the area. He suggested either an Italian joint four blocks down or a German place called the Rattskeller over on Dorset. It's closer and it's getting damned cold outside. The wind is coming in off the North Sea."

"Rattskeller, it's. Besides being from Texas, I just can't take this type of cold weather. Lead the way, Navigator," Bart said as he offered an open door.

The trio walked quickly over Dorset Street in the cold wind. They saw the empty tables and chairs just outside the restaurant. They went into a dimly lit room where there were about a dozen locals drinking at the bar or eating at one of the four booths and four tables along the back and right side wall.

West leaned over to Bart and asked, "Do we want an outside table?"

The heavyset man behind the bar saw them and waved them to an open booth at the very back of the bar.

"Greetings, Gents! I take it you're here for the tourist sites," quipped the barmaid who was in her late thirties, but beautiful by any standard.

Bart replied at once, not taking his eyes off the buxom blonde's well-developed chest, "You bet! We're here on the American plan. Tomorrow it's the Buckingham Palace tour if the damned Germans don't bomb it first."

"You're Yanks, great! How about something to warm you up?" She asked them looking at Bart and said... "And I'm not on the menu."

"Killjoy! How about a double of your famous single malt scotch," he retorted.

"Right-O" she said then turned to the others and asked,"Now how about you lads?"

"Make that three," Sharp said, "shots, that is. I have no idea what junior here wants. Better check his ID to see if he's old enough to be here."

After the second round they looked at the menu. There were very impressed at the wide variety of foods and the almost total omission of the traditional fish and chips. It even had a breakfast menu on the backside.

The lady came back without another round and asked, "What's your pleasure, gents?" Then looked at Bart and said, "Forget it."

Bart looked up at her blue eyes and smiled, "I don't get it. The world is under attack by the damned Germans and this German bar is going great in downtown London. What's the story, if you don't mind my asking?"

"Fair question," she said. "The owner is Heinrich Hoff, the big guy behind the bar. He came here in 1913 with his parents and sister. When the first war broke out, he volunteered to help Whitehall with translations and advised them on the German culture. He even helped recruit spies to go into France and Germany. Needless to say, he became a popular man to the government. After the war, he went into Germany to assist with the transition and implementation of Versailles Treaty. He had a little money and he took advantage of the war-torn situation. He made a lot of money over there. He came back after two years and bought this place. People really don't think of him as a German. Besides, he runs a great kitchen and hotel. You'll find the food to be outstanding."

"Did you say hotel?" Sharp interjected.

"Yes, he's eight apartments that he rents upstairs. They're large in size and have very nice furniture. He gets good money for them too," she said.

The crew looked silently at each other then quickly ordered supper. Sharp was the first to say what was on everyone's mind. "Are you guys thinking what I'm? "That dump we're in is really bad. This isn't. This could be real great for us. Good place to live and food that doesn't make you want to throw up. With what we're getting for housing allowance and per diem, we could afford this, I think."

When the barmaid came back, Bart asked, "Are there any available flats upstairs?"

"Sure, we've four open. They rent for five pounds per night or 120 pounds a month," she responded. "That includes breakfast."

Great, that's within our housing allowance. Could we see the space after we eat?"

Sure, I'll tell Heine. He'll take you up for a show," then she looked at Coltrane and waved a finger at him. "No, no, not me, forget it. I'm not on the bloody playbill."

Bart smiled warmly, almost laughing. "Who are you?"

"I'm Regina Whitehurst. Everybody calls me Reggie," and who are you blokes?"

Bart introduced the trio. She was genuinely warm in her response. Then she turned to get the waiting food order.

Later, Heinrich Hoff finished showing the available flats to the three aviators and turned to them in anticipation of an answer.

Sharp was the first to say anything. "The bathroom is larger than my current bedroom. This is a palace compared to what we've now. I'm in!"

A smile came over Heine's face, then Bart and Robby West chimed in with their agreement to rent.

"Can we move in tomorrow?" asked Bart.

"Tonight if you wish," Heine said. "Now Yanks, how about a drink on me?"

CHAPTER 14

On the night of December 29th 1940, President Roosevelt sat at his desk in the oval office. A bank of radio microphones had been placed before him. It was obvious that he was preparing to give one of his fireside chats to the American people.

However, as Roosevelt began, he made it clear that this night there would not be a typical speech.

"This is not a fireside chat on war," the President said with emphasis. "It is a talk on national security; because the nub of the whole purpose of your President is to keep you now, and your children later, and your grandchildren much later, out of a last-ditch war for the preservation of American independence, and all of the things that American independence means to you and to me and to ours.

Tonight, in the presence of a world crisis, my mind goes back eight years to a night in the midst of a domestic crisis. It was a time when the wheels of American industry were grinding to a full stop, when the whole banking system of our country had ceased to function. I well remember that while I sat in my study in the White House, preparing to talk with the people of the United States, I had before my eyes the picture of all those Americans with whom I was talking. I saw the workmen in the mills, the mines, the factories, the girl behind the counter, the small shopkeeper, the farmer doing his spring plowing, the widows and the old men wondering about their life's savings. I tried to convey to the great mass of American people what the banking crisis meant to them in their daily lives.

Tonight, I want to do the same thing, with the same people, in this new crisis which faces America. We met the issue of 1933 with courage and realism. We face this new crisis, this new threat to the security of our nation, with the same courage and realism. Never before since Jamestown and Plymouth Rock has our American civilization been in such danger as now. For on September 27th, 1940 -- this year -- by an agreement signed in Berlin, three powerful nations, two in Europe and one in Asia, joined themselves together in the threat that if the United States of America interfered with or blocked the expansion program of these three nations -- a program aimed at world control -- they would unite in ultimate action against the United States.

The Nazi masters of Germany have made it clear that they intend not only to dominate all life and thought in their own country, but also to enslave the whole of Europe, and then to use the resources of Europe to dominate the rest of the world. It was only three weeks ago that their leader stated this: "There are two worlds that stand opposed to each other." And then in defiant reply to his opponents he said this: "Others are correct when they say: 'With this world we cannot ever reconcile ourselves. I can beat any other power in the world." So said the leader of the Nazis!" The President paused momentarily to adjust his glasses then continued in a scholarly tone of voice.

"In other words, the Axis not merely admits but the Axis proclaims that there can be no ultimate peace between their philosophy -- their philosophy of government -- and our philosophy of government. In view of the nature of this undeniable threat, it can be asserted, properly and categorically, that the United States has no right or reason to encourage talk of peace until the day shall come when there is a clear intention on the part of the aggressor nations to abandon all thought of dominating or conquering the world.

At this moment the forces of the States that are leagued against all peoples who live in freedom are being held away from our shores. The Germans and the Italians are being blocked on the other side of the Atlantic by the British and by the Greeks, and by thousands of soldiers and sailors who were able to escape from subjugated countries. In Asia the Japanese are being engaged by the Chinese nation in another great defense. In the Pacific Ocean is our fleet.

Some of our people like to believe that wars in Europe and in Asia are of no concern to us. But it is a matter of most vital concern to us that European and Asiatic war-makers should not gain control of the oceans which lead to this hemisphere. One hundred and seventeen years ago the Monroe Doctrine was conceived by our government as a measure of defense in the face of a threat against this hemisphere by an alliance in Continental Europe. Thereafter, we stood guard in the Atlantic, with the British as neighbors. There was no treaty. There was no "unwritten agreement." And yet there was the feeling, proven correct by history, that we as neighbors could settle any disputes in peaceful fashion. And the fact is that during the whole of this time the Western Hemisphere has remained free from aggression from Europe or from Asia.

Does anyone seriously believe that we need to fear attack anywhere in the Americas while a free Britain remains our most powerful naval neighbor in the Atlantic? And does anyone seriously believe, on the other hand, that we could rest easy if the Axis powers were our neighbors there? If Great Britain goes down, the Axis powers will control the Continents of Europe, Asia, Africa, Austral-Asia, and the high seas. And they will be in a position to bring enormous military and naval resources against this hemisphere. It is no exaggeration to say that all of us in all the Americas would be living at the point of a gun -- a gun loaded with explosive bullets, economic as well as military. We should enter upon a new and terrible era in which the whole world, our hemisphere included, would be run by threats of brute force. And to survive in such a world, we would have to convert ourselves permanently into a militaristic power on the basis of war economy.

Some of us like to believe that even if Britain falls, we are still safe, because of the broad expanse of the Atlantic and of the Pacific. But the width of those oceans is not what it was in the days of clipper ships. At one point between Africa and Brazil the distance is less than it is from Washington to Denver, Colorado, five hours for the latest type of bomber. And at the north end of the Pacific Ocean, America and Asia almost touch each other. Why, even today we have planes that could fly from the British Isles to New England and back again without refueling. And remember that the range of the modern bomber is ever being increased.

During the past week many people in all parts of the nation have told me what they wanted me to say tonight. Almost all of them expressed a courageous desire to hear the plain truth about the gravity of the situation. One telegram, however, expressed the attitude of the small minority who want to see no evil and hear no evil, even though they know in their hearts that evil exists. That telegram begged me not to tell again of the ease with which our American cities could be bombed by any hostile power which had gained bases in this Western Hemisphere. The gist of that telegram was: "Please, Mr. President, don't frighten us by telling us the facts." Frankly and definitely there is danger ahead -- danger against which we must prepare. But we well know that we cannot escape danger, or the fear of danger, by crawling into bed and pulling the covers over our heads." He glanced over to the expressionless Secretary of State Cordell Hull before resuming his speech.

"Some nations of Europe were bound by solemn nonintervention pacts with Germany. Other nations were assured by Germany that they need never fear invasion. Nonintervention pact or not, the fact remains that they were attacked, overrun, thrown into modern slavery at an hour's notice -- or even without any notice at all. As an exiled leader of one of these nations said to me the other day, "The notice was a minus quantity. It was given to my government two hours after German troops had poured into my country in a hundred places." The fate of these nations tells us what it means to live at the point of a Nazi gun," he said as he raised and lowered his right hand as point of personal emphasis.

The Nazis have justified such actions by various pious frauds. One of these frauds is the claim that they are occupying a nation for the purpose of "restoring order." Another is that they are occupying or controlling a nation on the excuse that they are "protecting it" against the aggression of somebody else. For example, Germany has said that she was occupying Belgium to save the Belgians from the British. Would she then hesitate to say to any South American country: "We are occupying you to protect you from aggression by the United States"? Belgium today is being used as an invasion base against Britain, now fighting for its life. And any South American country, in Nazi hands, would always constitute a jumping off place for German attack on any one of the other republics of this hemisphere.

Analyze for yourselves the future of two other places even nearer to Germany if the Nazis won. Could Ireland hold out? Would Irish freedom be permitted as an amazing pet exception in an unfree world? Or the islands of the Azores, which still fly the flag of Portugal after five centuries? You and I think of Hawaii as an outpost of defense in the Pacific. And yet the Azores are closer to our shores in the Atlantic than Hawaii is on the other side.

There are those who say that the Axis powers would never have any desire to attack the Western Hemisphere. That is the same dangerous form of wishful thinking which has destroyed the powers of resistance of so many conquered peoples. The plain facts are that the Nazis have proclaimed, time and again, that all other races are their inferiors and therefore subject to their orders. And most important of all, the vast resources and wealth of this American hemisphere constitute the most tempting loot in all of the round world.

Let us no longer blind ourselves to the undeniable fact that the evil forces which have crushed and undermined and corrupted so many others are already within our own gates. Your government knows much about them and every day is ferreting them out. Their secret emissaries are active in our own and in neighboring countries. They seek to stir up suspicion and dissension, to cause internal strife. They try to turn capital against labor, and vice versa. They try to reawaken long slumbering racial and religious enmities which should have no place in this country. They are active in every group that promotes intolerance. They exploit for their own ends our own natural abhorrence of war. These trouble-breeders have but one purpose. It is to divide our people, to divide them into hostile groups and to destroy our unity and shatter our will to defend ourselves.

There are also American citizens, many of them in high places, who, unwittingly in most cases, are aiding and abetting the work of these agents. I do not charge these American citizens with being foreign agents. But I do charge them with doing exactly the kind of work that the dictators want done in the United States. These people not only believe that we can save our own skins by shutting our eyes to the fate of other nations. Some of them go much further than that. They say that we can and should become the friends and even the partners of the Axis powers. Some of them even suggest that we should imitate the methods of the dictatorships. But Americans never can and never will do that." The President paused slightly as he looked over to the beautiful Carol Lombard who was obviously enjoying the speech.

"The experience of the past two years has proven beyond doubt that no nation can appease the Nazis. No man can tame a tiger into a kitten by stroking it. There can be no appeasement with ruthlessness. There can be no reasoning with an incendiary bomb. We know now that a nation can have peace with the Nazis only at the price of total surrender. Even the people of Italy have been forced to become accomplices of the Nazis; but at this moment they do not know how soon they will be embraced to death by their allies.

The American appeasers ignore the warning to be found in the fate of Austria, Czechoslovakia, Poland, Norway, Belgium, the Netherlands, Denmark, and France. They tell you that the Axis powers are going to win anyway; that all of this bloodshed in the world could be saved, that the United States might just as well throw its influence into the scale of a dictated peace and get the best out of it that we can. They call it a "negotiated peace." Nonsense! Is it a negotiated peace if a gang of outlaws surrounds your community and on threat of extermination makes you pay tribute to save your own skins? For such a dictated peace would be no peace at all. It would be only another armistice, leading to the most gigantic armament race and the most devastating trade wars in all history. And in these contests the Americas would offer the only real resistance to the Axis power. With all their vaunted efficiency, with all their parade of pious purpose in this war, there are still in their background the concentration camp and the servants of God in chains.

The history of recent years proves that the shootings and the chains and the concentration camps are not simply the transient tools but the very altars of modern dictatorships. They may talk of a "new order" in the world, but what they have in mind is only a revival of the oldest and the worst tyranny. In that there is no liberty, no religion, no hope. The proposed "new order" is the very opposite of a United States of Europe or a United States of Asia. It is not a government based upon the consent of the governed. It is not a union of ordinary, self-respecting men and women to protect themselves and their freedom and their dignity from oppression. It is an unholy alliance of power and pelf to dominate and to enslave the human race.

The British people and their allies today are conducting an active war against this unholy alliance. Our own future security is greatly dependent on the outcome of that fight. Our ability to "keep out of war" is going to be affected by that outcome. Thinking in terms of today and tomorrow, I make the direct statement to the American people that there is far less chance of the United States getting into war if we do all we can now to support the nations defending themselves against attack by the Axis than if we acquiesce in their defeat, submit tamely to an Axis victory, and wait our turn to be the object of attack in another war later on.

If we are to be completely honest with ourselves, we must admit that there is risk in any course we may take. But I deeply believe that the great majority of our people agree that the course that I advocate involves the least risk now and the greatest hope for world peace in the future.

The people of Europe who are defending themselves do not ask us to do their fighting. They ask us for the implements of war, the planes, the tanks, the guns, the freighters which will enable them to fight for their liberty and for our security. Emphatically, we must get these weapons to them, get them to them in sufficient volume and quickly enough so that we and our children will be saved the agony and suffering of war which others have had to endure.

Let not the defeatists tell us that it is too late. It will never be earlier. Tomorrow will be later than today.

Certain facts are self-evident.

In a military sense Great Britain and the British Empire are today the spearhead of resistance to world conquest. And they are putting up a fight which will live forever in the story of human gallantry. There is no demand for sending an American expeditionary force outside our own borders. There is no intention by any member of your government to send such a force. You can therefore, nail any talk about sending armies to Europe as deliberate untruth. Our national policy is not directed toward war. Its sole purpose is to keep war away from our country and away from our people.

Democracy's fight against world conquest is being greatly aided, and must be more greatly aided, by the rearmament of the United States and by sending every ounce and every ton of munitions and supplies that we can possibly spare to help the defenders who are in the front lines. And it is no more un-neutral for us to do that than it is for Sweden, Russia, and other nations near Germany to send steel and ore and oil and other war materials into Germany every day in the week.

We are planning our own defense with the utmost urgency, and in its vast scale we must integrate the war needs of Britain and the other free nations which are resisting aggression. This is not a matter of sentiment or of controversial personal opinion. It is a matter of realistic, practical military policy, based on the advice of our military experts who are in close touch with existing warfare. These military and naval experts and the members of the Congress and the Administration have a single-minded purpose: the defense of the United States.

This nation is making a great effort to produce everything that is necessary in this emergency, and with all possible speed. And this great effort requires great sacrifice. I would ask no one to defend a democracy which in turn would not defend everyone in the nation against want and privation. The strength of this nation shall not be diluted by the failure of the government to protect the economic well-being of its citizens. If our capacity to produce is limited by machines, it must ever be remembered that these machines are operated by the skill and the stamina of the workers.

As the government is determined to protect the rights of the workers, so the nation has a right to expect that the men who man the machines will discharge their full responsibilities to the urgent needs of defense. The worker possesses the same human dignity and is entitled to the same security of position as the engineer or the manager or the owner. For the workers provide the human power that turns out the destroyers, and the planes, and the tanks. The nation expects our defense industries to continue operation without interruption by strikes or lockouts. It expects and insists that management and workers will reconcile their differences by voluntary or legal means, to continue to produce the supplies that are so sorely needed. And on the economic side of our great defense program, we are, as you know, bending every effort to maintain stability of prices and with that the stability of the cost of living.

Nine days ago I announced the setting up of a more effective organization to direct our gigantic efforts to increase the production of munitions. The appropriation of vast sums of money and a well-coordinated executive direction of our defense efforts are not in themselves enough. Guns, planes, ships and many other things have to be built in the factories and the arsenals of America. They have to be produced by workers and managers and engineers with the aid of machines which in turn have to be built by hundreds of thousands of workers throughout the land. In this great work there has been splendid cooperation between the government and industry and labor. And I am very thankful.

American industrial genius, unmatched throughout all the world in the solution of production problems, has been called upon to bring its resources and its talents into action. Manufacturers of watches, of farm implements, of Linotypes and cash registers and automobiles, and sewing machines and lawn mowers and locomotives, are now making fuses and bomb packing crates and telescope mounts and shells and pistols and tanks.

But all of our present efforts are not enough. We must have more ships, more guns, more planes -- more of everything. And this can be accomplished only if we discard the notion of "business as usual." This job cannot be done merely by superimposing on the existing productive facilities the added requirements of the nation for defense. Our defense efforts must not be blocked by those who fear the future consequences of surplus plant capacity. The possible consequences of failure of our defense efforts now are much more to be feared. And after the present needs of our defense are past, a proper handling of the country's peacetime needs will require all of the new productive capacity, if not still more. No pessimistic policy about the future of America shall delay the immediate expansion of those industries essential to defense. We need them.

I want to make it clear that it is the purpose of the nation to build now with all possible speed every machine, every arsenal, and every factory that we need to manufacture our defense material. We have the men, the skill, the wealth, and above all, the will. I am confident that if and when production of consumer or luxury goods in certain industries requires the use of machines and raw materials that are essential for defense purposes, then such production must yield, and will gladly yield, to our primary and compelling purpose.

So I appeal to the owners of plants, to the managers, to the workers, to our own government employees to put every ounce of effort into producing these munitions swiftly and without stint. With this appeal I give you the pledge that all of us who are officers of your government will devote ourselves to the same whole-hearted extent to the great task that lies ahead.

As planes and ships and guns and shells are produced, your government, with its defense experts, can then determine how best to use them to defend this hemisphere. The decision as to how much shall be sent abroad and how much shall remain at home must be made on the basis of our overall military necessities.

We must be the great arsenal of democracy," said the President in a firm and decisive tone as he looked over to see the reaction on the face of General Arnold.

For us this is an emergency as serious as war itself. We must apply ourselves to our task with the same resolution, the same sense of urgency, the same spirit of patriotism and sacrifice as we would show were we at war.

We have furnished the British great material support and we will furnish far more in the future. There will be no "bottlenecks" in our determination to aid Great Britain. No dictator, no combination of dictators, will weaken that determination by threats of how they will construe that determination. The British have received invaluable military support from the heroic Greek Army and from the forces of all the governments in exile. Their strength is growing. It is the strength of men and women who value their freedom more highly than they value their lives.

I believe that the Axis powers are not going to win this war. I base that belief on the latest and best of information.

We have no excuse for defeatism. We have every good reason for hope -- hope for peace, yes, and hope for the defense of our civilization and for the building of a better civilization in the future. I have the profound conviction that the American people are now determined to put forth a mightier effort than they have ever yet made to increase our production of all the implements of defense, to meet the threat to our democratic faith.

As President of the United States, I call for that national effort. I call for it in the name of this nation which we love and honor and which we are privileged and proud to serve. I call upon our people with absolute confidence that our common cause will greatly succeed.

Thank you and good evening."

The radio technician sitting behind the control panel said, "You are off, Mr. President."

Roosevelt immediately moved from behind the desk to meet his special guests and get their reaction to his speech.

A short time later, in a parlor in the White House, a select group of people who had been invited to sit in on the fireside chat, now sat with cocktails and hors d'oeuvres.

Roosevelt talked with several of the people, General Arnold being one of them, along with the two reporters. Secretary Hull finished shaking hands with one of the VIPs present for the broadcast then walked over to the President.

"An excellent speech, Mr. President," Hull said. "That should give our people in the Congress something to work with when Lend-Lease comes up for debate."

President Roosevelt grinned. "Well…let's hope so, Mr. Secretary," He turned to the reporters. "The American people ought to realize how vital it's to our own future security that England holds out against Hitler. Britain is bankrupt, but Churchill leaves no doubt they'll fight on…if they can be supplied."

"And… our American industry can do that?" A reporter asked. "What about the Neutrality Act, Mr. President? Wouldn't directing aid to Britain, a belligerent in a war, be a violation?"

"The Lend-Lease proposal I'm sending to the Congress would allow us to lend England unlimited supplies and equipment, in some cases in exchange for leases on advanced bases of operation, all without violating the Neutrality Act or any other constitutional provision the isolationists try to use against us," Roosevelt said.

Well, Lend-Lease notwithstanding, it was a great speech, Mr. President. The Arsenal of Democracy…is the kind of phrase that finds its way into the history books!" one man said.

"Thank you, John,"

Gable and Lombard detached themselves from a small knot of people, and approached the President.

"Great speech, Mr. President," Gable said.

"Thank you, Clark," President Roosevelt said, He turned to Carole Lombard "You look positively ravishing tonight, Carole."

"Why, thank you Mr. President. You don't look so bad yourself,"

Roosevelt laughed. "Come now!"

Lombard held her champagne glass aloft before the guests. "A toast everybody." She turned to the President and smiled. "To the President of the United States.

"May America indeed be the Arsenal of Democracy, Mr. President, in spite of Charlie Lindbergh and the isolationists!"

The guests raised their glasses, and some exclaimed, "Here! Here!"

A smiling President Roosevelt acknowledged the toast and then thanked his guests. "A President's day doesn't end at sundown, you know."

Roosevelt nodded to a secret service agent who stood nearby, indicating his readiness to leave the room.

The agent went to Roosevelt's wheel chair, grasped the handles to push the President from the room, all of this as Roosevelt spoke softly to Ann Roosevelt who had crossed to kiss the President on his cheek.

"Harry will be along with the initial press reactions momentarily. I'll be in the library. Send him in there, will you?"

"Of course, Pa." She gazed at her father admiringly. "It was really an electrifying speech, you know."

"Thank you, my dear."

President Roosevelt turned to General Arnold, "Oh, Hap."

"Yes, Mr. President."

"I've got some work to finish off. Do you mind coming along for a few minutes?"

"Not at all, Sir."

Roosevelt emerged from the oval office, being pushed by the Secret Service Agent, General Arnold walked alongside the wheel chair. They proceeded through the reception area and on down a long corridor leading to the library, the President talking all the while.

You know, Hap, we've got a long way to go in overcoming public apathy," Roosevelt said.

Yes, Mr. President," General Arnold said.

President Roosevelt thought for a moment. "Well, anyway...Marshall approved the Kilner-Lindbergh Five Year Plan. The Air Corps finally has *its* mission."

General Arnold grinned. "That's right, Mr. President."

"And…we've got Air Corps observers in England?" Roosevelt asked.

"General Chaney is there with a staff, construction of airbases all over England has started and that B-25 experiment with the Special Operations Executive, Code name Black Bart is in place. Black Bart flew their first mission yesterday. It made a supply drop to the resistance and shot down a ME-109 as well."

"Excellent. Keep me informed on that operation. I'm very curious on how that works out." The President paused, becoming reflective. "Hap, there's talk up here about a reorganization plan for the Air Corps. It's what we had in mind when we made you Acting Deputy Chief of Staff last March, and kept you on as Chief of the Air Corps at the same time. I'm directing Secretary of War Stimson to place our Army Air Corps under a *single commander."*

"We've needed that kind of unity of Command, Mr. President," General Arnold said.

"We're reviving the office of Assistant Secretary of War for Air. I've been thinking Robert A. Lovett would be an asset there. He's done a fine job as our special assistant on Air Matters."

General Arnold found it hard to believe what he was hearing.

"Excellent choice, Sir!"

"The way we've got it planned, you'll become Chief of the Army Air Forces at that time, but, you'll retain the title of Deputy Chief of Staff." He paused to gauge Arnold's reaction." That way, of course, you'll be able to serve as contact between the War Department General Staff and the Army Air Forces."

"I'm not so sure I agree with my involvement in the matter, but I think the plan itself is excellent! It certainly should help eliminate our perennial problems with the war department general staff."

"Exactly… something we should have done years ago."

They arrived at the library door and General Arnold opened the door as the Secret Service agent wheeled the President into the library. The President gestured to a desk across from the library door and the secret service agent pushed the wheel chair to the desk where he was dismissed by the President.

"Thank you," President Roosevelt said. "I'd like not to be disturbed except when Hopkins comes up, of course."

"Yes, Sir," the agent said and left.

The President wheeled himself into position behind the desk where a stack of paper work had been carefully laid out for his perusal and action.

The President gestured to one of the several large chairs by the desk. "Sit down Hap." He pointed to a decanter on the corner of the desk. "Care for one?"

"Why…yes of course, if you are, Sir." General Arnold said.

Roosevelt began pouring the drinks, talking all the while.

"Hap, Churchill's chiefs of staff are coming over here next week. They want to discuss grand strategy with our chiefs and their representatives."

The President passed the drink to Arnold who took the glass and settled back into his seat. Roosevelt contemplated his glass for a moment, then he gazed at Arnold:

"Of course, if the press gets hold of this they'll accuse us of making secret plans to go to War! Our goose would be cooked, you know!" President Roosevelt said.

"I understand, Sir." General Arnold said.

"The military consensus seems to be that we'll be forced into the war eventually. The mutual pact between Japan, Germany and Italy provides a pretty sound basis for their judgment," FDR said

"Seems rather obvious, Sir."

"In that event, our combined efforts would be directed against Germany first." Roosevelt said. "Any action against Japan being fought more or less on an attrition basis until Germany is defeated."

Roosevelt leaned forward as he spoke, emphasizing the gravity of his words.

"Hap...the War Department strategists are talking about conducting a massive air offensive against German industry... if not Germany itself. It will be done from airdromes that we've started building in England. Heavy bombers will drop hundreds of thousands of tons of bombs deep into enemy territory. They feel German morale can't withstand the pressures of aerial bombardment as the British have for so long now. Can we do it?"

"Of course, Mr. President. Given the time," General Arnold said. "The strategic bombardment mission is what we've been working toward ever since Billy Mitchell and our tactical school developed the concepts."

"How much time?" President Roosevelt asked.

General Arnold paused. "Three years."

"Three years! You're talking about 1943!"

"Mr. President... it'll be late in forty-one before sufficient numbers of B-17s and B-24s are available to begin basic four engine training programs here in the United States."

"But...*three years, Hap?"*

"Well...we're looking at another year to a year and a half to equip and train a sufficient number of combat groups to efficiently mount a strategic air offensive." General Arnold began to speak slowly to emphasize the importance of what he was saying. "Gunners...bombadiers...entire crews...they've to be trained in the equipment they'll fly in combat. Otherwise, our combat losses would be unacceptable." He was silent for a moment, knowing the President was thinking about his words. "In the meantime, we've still to equip our heavy bombardment groups in Alaska, the Caribbean and Hawaii with B-17s, not to speak of the possibility of placing a heavy bombardment group in the Philippines. Most of those groups are still flying obsolete B-10's."

President Roosevelt gazed at General Arnold for a long moment. "Prime Minister Churchill wants a hundred B-17s the minute the Lend-Lease proposal passes the Congress...if indeed it does."

General Arnold stares at the President incredulously. "But Mr. President! That would be impossible!!"

General Arnold deposited his glass on the end table by his chair, leaned forward to emphasize his concern.

"The Air Corps has developed its entire strategic mission around the B-17. Production schedules will be strained to the limit in meeting our own requirements."

President Roosevelt frowned. "The whole idea is to keep England in the battle, General. The longer they hold, the more time we buy."

"But, if England falls, Mr. President. What then?" General Arnold asked. "We're apt to find ourselves in a damned ticklish position over here if we're called on to fight or even to defend our own hemisphere. We've only got forty in the entire Air Corps inventory right now...that's throughout this hemisphere and the Pacific."

Roosevelt's anger subsided as he gazed at General Arnold, and realized the integrity of his response. "Can't something be done to increase heavy bomber production, even before year's end?"

"I've got the Douglas and the Vega people talking with Boeing. We're hoping to sub contract B-17's production to them. They both have the capability."

"And..."

"I'm optimistic, Sir. But it'll be early summer before any scheduling projections can be made realistically."

"Then I'd say we've got a serious problem on our hands, Hap," the President said.

Years of frustration weighed heavily in General Arnold's voice. "If you'll excuse me Sir, that's what we in the Air Corps have been trying to demonstrate to the war department general staff for the past ten years now."

"Of course…of course," the President said. "Well, nothing has been approved between the Prime Minister and me at this point." He stopped talking to gather his thoughts. "Hopkins is off to England next week to begin arrangements for a meeting between Churchill and me -- he'll be reporting on what the most pressing needs are over there -- and what kind of a time table we're looking at," the President smiled. "I appreciate your candor, Hap."

"Thank you." General Arnold stood up. "Good night,Mr. President."

The President nodded, smiled briefly and then delved into the paper work before him,

General Arnold crossed to the door, opened it, then turned back to the President.

"Oh, and by the way, Mr. President. It was a whale of a speech."

Roosevelt nodded, and smiled again, then watched as General Arnold left the room. In the hallway adjacent to the library, Harry Hopkins hurriedly approached the library door just as General Arnold had moved a few steps down the hallway.

"Well, General Arnold, are you prepared to deal with forty-thousand airplanes a year?" Harry Hopkins asked and waved a sheaf of telegrams. "They say you're going to get them."

"I'm prepared…if we don't give them all away before the Air Corps gets what it needs," General Arnold said.

"He told you about Churchill and the B-17s?" Harry Hopkins asked

"Yes." General Arnold said. "I've got heavy bombardment groups sprouting up all over the hemisphere, Harry They don't have a damned thing to fly!" The General continued. "We *must* keep *all* of our B-17s over here… at least until late next year."

"That may be a tough request to follow through on, General. Anyway… nothing's been agreed to yet." Hopkins clasped the General's shoulders. "I'll confer with you before I leave for England, all right?"

General Arnold only nodded, and then walked on down the hall. Hopkins gazed after him momentarily as he entered the library.

It was just a matter of weeks before President Roosevelt was at his desk in the oval office, signing the HR 1776 Bill. Secretary Hull, General George Marshall, Admiral Stark and three Government VIPs gathered behind the desk witnessing the signing of the bill, HR 1776, known as the Lend-Lease Act. The HR 1776 empowered the U. S. to provide her Allies with weapons of war. Twenty-one of our mighty B-17 Flying Fortresses were already on the way to England. The President asked for an increase in overall aircraft production to forty thousand planes a year.

The production of virtually all military items had been increased tenfold or more. All over America, industry responded by gearing up to meet production quotas that were considered impossible by some, but not by America's workers. For the young and the old alike, skilled and non skilled, there was no question that the job would be done. Churchill asked for tools to finish the job against Hitler and the American people would build them for their British friends.

CHAPTER 15

A gust of wind came into the Rattskeller at the same time that Bart and two crewmen entered.

"Damn, it's cold! That humid cold air off the North Atlantic goes right through me," Sharp said. "Reggie, dear, could we have a round of whiskeys, please?"

"Sure, love," she replied as she stopped Bart. "You've a visitor waiting for you in the back booth."

"Thanks, male or female?" he replied.

"Male, you sexual pervert," Reggie answered with a sexy smile. "I saw you and that redhead over at the Barley Mow last night. Nice looking woman. Since she was out with you, I assume that she's no morals."

Bart winked as he went to meet the unknown visitor.

As Bart got close to the booth, he saw the head of the SOE, Hugh Dalton himself.

"Welcome back, Bart. Another great flight I understand. What does that make the total, twelve over Belgium, one flight into Spain and four over France, right?"

"That's correct, Sir," Bar said as he sat down. He was handed his drink by Reggie as soon as he sat down.

Dalton looked up at Reggie and asked, "Don't let anyone disturb us, love."

She nodded and left. She knew who Dalton was. Now she wasn't sure about Bart Coltrane and his friends. The head of the Special Operations Executive doesn't just talk to anyone, especially some American instructor pilots. "They must not be just pilots," she thought.

"I hope that you don't mind this bit of intrigue and informality. I understand that you and Rupert Chapman don't always see eye to eye these days," he said, then continued without letting Bart comment. "Rupert can get under one's skin, but he's a professional. I know that he means well, at least." Dalton stopped and looked Coltrane in the eyes. Bart knew to keep his mouth shut. Then Dalton continued, "I have a very pressing problem in Norway. I need a special delivery that will be more than difficult. You're my only real chance of getting some very critical supplies and two SOE personnel into the area in time for a very critical operation. The Germans have a new heavy water processing plant in Norway that could eventually have a serious impact on the war and Jens Christian Hange is trying to form a coordinated underground resistance movement in Norway. The two SOE agents and supplies are going there for those two purposes.

"I can't afford delays, differences of professional opinions or obvious office conflicts. So if you agree to take on the mission, I'll make sure Rupert is on a trip for me. A valid trip, and out of the office anyway. That prevents office or internal problems to affect the mission. You understand where I'm going with this, Bart?"

The only question is where and when are we going?

"Not that simple, Bart," Dalton interjected. The weather over the entire U.K. area and the North Sea is absolutely abominable. Nothing is flying for the next two or possibly three days. I need the delivery to be made tomorrow afternoon."

Coltrane sat back and finished off his drink without saying anything.

Dalton casually looked around to insure there was nobody eavesdropping. "Bart, you'd have to take off in almost zero-zero conditions in the dark and fly on instruments to a point off the Norway Coast where the weather isn't much better.

"It seems that the base of the clouds is around 400 or 500 feet off the ocean some three to four miles offshore. That means your flight would have to stay at altitude above the clouds to keep out of icing conditions then descend to 300 feet exactly three miles off the coast. Then fly to the drop point through the valleys and avoid the cloud covered mountain peaks and return. The weather in Norway is also trashy but better than we've here. It's bad enough to keep the German fighters on the ground. The last part of the problem is where in the U.K. you could land given the adverse conditions. Sort of a bloody challenge isn't it?"

Coltrane looked at Dalton as he thought through the problem. Then he spoke in a soft deliberate tone, "This must be damned important for you to even be here much less asking us to fly this type of mission. What do you say we go over to the office and plan this adventure? I doubt that anyone would be around to disturb us or ask unnecessary questions."

"Great idea. After we go over the details, I'll buy you blokes a well-deserved supper."

Bart got up and looked at his two friends at the bar. They watched him stick his finger into the air and give the crank up sign. They quickly downed their drinks and got their coats on as Dalton and Coltrane walked to the door.

Fifteen minutes later they were in the warm SOE office. They sat at the Black Bart conference table as Dalton went over the details of the mission. At the conclusion of his briefing, there was a sigh from the crew.

"That's a tall order, Sir," Dalton said. "How much of a cloud base will you really need to do some sort of instrument landing back here?"

"If it was a flat area with no towers, obstructions, hills or buildings, I could put us a mile off the end of the runway at 300 feet, possibly 200 if our altimeters are not too far off. We would need the help of someone to call around the selected airfields to see what they actually have for weather conditions and let us know."

"Smashing!" Dalton said, as he slammed his fist into the other hand. "We can do that easily."

"I can do my part if the boss is comfortable with it," Sharp said as he turned to Bart.

"Hell, I'm just a truck driver going where I'm told to go. It's almost as bad as being married," Bart said in a mock serious tone.

Robby West was at the wall map looking at the probable course and return conditions. "Yeah, you're really on target with *smashing*."

Bart turned to Dalton, "Sir, we'll have this planned and into your hands by 0500. We'll be off Tempsford by 0900. Sir, on our return course – we'll need the airfield weather conditions updated every 30 minutes starting at 1200 hours. We'll call RAF Sumburgh operators to get the report. Perhaps we can even get in there. They'll probably clear before Scotland or the Midlands. At any rate, we'll depend on the weather report. Since we'll be almost the only aircraft in the sky, we shouldn't have to worry about any midair collision."

"You can depend on the very best report possible when you call in to Sumburgh," Dalton said with a tone of commitment.

"Well, then Sir, if you'll give us a rain check on that meal, we've work to do. Please have your drop pods to our hangar by 0700 and your passengers there by 0800. We'll take things from there, Sir," Coltrane said as he looked at Dalton.

"Bloody good! I shall leave you to your planning," Dalton said as he went to the door. "Gentlemen, thank you for your effort." Then he left.

"Okay, Prince Henry, how do we do this?" Coltrane asked.

"Actually, it's a piece of cake until we get to the landing part. That could be a little dicey. But, fearless commander, I have a plan!" Sharp said with fanfare.

Coltrane dropped his head and shook it a couple of times before looking back up at Sharp. "Why do I get the feeling this will be far beyond normal flying and established instrument landing procedures?"

"Take a look at this idea," he said as he went to the blackboard. He drew a horizontal line then four perpendicular lines. "Now," he stated his explanation, "this only applies to Tempsford. If we return slightly to the west of RAF Bedford turning towards their HF Non-directional Beacon (NDB) at one thousand feet, we would cross over it on an established course of 128 degrees at 120 mph. Immediately after crossing we establish a 185 feet per minute descent. That rate is critical as is the heading. You'll fly 128 degree inbound heading on the Tempsford NDB, but it's the Bedford NDB (X3TH) that's important as that gives you the time to decision point. Winds should not be a factor in this trashy weather. Three minutes and forty-eight seconds we should be over the town of Tempsford. We might break out and see the runway a little over one half mile ahead, but I doubt it. Four minutes and nine seconds after Bedford, we should be at 200 feet above the road west of the runway. We should be able to see the runway a quarter of a mile away. If you can't after four minutes and fifteen seconds, you put the power to her and we fly out over the channel and bail out. We'll be almost out of fuel and options by then. So how do you like the plan?"

Coltrane looked over at West who was hanging to every word said by Sharp. "Smashing, I guess," West said with a look of amazement on his face. Then he looked over to Coltrane and asked him in return, "Can you fly that close to tolerances?"

Yes, but I'll need to focus totally on the instruments you'll need to be looking outside at all times to spot the runway and maybe the two checkpoints. When you see the runway, you'll take the controls and land. I won't be able to transition from the gauges to looking for the runway in time to land. Not at 120 mph for sure," Coltrane said as he leaned back in his seat and put his hands behind his head.

"I guess we'd better call Royston and tell him to get the bird ready to go. Okay, let's work up a flight plan for our three options. Then get some sleep before we launch into the white abyss," Coltrane said, as he got up to get closer to the wall map.

The visibility was absolute zero-zero when the Black Bart crew got off the train at Tempsford. Sergeant Royston was there with a jeep. Where and how he got it, Coltrane didn't want to know. He was just thankful that he had "requisitioned" it. That British Lorrie was a rough riding machine.

Coltrane hadn't fully gotten into the jeep when Royston started talking. "Both passengers and cargo arrived before 0600. They don't say much, nor have they really identified themselves. They went through the Gibraltar Farm Barn to get special equipment, so I assume that they're section D spooks. They've three delivery pods which weigh a total of eight hundred sixty pounds. The Black Bart is ready to go except for the deicing boots. That hot air modification that you came up with is probably too much heat for the rubber and connectors. I wouldn't go up maximum anymore. They'll hold for now but I've put in a requisition for another complete set just in case. The radios and navigational instruments are good. I checked out the gyro compass and everything else I could think of. Apparently, we're going to fly on the gauges," he said as he took in a deep breath. Royston turned halfway in his seat as he directed his next comment towards Captain Sharp. "I put in two more map lights over your new table. I also put in a couple other modifications to make the ride better for you in that cramped area."

"Thanks, Sarge, it's rather tight in there and dark as hell," Sharp responded.

As they drove up to the make-shift hangar, Coltrane could see two men standing next to the left main landing gear looking at the pirate flag and name "Black Bart" painted on the nose of the aircraft.

"Good morning, gentlemen. I'm Major Bart Coltrane, your tour guide today," Bart said and he extended his hand. "May I see some identification?"

The smaller of the two stepped forward and gave him a leather bound identification card identifying him as an SOE agent from the Special Intelligence Service of Section D. He then said, "I'll vouch for this man. His identity needs to remain hush hush if you don't mind."

That peaked Coltrane's curiosity. "That's fine with me, Mr. X."

The man then said in perfect Southern Alabama English, "Thanks, it's just better that way. I work for Colonel Bill Donavan, if that helps you."

Coltrane immediately understood and nodded. "Okay, then. Did Sergeant Royston brief you on the flight and the way you'll depart?"

"Yes, Sir, he was very thorough. We jump out of the bomb bay immediately after the pods." He said that we would go out at 500 feet. That's a little tight on altitude for our chutes," the agent said.

"It's better that way. Your chutes will deploy very quickly at 150 knots and you'll only swing in the air twice before landing. We've done it many times before without so much as a sprained ankle. The Germans are less likely to see you or your pods. Besides, the weather won't let us get much higher. The takeoff may be a little different than you may have experienced before. We'll use a max power, short field takeoff procedure due to the very bad visibility. We want to get off the ground as quickly as possible, given that we can only see maybe three hundred feet ahead of the aircraft," Coltrane concluded. "Okay, if you'll go with Sergeant Royston, we'll get going in about 17 minutes," he said as he looked at his watch.

Coltrane climbed up into the forward entrance and looked at the three delivery pods hanging from the British type release hooks hanging from the top of the bomb bay. He checked to see if the parachute static lines which deployed the chutes immediately after leaving the bottom of the B-25 were attached properly. He then looked past the pods at his two passengers and Sergeant Royston in the rear compartment. All was ready. He climbed up into the cockpit and strapped himself into his parachute and safety belt. He looked out of his window to see Martin standing by the left engine with a fire extinguisher. Then he looked out to see if Lightfoot was next to the right engine. Fire guards were set and they were ready to crank.

It took almost ten minutes to start up and go through the checklist. Once satisfied with the aircraft's ability to fly safely, he hit the intercom, "Pilot to crew, confirm readiness." Then both pilots checked their altimeters to check accurate field evaluation. Then cross checked that against the reported barometric pressure. The difference was the adjustment or "K" factor.

One by one everyone checked in and confirmed that all aspects of their job and equipment were ready to go. Coltrane gave the signal to the two ground crewmen to pull the wheel chalks so he could move forward. Jack Martin quickly got into the jeep and slowly drove forward leading the B-25 to the end of the runway. He then went down the runway and turned around and parked next to the runway facing the aircraft so it gave Coltrane a visual reference as he took off. Coltrane set the parking brake and advanced the throttles to operating speed to check the magnetos and aircraft systems.

"Okay, Kelly, are you ready?" Coltrane asked.

"Just waiting on you," he said confidently. "Fly runway heading and climb to 9,000 feet."

"Roger, fly zero-seven-zero degrees, climb to and maintain nine thousand," Coltrane responded in a serious tone.

Black Bart was at the very end of the sixty-five hundred foot long runway seven zero at Tempsford. Coltrane advanced the throttles to maximum power. The aircraft shook as it strained against the brakes.

"Pilot to crew, prepare for takeoff," ordered Coltrane. "Okay, Robby, follow me up on throttles and controls," said Bart Coltrane as he looked ahead at the barely visible runway and dim glow of the jeep headlights. It was time!

Coltrane released the brakes and the aircraft lunged forward and quickly gained speed. He had to make a slight heading connection to keep the plane in the center of the runway. Suddenly, the jeep flashed past, then he pulled back on the control yoke and the aircraft leaped off the ground and into the rainy gray morning sky. Coltrane immediately adjusted his rate of climb and power settings to climb power. He kept his eyes on the attitude and airspeed indicators and cross-checking the compass to insure they didn't go off course. He turned on the autopilot which kept his wings level and on the zero-seven-zero degree heading. West had raised the landing gear and flaps when Coltrane gave him an indication with the palm of his hand. It was very dark and rainy. The plane became steady in its climb out to nine thousand feet.

Coltrane noticed that it was starting to get lighter about the time they passed through eighty-five hundred feet. Suddenly, they were above the clouds. It was mostly clear above with only a thin deck of clouds at 15,000 feet.

Bart was about to start leveling off at nine thousand feet when Sharp was heard over the intercom. "Turn to 027 degrees and climb to eleven thousand feet."

"Roger, zero two seven degrees, climbing to eleven thousand," Coltrane responded. "Wow that was solid cloud mass to 8,500. No wonder visibility was so bad."

About forty minutes after leveling off, Sharp came up to the cockpit. "We're on course and on time. I got three fixes and three RDF (Radio Direction Finder) fixes to confirm. We're on our way and where we want to be…I hope," Sharp said jokingly.

West looked at Sharp with a questionable look on his face.

"Relax, Robbie, I know where we're," Sharp said. "It seems strange to be up here and not another aircraft in sight." After a few minutes, he went back down to the navigator's table and prepared to run another set of position fixes.

Two hours and eight minutes after takeoff, Sharp called out to Coltrane, "Stand by to descend to five hundred feet on my mark descent at five hundred feet per minute." There was a pause, then Sharp said, "Descend now."

Coltrane adjusted the trim table to lower the nose for a power on descent to five hundred feet. When passing fifteen hundred feet, Coltrane reduced power and adjusted the altitude of the aircraft to continue the descent with the aircraft flying in a flat or level altitude. This would allow him to quickly advance power and stop the descent in case of emergency or premature sighting of the ocean surface or land mass.

The aircraft had almost reached seven hundred feet when they broke out of the ragged overcast. The visibility appeared to Coltrane to be about three miles or better. "This was good," he thought. He looked ahead and saw the Norwegian coast directly ahead. He could see the big island just to his left and the river directly ahead. "Bingo!" he called out. "Absolutely dead on, Kelly."

"Can you see the river valley ahead?" Sharp asked.

"Got it. Right where it's supposed to be."

"Good, stay in the valley for 29.5 miles. You'll over fly a lake. Then turn to 010 degrees for forty-eight miles to drop zone," he instructed.

West was looking on his map and watching for key land points to confirm their position. This was made difficult by Coltrane maneuvering the aircraft through the twists and turns needed to say in the valley and below the top of the surrounding hills and mountains." Suddenly, West called out, "There's the lake!"

"Okay, take up a heading of zero one zero. You'll be coming out of the narrow valley and be in more open area with lots of hills popping up."

Coltrane kept the aircraft 50 to 75 feet above the very rough terrain as he followed the course to the Drop Zone.

Coltrane hit the intercom, "Yank, get them ready. We'll be there in five minutes or so."

"Roger," replied Sergeant Royston.

Sharp came over the intercom, "You're three minutes to Drop Zone… can you see the lake yet, Robbie?" We drop just short of the lake."

"I've got the lake," exclaimed West. "It's five degrees to the starboard. Opening bomb bay doors! Stand by!"

"Okay to drop?" West asked Coltrane.

"You're cleared to drop," Bart replied calmly. "Stand by, 15 seconds to drop."

"Ready," then a pause, "Drop!" Bart said.

West toggled the release switches one at a time. The plane shuddered as each of the pods and two agents departed the aircraft and the static line went tight and deployed the parachutes.

"Five good chutes," reported Royston.

"Great," said Coltrane as he turned toward the valley to his left.

"It's only 11.2 miles to the end of this valley then turn to 267 degrees for 70.55 miles. Then we're home free," Sharp said.

"Home free," thought Coltrane. "We've had no enemy fire. We surely didn't catch them by surprise. Even if we did at the beginning, they would have communicated a general alarm. They'll be waiting at the coast for us! He hit the intercom, "Better be ready for some heavy fire at the coastline." Kelly, keep us in the least defended area and a route that we can go across the beach at treetop."

"Roger," Sharp replied. "You'll clear the hills about six miles prior to the beach on this course."

The next twenty minutes were silent as the B-25 weaved through the valley and hills until they hit the flat area near the beach.

The visibility was still about four to six miles which gave the enemy a clear shot at them. Bart put the bird down to 15 to 20 feet above the ground. This was a little unnerving to West who could see trees and other obstacles come screaming towards the aircraft at over 235 knots, then disappear suddenly. It took slightly more than two minutes to cross the coastal plain to the North Sea. Again, not a shot was fired at them.

"I don't believe it!" Coltrane said. "We caught them by surprise.

Maybe they thought we were just another German aircraft. Anyway, we cheated death once again…or should I say, so far!"

"Climb to ten thousand feet on a heading of 192 degrees. I'll contact Sumburgh for a weather report," Sharp said with a businesslike voice.

He came back up on the intercom about the same time the aircraft hit clear air again. The sun felt good on Bart's face.

"Stay on this course. Sumbough is visibility zero, sky obscured. We can't go there. Prestwick is about the same," Sharp said pausing to arrange his notes," Tempsford is reporting 200 feet overcast, winds less than 3 variable, visibility less than one mile. It looks like we get to use my new homemade instrument approach."

"Oh, Joy," Robby said, sarcastically. "Now we're back to that smashing idea."

"Robby, take the damned controls and fly his plan," Coltrane said with irritation. "You think too damned much about the bad and not the true genius of his idea." Put your HF-ADF upon the Tempsford frequency. That will be our 128 degree inbound approach course and our missed approach point if you can't find the damned runway. We're too far out to receive the signal, but we will in about an hour and a half. Kelly, keep him on course, I'm going to rest up for the approach."

"Come right to 205 degrees," Sharp said loudly over the intercom. Coltrane was suddenly awake from his semi-conscious rest. He sat up in his seat and turned the heading bug on the autopilot to 205 degrees. Start your descent to one thousand feet at 500 feet per minute."

Coltrane reduced the throttles slightly to get the desired 500 feet rate of decent per minute. He looked over at his and Robby's ADF. Both were registering their respective radio stations. "Okay, let's go through the pre-landing check while we aren't in a hurry. Prepare for landing."

As the Black Bart passed through two thousand feet, Sharp came on the intercom. "When I give you the word, execute a standard rate turn to the left. Establish yourself on a 97 degree inbound heading towards Bedford. You should be stabilized on course at 1,000 feet and 120 mph. Okay, look at your ADF. We're almost ready to turn. Get down to 1,000 feet, you're a little high and fast."

Coltrane made the needed adjustments. He saw the needle reach the turn point and quickly checked to make sure he was at 1,000 feet and 120 mph. All was where it should be.

"Turn," came the command from the navigator. Coltrane made the turn slowly and precisely. West had his sweaty hands loosely on the controls with Bart in nervous anticipation. Coltrane leveled up the plane on 128 degrees while still at 1,000 feet and 120 mph. "Very good, we're two miles from Bedford. Get ready to start your descent at 185 feet per minute," Sharp said.

"Give me gear and flaps!" Coltrane ordered West quickly complied.

The ADF needle in front of West fluctuated slightly then turned 180 degrees to the bottom of the instrument. He heard Sharp say "Station passage, start descent and start your stop watch." West quickly hit the timer function on the clock mounted on the instrument panel.

West directed his attention to the ground and in front of the descending aircraft. His eyes strained for any sign of the ground or runway. He became increasingly nervous as the altimeter slowly wound down to the 200 feet decision height.

'Are you sure there are no towers or church steeples around here?" West asked. Nobody replied.

Sharp said softly, "We should be over Tempsford now. Anything in sight?"

"Hell, no," Robby said. "We're at 200 feet, looks like we're going to hit the silk over the channel." Robbie felt an emotional letdown when he could not see the runway. "No joy!" he reported. Coltrane quickly pushed the throttles forward, raised the landing gear and started to climb to a higher altitude so they could bail out over the English Channel. An emergency procedure that he really didn't want to follow.

The aircraft was just starting to climb upward when he heard West call out. "I see the runway! It was just below us when we started up. I don't see how I could have missed it at decision height," reported West. "Let's try again. We were too close not to give it another try. I sure don't want to go swimming in the channel." Coltrane looked over at West then at the fuel gauges and shook his head. "We're getting real tight on fuel but we should be able to make one more try before we've to bail out." He leveled the aircraft off at 1,000 feet and put the autopilot back on before turning to Sharp. "What do you think, Prince Henry? Can you get us down to a 150 foot decision height just a little earlier than the last time?" Sharp turned toward Coltrane and with a broad smile said, "A piece of cake! As opposed to freezing my ass off in the channel I'm up for the challenge. Now turn to 280 degrees and let's get a little farther to the northwest of Bedford so we can get a solid 128 degree heading before we hit the NDB. Then we'll descend at 200 feet per minute until we get to 150 feet decision height a quarter mile before the runway. Don't go any lower than 150 and you may have to level off just a little before you've to execute missed approach."

"Sounds like a plan to me," Coltrane said as he turned to a 280 degree heading back to the northwest for another try. He and West went through the routine pre-landing check list as usual and waited until the word came from Sharp to start the left hand standard rate turn back towards the 128 degree heading to Bedford NDB. Coltrane smoothly completed his turn and was well established on course a good two miles from the Bedford navigation aid. "OK, give me the gear!" he commanded. Robbie moved the landing gear lever to the down position. The sound of the motors moving the wheels out of their wheel well and into the down position seemed to be louder than usual to Coltrane whose hands were once again sweating. One by one, he wiped his hands on his flight suit. Then he heard and felt the gear go into the down and locked position. He scanned his instruments and trimmed out the aircraft for smooth and stable flight. Satisfied he switched on the autopilot then waited for the station passage at Bedford.

Sharp said in a drawn out slow voice, "Stand by…start your time and start your descent."

Coltrane and West immediately started their respective stopwatch function on the clocks before them. Coltrane made a small power reduction on the two engines to establish the desired rate of descent and switched off the autopilot. He looked at the altimeter to verify his descent and then looked at his airspeed instrument and course indicator. He was exactly as he wanted as he reported to Sharp without taking his eyes off the instruments.

"Roger," replied Sharp, "you're thirty five seconds to decision height."

West was anxiously looking outside the cockpit for the runway but couldn't help steal a quick look at the slowly descending altimeter. They were passing through 200 feet and he was getting a little panic feeling come over him.

Sharp said with a firm voice, "Ten-seconds to decision point, we're at decision height."

"Time!" Sharp said loudly. "You should see something."

Robby West strained his eyes out front then something caught his eye. It was the road and then he saw the runway. "Runway in sight! I have the aircraft!"

Coltrane pulled his hand away from the throttles as Robby grabbed them and reduced the power as he corrected the path of the aircraft slightly to the right to the center of the runway. Then he chopped the power and the B-25 settled to the ground. The landing was a little rougher than what Robby liked, but very acceptable. Robbie remembered the old flyers axiom, "Any landing that you can walk away from is a good landing." The bomber slowed to a stop then turned on to the taxiway. The jeep suddenly appeared in front of the bird. "Follow Me" was on a large black and yellow lettered sign attached to the rear of the jeep.

Sharp came up behind the two pilots as they taxied to their hangar on the southwest end of the field. "Nice landing. Looks like my idea worked," he said with a big shit-eating grin.

Coltrane set the parking brakes and shut down the engines. As the propellers started to slow down, the ground crew replaced the chalks and started to look for the anticipated bullet and black holes. They were surprised to see none.

Sharp opened the hatch and lowered the built in ladder. He looked down and saw Hugh Dalton's face looking up at him. He had Major Grand with him.

"Have a nice flight?" he said in jest.

"Not bad, but the in-flight meals were terrible," Sharp said in a mock.

They got down and gathered at the front of the aircraft. Dalton shook everyone's hand with a big smile. "Bloody outstanding!" he said. "You bloody well qualified for the Tempsford Taxi Society. A dubious honor if I may say." "There will be no debriefing on this mission today. You can write it up tomorrow afternoon. I want to meet with you at half past three tomorrow in my office. We got a short wireless from our man that you landed them exactly on target and there were no injuries or damage to the equipment." Now go get a shower and head to London. I'll buy you that promised meal at 2000 hours at my club. Be sure to wear coat and tie. The Reform Club is real sticky about that. Now get out of here," he said like a proud father."

It was almost midnight when the crew of the Black Bart got back to the Rattskeller. Sharp closed the door behind the trio and started for the elevator at the back of the bar, when West said "I was so tired that I couldn't enjoy such a wonderful meal at one of the world's most exclusive clubs."

Sharp couldn't even find the energy to respond. He just kept walking to the elevator.

Bart was no better, but he did notice a gorgeous Reggie leaning on the bar accentuating her substantial cleavage.

"I may be dead tired, but I have to say how good you look tonight, Reggie," Bart said as he continued to walk to the elevator.

"I dressed up just for you, mate," she said. "I was going to give myself to you tonight, but you're too bloody tired to do me any good."

Bart smiled and turned back towards her and responded, "Got any strong coffee?"

"I'm afraid that you're far beyond coffee, love," she said as she got up and walked away laughing. 'You've had your chance."

"Thank you," Bart said as he entered the elevator and closed the door. "I'm grateful for the opportunity."

CHAPTER 16

Coltrane had just arrived at his office after their official meeting with Hugh Dalton congratulating them on their successful mission in Norway, when Major Annabel Beddows and Captain Balfour entered the office.

Bart was quick to stand up and walk over to them, "Good afternoon, and what do we attribute to having you join us today?" he said as he shook their hands.

"We came down to personally get your after action report on your 'unscheduled mission' yesterday," she said in a terse and professional tone. "You didn't bother to coordinate with us prior to your departure. That's not the way we do things here in Section D."

Bart was starting to get real irritated at this point. He moved closer and towered over the five-foot six Balfour and quietly said, "I do what I'm told by the Head of the SOE. If you don't like it, take it up with him."

Balfour quickly became intimidated and backed away saying, "Yes, of course. Now could we get the details on key points of intelligence?"

"Sure," Sharp said as he came over trying to defuse the situation, especially since Beddows had not given an inch. "Here is a copy of our actual flight path with times. We didn't see a single German the entire trip," he said as he handed the map to Beddows, who was still glaring at Coltrane.

"Thank you," she said as she and Balfour looked at the map.

Balfour looked at the map and pointed to the point where Black Bart left Norway over the North Sea. "Our information indicates that they had two anti aircraft batteries along this area."

"They could have, Sanford," Coltrane injected. "We may have caught them by surprise, or they couldn't see us due to weather and the low altitude that we were flying, or they hadn't been briefed on the B-25 and thought that we were one of theirs. No telling!"

"Beddows said in a cold and disinterested demeanor, "Well, it worked. There's nothing in your report that I need." Then she left without further comment.

Balfour and the others just looked at her as she left.

"What the hell's wrong with her?" Bart asked.

"Don't be offended, she's just that way. Her nickname around here is the "Ice Maiden." Her husband, the Duke of Estis, was killed in the initial Polish attack in '39. He was doing a threat assessment when he bought the farm," Balfour said in typical British form.

" 'Duke?' " Was she married to royalty?" Robby asked.

"Yes, quite. She's the Duchess of Estis, but she doesn't flaunt it like most of the bluebloods around here," responded Balfour. Her parents were killed in an auto accident when she was nineteen. They left her with a great deal of money, property and several large and successful manufacturing concerns.

"She was also left quite well off by the Duke," Balfour said as he took a shallow breath, and continued. "She has more money than God. You would never know that she was either a blueblood or very, very rich. She never uses her title or shows her wealth. She drives a ten-year old Bentley. On the other hand, the Duke always drove a new Rolls. She's just a very nice woman down deep. On the outside around here she's the Ice Maiden. I guess that I had better get back to work." He reached for the door lever when the door exploded open with Annabel Beddows storming in behind it. She marked in a direct line to Bart Coltrane and stopped just inches from his face.

"You said that if I don't like it, I could take it up with Hugh Dalton. Well, that's exactly what I'm going to do. This affront to myself and Rupert shall not go unanswered. I shall demand that you be formally rebuked for not following procedures and policies," she said in an angry and forceful voice. "Do you've anything to say?"

"You bet, lady, or should I say Duchess. You go to Dalton and you'll end up on the same shit list that Rupert is on," Bart said in a calm but commanding tone.

"What kind of bloody talk is that? Rupert Chapham is a brilliant professional soldier of the highest caliber. I seriously doubt he's on anybody's bloody list! He's everything that you should be as a military officer."

Coltrane almost broke into a laugh, which was noticed by Beddows and made her even madder. He then said "Rupert is a pompous REMF that has never seen hostile fire or ever lead men in combat. He's quick to send men in harm's way without considering what his orders could jeopardize. He's what combat officers fear more than the enemy."

This outraged Beddows. Others in the room were inching away before her next vocal assault.

She had reached a level of anger that she could not say anything then collected herself to ask, "Your arrogance is incredible! What is a REMF?"

He chuckled as did the others, "Well, you did ask. It means Rear Echelon Mother Fucker. It's a term used in the American military to express total professional disrespect for an incompetent officer. Now that you've heard nasty words from my mouth, let me help you out of our office and into the hallway that will lead you to Dalton's office." Bart gently grabbed her elbow and ushered her to the door. She was speechless.

Sharp turned to the others and said, "Okay, I'm taking bets on who calls Bart first. Dalton or Rupert. Any takers at twenty pounds?"

Balfour was the first to produce a twenty pound bill. "I'll take Rupert," he said as he gave Sharp the money. Then Robby put up his money on Dalton. Bart said, "That's a no brainer. Dalton will just laugh at her. Very silently, but he'll die laughing. Rupert is another thing. He may cause me more grief. He really is a sneaky shit."

"Bart," asked Balfour, "I'm curious as to why you haven't tried to get into the Ice Maiden's panties. She's just about the only female around here that you haven't tried to mount."

"That's easy, I only breed with warm-blooded mammals," Bart replied.

Balfour started towards the door shaking his head. "REMF, what a term."

"Now, if you get another midnight call to fly off, do give me a call. No matter what hour. It's my job to keep you alive, if possible. You obviously have enemies on both sides of the English Channel. Got to go now, chaps, Cheerio!"

CHAPTER 17

Senator Clay was sitting in his ornate rosewood paneled Washington D.C. office holding a copy of *The Washington Post* and staring at the headline that read: *Roosevelt and Churchill to Meet.* On the right side of page one an unrelated headline, caught the Senator's attention, *Draft Extension Bill comes before Congress.* Senator Clay laid the newspaper down in front of him, and reached for the telephone.

At the House of Representatives Office Complex, a secretary went to the inner office door, knocked lightly and then opened the door. Representative Clair looked up from his desk. Two colleagues were seated in front of Representative's desk reading copies of a document.

"Senator Clay on the line, Mr. Clair." The secretary said.

Clair nodded, reached for the phone as the Secretary walked away.

"Excuse me, please." Clair said to his colleagues who quietly smiled to each other when Clay's name was mentioned.

He spoke into the phone. "Hello, Titus. Why are you up to so early in the morning?"

"The Draft Extension Bill HR13111, how's it coming down there, Clair?" asked Titus Clay pleasantly

"Too close to call, Titus. It could go either way. How about in the Senate?"

"It'll pass up here. Nothing I can do to stop it. I have tried every trick in the book to stop it. We've just got to see to it that it's killed down there in the House."

"Well… I don't know, Titus. We've got three million men called up through the Selective Service Act now partially trained. Maybe we ought to extend the draft, for an additional year. If we let them all go back home now, we've accomplished nothing."

"If we let George Marshall finish the job, that would be just what Roosevelt and Churchill want!" Senator Clay yelled. He lowered his voice "The way I figure it, that bill's coming up before the House during their Conference out there in the Atlantic. If we kill it, it'll wipe out the basis for any further talks between those two war mongers. The surest way to peace is to deny Roosevelt and Churchill the tools for war that they want. Perhaps you could get Williams to vote no. He needs farm subsidy for his state. I'll get it for him if he votes no. As far as your buddy Wendt, his pet lumber project is dead if he votes for the extension. You let them know the political realities of this issue."

"Well, I… I don't know, Titus. Maybe we ought to soft pedal a bit. If Russia falls, England will sure as hell go. And there's the Japanese out there in the Pacific -- anything can happen out there."

"Well, I can see how it's with you, Clair!" Senator Clay said. "And, I'll tell you, there are some people who aren't going to like a turncoat Representative from our great state. You're forgetting where your support comes from. *The Lord giveth and the Lord taketh away.*"

"I'm afraid I'm just going to have to vote my conscience anyway, Titus. Sorry." Clair hung up the phone and turned to one of his colleagues.

Is he trying to muster support against the draft extension?" The colleague asked.

"Yeah," Representative Clark said.

"Frankly, I think the bill will fail anyway." The colleague said. "The opposition's really bearing down to kill it…national defense be damned."

"Well… that seems to be the preponderate attitude up here right now," Clair said. "I'm afraid that two political freight trains are about to collide. It'll be the nation as a whole that will be the real loser. I'm compelled by better judgment to vote for the extension, as it's what is best for the country. "

CHAPTER 18

It was almost five in Berlin when Admiral Wilhelm Canaris, head of the German Abwehr got a call from Reichsfuhrer Heinrich Hemmler, who was the head of the Gestapo, asking to come to his office. Upon arrival, he found Dr. Joseph Goebbles, the minister of public enlightenment and propaganda already there, seated in a leather chair before the fireplace.

"Good afternoon, Admiral," Hemmler said warmly, "Please take a seat. Could I offer you some Schnapps?"

"Thank you, Reichsfuhrer, that would be wonderful," Canaris said as he watched the two close Hitler confidants. He was always on guard anytime these two were friendly. It was totally out of character for them to be friendly to anyone.

Hemmler began, "During the past few months, we've been quite successful in keeping the Danish Resistance movement from becoming organized and cooperating with the SOE in London. Several of the SOE attempts to drop spies and supplies to various resistance groups have been stopped. This effort has discouraged both inter-group communications and coordination of attacks. They're also disappointed with London. Well, until recently they were disappointed. It seems the SOE has been quite successful recently delivering both large amounts of supplies and British agents. This has not only encouraged them, but they're starting to conduct more aggressive and damaging acts of sabotage. At first, we could not understand how this could be. We've been quite effective against the SOE Lysander aircraft. They're slow and very limited in capability. Our troops would joke about hearing them approach from the North Sea with enough time to smoke a cigarette before they were over land and shot down. Now there's a new aspect that has changed the equation. They're using a different aircraft.

"The Gestapo headquarters in Odense, Denmark has advised me of a new situation there that could be of interest to both of you," Hemmler continued as he walked up to the fireplace sipping his Schnapps. "It seems that one of the resistance members was captured last week. When he was interrogated he said that they were being supplied and supported by the SOE on a regular basis. We know it couldn't be by Lysander, so our man in Odense pressured the man to disclose that it was an American B-25 that was sneaking in and supplying them," Hemmler said as he carefully studied the facial expressions of his two guests. "That should interest you, Admiral, as there are four to six SOE agents operating in Denmark now. Dr. Goebbles, I'm not sure who is flying the B-25, but it's a clear violation of America's stated policy of neutrality. If it's flown by Americans instead of British pilots, that could be of significant use by your Information Ministry. It would certainly be embarrassing to Roosevelt if it wasn't just a Lend-Lease aircraft.

"I would suggest that Admiral Canaris contact his sources in Great Britain and the USA to determine where this plane is based and who is flying it. Meanwhile, the Gestapo will continue to investigate the matter. Perhaps we can set up a trap that will allow us to shoot it down and exploit the matter in the world press. I know that such an article would make our Fuhrer very happy. Do either of you've any questions or want to say anything?" Hemmler asked in a soft, but intimidating tone.

Canaris was the first to respond. "I think not, Reichsfuhrer. I understand the problem and shall take immediate action to find out who is flying these missions and where it's based. I shall keep the good minister informed of my findings as well as your office, Reichsfuhrer."

"Yes, that's most promising and I'll start to work on the structure of the news release while I await the Admiral's report," Goebbles said as he stood up and raised his hand and gave his perfunctory Heil Hitler!

CHAPTER 19

At the Wright Field Test Center in Dayton, Ohio a Wright twin radial engine was mounted on a test stand, its engine shaft linkage turning at cruise speed. The roaring, low frequency engine could be heard loudly. Carefully monitoring the test was Captain Victor Agather, a ready reserve officer and aviator who was called up from his Wall Street job as a merger and acquisition specialist with the Shields Company. He was momentarily startled by the arrival of General Echols and his aide-de-camp.

Captain Vic Agather, General Echols, a Lieutenant and a technician peered in from the opposite side of the control room window itself at the test engine.

"And the test was started…?" General Echols asked.

"Yesterday, twelve noon, Sir," The lieutenant said.

The general glanced at his watch. "Twenty-fours."

"Yes, Sir," The lieutenant said.

"Constant speed?" The general asked.

"Right."

"And all readings are stable?"

"Yes, Sir. All except the same upper line cylinder heads," The lieutenant said.

"Temperature increases?" The general asked.

"Yes, Sir. Three in the front and two in the rear. It's all there, Sir."

"Still perusing the data on the clip board? What about the oil temperatures?"

"They're stable. "

"It's the third prototype we've tested, Sir, not counting the ones that were installed on the B-29 airframe, of course." The lieutenant pointed to the clip board in the General's hand. "We've created all the standard stress factors but so far we haven't been able to duplicate the B-29 failures."

"I don't understand it," The General said. He continued to study the technical data. "Every time they took off in the Douglas test aircraft equipped with these same power plants, we had engine failures and even fires." He looked at Agather. "You know how long it took 'em to fly that ship from Long Beach out here to Wright?"

Captain Agather grinned. "Yes, Sir. We've all followed the development of the R3350 quite closely."

"They never could fly at prescribed altitudes because of the engine overheating problem. Have you discussed the problem with the Wright Company engineers?" the General asked.

"Yes, General," Agather said. "We're developing a crossover tube arrangement. It directs the combustible onto the exhaust valve in the affected cylinder heads."

"Using the compressed gasses as a coolant," The General said. Think it'll work?

"Their engineers are pretty optimistic," Captain Agather said

General Echols handed the clip board to the Lieutenant. "I believe we ought to go ahead with production. If we want design changes, the B-29s are going to start coming out of final assembly without engines."

"Well, we've got machine tools and material," Captain Agather said. "Allotments are all worked out, General. It's just a matter of releasing the prototype design to the factories so they can begin tooling up."

"What kind of time frame are we looking at?"

"Well, initial production capability by early next year." Vic Agather said.

"It'll be a neck and neck race even at that," General Echols said. He paused. "Better set it in motion, Captain."

"Right, Sir."

"You can shut it down now, Lieutenant," The general said.

"Yes, Sir."

"I'll want a complete written analysis of all the tests and testing procedures."

The lieutenant nodded and General Echols and Agather went into the control room. Then the Lieutenant turned to the technician and told him to shut it down. The technician nodded affirmatively, turned from the main test panel to a bank of switches to the left of the panel itself and began the shut down operation.

General Echols and Agather emerged from the test center, and walked toward the General's staff vehicle and Vic's jeep, both parked nearby.

"We've got a hundred P-40's sitting out in the Philippines without propellers and Lockheeds in England without engines," General Echols said. "China, England and Russia all screaming for immediate delivery on their Lend-Lease requirements, not to speak of the B-29 factories we got to equip and staffs and we' re rushing an engine into full production here before we're certain its design characteristics are stable. But, we've no alternative."

It'll all work out, Sir," Vic said.

General Echols smiled. "I guess it's to at that, doesn't it, Captain?"

"Yes, Sir," he said pausing then adding, "All this work, resources and urgency and the Congress still fights against us. What's the Congress really going to, shut all this down and wait for catastrophe to strike or get behind the President and get prepared for the inevitable?"

"Vic, the sting of the Great War is still fresh in the minds of some of the more seasoned Congressmen and Senators. They understandably want to stay out of war and hide between two oceans. They believe that if war comes, the Atlantic and Pacific oceans will buffer and deter any conflict. The Navy has everyone convinced that the battleships and the Navy armada will protect us from aggression on these shores. Yes, the politicians realize that taking such a position insures the defeat and occupation of England, our closest ally. They shamelessly would accept such a fate than to stand up and do what is the responsible thing to do. Vic, I can sense the shifting in the political winds on this matter. The American people will never let England be defeated without a fight. The President and those members of Congress who understand the realities of the explosive global situation will prevail."

"Thank you, Sir. That was really weighing on my mind."

The general smiled without comment got into his vehicle and drove away.

CHAPTER 20

It was just after lunch in Berlin when a knock was heard by Reichsfuhrer Hemmler on his office door.

"Come!" he said in his usual commanding voice.

"Sir," his aide-de-Camp said, "Admiral Canaris is here to see you. Colonel Feldcamp is still waiting to see you."

"Feldcamp can wait. I'll see him after Admiral Canaris," he said.

Admiral Canaris came into the office and gave his perfunctory "Heil Hitler."

"So good to see you, Wilhelm. Please have a seat," the Reichsfuhrer said in an attempt to be friendly. A personality trait that was hard for him to display to others. "I take it that you've news for me on that American B-25 that's disrupting our operations from France to Norway."

"Yes, Reichsfuhrer, I do. The British have just the one B-25. It's a loan to the RAF, as are the American crew. They're there to train the RAF on the B-25."

"But we're not certain who is actually flying the missions. We believe that the training is a mere cover story. We believe that the Americans are actually flying the support missions. They fly very differently than British pilots. We almost had supporting information and documents, but our agent in London was arrested," Canaris said, pausing slight. "They're not consistent on where and when these supply missions are flown. They've been of particular annoyance and problem to us in Denmark. The resistance attacks have more than tripled in the past four months. It's Colonel Feldcamp's position that it's a direct result of these impressive supply missions by the B-25. We've learned that it's a mission call sign of Black Bart. That's a historic British pirate. We've had reports that it's operated out of Tempsford and Tangmere. It's been seen refueling in the Shetland Islands as well. Our forces in France and Belgium have damaged the plane on numerous occasions, but have not been successful in knocking it down. We did learn that it was responsible for the shooting down of one of our ME-109's last December.

"It's a very formidable aircraft."

This was of great interest to the Reichsfuhrer. He was concerned that a medium bomber that could successfully win an air engagement with a ME-109. "What has been done to shoot this plane down?"

"Sir, it flies very low to the ground at over 250 miles per hour and usually at night or in the early dawn hours. Gunners have mere seconds to spot and shoot at the B-25 before it's gone or out of sight. We scramble fighters once the plane is spotted, but it's gone before they can find and destroy it," Canaris said.

"Very interesting," Hemmler said. "Do you think that Colonel Feldcamp has done a satisfactory job in Denmark in destroying this menace to the Third Reich?"

"Sir, there's always room for improvement for all of us. I would say that he's done an adequate job so far. I'm sure that he'll find a tactic that will work to destroy this B-25."

"Yes, yes, of course," Hemmler said. "I wasn't sure until now of that. Your report gives me hope that he won't need to be replaced just yet. He's outside waiting. Bring him in and let's see what new tactics he's planned to defeat this one aircraft that's becoming an embarrassment to the Third Reich."

Moments later a very scared commander of the German Gestapo in Denmark was standing at attention before Reichsfuhrer Hemmler's desk.

"Colonel, my time and patience is very short. What do you plan to do differently to destroy this B-25?" Hemmler said in an intimidating tone.

"Reichsfuhrer, I believe that our past efforts were based upon the conventional method of scrambling fighters to seek out the B-25 according to where the report originated. By the time we got our fighters up, the B-25 was gone and we had no way of knowing where to look. We're starting a new procedure when the alarm is given the fighters will fly out to the North Sea and from a line across the probable flight paths back to England. Once one of our fighter aircraft spots the B-25, he'll notify the others and it will engage so as to prevent it from escaping. This will give our forces a chance to find and destroy this Black Bart once and for all."

"Excellent, Colonel. See to its implementation immediately," the Reichsfuhrer ordered. "You're dismissed."

"Admiral, shall we walk down and advise the Fuehrer of our news about the American-flown B-25 and our plan to destroy it? I'm sure that he'll want Goebbles to get a worldwide news release on this violation of American neutrality," the Reichsfuhrer said as he got up from his desk. As they walked toward Hitler's office, Hemmler said to Canaris softy, "This is well-timed as the Americans are about to get into this war and they don't even know it. They're looking at us to start hostilities and it won't be us. Our allies, the Japanese will throw the first blow…and soon."

CHAPTER 21

Bart was looking at a series of bullet holes in the left side of the Black Bart. Much to his dismay, they damaged the pirate skull flag on the side. Had they been a foot higher, they would have gone right through him. Unfortunately, the rounds badly damaged the cartridge carrier that took the fifty caliber bullets from the ammunition can to one of the nose mounted machine guns. "That can be fixed," he thought as he continued to look at the damage from the last mission over Denmark. He turned to Sergeant Royston and asked, "Okay, how long will we be down?"

"Well, Sir, they did a lot of damage this time. Nothing really bad, but it's going to take us at least two days. Just a lot of little things that take time to fix right," he said with resignation.

"Very well, I guess we could use some time to catch up on the paperwork and try to plan ahead on the next mission," Bart said.

Sergeant Lightfoot came up to Coltrane, "Sir, you're to report to Major Grand's office immediately," Bart looked down with a sigh, "Yank, you had better cut some time off that time estimate. The boss apparently has a mission for us."

Coltrane reported to Major Grand at 1400 hours precisely. "Good afternoon, Sir," "I understand that you're looking for a fourth for poker."

Grand smiled and told Bart to sit down. "Our MI-5 friends across the hall have apprehended a foreign gentleman who has been asking a lot of questions about your operation. It seems Berlin isn't happy with your sterling performance and the moral lift that you've given some of the resistance units. He and his associates here in the U.K. have been instructed to check you boys out. We know that we couldn't keep you under wraps for long, but here we're," he said in a very happy mood. He became a little more serious. We've been handed a hot one from Hugh Dalton. It's a dicey one again. Back to Denmark I'm afraid. Well, as soon as you can repair your plane from the last trip there."

"I need to bring Lieutenant Zak Middleton into this," he said as he picked up the phone and called Middleton. "Be just a minute, he's just down the hall with Beddows and Chapman."

Moments later a stocky man in his late thirties came into the office.

"Ahhhhh, here he is now," Grand said as he got up to make the introductions. "Zak is a big fan of yours, Bart. He seems to think your chaps have given a great deal of encouragement to the resistance fighters in Denmark. From the look of the intelligence reports, there's a significant increase in sabotage and attacks on German supply convoys."

"It's a pleasure to meet you, Major. What he didn't tell you is that I would kill someone just to fly a mission in your B-25," Zak Middleton said with a lustful tone.

"You don't have to go that far. If you want to take a chance, you're welcome to fly with Black Bart any time," Coltrane said as he soaked in the praise.

"Actually," Major Grand injected, "Zak has been flying Lysanders for us into France and Belgium. Denmark is pretty much out of range except with drop tanks. Then the payload is minimal. He's flown over 200 missions. Some were real sticky wickets." He paused then continued, "On to the mission."

There are four key Danish resistance leaders and two of our own SOE agents over there that we need to bring back here to sort out the problems between them and to establish a coordinated program against the bloody Bosch. The bloody Germans have virtually closed off all air and sea routes for us to use. They can't go south into Germany or even go north to Norway. The Gestapo knows who these men are and are searching high and low for them. Especially, since they've increased their fight against the Germans with the supplies that you've been supplying them. We've a possible solution. Zak here can tell you his idea."

"Actually, it's quite simple. You fly in and pick them up," Zak initially said with a straight face then broke out into laughter when he saw the shocked expression on Bart's face." Let me explain. There's an island called Laeso just off the northeast part of Denmark. It's a fishing center where fishermen can bring their catch for further shipment down to Copenhagen. The Germans only have a platoon of 25 soldiers guarding the island. They're all at the seaport town of Vestero Havn. They have a daily patrol that drives around the island just before noon. This is all they do. To support them and provide for a rare visit from higher headquarters, they constructed an airfield in the center of the island. It's not guarded and can stand the weight of your B-25. Additionally, it's going to become one of the main operating and supply bases for the resistance if we can get them unified and coordinated at the meeting here in London. The mission is to get them back here and then return them a few days later before they're missed by the Germans. If we can get them organized and establish a supply distribution center there, it can be of enormous help. The fishing boats can deliver the supplies all along the coast.

Zak looked at Coltrane to see his reaction, then continued. "The plan would generally be that you fly in over the water to the tip of Denmark at dawn and land at the airstrip. Drop off more supplies and pick up the six passengers and return to Tempsford. You'd have to land and taxi all the way back to the end of the runway, so you'll have the wind on your nose. That's a short runway for a B-25. So the wind will be important. What are your thoughts?"

"Well," Bart said. "It's doable, okay. We'll be tight on fuel since we can't use a ferry tank. If all goes well, we can be on the ground at first light and off with the passengers in five minutes. If the Germans don't hear us come in, it will be a piece of cake. Even if they do, it will take them twenty or so minutes to assemble and drive out to the airfield. By then, we'll be long gone. The key will be to come in from the northwest over water and return the same way. I don't think there would be enough time for the Germans to get a report of our over flight in the north to scramble fighters from Alborg or Skrydstrup to intercept us. Even if they did, they still have to find us and catch up for the kill. Time doesn't work for them."

Major Grand asked, "What about going south instead of west and drop off some ammunition and explosives to that group you supplied yesterday? They really do need the rest of the supplies."

"Sir, the southern part of Denmark is getting to be extremely hard to fly through. They've significantly increased their heavy automatic weapons and Ack-ack. The holes in the Black Bart are testimony to their defenses. Beside the danger to your people that we're bringing back is too great. You sure don't want to get them killed or wounded on a supply mission." Bart said as he tapped the wall map.

"Right-O," the Major said as he looked at the map point shown by Coltrane's finger. "Well then, when can you fly the mission?"

"Sir, we got shot up pretty good yesterday in southern Denmark. I'd hate to try the mission of this importance before we complete repairs. Can we do it at dawn the day after tomorrow?" Coltrane asked."

"Yes, quite!" "Work out the details with Chapman and his people", ordered Grand. "I'll be gone for three days for a headquarters task.

"Make the best of it with Chapman. He'll be in charge in my absence. Say there, Bart, take Zak with you as an observer. Then I can get him off my back about flying with you."

"No problem, Sir. Black Bart will be glad to give him a thrill," Coltrane said with a smile as he slapped Zak on the shoulder.

As Zak and Bart walked down the hall, Zak asked Bart a series of questions about the B-25 and their tactics. Then he got a little more serious and asked "How many missions have you flown across the channel?"

Bart thought for a moment and responded, "Not really sure, but in the ten months we've been here we've averaged between ten and fifteen missions a month. A little less than that back in January and February due to bad weather and the ramping up of the resistance groups."

"That's bloody incredible! How many times have you been hit with ground fire?"

"Actually less than you might think. At first, when we weren't known and could fly past them at low level, it wasn't very often. Recently, all the Germans know about us and are really trying to knock us down. It's sort of a challenge to them, I think," Bart said calmly. "Yesterday was the worst. When we crossed the beach inbound, the alarm went out to the fighters to watch for us. They were better prepared this time and the longer we were over land gave the fighters a chance to get us. They even scrambled fighters out of Alborg trying to find us. Someday we'll have to deal with the fighters as well. The Germans aren't stupid."

"What about giving Chapman and his crew the mission requirements then go after a pint?" Zak suggested.

"Sounds good to me," Bart said as they entered the operations and intelligence section office.

Bart immediately saw the beautiful Ice Maiden standing next to Rupert Chapman.

"Good afternoon, Commander Chapman and Major Beddows," Bart said in a friendly and formal way. We've a mission for day after tomorrow to work out with you."

Rupert responded in his usually irritated and pontifical manner, "Yes, yes, I got the word of your high-priority hush hush mission. I'm busy right now, but Major Beddows can take down the details from you and we can meet at 1000 hours tomorrow morning with the flight briefing."

"Great, I'd much rather deal with her than you," Bart said in a warm tone.

For once there was a hint of a smile on Annabel Beddows face. "Come on, Cowboy, let's get the mission details," she said in a pleasant voice. This was the first time in all these months that she was remotely friendly.

Bart and Zak laid out the mission requirements given to them by Grand. "Given the importance of the passengers we'll get in and get out. Hopefully, we can avoid any hostile fire."

Bart looked up and saw that she was looking at him and not the map. He saw something in her face that had not been there all these months... warmth and tenderness. Then she suddenly became all business again and looked at the route outlined by Coltrane.

She thought for a moment then said "What if you flew to RAF Sumbrugh just after midnight and refueled. This time of year it's getting light about 0530 or so. Sunrise is somewhere around 0600, so you would take off from Sumbrugh about 0400 hours. That would put you about 30 miles south of Norway as you enter the Skagerrak Strait and away from any possible detection from either Norway or Denmark. Fly northeasterly until you clear any listening post or radar at the tip of Denmark, then still over water fly directly to Laeso. You would be there and undetected. Assuming you get there and pick up the passengers undetected, how would you return to Tempsford?"

"I would go a course of 250 degrees to the west. If I went south of Fredkerikshavn and north of Hjorring, I'd be put over flat farm land and away from any German forces.

"We could fly out about forty or fifty miles and then turn south to Tempsford. That's pretty straight forward. If we're detected as we pass over land, we'll be far out to sea before they can scramble the fighters and try to find us. Being at tree top altitude and 200 plus knots speed gives us a big advantage. We're hard to find that way. That's especially important given who we're bringing back," Bart concluded.

"Excellent, I'll work up your flight plan and threat assessment based upon this plan," she said in a professional manner. "Sanford is over at Whitehall getting the latest information and should be back here in an hour or so."

Zak Middleton was watching the uneasy interaction between Beddows and Coltrane. He thought he would help to break the ice between them. "I say, Major Beddows, you've some time before he gets back. Why don't you join us for a quick bite to eat over at the Rattskeller?"

Annabel immediately stiffened up and was about to say "no" when she changed her mind. "Why not?" she thought. It couldn't do any harm and she had missed lunch. "Very well, it would have to be quick, however."

The three of them walked over to the Rattskeller at a brisk walk. Zak and Annabel were walking ahead of Bart who was walking behind them trying to figure out why Zak would ask the Ice Maiden to join them.

Nobody took much notice as Bart and Zak entered, but the entrance of Beddows didn't go unnoticed by Robby West, Kelly Sharp and Reggie Whitehurst, who was washing beer glasses at the time. She almost dropped the slippery glass when she saw Beddows and who she was with.

They took a table near the front of the Rattskeller. Reggie was quick to get over to the table to get their order and to see how this oil and water mixture was working out. "Why would she come here with Coltrane?" she thought.

After ordering, Zak turned to Bart and asked, "Bart, how about telling us a little about yourself. Other than what's in your file, we know nothing about you."

"Not much to tell. I'm from Sweetwater, Texas, which is in the western part of Texas, some 220 miles west of Dallas. My father was a cotton farmer. We had very little money, so I got a job after school working for a crop dusting company. As I got older, I learned to fly and did crop dusting jobs after school and later through my college days at Abilene Christian College. I didn't want to be a cotton farmer, so I joined the Army Air Corps in 1934. That's about it," he said in a low tone.

Zak noticed that Annabel had not missed a single word of Bart's history. "I say, do you've a girl back in Sweetwater?" he asked, knowing that was a question on Annabel's mind.

"No girl back home," he said. "I never was in one place long enough to develop a relationship with anyone," Bart said with a sigh.

Reggie showed up with their order just as he finished. "What about you, Zak?" Annabel asked as if she really cared.

"Grew up here in London," he said. "My father was a solicitor for a while before becoming a Member of Parliament. The bloody devil is almost seventy-five and won't give it up. Especially, since there's a war on. After the usual prep schools, I went to Sandhurst and got commissioned a lieutenant. From there I went into the Intelligence Services. I never did put on a uniform, as I was officially discharged to perform the usual cloak and dagger lot. I got restless and got an appointment to flight school. After graduation, I flew transports for a while before flying the Hurricane fighters. I was just getting the hang of that beast when Mr. Hitler started his trouble. I got called in to volunteer for Lysanders and its bloody mission across the channel. After Hitler went into Poland, they pulled me back into uniform at my original lieutenant rank. They're trying to get my civilian time credited for promotion to lieutenant colonel with the rest of my Sandhurst mates."

Beddows had finished her meal and looked at her watch. "My, my time flies. This is really wonderful, but I must get back and get your mission planned out," she said with a slight smile as she stood up to go. "See you at 1000 hours tomorrow morning."

Both men stood up and but Bart walked her to the door. Then he returned to the table.

"I guess that she got an earful," Zak said as he picked up his scotch glass.

"Probably more than she wanted," Bart said as he looked at the front door that she went through.

A big smile went over Zak's face, "I don't think so, mate. Now, tell me about the B-25," he said changing the subject.

CHAPTER 22

Slightly after 0700 hours, Zak entered the Rattskeller and saw the crew of Black Bart eating a continental breakfast. He went over to the serving counter and poured himself a cup of coffee and sat down with them.

Robby West looked over at Zak and jokingly said, "Ahhhhh, our thrill seeker. You just weren't satisfied with certain death in Lysanders. You had to become a member of the Suicide Squad."

"Right-O, mate! Why wait for the grim reaper when you can do a bloody first rate job right away," he retorted. "Let's head over and get a head start on the operations and flight plan."

Coltrane was quick to get up and head for the door. The action was noted by Zak and Kelly Sharp. They looked at each other and smiled, Sharp said quietly, "That's a first. I wonder what's got his interest." It surely couldn't be Annabel!"

When they got to the Black Bart office, they were surprised to see Commander Rupert Chapham there with Balfour and Beddows.

"Morning, gentlemen, quickly take your seats," Chapham said in a monotone. "I have your revised mission plan and flight plan."

Everyone immediately noticed that he had the flight path marked differently than planned. It had the departure segment going due south to an unscheduled drop point then across southern Denmark to the North Sea, then to Tempsford.

"As you can see, I'm including an additional supply drop to the mission plan. It won't affect your fuel by any significant amount, and it will save an additional trip later," Chapham said as if the change was insignificant.

Coltrane stood up and went to the map with the route marked with red yarn and stick pins. He looked at the map then the printed flight plan. He looked at both Beddows and Balfour who looked away instead of looking him in the eye.

"You obviously realize that this route takes us over some of the worst flak and anti aircraft emplacements in all of Denmark. This one area here," he said pointing to a location on the map, "is where we got our ass shot up on the last mission. You obviously know this. You also are aware that this significantly jeopardizes our primary mission of safely delivering sensitive and important people to our higher headquarters," Coltrane said in a slight show of anger.

"Are you refusing to fly the mission, Major?" Before Coltrane could answer Chapham continued "Actually, Major, if you follow my flight plan you should be able to avoid the nastier areas."

"You idiot, that assumes the fucking Germans follow your plan and the four fighter squadrons don't get lucky and find us," Coltrane said with obvious anger. "I'm putting you on official record that this plan of yours endangers the primary mission and has a significant potential of failing all together," Coltrane said as he turned to Beddows and Balfour. "Do you two fully understand what I've just stated?"

"I suggest that you write up your own memorandums for the record to cover your ass later," he said in a calmer tone. Then he turned back to Chapham. "I'm personally holding you responsible for anything that happens after we depart the island. My officers and I'll be filing our own memorandums objecting to your decision. If Grand was here, he would override you, but he's not here to do so."

Chapham appeared unshaken by Coltrane's comments. "It would appear that you're afraid to fly a difficult mission. You've the right to decline the mission if you're too afraid to fly it," he said.

Beddows was shocked at what Chapham had said. She looked at Balfour and said "I do want to write a memo. Care to join me, Sanford?"

This did get a slight and unexpected reaction out of Chapham.

Coltrane walked up to Chapham with his face less than six inches from his. "I accept the mission!"

"Because to decline will set the whole SOE development plan in Denmark back perhaps a year. I have to fly the mission for the best interest of the war effort. I'll be back and you and I'll address the matter with Grand and Dalton," he said as he picked up the flight plan folder and handed it to Sharp. "Zak, you can't go. It's far too dangerous to put you into unnecessary danger."

"Hell, Major, I wouldn't miss this one on a bet. Count me in," Zak said.

Nobody said anything as Coltrane left the room followed by the others. Beddows saw him leave the room and go down the hall. She knew that he was going to fly the mission when she saw Sharp with the mission folder. She had a very sick feeling. The same feeling when General Langham and a Chaplin arrived unexpectedly at her home with the news of her husband's death in Poland. She turned away to hide the tears that were forming in her eyes.

"Bart, Bart, it's time to go," said Sharp as he shook Coltrane to awaken him. They had flown to Sumbrugh just after dark so everyone had time to get some sleep before the mission and avoid any potential ground fog developing in the early dawn hours at Sumbrugh.

"Scrub the mission, I want to sleep," he said jokingly.

"Yeah, right," Sharp said. "That would absolutely make Chapham very happy. I think he wants to get rid of us any way possible. This mission is just his first attempt."

"Yep, he's every combat pilot's worse nightmare," he said as he got up from the makeshift mattress made of three parachutes. He looked around and the others were getting up as well. "Robby made a quick walk around inspection with Sergeant Royston to make sure we still have two wings and two engines. I'll start the preflight checklist. Okay, folks, it's showtime!"

About an hour out of Sumbrugh, the cloud deck above them had gone allowing the moon to cast a shimmering glow on the North Sea below.

This gave the pilots an additional reference point to help keep them from crashing into the cold water below. There was a hint of sunlight showing on the horizon.

"Two minutes to the Skagerrak Strait turn. You'll turn to 030 degrees on my mark. Stand by…turn," ordered the navigator. "Nineteen minutes on this course."

The sunlight in the east continued to increase. The winds at the surface were coming out of the southwest. "That was good," thought Coltrane. They could make their approach from the east and not have to fly near the German garrison. The departure would be different. They would be close enough for anyone awake there to at least see them as they took off and turned south.

"Turn to 185 degrees on my mark…turn," came the familiar voice of Kelly Sharp. After Coltrane made the turn, he turned to Robby. "Call the Reception Committee and tell them we're five minutes out. Be on the northeast end of the runway."

Zak Middleton was between and to the rear of the pilots. "There," he said, slightly to the right. "You're on an almost a perfect alignment for your approach."

Coltrane nodded as he saw the short runway. As he turned to line up on final approach to land, he said to Robby, "Gear and full flaps." The plane slowed to 120 mph and slowly decreased its speed until it made contact with the very east end of the runway. Bart quickly slowed the plane and made a 180 degree turn so he could quickly return to the east end of the runway. He got to the end and turned around again facing down the runway ready to take off quickly if attacked. Robby had already opened the bomb bay doors as a dozen men came running up to the plane.

"I hope those are our friendly chaps," Zak said as he looked out the cockpit side window. Then he turned around just in time to see three of the four delivery pods drop to the ground. The men on the ground quickly carted them away to a grocery truck that had driven up. At the rear of the aircraft six men climbed up the rear ladder into the compartment.

Coltrane was looking at the last pod being carried away when he heard Sergeant Royston report, "We're ready in the rear. Six souls on board."

"Close bomb bay doors," Bart ordered as he advanced the throttles to the maximum setting allowable in these condition. Okay, Robby, you've the aircraft, take us to Horsens," Coltrane ordered.

The chance of a tactical takeoff was a thrill to Robby West. "Roger on the go," he said as he released the brakes. The big bird started down the short runway. Coltrane read off the ever increasing airspeed to West. Then West gently pulled the control yoke back and the plane leaped off the ground.

Sharp called out, "Turn left to 168 degrees for eighteen minutes then 205 degrees for eleven minutes. Your drop course will be 255 degrees. Robby started his turn once he was fifty feet off the ground. "Roger, one six eight degrees."

Three miles to the west, German Private First Class Claus Herbert was taking a moment from walking his guard post on the Vestere Havn dock to relieve himself when he heard the B-25. He quickly turned to see the aircraft turning south. He immediately ran to the guard shack telephone some 1,100 feet away. He was out of breath when he got to the phone. He lifted the phone and contacted the Sergeant of the Guard. "This is post number three. Black Bart, Black Bart," he screamed into the phone. The voice on the other end told him to slow down and tell him again what he saw over five minutes ago. When the Sergeant understood that post number three had an actual sighting of Black Bart, he too became excited. He hung up the phone and called his platoon leader at the local headquarters. He did not answer. The Sergeant thought for a moment then called the local restaurant where the German Lieutenant took his morning breakfast. It took what seemed forever to the Sergeant for that damned officer to get off his ass and answer the phone. Precious time was being wasted.

"Ya, ya, this is Lieutenant Hoenfelds, Heil Hitler," replied the unexcited officer.

"Sir, this is the Sergeant of the Guard – post number three - saw Black Bart back towards the east about eight minutes ago," the Sergeant said as he looked at his watch.

With a little more interest, the officer asked which direction he was flying. "It was to the south, Sir," said the Sergeant.

"Very good, Sergeant, I shall call headquarters." The German officer then dialed a number in Alborg. It took eight rings before the phone was answered. "Gestapo headquarters, Alborg, Schultz speaking."

"This is Lieutenant Hoenfelds, Heil Hitler. I'm the commander of the guard detachment at Laeso Island. Black Bart was seen twelve minutes ago over the island heading south or southwest."

"Excellent, Lieutenant! I shall handle it from here. Goodbye," said the Gestapo agent.

By the time the Gestapo agent had called his superior and the alert fighter squadron at Alborg it was time for Robby to make his turn towards Hersen. He was still far offshore and flying about fifty feet off of the ocean. This was a real thrill for him.

Most of his flying the past few months had been the easy long over water segments of the flight which were boring. He did do a couple of drops over Belgium and France, but they were not in bad anti aircraft areas. He was a happy camper today. This was a hot mission and he was on the controls.

"Okay, Robby, turn to a heading of 205 now," came the voice of Kelly Sharp who was recalculating the final course to the drop zone that would keep them away from the effective range of the higher concentration of anti aircraft fire. The preferred course was still going to be bad enough. Zak had squeezed around so he could look over his shoulder at the map.

Zak looked at the map and pointed to an area just to the east of Hersen. "Stay away from this point. That's a bad flak area. I don't care what Chapham said. That's a real bad area. Fly to the south a little and it will be better…not good, but better."

"Hey, Bart," called Zak over the intercom. "If we cut short this next leg by about five miles and turn inland near Samas Island, we can miss some of that heavy Flak on the west side of Hersen. We would approach the drop zone from the north instead of the east. That will minimize the AAA near Rask Molle. What do you think?"

"Good idea. I wasn't looking forward to flying over the top of those emplacements near the drop zone. Kelly, go with his plan," Coltrane directed. "Okay, Robby, you'll turn to the new course just before you get a beam of that island. What's his new course, Kelly?"

"It will be 198 degrees. You'll have flak on your right, so don't cut the corner," Sharp advised.

"Strange that we haven't seen any fighters up looking for us," Bart said as he scanned the sky.

The phone rang on Colonel Feldcamp's desk in his Odense headquarters. "Colonel Feldcamp, Heil Hitler."

"Sir, this is the duty controller at Alborg. Two squadrons are airborne and are headed for their position across the western side of Denmark. We've another squadron ready to launch in thirty minutes to replace aircraft that are running low on fuel. Times are staggered for fuel concerns. Each aircraft will have a twenty-five mile area to cover. We should be able to spot and destroy the B-25 on its homeward leg, Sir."

"Very well, keep me informed," he replied.

CHAPTER 23

Sharp's voice came over the intercom "Stand by for right turn to 198 degrees. Ready…turn!" Robby West made a smooth turn and descended to twenty or so feet above the ground.

The two pilots saw the tracers coming up towards them as soon as they crossed over the shore line. It was heavy and getting worse. Coltrane felt a few hits.

"Crew Chief to pilot, we've taken hits in the rear. One of the passengers got hit. Not serious. Wow, we just got hit again," Royston said.

Black puffs started appearing in front and to either side of the B-25. Flak from the anti aircraft battery located just outside the small town of Rask Molle. Suddenly, the aircraft shuddered as the close-by flak detonation sent pieces of hot metal into the right side of the fuselage. Coltrane looked at the instruments searching for signs of damage to systems that operated the airplane. Then another hit and another. Several bursts of machine gun rounds hit the aircraft.

"Kelly, contact the reception committee and see if they're ready for the drop," Coltrane ordered. "We're three minutes out!"

"Roger, contact made. Ready for drop. Prepare to turn to 225 degrees in about one minute," Sharp said.

Coltrane was almost deafened by a loud explosion just outside the right side of the cockpit. He felt a warm liquid on his face along with little Plexiglas cuts. The aircraft jumped up then down. It was about to hit the ground when Coltrane grabbed the controls from West. "Dammit, Robby, you're getting too close to the ground!" There was no reply or the feeling of Robby on the controls. He looked at West and saw that he had massive facial wounds with blood spurting out of his face, neck and chest. The blood stopped spurting. He was dead! "We lost a passenger back here. He took one in the chest, Royston responded.

"Zak, get up here and pull Robby out of his seat. He's bought the farm."

"Turn to 225 degrees – now," Sharp said. "You're four miles to drop."

Coltrane opened the bomb bay doors as Zak and Sharp pulled Robby West's mangled body out of the co-pilot seat. Zak got into it and strapped himself in.

"Zak, look over there at one o'clock. Is that the drop zone?" Coltrane asked as he gained a few feet of altitude for the drop.

"No, it's right on the nose. You're shooting for that open area in the middle of those trees," he replied as another stream of tracers reached up for them.

"Get ready, Drop!" Coltrane said as he hit the solenoid release system. The last delivery pod departed normally.

"Good chute!" cried Royston.

"Turn to 233 degrees, 62.5 miles to coastline," responded Sharp.

The Black Bart had almost continuous ground fire. Hits were felt, but no systems failure as of yet. Flak bursts started appearing in front of them as they approached the coast line. Coltrane kept the aircraft as low as possible to reduce the exposure to hostile fire.

The coast line flashed behind them. The ground fire ended. They had made it…so far.

Zak tapped on the starboard fuel gauge. "Hey Bart, I think we've a problem. There are holes in the starboard fuel tank. We're losing fuel," he said.

"Great, just what we didn't need. Coltrane retorted. Use the fuel cross feed system and use up that fuel before it leaks out."

A flicker in the distance caught his attention. It was much higher and getting closer. "It was a fighter! Just like before, only there had to be more than this guy," Coltrane thought. He had to do his best to get away from the coast line and this ME-109. He advanced the throttles and prop pitch to gain as much speed as possible. Like before, he would get as low as possible so the fighter couldn't get below him and his unprotected belly. "Close off the cross feed system. I don't want to risk an air bubble while we're maneuvering," he said to Zak.

"We've to take his first pass," Coltrane said to the crew. Yank, you get on one of those waist guns and get a passenger on the other. You have to keep the 109 from getting a clean shot. I'll swing the tail when you need it so you can have a good shot. Once he's passed, I'll see what I can do with the weight fifties up here. I'll be doing some wild maneuvering, so be careful."

As predictable as sunrise, the ME-109 flew over the B-25 and made a steep diving turn to get on the tail of the B-25. As he got closer, Coltrane moved the plane back and forth with the rudder controls to make them a hard shot for the German.

Royston yelled, "Give me some right pedal!" Bart did so which gave a clear shot at the ME-109 who was now starting to fire. Royston's aim was good, but he had not hit the 109. Tracers were flying by the cockpit window and making splashes in the sea in front of them. "He's almost on us," Royston said. "He'll overfly on the left."

Coltrane chopped his power and dropped the landing gear to quickly reduce speed and then he raised the gear just as the ME-109 flashed by above. Bart added power and the speed started to increase quickly. The 109 started to make a climbing right turn just as Coltrane had hoped that he would. He immediately made a tight right climbing turn and pointed his eight fifty caliber machine guns just ahead of his flight path. He pushed the fire button and eight streams of tracers bolted out ahead of the 109. It literally ran into a wall of Coltrane's fifty caliber bullets. Just like the first German he shot down, this one broke apart as the rounds tore through the aluminum skin and fuel tank. The explosion finished off the kill.

"Now, let's get some distance between us and the other fighters that had to be en route," he said as he straightened out the Black Bart for Tempsford. "Zak, open up the cross feed system. We won't be maneuvering anymore."

They had barely crossed the English shoreline when the right engine quit from the fuel running out. The holes made by the Flak had emptied both main and auxiliary fuel tanks in the right wing.

"Feather Number 2," Bart said to Zak, who pulled the throttle and mixture lever to the full rear position and then pushed the feather button. He then turned off the ignition switch on the console. Black Bart flew very well on one engine, he thought.

"Okay, everyone get strapped down, this could be a rough landing with one engine and this amount of weight."

Zak made the radio calls to Tempsford advising them of their condition and the need for an ambulance for a wounded passenger and two dead comrades.

Bart made a long, slow turn to the left so as to not induce a spin by turning into a dead engine. He straightened up on a long final approach for runway 070 just like he did returning from the Norway mission. He kept his speed up for safety given his bad engine. As he crossed the runway threshold, he slightly reduced power and let the Black Bart settle on to the runway. They were home!

It was almost noon by the time they got Robby's body off and into the ambulance. Coltrane took a shower and went back down to the hanger to get a detailed list of the damages to the aircraft. The list was three pages long. It would be at least a week before Black Bart flew again. That was fine with Bart. He was tired and very depressed at the recent events. They had been over here eleven months. They had flown over 120 missions behind enemy lines and were credited with two ME-109 kills. Not bad, he thought, especially since the United States wasn't even at war…yet. Judging from the news reports and the classified Intel that he got from Sanford Balfour, America's entrance into the war was not far off.

Coltrane walked over to Sergeant Royston. "Go get a drink or twenty. This will wait until tomorrow," he said holding up the damage list.

Royston nodded, then pointed his thumb over his shoulder and said "They'll get started right now. I'll join them in the morning. After a big success like this, the brass will only be pushing harder and we have to deliver."

Coltrane smiled and reached out to shake the Sergeant's hand. "See you tomorrow, Yank."

The train ride back to London was usually a time for sleep, but this afternoon there was only silent reflection and grief. When they got back to the Rattskeller, Reggie ran up to the three men and hugged each of them. They had no idea what prompted the affection. "What's the big deal, Reggie?" Zak asked.

She held up the afternoon newspaper. The headlines read "YANKS FLYING FOR RAF." The news article generally described the B-25 and the behind the lines supply mission. While vague, the German news release was fairly accurate. This proves that America had violated the Neutrality Act and had taken Britain's side in the war.

I knew that you chaps were something more than instructor pilots, Reggie said, as she and Heine came out from behind the bar with a tray of caviar and champagne.

Bart and Sharp tired to put on a happy face, but their heart just wasn't in it. Zak told them of Robby's death which promptly put a damper on the celebration.

The trio was a little livelier after supper. Zak was describing the maneuver that allowed them to shoot down the ME-109. Heine was totally elated at the story. He was proud to have the crew of Black Bart staying at his hotel. Heine knew that he and Reggie could not tell anyone without the risk of the crew being killed by German agents. That was fine with him. He could keep a secret.

It was a little after 2100 hours when Rupert Chapham came into the Rattskeller. He made a direct course to the bar where Bart was having another scotch. It was by no means his first.

"Well, you survived," he said to Bart who had his back turned to him. The sound of Chapham's voice stirred an angry emotion deep inside him. He didn't reply or react. He just remained there leaning on the bar.

Well, Major, if you had followed my flight plan in detail, your mission would have been totally successful. You probably would not have lost anyone as well. You didn't follow my instructions and flight plan; therefore, you must bear the full responsibility for the losses and failure."

Coltrane was enraged, but still had not moved or said anything. Others in the room had started to take notice of the situation. Zak and Sharp stood a little closer, but were not about to interfere.

"I say, turn and face me, you bugger," Chapham said as he pushed on Bart's right shoulder. Bart still didn't move.

"What's wrong, can't you face me and admit that you failed to follow my plan which got your mate killed?" "It's your fault and yours alone that Lieutenant West is dead. Admit it!" he said as he once again jabbed at his right shoulder.

This time Coltrane spun around like a coiled spring to his left and unleashed a powerful punch to Chapham's left jaw and cheekbone. Those close by could hear the bones shattering. Blood from his nose and three inch cut on his cheek sprayed everywhere. Chapham fell to the floor unconscious and bleeding badly. The left side of his face was gruesome and deformed.

Coltrane turned back to the bar and picked up his drink. After taking a big gulp, he looked over at an astonished Reggie and said, "Perhaps you should call him an ambulance."

Heinreich Hemmler was walking down the hall of Gestapo headquarters at Prinz-Albrecht-8 when he saw SS Colonel Knoff. Knoff, had a reputation for strict allegiance to his admired Superior Hemmler and for his cruelty. Hemmler stopped him in the hall.

"Colonel, I have a special assignment for you. You're to go immediately to Odense and arrest Colonel Feldcamp for disobeying my order to terminate the Black Bart operations. He failed. You're to place him in Schutzhaft (protective custody). In my name, you're to appoint his second in command to commander. He is to take whatever actions necessary to kill or terminate the Black Bart missions. If he fails, he'll be joining Feldcamp. Do you understand?" Hemmler asked in a harsh command voice.

"Yes, Reichsfuhrer Hemmler. What do you want me to do with Colonel Feldcamp?"

Hemmler gave him a cold, hard look without saying anything. Knoff saw the look and replied, "I understand."

Eight thousand miles to the west Helen Lemay sat at her bedroom vanity brushing her hair, her eyes fixed on Lemay, who stood in the background buttoning the last button to his pajama top.

"You've been preoccupied all evening darling," Helen said. What's troubling you?"

"General Krogstead thinks war is inevitable."

Helen paused momentarily. "Do you think it is, Curt?"

Lemay began to place parts of the uniform he'd just removed on a hanger. "Yes. No question about it." He went to the closet. "It's just that we're in a helluva shape to go to war. No airplanes, nothing to train with. Not even a training area or a bomb range to practice it on. I don't even know what I'm supposed to be doing to get us ready. And… even if I did, we don't have what we need to do it with. We're divided out forty ways from Sunday. New B-17 groups sprouting up every day."

What bothers me the most is the political infighting we in the Air Corps have with a few congressmen and senators who are fighting side by side with the Battleship and tank boys in the Pentagon. They'll do anything to slow or stop us from acquisition of aircraft and war preparation funds. I've seen some of the most subtle and devious attempts to hold us back even with this country heading towards war in Europe. They don't care about the potentially catastrophic effects on the country and our ability to fight the war in Europe and perhaps even here. They're only concerned about their prestige and little kingdoms.

Helen turned and faced Lemay. "But darling, those things are beyond your control. You're doing your job."

Lemay moved to the bed. "I'm not so sure I could convince myself of that if my group had to fly over Germany tomorrow."

Helen got up and went to her husband. "Curt, what else could you do?"

Lemay threw up his hands. "Wish I knew."

Helen put her arm around Lemay's shoulder. "I love you darling."

Lemay gazed deeply into Helen's eyes, and then kissed her.

CHAPTER 24

On Placentia Bay in Newfoundland, a U.S. Navy PBY split the waves and then settled into the water as its landing speed reduced. The PBY continued to water taxi towards a U.S. Navy cruiser. A motor whale boat stood nearer to the PBY and maneuvered closer to it to receive its passenger.

The Presidential mail courier emerged onto the gangway, paused to salute the ship's flag and then turned to the ship's duty officer, who stood waiting.

"Follow me," the duty officer said.

The courier, a U.S. Navy lieutenant followed the duty officer to a compartment adjacent to the main ward room. The duty officer opened the hatch and the courier entered the compartment, and approached a senior staff officer, who was seated behind a desk opposite the hatch. Two armed guards stood on either side of the hatch and another stood by the senior staff officer's desk.

The staff officer rose as the courier reached the desk, produced a set of keys from his pocket, unlocked the briefcase from the courier's wrist and greeted the courier.

"Good morning," The staff officer said.

"Good morning, Sir,"

"The Churchill flotilla is due to enter the bay here at 1400 hours," The senior staff office said. "You're to stand by. There may be further dispatches for Washington after the initial meeting of the President and the Prime Minister."

"Yes, Sir."

The Staff Officer opened the briefcase and looked at the contents, an official folder containing several dispatches, crossed to the hatchway where the

Marine Guards stood, opened the hatch and entered the smoky ward room.

The Senior Staff Officer went to President Roosevelt who was seated in his mobile chair at the head of a long conference type table. A world map and an adjacent map of the Western Hemisphere reached along the back bulkhead, ceiling to floor.

General Marshall stood before the map, pointer in hand, obviously in a briefing session, but paused as the Staff Officer quietly handed the folder of dispatches to the President. The President nodded his thanks quietly. General Arnold, Admiral Stark, and Admiral King were seated at the conference table with the President.

"In summary, our Grand Strategy and military policy in the Far East will continue to be developed along the general intelligence theory that the Japanese will sweep South from their present bases here between Hanoi and Saigon," General Marshall said.

Admiral Stark pointed to the relevant area of the map. "What's the latest on their troop concentration down there?"

"They've moved a total of thirty Infantry Divisions and supporting equipment into the area since the Vichy French Government granted "limited" use of their Colonial territory there earlier this year," Marshall said.

"Three additional Divisions since the last report," Admiral Stark said. "That's limited use all right; limited by insufficient land mass to contain more troops."

"There's no doubt the Japanese are preparing to invade Thailand… then British Malaya and finally the Dutch Netherlands' East Indies down." General Marshall said. He indicated the relevant areas. "There, firmly based on an immense reservoir of natural resources--oil--rubber--tin, they'll attempt to play for time to balance their economy. It's been badly depleted by the War Party's lingering and costly expeditions up in Manchuria and China."

"An invasion of the Malaysian Peninsula and the Dutch East Indies would almost certainly provoke the British and Dutch into some kind of military action against the Japanese," Admiral Stark said.

"Of course. They'd have no choice."

"Churchill will want to know what our position would be in such a case," Roosevelt said.

"Well, it seems to me the American people would be reluctant…at best, to become involved in a bloody War in such a remote area,"

"I agree, Admiral Stark," President Roosevelt said "Therefore I intend to propose that we issue a joint communication to the Japanese, directing them to neutralize Indochina immediately; that's, pull out all of her troops and equipment. Further, we would propose that they begin treaty negotiations with Premier Chiang Kai-Shek in an attempt to settle the Chinese situation."

"And what is our leverage?" Admiral Stark asked.

"Failure to comply would result in a boycott of imports to Japan... Supplies raw materials… petroleum. And I would order all Japanese assets in the United States frozen," the President said

General Marshall seated himself contemplatively and Admiral King stepped up to the map, and gazed at it thoughtfully.

"That would narrow the Japanese options down to two: withdraw from her pattern of conquest - all the way back to the Home islands," he said, indicating the area, "leaving her totally dependent on world imports for future existence, or risk everything in an all out effort to establish her cherished dream: the conquest of East Asia and the establishment of Japanese controlled Greater East Asia." Admiral King indicated the relevant East Asia area with the pointer.

"That's about it, all right," President Roosevelt said.

"Suppose they invade Thailand?" Admiral King asked.

"I think we turn a deaf ear to that," President Roosevelt said "But, if they move on into Malaysia, we'd be compelled to protect our interest in the region." The President wheeled himself into position before the map. "If the Japanese gain control of the Malaysian Peninsula and Singapore they could choke off the entire area, including Australia." He indicated another area with the pointer. "By intelligent use of their base in the Mandated Island chains spread across the Pacific here between the United States and this general region, they could easily control the entire South Pacific."

Admiral King seated himself. "Sea communications upon which logistical support of those widely scattered regions depends ought to be the concern of all three powers: the Great Britain, the United States and…"

"A Japanese occupation of the area would vitally affect the ability of Britain to maintain her position in the European Balance against Hitler," the President said. "Much of her raw materials and petroleum comes from that general area."

"War Department Policy with regard to our defense posture in the Pacific, particularly the Philippines area, is undergoing a drastic change since the ABO-l and Rainbow Plan had been put in place by the combined chiefs of staff earlier this year." General Marshall said. "Rapid expansion of the aerial defenses in the Islands is becoming one of the more important elements of that changing attitude. The placement of four heavy bombardment groups in the Far East Air Force by year's end is being considered in order to emphasize U. S. opposition to further Japanese aggression in East Asia."

General Arnold was suddenly startled. "We simply equip four heavy bombardment groups with B-17s by the end of the year."

General Marshall stood up and went to the map. "Even if we divert B-17's from the Hawaiian Air Defense plan for Pearl Harbor and Oahu, we could possibly get only thirty or forty B-17s out to the Philippines by the end of December." He gazed at the group. "I think we ought to give such a decision a long, hard look.

"Why, Hap?" President Roosevelt asked.

"Well, Mr. President; we've considered carrier based air attacks against Pearl Harbor and other military installations in the Hawaiian Islands as being eminently possible. Just as historically, most military strategists consider the Philippines to be somewhat indefensible. Of course, the present circumstance out there changes all of that to some degree."

"How would you use bombardment aviation in the defense of Pearl Harbor?" Roosevelt asked.

"By daylight reconnaissance missions throughout a nine hundred mile circumference of Oahu here, each Fortress covering a sector," General Arnold said as he indicated with a pencil the area to be flown. He then turned to the President. "Our Fortresses are the only airplanes with sufficient operating range for that kind of reconnaissance out there."

"And?" President Roosevelt said.

"A B-17 attack force, on stand by could be called out to destroy the enemy, at least two days before their carriers could get close enough to launch an air strike against Oahu… Pearl Harbor." General Arnold said.

"What have we got out there now?" President Roosevelt asked.

"The 19th Heavy Bombardment Group has twenty-one B-17s," Arnold said.

"Hap, the War Department rejected the Hawaiian air defense plan before you got back to Washington last week," the President said. "It would have required more B-17s than will be available in the near future. You'll be advised to transfer the 19th Bombardment Group to the Philippines, probably before our conference here with Churchill has ended."

"But…" General Arnold said.

"The Navy will assume the responsibility for off shore reconnaissance and defense of the Hawaiian Islands," General Marshall said.

"What about Guam… Wake?" Admiral King asked. "We can't cover those outposts without some help, General."

President Roosevelt suddenly became aware that the discussion was about to become heated, which he hoped to avoid.

"Well, it's the same problem that plagues us is in the zone of the interior and in Europe… and now in Russia!" The President passed a dispatch to General Marshall. "This just came in to Sumner Wells and Harriman: Russia wants B-17s. General Marshall, you and Hap had better get your heads together on this one." He turned to General Arnold. "Hap, I'd like you to conclude this morning's session by briefing the Joint Chiefs on our recent decisions regarding the Boeing flying fortress."

General Arnold turned to the map, secured the pointer and began.

"As you know, there aren't any aircraft types operational in the Air Force inventory today that are designed to the strategic requirements of range and payloads that would be necessitated by an outbreak of hostilities in the Pacific area." The General indicated the related general area on the map. "Nor do the British have such an operational ability."

"The Boeing aircraft company's progress in the engineering and development of the B-29 prototype has prompted the relevant committees of Congress and the Air Corps to place orders for two hundred and fifty B-29 flying fortresses on a more or less sight-unseen basis. Our decision of course, is based on the accumulated theoretical engineering data generated by Boeing's technical people." General Arnold continued. "We feel the aircraft will exceed the original recommendations released by the Kilner Board for the development of a long range, precision bomber with a three thousand mile operating range and a twenty thousand pound pay load."

Admiral King frowned.

"All of this, together with the absolutely critical requirement for such an aircraft to successfully conduct a war operation in far flung areas, prompted us to proceed with the utmost haste," General Arnold said. "Obviously there's a very real element of risk involved… but we're in no position to compromise."

Concern appeared on the faces of the chiefs and staff and the President himself. General Arnold looked at them and kept talking.

"Therefore, the B-29's have been given first call top priority on raw materials; machine too, equipment, manufacturing facilities, technical staff and engineering personnel."

Everyone exchanged sharp, perplexed glances.

"We've authorized the construction of four major production plants in the country to produce the aircraft in quantity." General Arnold moved to a second map of the U. S. and indicated the relevant position. There are two Boeing plants. One Boeing plant at Renton, Washington and the other at Wichita, Kansas. We also are using a Bell plant at Marietta, Georgia, and a Martin plant at Omaha, Nebraska. That plant construction has already begun. It's being coordinated out of a War Manpower and Machine Tool Allocation office we've set up out at Wright." He looked at Roosevelt. "Mr. President."

"Thank you, Hap." There was a general and contemplative silence as Arnold took his seat. "Gentlemen, we still don't seem to be able to figure out just exactly what the Japanese are up to. They simply can't afford sustained confrontation without further access to raw materials and resources. Therefore, I believe we ought to approach this conference with candor. Churchill will press for a commitment from us in the event of a Japanese invasion of Malaysia.

We'll just have to feel our way through that one."

Roosevelt nodded at an aide, indicating his readiness to leave the ward room. The aide approached as the entire group rose to their feet.

"Well gentlemen," President Roosevelt grinned happily as he was being wheeled out, "our next conference will be with the Prime Minister himself. We're to dine with him on board the Prince of Wales tonight. Harry has persuaded him to make one of his famous after dinner speeches."

The President and his aides left the ward room and Admiral King turned to General Arnold.

"Henry, where do you propose to base your B-29's should there be an outbreak of hostilities in the Pacific?"

General Arnold and Admiral King went back to the map as the other Staff members looked on interestedly.

"Well…of course that depends on target priorities," General Arnold said. He indicated a general area on the map along the equator and west of the 180th meridian that comprises parts of both India and China. "But our only possibilities lie in this general region. Even then, targets in the Dutch East Indies or Japan itself would still remain beyond our operating range." He looked at Admiral King and grinned. "We're working on a system of advance refueling bases."

"Well, I don't know, Henry," Admiral King said. "It just seems we're putting a great deal of strategic dependence on an airplane that hasn't even been test flown yet."

"The Air Forces have no other alternative, Admiral," the General said. "We recognize the practicality and the potential of aircraft carriers used along a far flung battle front such as this one would be. However, carrier based bomb loads simply aren't sufficient to incapacitate large segments of an enemy's industrial capability. That role must be filled by the bombers. The B-29's are the only hope for such a capability in the Pacific and Far East."

"And if it fails?" King asked

"Then…we've got problems…and they won't be confined to the Army Air Corps."

Admiral King gazed at the map for a moment, and then, without further words walked out of the room. The others followed.

General Marshall paused a moment, and turned back to General Arnold:

"You know, Hap; every dollar you're spending on your B-29's have *In God We Trust* engraved on it somewhere. Perhaps that's the only option we've left open to us at the moment, and, I'll tell you something else: if congress fails to pass the draft extension, well I'm reluctant to contemplate the consequences."

A staff officer was waiting for the two generals when the left the ward room. Marine guards stood at attention as they emerged. The staff officer who was obviously waiting for them spoke urgently.

"General Marshall, there's a radio broadcast coming in from New York. We thought you'd be interested. We've had it piped into the executive's quarters here."

General Marshall nodded, and followed the Staff Officer into an adjacent compartment. They entered the compartment and found a Navy lieutenant adjusting the radio speaker where Senator Titus Clay's voice was heard in a static ridden broadcast.

"...And so my fellow Americans, I urge you to contact your Congressional Representatives today, before it's too late, and urge them to vote against extending the draft. American mothers, if you allow the Congress to extend the draft, even for one more year, you may as well agree to plow under one out of every three of America's finest young men. Flanders Field will not hold the dead that will fall in the war being planned by our own President and Mr. Churchill at this very moment. We must put an end to this mad, headlong rush into the carnage of a Second World War. Do not let the red blood of our youth drip from our own hands. Thank you."

"Ladies and Gentlemen - the honorable Senator Titus Clay. This broadcast was presented as a public service and does not necessarily reflect the views of this station," the radio announcer said.

"The man is mad!" General Marshall said. "The storms gather around us and he wants to open the windows." General Marshall looked down and shook his head as he walked to the hatchway and abruptly left.

CHAPTER 25

The HMS Prince of Wales emerged through wisps of Arctic fog as she steamed into Placentia Bay. Martial music could be heard loudly on the Augusta. President Roosevelt, Elliot Roosevelt, Franklin Roosevelt Jr., General Marshall, General Stark, Sumner Welles and Averill Harriman observed the majestic entry of the Prince of Wales, occasionally raising their field glasses to their eyes. President Roosevelt wore the familiar felt hat, its brim turned up jauntily and a black cape about his shoulders.

The Prince of Wales glided past the Augusta, flags flying, sailors parading, side boys up and a contingent of British marines present arms.

The indomitable Winston Churchill stood on the bridge, the familiar cigar clamped firmly in his mouth. The President smiled happily and the USS Augusta Band continued the martial music. Harry Hopkins passed through the honor guard and greeted the President. Admiral Stark, General Marshall, General Arnold, Admiral King, Franklin Roosevelt Jr., Averill Harriman and Secretary Welles made up the reception line.

"Harry, I do believe the voyage was good for you," President Roosevelt said.

"Well… at least I was able to get some work done," Hopkins said.

Hopkins shook hands with Elliot Roosevelt who stood by his father, supporting him.

Winston Churchill emerged onto the USS Augusta gangway, passed through the Honor Guard that stood on each side of the gangway, and stepped up to President Roosevelt. Churchill wore a Navy cap and uniform and was followed by Admiral Pound, Sir John Dill and Vice Admiral Freeman. Churchill and Roosevelt shook hands warmly.

"Mr. President," Winston Churchill said.

The two leaders gazed at each other, smiling. "This is a historic occasion for Great Britain and the United States, Mr. Prime Minister."

Churchill extracted a letter from the breast pocket of his uniform. Their majesties ask me to hand this to you personally."

Roosevelt took the letter. "I'm honored. May I introduce my sons Elliot and Franklin Jr., Mr. Prime Minister?"

Churchill and his entourage moved along the reception line, their words lost in the sweeping music of the Augusta Band.

That evening in the main ward room of the Prince of Wales, Churchill spoke to the collective group, all obviously having finished dinner. A world map covered the Bulkhead behind Churchill and Churchill referred to the map occasionally during the evening speech.

"Thus England has been given respite from Hitler's strange, unpredictable strategy that drove him to attack the Russians. Whilst he fights on the steps of Russia, we retrench and refurbish," Churchill said.

"Our continuing strategy is to engage Hitler's armies along their extended lines of conquest...North Africa...the middle East...believing them to be his weakest points of encounter due to the necessarily long and strenuous lines of logistics and supply -- looking forward to that day when we'll darken the skies over Germany with armadas of strategic bombers that will destroy the German industrial apparatus and the German will to make war."

"We shall not send waves of human flesh against German military might as we did in World War One... a tactic that resulted in a carnage unimaginable. Instead, we shall attack and destroy the enemy with strategic air power, while our navies blockade his shores and our armies force him back into his own boundaries. Then, with the jackal thus weakened, we'll invade."

Everyone applauded.

A short time later, General Arnold and General Marshall sat thoughtfully in the moderately lighted interior of the motor launch.

"An inspiring speech," General Arnold said.

"Yes, but a cold and dismal fear welled up in me when I wondered if the Prime Minister, or the President, really knows how far we've to go to equip and train an Air Force large enough to realize their Grand Strategy," General

Marshall said.

General Arnold grinned. "An officer on my staff put it in rather startling terms awhile back. 'Damn, General, he said. "What you're asking for is like telling a college that's been graduating three hundred upper classmen a year to begin graduating *fifty thousand…in three years* or… a company that's been manufacturing a thousand items a year to produce *fifty thousand* items a year… all without experienced administrators."

General Marshall chuckled. "Well, the issues are being clearly drawn. Issues that involve the most cherished aspects of a free society. America will produce and fight if needed. But, I do not believe that we can bomb the fight out of the Germans."

Arnold gazed at Marshall, momentarily disappointed in his assessment. He clearly understood what was happening to the countries of Western and Eastern Europe and what was about to happen to England. The monster war machine created and unleashed by Hitler could only be stopped by destroying its ability and will to fight. That could only be done through a massive bombing campaign. The resolution by conventional means would be costly in time, resources and an unacceptable loss of American and British lives. Arnold's thoughts continued to what was happening right here in Placentia Bay. Few had ever heard of Placentia Bay, Newfoundland until President Franklin D. Roosevelt and Britain's Prime Minister, Winston Churchill, met there for their historic Atlantic Conference.

"The Atlantic Charter," hammered out by the two indomitable world leaders during the conference, was a document that set forth the fundamental aims and objectives of both countries in a war ravaged world. It would most certainly become one of the most historic documents of our times. The great leaders hoped for enough time to allow America to build up its wartime manufacturing capability and the development and training of sufficient military troops to aid in the war in Europe.

The President and Mr. Churchill joined in a Sunday morning worship service with British and American seamen alike on board the HMS Prince of Wales. Arnold knew that this was to be a war undertaken by two nations of brothers for the common good. It would take everything that both countries could muster and deliver against the dedicated and dynamic force that Germany had deployed against the world. "Yes," Arnold thought, "This was to be a war that would be won or lost by the battles fought in the sky." He had a sudden chill come over him as he realized the awesome responsibility that he had before him. His actions and decisions could potentially affect the outcome of the battles ahead and ultimately the war itself. He slowly got up shaking inside from the realization of his massive responsibility. He looked around the room to see if anyone had seen him before he went to his quarters.

Meantime, in Washington, scores of members of the U. S. House of Representatives presided over by Sam Rayburn, wielding his gavel, voted on the Draft Extension Bill. The Bill that extended the draft law for an additional year passed Congress by one vote. Failure to extend the draft law would have dealt the U. S. Army a devastating blow. Still only partially trained, the draftees made up the bulk of the that Army General George Marshall has struggled to mobilize, equip and train. War would be difficult at best to wage at this time.

CHAPTER 26

On December 6th, 1941, the late afternoon sun rays silhouetted three B-17's parked on the ramp at Hamilton Field in San Francisco. In the briefing room a number of B-17 crew members were sitting in the audience listening to General Arnold give a short briefing.

"You all read the newspapers," General Arnold said. "You know the Japanese Ambassador's have asked for one last meeting with Secretary Hull tomorrow, ostensibly to head off war." The General turned to the map. "Our intelligence informed us there are massive Japanese shipments of supplies and troops moving in this general area." General Arnold indicated the area around Indochina. "We've just about decided they're going to hit the Philippines in order to knock out our reinforced command there under General MacArthur, but we don't know when... or how."

Crew members in the audience, including Captain Raymond Swenson and flight surgeon William R. Shick listened closely to the General's words.

"In summary, you may run into trouble along the way." General Arnold turned to the map again and pointed to the related areas anywhere along the Japanese mandated Islands. "The thirteen B-17's that we're sending to MacArthur and General Brereton... they're critical to all of us. Get them through." General Arnold nodded at flight surgeon Shick. "Besides, you're carrying an important passenger. You may need flight surgeon Shick somewhere down the line."

Everyone laughed.

"Your scheduled refueling stop at Hickman in romantic Hawaii in the morning should provide some beautiful scenery. Too bad you won't have time to take proper advantage of it," General Arnold said. "That's all gentlemen. Good luck."

Later that afternoon, General Arnold watched Captain Swenson, his crew and flight surgeon Shick board one of the last B-17's that were on the parking ramp. Both Captain Swenson and the flight surgeon stopped to shake hands with General Arnold before boarding their ship.

General Arnold smiled at both of them. "Captain, you tell Lewis Brereton to take care of these ships. He's got more B-17's than anybody else in the air force."

"I'll tell him, Sir," Captain Swenson said.

"And get those Japs in line out there, Captain," General Arnold said.

"Count on it," Captain Swenson said.

Captain Swenson continued on to the B-17 and General Arnold gazed after him momentarily before turning back to shake hands with flight surgeon Shick.

"Take care of my boys, doc," General Arnold said. "I worry about them, you know."

"Right now it, it's you I'm concerned about, General."

"Well, as a matter of fact, I'm going up to the mountains with Donald Douglas tomorrow. We're going to do some deer hunting up there."

Shick extended his hand. "Good luck, General," He gestured toward the flight crew. "Don't worry. I'll take good care of them."

General Arnold nodded and watched as Shick walked to the B-17 and entered through the nose hatch. A moment later, Captain Swenson looked out the cockpit window as the engines began firing to life. Swenson glanced down at General Arnold and raised his hand in a casual salute, and then began turning the B-17 into the taxi ramp. General Arnold returned the salute and watched as the last of the B-17's became airborne, now headed west into the evening sun.

Captain Swenson made some minor adjustments to the trimming

tab, surveyed the instrumentation, and then gazed out into night beyond the cockpit. Flight surgeon Shick entered the compartment where the Navigator was busy making dead reckoning projections on a chart spread out on the navigator's table before him. Shick, carrying his parachute pack, looked over his navigator shoulder at the chart where the course was being laid out from California to the Philippines. The navigator tapped his divider on the chart at the Philippines location, all the way across the Pacific and looked up at Shick.

"We're going to be a hell of a long way from home, doc,"

Shick propped his parachute pack in the corner of the compartment. "Does that bother you?"

"No… not really."

"Family?" the flight surgeon asked.

"Yeah a wife and three kids. How about you?"

Shick extracted a small leather picture holder from his breast pocket. "A daughter that's sixteen now. She's a top student and damned pretty too, even if she is my kid."

The navigator took the folder, opened it and gazed at the two pictures there. "Your wife?" he asked as he looked at one photograph." Shick nodded. "Nice family." He closed the folder and handed it back to the doctor. "I hear you were a big name back home. How you get mixed up in all this?"

Flight surgeon Shick thought for moment. "I've always been fascinated with aviation, I guess. I accepted my commission just feeling that I could make a greater contribution here, that's all." He gazed at the young navigator, smiling. "Are you a career officer?"

The navigator grinned proudly.

The flight surgeon struck the side of his parachute as if it were a pillow, then laid his head back against it. "Wake me up before we hit the islands. I wouldn't want to miss that, you know." He paused. "Saw it a few years ago from a Matson Liner, never from the air. It should be breathtaking."

The navigator grinned and then turned back to his work. Shick adjusted his torso to the crude parachute bed, and closed his eyes drowsily.

Secretary of State Cordell Hull's vehicle pulled up to the State Department Building and Mr. Hull stepped out of the car, and noticed that the massive white columns of the State Department Building were bathed in the warm, early morning sun rays. He walked to the private entrance, briefcase in hand, and went inside. Mr. Ballantine, Mr. Hornbeck, and Mr. Hamilton, advisors to the Secretary on Far East matters were obviously awaiting the secretary's arrival.

"Good morning, Mr. Secretary," Mr. Ballentine said, proffering several sheets of teletype material. "This just came up from the Intelligence decoding section, Mr. Secretary."

Secretary Hull read the message. "It appears to be an answer to our November 26th proposals." He looked at Ballentine." When did intelligence intercept this?"

"Started coming out of Tokyo about two A.M. this morning our time. Intelligence took awhile to decode it. The fourteen parts came in separate."

"It looks like their final response," Secretary Hull said. He continued to pursue the message. "*Ignore their sacrifices in China!?* He looked at all three men. "Rubbish." He struck the message with the back of his hand. "The document is obviously intended as an insult. Their so called *sacrifices* in China were downright *aggressions* of the cruelest nature. They conspired to block the Japanese effort to establish a new order in the Far East." He faced the assembled men bewildered and perplexed. "What on earth makes them think they've a right to occupy Malaysia… the Dutch East Indies… lands that are not even remotely related to them in ethnic or cultural history?"

"But the document says nothing about breaking off diplomatic relations with us… nor does it imply a declaration of war," Mr. Hamilton said.

"This last paragraph?" Secretary Hull said. "Why would Tokyo want Ambassadors Nomura and Kurusu to deliver this to me at precisely one o'clock this afternoon?"

"Intelligence feels that's some kind of zero hour." Hornbeck said. "That will be early morning throughout the Eastern Pacific. They figure the

Japs are going to hit us out there somewhere."

"Has the President been notified?" Secretary Hull asked.

"Yes, Sir," Ballentine said. "And the Secretary of War and the Secretary of the Navy are on their way over here now."

The telephone rang and Mr. Hamilton answered it. "State Department," He said and handed the phone to Secretary Hull. "Ambassador Nomura,"

Secretary Hull hesitated, organizing his thoughts, then took the phone.

Yes Mr. Ambassador…this is Secretary Hull." He paused while exchanging perplexed glances with Ballentine, Hornbeck and Hamilton, "Yes, I'll be in my office this afternoon." He was silent for a moment, listening. "Yes, I'll see you at one o'clock." Secretary Hull replaced the receiver in its cradle solemnly.

Presently, Mr. Hamilton approached the Secretary and held out a black note book. "The morning intelligence reports on the Far East, Sir,"

Secretary Hull took the note book. "Thank you."

Secretary Hull went to the window and gazed out, his mind heavy with the events at hand.

Early the following morning, Captain Swenson looked out the cockpit window at the bright blue Pacific waters that stretched out below and beyond.

"There it's, Diamond Head," The co-pilot said.

Captain Swenson rose up in his seat and peered out threw the windscreen. "Right on the button!"

In the navigator's compartment, flight surgeon Shick and the navigator looked out onto the exotic scenery below. Shick nudged the navigator and pointed upward to the left and ahead of the B-17. They saw two Val type Japanese aircraft in front and above the B-17 at a distance of three or four thousand feet.

"Looks like some kind of welcoming committee," Shick said. "But who? They aren't Army or Navy."

The navigator shook his head negatively and then looked back to his right and ahead of the B-17. "Looks like a pretty big group over there by Pearl...." He pointed through the nose canopy at a huge black smoke column that was extending upward. "That smoke column must be three hundred feet high."

Shick looked toward the smoke column and then back toward the two Japanese aircraft, a puzzled expression was noticeably formed by the wrinkles in his face.

Captain Swenson began initial radio contact. "Hickam Tower, this is Captain Swenson -- Boeing B-17. Flight *three*. Repeat Flight *three* from Hamilton Field. We're approximately fifteen miles East of Diamond Head and standing by for landing instructions. By the way...who's our escort?"

"Flight three...Hickam Tower...field under." The voice faded and was replaced by static. Suddenly the voice was clear again. "Proceed." And, then more static.

Swenson and the co-pilot exchanged perplexed glances. Captain Swenson tried the radio again.

"Hickam Tower, this is Army flight three. Unable to read you clearly. We're low on fuel... unable to proceed beyond Hickam. Request landing."

Suddenly the co-pilot ducked and yelled, "Look out!"

A Japanese Zero hurtled through the visible area beyond the windscreen, passing above the B-17, even as several bullets shattered the windscreen. Both pilot ducked wildly.

"What the hell?" The pilot said.

The navigator looked out through the side window of the compartment in disbelief. "Those Bastards are Japs!"

Flight surgeon Shick pointed urgently. "Here comes another one," he said with a sudden chill of fear coming over him.

A Zero peeled down toward Swenson's B-17 in a forty-five degree, front approach from the right. Two machine gun bullets struck the navigator across the chest almost simultaneously, hurtling him back across the chart table and then into a crumpled mass in the corner of the compartment, his blood splashing grotesquely across the chart. Flight Surgeon Shick leaped across the compartment to help the navigator. He pulled the navigator up and then stared in disbelief.

"Oh God!" he cried out as he became sick and threw up.

Captain Swenson struggles to steady the B-17." He spoke into the intercom. "We're going to try for Hickam. Hang on."

The co-pilot looked out the right side of the ship, down at Hickam below and to the right. Wisps of smoke from bursting ground Flak and aerial combat flashed by the cockpit window.

"Runway's clear," The co-pilot said.

As they approached the Hickam runway the co-pilot could see several fires scattered here and there. As Swenson's B-17 flared its nose up slightly to land two zeros kept firing at them sporadically then they peeled up and away in opposite directions. The B-17 struck the runway, careening to the left then straightening out. It started to roll out as it rushed past burning aircraft wreckage. The B-17 finally stopped at the end of the runway. Swenson, the co-pilot and flight surgeon got out and started running to the shelter of a nearby machine gun bunker.

A Zero was screaming in no more than ten feet off the ground as it started to strafe the field. Suddenly the Zero's bullets slammed into Flight surgeon Shicks' back, pitching him forward in a grotesque somersault. He lay face up, his arms extended—a death stare in his eyes. The leather photo holder lay beside him, the faces of his wife and daughter smiling serenely.

The level of gun fire diminished as the first attack wave had ended. The battleships California, West Virginia, Nevada, and Arizona were all smoking and lying on the bottom of the Pacific Ocean. The Oklahoma was still in the process of capsizing.

Two Marines in a machine gun emplacement on Ford Island surveyed the carnage.

"Every damned battleship in the Pacific Fleet," the first marine said.

"And they were sent out here to scare the Japs," the second Marine said. "Looks like we're the ones who got scared."

The telephone rang in Secretary of State Cornell Hull's office in Washington D.C. at 1:14 P.M. on December 7th, 1941 and Mr. Ballentine went to answer it. Secretary Hull stood in the center of the room. Green H. Hackworth, legal advisor to State walked from the office doorway to Secretary Hull.

Mr. Ballentine picked up the telephone. "State…"

Hackworth turned to Secretary Hull. "The Japanese ambassadors are here, Sir."

Hull nodded, lifting his hand in momentary restraint as he gazed toward Ballentine.

"Yes, Mr. President, one moment," Ballentine said. He looked at Secretary Hull. "It's the President."

Secretary Hull took the telephone." Cordell, Mr. President. He squared his shoulders. "Has it been confirmed?" Hull paused and listened. Yes, Mr. President. Their ambassadors are waiting outside now." He was quiet and listened again. "Very well… I'll see them. Yes …yes I'll see to it."

Secretary Hull turned to Hackworth and Ballentine as he hung up the phone. "The President said there's an unconfirmed report Pearl Harbor out in the Hawaiian Islands has just been attacked."

He paused thoughtfully, and then he gestured to Hackworth to admit the Japanese ambassador's. Hackworth opened the door to admit Ambassadors Nomura and Kurusu who handed Secretary Hull a lengthy, typewritten document.

"I have been instructed by my Government to deliver this document to you at one o'clock," Nomura said. He and Secretary Hull stared at each other. "Difficulty in decoding has delayed our ability to carry out that instruction, Sir."

"Why did you specify 1:00 P.M. in your request for an interview, Mr. Ambassador?" Hull snapped.

'I do not know, Sir. It was my instruction."

Secretary Hull pretended to glance through the document, and then gazed at Nomura. "Are you're presenting this…He indicated the document. "Under instruction from your government?"

"That's correct, Sir," Nomura said.

Secretary Hull scanned a few more pages, then, explosively, all his pent-up emotion released at once. "I must say, Mr. Ambassador, that in all of my dealings with you I have never uttered one word of untruth. This is borne out, absolutely, by the record." He shook the document in Nomura's face. "In all of my fifty years of public service, I have never seen a document that was more crowded with falsehoods and distortions on a scale so huge that I never imagined until today that *any* government on this planet was capable of uttering them."

Nomura started to speak but had to cough slightly before he resumed his impassive task.

Secretary Hull continued, unable to control his anger. "Your government invaded China, Manchuria and Korea in the cruelest aggression in recent history. You occupied Indochina and you've continued to make plans to occupy Malaysia and the Dutch East Indies. Yet, you've the fortitude to present such a document as this to me."

Secretary Hull stopped speaking, motioning them to leave his office at once. He watched the Ambassador walk away.

Secretary Hull sadly gazed after the departed ambassadors. Nomura and Kurusu walk out Secretary Hull's office only to be surrounded by newsmen.

Nomura and Kurusu moved through the reporters—not speaking, their faces a study of frozen passivity.

CHAPTER 27

There was a knock on Coltrane's door. Heine spoke loudly through the door so Bart could hear him. "Bart, you're wanted at the office. You need to go see Lieutenant Colonel Grand."

"Okay," Coltrane said as he rubbed the sleep from his eyes and tried to fully wake up. He finally got up and headed to the shower.

Thirty minutes later he arrived at Grand's office. His orderly told Bart that Grant had been promoted to lieutenant colonel yesterday. He knocked on the door and announced Major Coltrane.

"Good morning and congratulations, Sir," Bart said with genuine warmth in his voice.

"Thanks. I might be a bloody private by sundown. We've no time to talk. Sir Hugh is waiting and he's livid over the mission and subsequent events," Grand said as he led Bart out the door.

The two quickly entered the office of the head of Special Operations Executive (SOE) and took seats as directed.

"I have read the reports, memorandums and various stories about yesterday. What the hell happened to your command, Lawrence?" Dalton asked with stress and irritation.

"Sir, it seems that Commander Chapham exceeded his authority as acting commander to change Major Coltrane's mission and flight plan to accommodate an additional supply drop in southern Denmark," Grand said somewhat matter of factly.

"Knowing the critical importance and sensitivity of the primary mission, I can't understand why he would bugger the mission with a routine supply drop. His decision caused two deaths, one wounded, not including him, and a badly shot up B-25. Why did Beddows and Balfour inject themselves into the matter? They're just as responsible as far as I'm concerned."

Coltrane interrupted Dalton. "Sir, they tried. They did attempt to explain the problems with this mission. They did all that was possible under the circumstances. Chapham was in command and he wasn't going to change his decision or listen to his subordinates even if it was a temporary command. I suspect that there was a certain amount of personal animosity as well."

"So you feel comfortable with Balfour and Beddows?" he asked.

"Absolutely, Sir. They make a great team. I'm speaking for the others when I say that we've full faith and confidence in them. The problem was Chapham," Bart said with confidence.

Dalton leaned back in his chair and looked directly at Coltrane. "Why did you accept the mission given the unwarranted dangers?"

"Sir, it's really simple. First, the primary mission was critical and beyond the good of any one man or crew. Secondly, I'm regular army, therefore I always obey those appointed over me. I sure wasn't going to give the son-of-a-bitch the personal satisfaction of declining in fear or disobeying a lawful order."

Dalton was silent for a moment, then he spoke in an official tone, "Then I can tell the Prime Minister that the problem is isolated to one person, and he's going to be in the hospital for months prior to his discharge from active duty for medical reasons." Grand and Coltrane both agreed.

"Very well, the matter is closed," Dalton said authoritatively. "Now the matter of a new co-pilot for you."

"Sir, can we keep Zak Middleton? He was great on the last mission and fits in with the Black Bart crew?" Coltrane asked.

"Bloody good idea. Done! Now about the two bodies. The American Embassy will take charge of Lieutenant West's arrangements. It seems that we must bury the Dane here. It would be difficult to send him back to Denmark."

"Sir," said Coltrane. "Black Bart would like to take him back when we take the Danish underground back. That type of support would go along way with the Danish underground."

"First, what makes you think that you're taking them back instead of a submarine?" "Secondly, can you get a coffin in the aircraft?" Dalton asked with a degree of authority.

"Logic says it's a Black Bart mission. A sub would take a long time and they'll be anxious to get the new operation into action. We took them out under fire and we have to show our resolve to fight with them despite the danger. Besides, Sir, we want to," Coltrane said respectfully. "And yes, the coffin will fit into the bomb bay."

"Very well, it's your mission," Dalton commanded.

"Do you've anything to add, Lieutenant Colonel Grand?" Dalton heavily emphasizing the Lieutenant Colonel part.

"No Sir, we're ready to move forward."

"Good hunting, gentlemen!"

Grand and Coltrane went back to their office chatting about the problems dealing with the new German tactics employed to get Black Bart. As they got to the fourth floor, they ran into Annabel Beddows in the hall. Grand excused himself and left Bart and Annabel talking.

"How did it go with Sir Hugh?" she asked.

"Very well, I guess. I'm not scheduled for a firing squad. We'll be taking the body back to Denmark when they're ready to go," Bart said softly.

"Good, I'll look forward to making up that flight plan," she said as she started to walk away.

"Wait," Coltrane said, "how about joining me for supper at the Rattskeller tonight? We can eat early and then go our separate ways. Strictly platonic!"

She smiled as she lowered her head and started off down the hall. "I don't think so, thanks anyway."

It was almost 1900 hours. Coltrane was sitting in his usual booth at the back of the Rattskeller, drinking scotch and reading about the Japanese diplomats negotiating in Washington, D.C., when a woman walked up. At first he thought it was Reggie, until he looked up and saw Annabel Beddows.

"The supper offer still good?" she asked.

"Absolutely," he said as he got up. "Please have a seat. Can I offer you a drink?"

"Sure," she said. "Scotch neat."

"Reggie," Coltrane said, "could we've two single malts, neat, please?"

"I understand that you stood up to Sir Hugh in behalf of Sanford and me. Thanks. I thought certain that we would be political casualties. I really do like what I'm doing and I wouldn't want to be transferred to a regular unit."

They had just finished the first round and reviewed the menu when Bart waved towards Reggie. She and Heine were listening to the radio. Reggie looked over and said, "Come quickly. The Japs are bombing Pearl Harbor!"

"Well we're in it now!" Bart said.

"It's about bloody time. You've been at it almost a year," she said with a warm smile.

Coltrane looked at her smile and then into her eyes. He saw what he had hoped for in them.

"I have to go,' she said abruptly. "I have two Lysander missions to prepare for." She got up and departed unceremoniously.

At first, Bart just stood there watching as she went out the door. Then he went after her. He worked through the unusually crowded sidewalk to catch up with her a half a block away. He gently grabbed her arm and turned her around kissed her passionately. She did not react at first then suddenly she threw her arms around his neck and returned his kiss.

The props were still turning when Zak turned off the two engine ignition switches after his pilot in command and crew competency check ride. Zak turned to Bart who was standing on the steps behind the two pilots and asked, "Will that pass muster?"

"Zak, you and your crew were qualified long before the check ride. This is a formality and you know it," Bart said as he started down the ladder to the airfield tarmac. "You're cleared to start flying missions starting tomorrow. It will be nice to have help. I'd say that it would give us a break, but if I know Dalton and Grand, they'll just increase the mission load."

"No doubt," Zak replied. "What do you've planned for the next 72 hours? It must be nice to have some time off."

"Annabel is taking me up to her family house up near Bolton. I think she's a little concerned about my reaction to her obvious wealth," Bart said with concern.

"How do you feel about being in love with a woman that's worth over one hundred million British Pounds Sterling?"

"Hey, you know where I come from. I'm happy just being with her. The money really doesn't excite me. It's her money, not mine. I don't want any of her money either," Bart said.

"Well, like it or not you'll be around nice things and with a long list of British Royalty and bluebloods. She can't change that either," Zak said as he started walking to the operations building to get a shower. "Can you adjust to that environment from time to time?"

"Yes, I can spit out my chewing tobacco, clean the cowshit off my boots, and take a shower every Saturday," Bart quipped. "I can do anything required to be with her."

"Right-O!"

CHAPTER 28

Bart was enjoying the ride through the English countryside. He loved the rolling hills and diversified trees, cultivated fields and pastures. It was a far cry from west Texas that was as flat as it was desolate. "Cotton fields for as far as the eye could see," he thought.

They passed through a large stone gate and on to a blacktop road that went across a beautiful pasture with cows and a half dozen beautiful horses. He looked ahead for the house, but it wasn't in view. Perhaps it wasn't as big as he thought.

"How big is the estate?" he asked.

"It's slightly less than 4,500 hectares," she replied.

"That's over 9,000 acres, very impressive," he said. Just as they went over a hill and the house came into view. "It's a monster," he thought. It was a three-story mansion that looked very much like the Schonbrunn Castle in Vienna, only much smaller. Its size was still humbling to Coltrane. "Do you've parties here very often?"

"Before the war we would have three parties a year and formal suppers six or eight times a year," she said softly. "This year the annual Children's Christmas Party was held in London due to the war. You were on a mission or I would have put you to work at the party. It's a social occasion that raises funds for Christmas presents given to children in hospitals and orphanages. The other annual charity ball that I host is the St. Dwynwen's Day celebration. It's a Welsh holiday for the Patron Saint of Lovers. The Duke was part Welsh. It raises funds for disabled veterans from the Great War. It comes up on the 25th of January. I'll have it in London this year as well. The war you know. I hope that you'll be my escort and host," she said with a smile, looking at him briefly.

"I'd be honored, but I'm not sure that I could be polished and sophisticated enough for the occasion," he said with a tone of reservation. I'll do what I can. You'll have to educate me on proper etiquette and customs."

"Just be yourself. If you're honest and sincere the rest will take care of itself. Do you have your formal dress uniform here or is it in the States?"

"It's in the States," he said. "It's packed away at March Field. It doesn't fit very well. I bought the cheapest uniform that I could get. We don't wear them often and I didn't want to pay a bunch of money for something that wasn't worn more than once or twice a year."

She thought for a moment then said "You've a birthday in March. My present to you'll be a new dress uniform. Okay with you?"

"That's a little much for a birthday, but I'll need it if I'm going to help you with the St. Dwynwen's fundraiser," he said in appreciation.

"Then it's settled. When we get back to London you can go over to The Huntsman and Charles will fix you up. He's done uniforms for many, many officers including Black Jack Pershing."

"Where is this tailor shop?" he asked.

"Why Saville Row, of course. You certainly don't want something off the rack that will make you look like a potato," she said almost laughing.

Bart laughed as her analogy. He knew about Saville Row. A necktie there would cost more than a month's pay, much less an officer's dress uniform.

They came to a stop in front of the massive home. She looked at it then said "I'm thinking of selling it and buying a larger place in London. Elizabeth's uncle Henry made me a very nice offer last week."

"Really, last week you say? The devil! He knows that American combat units will be renting houses like this for their headquarters. They'll pay very, very well for a place like this. I'd hold on to it until after the war to sell. You'll make a nice rental fee until the duration," he said.

I bet that you're right. He's quite the businessman. I was wondering what possessed him to buy a place like this during a war. I should have thought about the U.S. military. Damn, that was so obvious and I didn't see it. I guess I'm not as good an intelligence agent as I thought I was," Annabel said in a mock terse tone. "Now, lover, collect the bags in the boot while I open up. I gave all the employees the weekend off, so we won't be bothered. Now let's go see if you're as good on the ground as you're in the air."

CHAPTER 29

A 306th Bombardment Group B-17 approached the Wendover landing strip and the aircraft rolled into the turn onto base leg. Captain Taylor, the 306th Operations officer, stood up in a jeep with other USAAF flight officers as they observed the B-17 landing approach.

"On these 'power off' landings," Captain Taylor said, "you'll throttle down to 2100 rpm on base leg, twenty-three inches manifold pressure with turbo controls 'full on'…all before you turn into final." Captain Taylor looked down from the Jeep and scanned the group. "Once you roll out on final, you'll be coordinating several characteristics of the airplane simultaneously."

On board the approaching aircraft, a young lieutenant sat in left seat of the 306th Bombardment Group B-17 and Lieutenant Colonel Lemay sat in the right seat. When the final turn was completed, the lieutenant began his final landing procedure.

"Flaps full down," the lieutenant said. Lemay lowered the flaps. "Flaps full down."

"Prop controls full high rpm," the lieutenant said.

Lemay set the prop controls. "Props full high rpm," he said.

The lieutenant and Lemay looked out onto the Wendover runway which stretched out in front of them.

"Nose up a little. You're looking for a constant hundred twenty miles per hour glide speed now," Lemay said.

The air speed indicator settled on one hundred twenty miles per hour. Lemay lifted his eyes from the air speed indicator to look out on the approaching runway.

"That's it," he said, then continued. "That's better." Then, he glanced at the altimeter.

"One hundred seventy feet...one hundred sixty feet...begin leveling off now...smoothly...that's it..."

The B-17 touched down, suddenly lurching to the right wildly.

"Stay off those brakes!" Lemay said.

Smoke began to pour from the locked wheels of the wildly lurching B-17. Captain Taylor closed his eyes, and winced at the violence of the landing.

The pilot recovered alignment to the runway.

Captain Taylor turned from the landing to speak to the assembled group.

"B-17 pilots report to the flight line at one o'clock this afternoon, ready to fly. We'll begin in alphabetical order...landing and takeoffs in the number two ship." Captain Taylor continued. "Lieutenant Haggerty, you'll take my place here with the observer pilots."

"Yes, Sir."

Lemay exited the parked 306th Bombardment Group B-17. The pilot followed him.

"Sorry about the brakes, Colonel," The lieutenant said

Lemay turned to gaze at the lieutenant for a moment, then, grinned. "The first four-engine landing's always a little rough. You'll do better next time."

"Lemay walked to the ship's mechanic who had just finished positioning the wheel chocks.

"Better give the tires and the landing gear the once over. We may have done some damage on that one."

"Yes, Sir," the mechanic said as he started looking at the landing gear.

Lemay climbed into a parked jeep, started the engine and drove away, realizing how much more training his pilots and aircrews desperately needed before deploying to Europe and life and death combat.

CHAPTER 30

Coltrane had just arrived in London from a mission to take the Danish Resistance leaders and their fallen comrade back to Laeso Island. This time they were over water with no fighters to tear up the repaired Black Bart. He went into the Section D building on Baker Street and ran into Sanford Balfour just inside the entrance.

"I take it that you had a good mission," he said smiling. "The boss wants to see you. Better not keep him waiting."

"Right," Bart said as he gave Balfour a friendly slap on the arm. He went to Major Grand's office where Dalton and Beddows were already in the office and seated.

Seeing Coltrane, Grand motioned him on into the office and to a chair. "I take it the mission went off as planned?" he asked.

"As you would say, it was frightfully boring," Bart said lightly. "It went just like Major Beddows planned it, Sir."

"We were discussing the fact that you've been here for a year without any holiday at all and Christmas is coming. Ho, Ho, Ho and all that rubbish. I have a mission for the Black Bart and three of our staff officers here. It seems that our second B-25 is ready for pick up in California. It's just like yours except it's the suggested improvements that you forwarded to North American Aviation. The next two that are ordered will be ready in March. That will give Black Bart four aircraft for its mission," said Grand, pausing to cut the tip off his cigar.

Dalton who was already sitting in the chair to Bart's right then spoke. "You and your crew will fly back to California day after tomorrow on a Military

Air Transport B-24 that they're using to shuttle VIPs and diplomats back and forth between London and Washington. You'll find your own transportation from Washington to Los Angeles. Use your 'Silver Fox' priority. That should work rather well for you."

"When you get to Washington, please assist Major Beddows and the three other SOE staff over to the Pentagon. They've a series of intelligence coordination meetings to attend. Once the Major is finished at the Pentagon, she'll catch a commercial flight to Los Angeles. She'll deliver the final purchase documents for your last two B-25s. Perhaps they'll make a right hand drive version," he said joking. I would appreciate it if you would give her a lift back to Washington Boling Field in the new B-25. She's wanted to fly in your Black Bart aircraft for some time but her combat loss would be far too great to SOE. She'll take the B-24 back," Dalton said, then remembering another item. "Oh yes, while you're at the Pentagon you're to stop by General Arnold's office. He wants to see you again. Now don't let him take you back. You've another year with us by agreement."

"Not to worry, Sir," Bart replied. "They couldn't get me out of SOE with a crowbar."

Dalton being a sly and cunning intelligence officer had become aware of the budding relationship between Coltrane Major Beddows. That pleased him. She deserved another good man in her life.

Major Grand interjected, "Her flight is on 20 December. She can't miss that flight. Seats are hard to come by and she's certain social obligations at Christmas time as the Duchess of Estis."

"Not a problem, Sir," Coltrane replied.

"Well, we have our plan then, thank you," Dalton said as he got up.

Everyone started to leave the room. Dalton grabbed Bart's arm and leaned closely and said "May I suggest that you've a refuel stop in Sweetwater. I think your parents would like to meet your crew."

Coltrane looked Dalton in the eyes and knew immediately who he really wanted him to introduce to his parents. He smiled and said, "That's a great idea, Sir."

The B-24 came to a stop in front of the Boiling Field Transit Aircraft operations building. The weary passengers deplaned and went into operations to check in and get individual instructions or travel orders. After the long and bumpy ride across the Atlantic, the group wanted to get a room at the visiting officer's quarters, take a shower and sleep. Before departing the field, Coltrane arranged for he and his crew to fly out the next afternoon to the west coast.

The next morning, Coltrane and the four British officers met in the VOQ office to arrange transportation to the Pentagon.

Beddows looked at the message attached to her arrival package. It directed her group to go to an office building near the White House where they would meet the President's Coordinator of Information, a Colonel Donovan. He would take care of all arrangements from that point. She looked at Coltrane with a confused expression.

"Don't worry or say anything. You're going to meet this country's top spy. He's a real leader and knows his business. Work with him as he's the President's ear. You can be sure that you'll see a lot of his personnel in the near future," Coltrane said softly. "I have a meeting with General Arnold, before I have to catch my flight to LA. I won't see you until you get to Los Angeles. I'll meet your plane." Bart looked around to see if there was anyone around them, then he kissed Annabel.

Promptly at 0900 hours, Coltrane entered the outer office of General Arnold. The sergeant escorted him to a small conference room where there were six officers. Also, there was a full colonel named Bradshaw, who introduced himself and the other staff officers around the table. Coltrane did his best to remember their names and respective staff functions.

"Major Coltrane," the Colonel said, "We've been reading your operational reports and reports from the SOE. They're very impressive to say the very least. Your program has exceeded the highest expectations. We understand that you're here to pick up a second B-25 and two more in April.

"We're in the war now and Colonel Donovan expects to participate with the SOE in developing resistance activities. We're currently designing the force and operational procedures for what we're calling 'Operation Carpetbagger.' We should be deploying to RAF Harrington airbase in July of next year. Sooner if we can get delivery of our B-24s and our agents trained. Today, we would appreciate you talking to our planning staff so they can draw on your experience. The men around the table have been excitedly awaiting your arrival. But first I need to take you to see General Arnold. Please follow me."

Bart entered the General's office and marched to a position directly in front of his desk, saluted and reported, "Sir, Major Coltrane reporting as ordered."

Arnold returned his salute as he came out from his desk. It's a pleasure to meet such a distinguished combat aviator. Your outstanding operations for the SOE have made us proud. You've done a wonderful job over there this past year. We've a team anxiously waiting to debrief you in the conference room.

"We sure could use you here right now training our guys headed over there soon. But you're under an agreement with the Brits for another year unless you want to be relieved of the assignment.

"No, Sir, I'm doing a lot of good for the war effort there. I'll be ready to join up with one of our B-17 Groups when I'm finished."

"Very well, then. I'm delighted that you feel that strongly about what you're doing…and we'll have a B-17 waiting for you," Arnold said as he turned to his desk and picked up a sheet of paper. "It's with pleasure that I present you with your orders promoting you to the rank of Lieutenant Colonel. If there is anyone who has earned this promotion, it's you. Now, please help my staff gear up for the war."

"Yes, Sir," Bart said as he saluted and returned to the conference room. Coltrane barely got away from the endless questions in time to catch his flight west.

A couple of days later, the military C-47 stopped and the passengers deplaned at the March Field transit terminal. Annabel was the first off the plane. Bart's heart started beating more rapidly. As soon as she entered the building, he pulled her into the empty room adjoining the main reception area and kissed her passionately. "I've missed you," he said.

Annabel looked at him and said in a formal and proper tone, "And who are you? Yes, you idiot, I've missed you too." Then she noticed the silver leaves of a Lieutenant Colonel on his jacket. "My, my, they're giving away rank in the Army Air Force, aren't they," she said jokingly.

"So true. Now let's get you checked in at the visiting female officer's quarters. Then we need to go over to North American. They're expecting you today instead of tomorrow. I can't explain the screw up. The war you know. If we get the aircraft signed for today, I can show you Southern California tomorrow. We'll head back to Washington the day after," Bart said without taking a breath.

The wheels of the B-25 barely squealed as they landed in Sweetwater, Texas. They parked the B-25 in front of the civilian fixed base operator. Several civilians came out of the old hangar to take a closer look at the new B-25. It was a novelty to them as military aircraft seldom landed in Sweetwater. Bart asked the fuel truck driver to fuel the aircraft while they went to get a bite to eat.

The young kid nodded as his wide open eyes took in the B-25.

His parents had walked out to meet them. I'd like to introduce my parents, Frank and Doris Coltrane. This is Major Annabel Beddows of the RAF who we work with very closely over there." He then introduced the crew of the Black Bart.

"Nice to meet you all," they responded. Now I understand you're limited on time, so let's head over to Lowaki's for some Texas hospitality and a damned good steak dinner," Frank said.

The hurried steak lunch conversation was dominated by Bart's mother and Annabel. That was fine with everyone else, as they just wanted to concentrate on the delicious sixteen ounce steak and trimmings. They hadn't had a steak that delicious before and they savored every bite.

After they stuffed dessert down, they returned to the airfield. As they walked out to the plane, Bart's mother hugged him goodbye and whispered into his ear. "She's the one, isn't she?" Bart smiled and nodded. Then Bart shook his father's hand before climbing up the ladder and into the cockpit.

CHAPTER 31

January 25, 1942 was a typical winter evening in London. It was cold, damp and overcast, with the persistent wind which had a way of going through any clothing and chilling a person to the bone. The ballroom of the Connaught Hotel in Mayfair was warm and alive with a host of political and business dignitaries from all parts of Great Britain, all of whom had come to this annual event to leave large amounts of money to support the less fortunate and disables soldiers and sailors that fought in World War I or the Great War, as it was more popularly referred to.

Duchess of Estis, Annabel Beddows of Bolton headed the official receiving line with her official escort, Lieutenant Colonel Bart Coltrane, U.S. Army Air Force. At first Bart felt out of place, but quickly adjusted to the situation and became a warm and genial figure standing next to the chairwoman of this traditional charity gala in his new dress uniform. He was impressed at how well it fitted him. His attention snapped back to a tall, handsome military man being introduced to him.

"Colonel Coltrane, may I introduce a very good friend of mine, Henry, the Duke of Gloucester."

Bart was quick to look this famous English figure in his eyes and extended his hand to his. "An honor to meet you, Sir," Bart said with obvious respect and admiration.

"So you're the bugger that figured out my land deal with Annabel. Very shrewd, young man," he gently leaned over and quietly spoke in Bart's ear. "I'm grateful to you for bringing happiness to Annabel. She was a hermit and very depressed until you came into her life. All the best to you two."

Then the Duke continued down the receiving line.

The official receiving line was about to close when two men in plain business suits came into the room and looked around the room then took posts at the door and midway along the wall. Bart was concerned as he couldn't figure out why two obvious bodyguards would be at a charity function. Then he saw why. His boss, Sir Hugh Dalton, had entered with the U.S. Ambassador, the Foreign Minister and a short man he could not identify.

Suddenly, he was shocked to see the Prime Minister himself. It was Churchill!

Churchill and Annabel exchanged hugs and the traditional kiss on both cheeks like they were long-term close friends, and they were. Then Annabel turned to introduce Bart.

"No introductions necessary, my dear. I hear about this young man almost daily. Black Bart, it's an honor to meet you and to thank you on behalf of the British Empire. You've been of great service to our island nation and do great a service to your country," the Prime Minister said in his unmistakable voice which had been overheard by those close by. This brought spontaneous applause from the guests. Churchill being the consummate politician saw a political opportunity and grabbed Coltrane's hand and raised it high. "Ladies and gentlemen, I give you Black Bart, the man whom the Germans fear more than their own leader." The applause became louder and then died away when Sir Winston continued down the receiving line.

Right behind the Prime Minister was Sir Anthony Eden, the wartime Foreign Secretary. "My congratulations, Colonel. My sources in Berlin tell me that you've become the most hated bunch of pirates to Hitler and The Third Reich. Hitler has lost a lot of sleep thanks to you and your men. Keep up the good work and we can bring an end to this bloody mess."

"Thank you, I shall take your news to the pirates," Coltrane said proudly.

The American Ambassador was next to pass through the line and expressed the President's appreciation to Black Bart for their efforts prior to and post declaration of war.

Sir Hugh Dalton came through considerably quieter than the others.

"There's nothing that I can say to top the Prime Minister. Looks like you've won in the air and on the ground," nodding to Annabel. "I take it that you did stop in Sweetwater."

"Yes, Sir, it was a great place to refuel and get lunch."

Annabel made like the regal social butterfly and went from guest to guest greeting them and making social conversation. She kept looking over at Bart to see if he was doing okay with the guests. She saw him talking to the various guests as well, and without any difficulty. Any question that she may have had about him not fitting into the social strata was soon dispelled. He was working the crowd like a professional.

On a cold February morning in 1942, an Army C-47 approached the runway at Wendover Field in Utah, its landing gear settled down on the runway. Sagebrush bent with the mild desert wind, and from the cockpit window Colonel Curtis Lemay looked out onto a mountain range and at the rows of military tents that were alongside the runway as the C-47 braked and turned onto a parking ramp.

Lemay stepped from the C-47, a well-worn Army B-4 clothes bag in hand. He made his way to a waiting jeep, climbed into it and drove away. Moments later, he pulled up in front of one of the tents, and quickly got out of the jeep.

Colonel Chip Overacker rose from his desk to greet Lemay, extending his hand.

"Welcome back to the 306th, Colonel," Overacker said.

"Where…uh…where is it?"

Colonel Overacker grinned and pointed to a steel file cabinet. Why, it's all right there…paper!"

Colonel Overacker motioned Lemay to a chair as he sat down.

"Drink?" Colonel Overacker asked. He lifted a bottle from his desk drawer.

"No," Lemay said.

Colonel Overacker placed the bottle back in the drawer. "Before you've finished here, you'll welcome one occasionally." He glanced at an open file on his desk. "Well Curt, they've hustled you around a bit since Pearl… Westover to Pendleton with the 34th Bomb Group." He looked up at Lemay. "The big West Coast invasion scary up there?

Lemay nodded.

Colonel Overacker looked at the folder again. "Accelerated service test on B-24s out at Wright Field…back to Pendleton…and now here as Group Exec! All in a couple of months."

Lemay grinned slightly. "War Department's got a bad case of the jitters."

"Their judgment hasn't been too accurate recently." Colonel Overacker paused. "How'd you get involved in B-24 service Test?"

"I flew one of the first B-24s delivered from the factory." Lemay smiled at the memory. "As a matter of fact, the second time I flew the beast, I flew it all the way across the North Atlantic."

"Ferry?"

"Passengers...British and American Diplomats…businessmen on Government assignment. I even had Lady Halifax on board. No toilets… pretty primitive accommodations. When we landed in Prestwick, she came up and complimented me on the flight, told me I'd done quite well for my second time behind the controls of a B-24."

Colonel Overacker laughed. "She knew!"

"They all did." Lemay said. "I was the only one scared, I guess. Well I'd like to go over the aircraft availability projections… training programs, that's, with your permission of course."

"You've it, Colonel, But…projections? Training programs? The pilots coming into this outfit are coming straight out of single engine training. Most of them have never even seen a B-17."

"What about airplanes?" Lemay asked.

"We've been promised a couple of 17s by the end of the month," the Colonel said.

"It looks as if we're a little like Boy Scouts, trying to build a fire without matches." Lemay said.

Colonel Overacker nodded affirmatively and got up from his worn out chair. "Well, with all eight battleships in the Pacific Fleet still out there on the bottom of Pearl Harbor, the Prince of Wales and that other British battleship sunk off Singapore, it must be pretty clear to everyone by now that battleships aren't our first line of defense any longer. The way I see it, we're. Funny thing about the Boy Scouts, you know. They just keep rubbing those sticks together and pretty soon…" Overacker snapped his fingers. "Sergeant," he yelled as he turned to Lemay. "I've called a Staff meeting for 1600. Give you a chance to get acquainted."

Lemay nodded. "What about living quarters? "Great choices. A tent or the State Line Hotel. Your family coming out?"

Lemay nodded affirmatively.

The jeep driver entered the room.

"Show Colonel Lemay to his tent, Sergeant."

"Yes Sir," The sergeant said.

Colonel Overacker extended his hand to Lemay. "Let me know if you need anything."

Lemay nodded, shook hands with Overacker, and then left with the driver. Colonel Overacker gazed after Lemay as he walked away, somberly.

Two Army trucks pulled up alongside the tent area, and soldiers began spilling out of the trucks and forming up in mildly undisciplined rowdiness. Lemay watched the incoming troops, still in front of Colonel Overacker's tent.

"Who are they?" Lemay asked the driver.

"Gunners. Coming up from Fort Sill, I think."

Lemay walked to the small troop formation, and spoke to one of the privates casually.

"What's your MOS Private?" Lemay asked

The private saluted. "Gunnery, Sir."

"Gunnery school?"

"Oh no, Sir!" He gestured towards the rest of the troop. "We just finished basic last week, Sir!"

Lemay gazed at the private for a long moment as he slowly turned back to the driver who was waiting in the jeep.

CHAPTER 32

Lemay and Colonel Overacker watched as a USAAF C-47 touched down and rolled out. The nose of the C-47 pulled up, its nose dipping with the braking action, and then the engines wound down. General Olds dropped down from the airplane and headed straight towards Lemay and Overacker.

General Olds offered his hand after exchanging salutes, and they shook hands.

"Curt...Chip. Well, according to the reports, you fellows have done quite a job out here with two airplanes." They all began to walk to a jeep parked nearby. "At least you've got your pilots where they can get up and down without killing themselves."

"What about our bombardiers...navigators, General?" Lemay asked.

"Doing the best we can Curt," General Olds said. "They're beginning to come out of the training schools but they're green as hell. Most of them have never even seen a B-17 or a Keystone," he said as they got into the vehicle.

"Chip, I'd like to have a few minutes with Lemay if you don't mind."

Colonel Overacker started the jeep. "Not at all, Sir,"

Lemay and General Olds walked away.

Lemay and General Olds entered Lemay's tent office at Wendover Field and General Bob Olds removed his cap and seated himself while Lemay sat down at his desk.

"Curt, we're transferring you up to the 305th at Salt Lake. We're making you the Group Commander up there," the general said.

"What's their strength?" Lemay asked.

"Same as here - mostly a paper outfit right now," The General said. He settled back in the chair. "The War Department's jittery about the possibility of a Japanese invasion of our West Coast. So we're going to equip the 305th as best as we can. You'll get whatever we can find to loan you on a temporary expediency basis. We'll be moving you up to Geiger Field at Spokane in a few weeks. You'll continue whatever training programs they may have underway out there in Salt Lake until we find the additional airplanes to loan your outfit."

"Group strength? B-17s?" Lemay asked.

"Nobody's at group strength now, Curt. Certainly not with the B-17's. There'll be some B and F models soon. We'll have to return all the airplanes assigned to you on temporary expediency." He paused. "When the invasion scare dies down a little, you'll probably come back to Murdock for whatever time there's left before going overseas."

"Europe, Eighth Air Force?" Lemay asked

"That's the way it stands now, "General Olds said. The time, of course, is all geared to B-17 availability. You'll turn in your old aircraft at Nuroc and pick up new ones somewhere on the East Coast just before your departure.

We're sure as hell going to be a rag-tag outfit, General," Lemay said.

"We'll train purposefully without airplanes... bombardiers... navigators... gunners. I think everybody understands the problem. Some training will have to be accomplished over there...especially the advanced formation work." The General grinned. "Oh...By the way Curt you've been promoted to full Colonel."

Lemay laughed incredulously.

"What's the matter?"

"It's just that I was a Second Lieutenant for seven years now I've gone from Captain to full Colonel in sixteen months."

"It's happening all over...particularly to the old Second Bombardment Group. You people are the backbone of heavy bombardment today, you know. Too bad there were only a handful of us. Frank Andrews is back from oblivion. He had been reduced to a Colonel at one time by the old Guard up at the War Department you know," General Olds said. "He s a Lieutenant General now, headed for England." He sighed. "I've got the Air Command and God how I wish it were a combat command. But...they say training administrators are necessary in this business."

"I learned more from you in thirty days than I'd learned the entire twelve years I'd been in the Air Corps previously, General," Lemay said. "That operation job out there at Langley was a real eye opener. I was brand new at it, a real novice." He shook his head. "I'll never forget the first morning that you came in after I had taken over."

"Lemay, what's the weather out in San Antonio?"

"Hell, I don't know. San Antonio's twelve hundred miles away."

"You should know. A B-17 can fly that far! What if we had to schedule a mission to San Antonio this morning?"

"You scorched my tail pretty good, you know. Never made that mistake again."

General Olds said, "I knew the weather within a fifteen hundred mile radius of Langley Field every morning before seven o'clock and the status of every airplane in the Second Bombardment Group."

The General stood up to leave. "Curt... I... I think it's important that you be made aware of a high level disagreement up in the War Department on the conduct of the War. Some people up there want to scrap the combined Chiefs' RAINBOW-5 plan for a European offensive and concentrate our total War effort in the Pacific instead. If that should happen, then everything I've told you would change, of course." He extended his hand. "Well... No need for you to see me out. I can find Chip's quarters. Good luck Curt."

"Thank you, Sir," Lemay said.

CHAPTER 33

The Boeing B-29 Super Fortress filled the blue sky, and the inherent beauty of the aircraft was heightened by a lyrical sequence of gentle turns.

The command pilot, Eddy Allen, was seated at the controls, grinning broadly, obviously pleased with the control response and handling characteristics of the mammoth bomber.

"Boeing B-29... this is Renton Control ... over."

"Renton Control... this is Boeing B-29 test," Eddy Allen said.

A group of men, obviously Boeing engineers, technicians and executives, stood by a mobile control unit, all of them gazing upward at the B-29.

The chief engineer, Ed Wells, grinned triumphantly. "The chase plane's going to make one more photographic pass under you Eddy and then we want you to bring her in, okay?"

The chase plane flew alongside the B-29. The B-29, in a gentle turn, leveled out.

"Understood, Renton Control," Eddy Allen said.

"Those turns, Eddy... do they feel as smooth as they look?" Ed Wells asked.

"Smooth as silk, Ed... control responses are really clean... no rambling vibrations nothing... just like a magic carpet."

Then came the key question that Wells almost afraid to ask. All eyes were now glued on Wells. "The…uh... the predicted stability curves, Eddy... what's your feel there?"

"Well, Ed... pitch and roll... they... they feel real good. May be a little bit more than we'd expected ... but I ... " Eddy Allen paused again. "I don't sense any major stability problems at all."

A collective and exuberant cheer emanated from the group gathered around the Mobile Control Unit.

"Excellent, Eddy… excellent!" Ed Wells said

Several of the engineers shook hands with each other, then with Wells. After a few moments of this, Wells continued the radio transmission.

"We'll be interested in alignment characteristics on final, Eddy. Give us your reactions as often as you can."

"Understood, Renton Control."

The B-29 began to turn into final approach in the distance. The B-25 chase plane, tiny in comparison, remained alongside the B-29 and the mobile control group watched both aircrafts closely.

"Renton control... We're lining up on final…" Eddy Allen said.

Tension appeared on the faces of the group as they gazed out at the runway that stretched out away in the distance and watched the final approach. Eddy Allen made the necessary control corrections and then lined up with the runway.

"Looks like she wants to drift a little, Ed," Eddy Allen said. "Nothing serious, just a little bit difficult to hold alignment, that's all."

"That's great... you're looking good Eddy, real good," Wells said.

After the B-29 landed, the mobile control personnel began to cheer, exchanging back slaps and handshakes, all in sheer exultation. Eddy Allen dropped to the ramp, only to find himself besieged by the Boeing executives and engineers.

"She flies!!" he said.

The President of Boeing and Ed Wells watched Eddy Allen being congratulated and both of them grinned broadly.

"This calls for a celebration, Ed," the president of Boeing said. "I'd like all of you over at the main conference room for champagne after you've finished the debriefing." He looked at Ed Wells with deep respect, and then continued. "You and your people have really pulled one off here you know." He looked at the group assembled there. "I only wish the entire nation could share this with you. I know they'd be as proud as I'm."

The president of Boeing grasped Ed Wells' shoulder in a spontaneous gesture of gratitude, then crossed to a waiting chauffeur-driven car, as Ed Wells looked after him. The Boeing executive closed the door made a thumb up gesture to Wells accompanied by a smile and a wave as he left.

Inside a hanger type briefing room at Boeing, Ed Wells stood at the podium.

"Well... I guess that's about it gentlemen," he said.

Wells stood in front of a large board which bore a mass of technical expressions -- both literal and numeral -- chalked across its surface. Eddy Allen sat informally -- behind a scarred conference type table which stood immediately in front of the blackboard. He listened to Wells as he addressed the collective engineering group.

Ed Wells stood with a piece of chalk in his hand."...Assuming there are no further questions..."

Many Boeing engineers were seated with various kinds of manuals and note books on the small desk tops before them. There was no response from the group.

"Very well then," Ed Wells said. "The... the second test flight will be scheduled just as soon as the ground inspections are completed a assuming, of course, we don't encounter anything serious there." He put the chalk down and wiped his hands on handkerchief. "Gentlemen, I needn't remind you that time is of the essence."

He sat down next to Eddy Allen and continued.

"The Renton Plant here has already begun fabricating sub-assemblies - with the main assembly lines staffed and waiting. Our plant in Wichita is equipped, the inventory of raw material completed and... they're fully staffed with manpower. Marietta is equipped and receiving raw materials... with manpower allocations nearly completed. Construction on the Omaha facility is complete. They're setting machine tools out there now. Since they're all waiting on us now, it's imperative that engineering changes resulting from these initial test flights be processed into approved EOs and integrated into the master production line blue prints as expediently as possible. The next three or four flights should give us a pattern of what to expect." Ed Wells grinned broadly. "But... at this point, gentlemen, I think it pretty safe to assume according to preliminary indications..." he gestured towards the blackboard. "We've exceeded the original Air Corps Specs – ACROSS THE BOARD!!"

Spontaneous applause broke out among those present and Ed Wells stood up and continued.

"The president of the company has invited all of us to a brief celebration in the main conference room." The group rose and gathered their documents and note books.

"Eddy and I'll join you there shortly."

"Eddy, I'm afraid I've got to spring something on you that you aren't going to like," Ed Wells said. "We're putting your regular crew aside for the second test flight. All flight crew positions will be manned by the Engineering Department Heads themselves, eight of them in fact."

Eddy Allen paused and sighed. "You're right... I don't like it! For one thing, you're risking irreplaceable technical personnel."

"We trust your professionalism, Eddy... your ability to... to get us back alright. What's more... we trust the airplane." Wells took a deep breath, expelling it slowly, as he looked at Allen squarely in the eye.

"General Arnold, the Air Corps committees, the president of our company ...and... myself as well... we're all aware of the risk involved. But if we can get the engineering staff into a position to observe and record information first hand, then we'll save precious weeks of communication time in achieving whatever engineering changes are found to be necessary from these initial test flights."

"But, Ed... as an experienced test pilot... I'm…"

Ed Wells interrupted. "Eddy, try to understand my position. Because of the developments in the Pacific and the Far East, this airplane has become absolutely critical to the successful conduct of the War out there. IT MUST be developed and delivered... ON TIME !"

"What other choices do I have?" Eddy Allen asked

"None, I guess. You can count on my cooperation," Ed Wells sighed. "I guess I already knew that, Eddy."

Eddy Allen grinned wryly as they both rose and walked out of the room.

Eddy Allen and Ed Wells entered the typical, mahogany paneled conference room, where all eyes became focused on them, and then, without cue, everybody raised their glasses in salute, and began to sing: *"For they're jolly good fellows,"* as glasses of champagne were handed to Wells and Allen, who joined the group in a collective toast as the song lyrics were completed.

CHAPTER 34

Lemay pulled up to the base in Syracuse, New York in a jeep, stepped out of the vehicle and walked into the headquarters building. He walked into an office complex, obviously headed for an adjacent office. A group staff sergeant stopped him.

"Colonel Anderson's up here from Washington, Colonel Lemay, and is waiting in the Ops Office, there." He gestured towards the temporary 305th Ops Office in the adjacent room.

Lemay nodded and headed towards the temporary 305th Operations Office and walked inside where he found Colonel Fred Anderson sitting and talking with the 305th Ops Officer, Lieutenant Colonel John DeRussey.

Colonel Anderson looked up at Lemay as he entered the room, then he stood up. "Curt! The Sergeant said you'd be along shortly." He shook hands with Lemay. "Thought I'd wait in here with Colonel DeRussey." He searched Lemay's somber features.

Lemay sat down and Colonel Anderson did the same.

"How about you?" Lemay asked. "Still Deputy Director over at Bombardment?"

"No. Matter of fact, I'm assigned to General Arnold's office now,' Colonel Anderson said.

Lemay smiled. "Can't get much closer to the heart of things than that."

"Too close, sometimes," Colonel Anderson paused for a moment. "Curt, General Kinney's screaming for more Heavy Bombardment Groups out in the Pacific."

"Who isn't?" Lemay asked

"It's a little closer to home than that Curt. They… they're about to divert the 305th out there. They're ignoring the heavy losses the first groups are encountering in Europe. I understand they're sustaining between twenty and forty percent combat losses. The training was insufficient and the current tactics are inconsistent with the German fighters and anti aircraft tactics being used. We're needed most in England, not the Pacific."

Lemay rose from his chair abruptly, gazing incredulously at Colonel Anderson. He went to the window, looked out for a moment, and then turned back to Colonel Anderson. "That doesn't make sense, Fred. I have reports that the loss rate on the groups' already flying combat is three times higher than projected. Those are unacceptable loss rates. They can't sustain operations at that rate much longer. We need to get to England and help the effort. Don't they realize my ground echelon left Muroc a month ago? They've already sailed for England."

"It's the B-17s they need out there, Curt," The Colonel said. "You've got thirty-five of them, brand new, all of them sitting here in Syracuse. That's pretty damned tempting."

"If we're transferred out there under the circumstances, the 305th would cease to exist. Our planes... crews... they'd be used as replacements." Lemay turned back to the window and gazed out for a few moments. "Can you stall the decision Fred?"

"Maybe. I could try anyway," Colonel Anderson said.

"How long?" Lemay asked.

"A couple of days at the most."

Lemay turned from the window, walked to Colonel Anderson, who was standing now, and offered him his hand.

"Thanks Fred."

"I don't even want to know what you're thinking, Curt," Colonel Anderson said. "I've got business in New York, and should be back in Washington, tonight. I'll do what I can." He glanced at his wrist watch. "Time for lunch?"

"Rain check?" Lemay asked.

"Sure." The colonel grasped Lemay's shoulder briefly. "Good luck, Curt."

Lemay nodded as Anderson turned to Colonel DeRussey.

"Take care of him, John."

DeRussey gestured thumbs up. "Count on it, Colonel. And thanks."

Colonel Anderson left the office.

Lemay turned to DeRussey. "Can you get all of our flight crews assembled here by five o'clock this afternoon?"

"I think so, Colonel."

"Tell them to come packed and prepared to remain on base until further notice."

DeRussey nodded.

"Cancel all navigator and bombardier training flights that were scheduled for this afternoon," Lemay said and walked to the door. "I want you, Preston, Fulkrod and Cohen in my office as soon as possible."

Lemay exited and Colonel DeRussey gazed after him momentarily, and then picked up the telephone.

"Sergeant, get in here with a personnel roster, on the double!" DeRussey said.

"Yes, Sir."

The Sergeant hung up the phone abruptly, went to a temporary cardboard file case, extracted a folder and hurried into Colonel DeRussoy's office.

Lemay was sitting at his desk engaged in paper work when Captain Fulkrod, Captain Cohen and Major Preston filed into the room. He motioned them to chairs.

"What's up, Colonel?" Ben Fulkrod asked.

"How do we stand on the ball turret modification Ben?"

"Going pretty slow, Colonel, but we're nearly through," Fulkrod said. "With our own flight crews having to do the work it's... "

Lemay interrupted. "How about the airplanes themselves? They ready?"

"Ready for what, Colonel?"

"A North Atlantic crossing," Lemay said.

Ben Fulkrod grinned as he sensed the situation coming. "I think so,

Colonel."

How soon can you've the entire group serviced out and ready to go—the earliest possible time?" Lemay asked

"In the morning," Ben Fulkrod said.

"Then, do it!" Lemay said.

"What about the modification kits?"

"I thought I just heard you say they'd be finished tonight. I don't think I'm going to have time to make an installation inspection," Lemay said.

Yes Sir," Ben Fulkrod said. "I understand."

John DeRussey entered the office and sat down. "Our standing orders are to proceed to Prestwick as soon as we're ready to go. Unless we button up and get the hell out of here damned fast, going to end up in the Pacific with only half of our outfit," he said.

"We've still got two airplanes en route, Colonel." Major Preston said.

"That fills us up?" Lemay asked.

"Right, thirty five," Preston said

"When are they due in?"

"In the morning."

"John, can you be ready for departure by tomorrow morning?" Lemay asked.

"Yes," Colonel DeRussey said.

"Cohen?" Lemay asked

Captain Cohen nodded in the affirmative.

"Ben?"

"Yes, Sir," Ben Fulkrod said.

Lemay turned to Major Preston. "Assuming we receive the last two airplanes in the morning, Joe?"

"I'll be ready, Colonel."

"Then, let' s get the hell out of here, I want everybody working on each airplane, getting it ready to go, then moving on to the next."

"We'll be ready," Captain Cohen said.

The group got up to leave and Fulkrod paused, then turned to Lemay.

"By the way Colonel, there are some things I'd like to take along. Wing bushing reamers for instance. They're not on the regulation list, but we'll be changing a lot of wings over there. If we've to wait for the service command to do it, our 17s are going to be in the shop more than they're in the air."

"Take everything you can get your hands on Ben, whether it's on the regulation list or not! Tools, medicine, drugs - anything we may need!"

"My lathe?" Fulkrod asked

"Find room for it!"

Ben Fulkrod smiled. "Yes, Sir."

They left Lemay's office.

Two hours later, Lemay and Helen emerged from the hotel entrance, and Lemay tossed his baggage in the back of the jeep. Janie tagged behind with two bell boys who were carrying Lemay's foot locker. The bell boys placed the locker in the rear of the jeep, and then crossed back to the hotel entrance with Janie following happily. Moments later, Janie returned to Lemay and Helen, who were both visibly shaken.

Helen struggled to maintain her composure, wiping her eyes with the back of her hand, and speaking apologetically.

"I'm sorry, Curt, It just that I thought we had more time." She suddenly lost control and held Lemay closer. "Oh God, Curt! I may never see you again!"

Lemay held Helen close and stroked her hair, too overcome himself to speak.

Janie observed her mother's tears, and went to her, put her arms about her protectively and looked up at Lemay angrily.

"Why are you making Mommy cry?" Jane asked.

Lemay bent down to the perplexed Janie, clasped her close in his arms and kissed her. Then he got into the jeep and left. Helen gazed after him, the tears running down her cheeks.

"Goodbye, darling."

The aviator's tactical map of the Northern Hemisphere on the wall of the briefing room in Syracuse had everyone's attention. There was red tape outlining the 305 Group route of flight to England. Colonel DeRussey was winding up a briefing with the thirty five flight crews of the 305th. The flight crews themselves listened intently, not wanting to miss one little detail of the mission to Europe.

"I guess that's about it," Colonel DeRussey said. He looked around the room. "Any questions?"

The flight crews sat silently; contemplating the gravity of the briefing they'd just been given.

"Ten... shun!" an officer said.

The flight crews came to attention when Lemay strode up to the briefing Officer's podium. He turned to the group, his face more stern than normal, the partial paralysis giving it an unusually serious expression. He motioned the flight crews to take their seats,

"Well, this is it," he said. "Each crew will spend the rest of the evening checking their individual aircraft thoroughly. We've got extra maintenance people on the line to help you with any last minute problems that may show up. Takeoffs will begin at seven A.M. See you in Gander tomorrow evening. Good luck!"

Lemay walked off the podium.

The crews rose to depart, and a roar of excited conversation reverberated through the briefing-room. Lieutenant Walker and his co-pilot, Lieutenant Longmire, made their way toward the door.

Well, Old Iron Ass was eloquent as usual," Lieutenant Longmire said.

"What did you expect him to say?" Lieutenant Walker asked.

"How about have a wild night on the town, boys? It's my reward for three months at hard labor in the Muroc Compound!"

Lieutenant Walker looked at Lieutenant Longmire disdainfully. "Come on! What's with you? In the three months we were out at Muroc, we had exactly two weekends off! The guys from those other outfits out there went in every night!" He gestured towards Lemay. "You want to know something? I'll bet when he goes to the bathroom, it comes out cast iron!"

"Look, Ralph, at the risk of offending your overwhelming lust for females, you'd better be damned glad it's Lemay that's taking us into combat! You may live long enough to enjoy bedding down with a broad someday."

Lieutenant Longmire gazed at Lieutenant Walker darkly as he continued making his way to the door.

The first rays of the morning sun were seen in pastel relief on the horizon. One B-17 roared down the runway, lifted off, and then a second one did the same. Lemay sat in the pilot seat of the first B-17 with DeRussey as his co-pilot.

"Gear up," Lemay said.

"Gear up," DeRussey said as Lemay's B-17 flew into the sunrise.

CHAPTER 35

In High Wycombe, England, at the Eighth Air Force Headquarters in October 1942, a first lieutenant ripped a telex message from a teletype, gazed at it for a moment, then placed it with a previous message he held in his hand. He then walked to an inner office where the sign *Eighth Air Force Command Operations* was seen on the door.

The lieutenant went to a desk where an Air Force colonel sat busily engaged in paper work details on his desk. The lieutenant handed him the message.

"This came in about an hour ago, Colonel."

The colonel took the message and read it as a perplexed expression crossed his face.

"But I thought they'd been shunted out to General Kenney in the Pacific?" asked the colonel. He glanced at the lieutenant questioningly. "Have you confirmed this?"

"Yes, Sir," the lieutenant said. He began to read from the second telex message. "Thirty B-17s of the 305th had landed at Prestwick when this was sent out. One ship ditched off Gander. Crew made it out okay. They'll be picking up a new ship tomorrow. Another ship lost two engines on the way over. It landed somewhere up in Northern Scotland." He handed the colonel the second confirming telex. "That's the word from Ops up at Prestwick."

I'll be damned," the colonel said. He paused. "Well... you'd better get word to Lemay's ground echelon up at Grafton-Underwood. Their reassignment orders went out this morning,

"Yes, Sir," the lieutenant said and walked away.

The colonel rose from the desk, thought for a moment, undecided as to what he was going to do. He then left with a slight frown on his brow. He made his way through a maze of desks and clerical groupings to a hallway leading to what was once the dining area of the complex but was now identified as the main conference area. The strong stench of body odor and stale cigarettes smoke was repulsive to the colonel. Two armed and smartly uniformed MPs stood by the conference hall entrance, one on each side. As the colonel approached, one of the MPs moved slightly in a restraining gesture.

"Colonel, that Senate investigating committee's still in there. General Spaatz and General Baker both left word they're not to be disturbed. They don't seem like they're in a very good mood, Sir."

The colonel waved the telex happily. "This will improve their outlook!"

The colonel entered the conference area where General Spaatz was standing at the head of a long, scarred oak conference table with General Eaker seated to his left at the conference table. Three U.S. Senators sat across from General Eaker, one of them being the usually repugnant Senator Titus Clay.

A large flow chart outlining the mounting percentage of battle damage being sustained by the Eighth Air Force Heavy Bomber Command, and the attrition resulting from an inadequate flow of replacement equipment, men and material was located behind General Spaatz. Five Heavy Bomber Groups were depicted on the chart: the 91st, 303rd, 44th, 306th and 93rd. A large world map reached from ceiling to floor. The colonel paused unobtrusively as General Spaatz completed his statement in progress.

"…Furthermore, I'm not sure the Eighth Air Force can continue sustained operations here with our remaining combat units," General Spaatz said.

The Senators registered their bewilderment at General Spaatz's matter-of-fact statement.

General Spaatz continued. "Units that were to be initially assigned to us here are being sent to the Pacific and to North Africa. Even our replacement crews, equipment and service personnel are being diverted to those areas."

Senator Connally from Texas rose and went to the wall map, indicating the relevant areas as he spoke.

"General, are you suggesting that it would be better to allow the Nazi forces in North Africa to link up with the Japanese there just in order for you to continue to build up the Eighth Air Force here?" the Senator asked.

"No, Senator. Nothing like that," the General said. "The invasion of North Africa has obviously become a military necessity." He paused. "However, if we had entered the war with a larger nucleus of heavy bombers and trained crews, our Eighth Air Force strategic air offensive here in Great Britain would have already begun to reduce the German industrial output to the point Hitler would have had to begin pulling out of North Africa by now. He simply wouldn't have been able to supply his North African front and the Russian front also!"

"As it is, gentlemen, Sledgehammer and Round-Up, the proposed ground invasions of France and Germany that are being planned in lieu of our Strategic Air offensive…an offensive that was conceived and approved by the combined Chiefs in the Rainbow-5 and in Air Plans Division One... Those invasions will be infinitely more costly in ground forces and material... <u>if</u> they're undertaken before we've been able to achieve significant results in our Strategic Air offensive against German industrial and military targets."

"Churchill's working hard to pull the plug on the Sledgehammer Plan. Seems to feel it'll be too costly to justify its use simply as a diversionary tactic designed to draw Hitler's attention away from the Russian and African fronts. He wants to hit the 'soft underbelly' of the European continent, as he calls it Turkey...Greece... Italy. Joe Stalin's not too happy about that, of course."

"It seems to me you're placing an exaggerated importance on the Eighth Air Force potential here, General," Senator Thomas said. "For instance!" He indicated the relevant areas. "Why couldn't we put B-29s in North Africa and carry out a Strategic Air offensive from there?"

General Spaatz sighed. "The B-29 is still a long way from service Senator. Hitler could easily win on one… or both... fronts by that time!" He paused again. "I believe the British Isles are the only place available to us from which we can successfully launch a major strategic air offensive against German industry…an air offensive that will gain us superiority in the air over Europe. Without such air supremacy, the war with Germany might very well be lost!"

Senator Clay, who had sat by sullenly and quietly, now exploded. "That's highly imaginative, General! But then, you Air Force people have always been ridden with super egos. You've always thought you were the only military element that could win a war! Well… our soldiers can cross the Channel. They can invade and occupy. And that's what's being planned. Planned because you've failed to fly a single mission of any significance since you've been over here! Yet, you sit here and have the temerity to tell us you could win the whole damned shebang! Only you don't have planes. You don't have trained crews! You don't have maintenance! You don't have replacements! What do you have, Sir? I'll tell you? An undeserved huge ego!

Senator Thomas frowned when he heard Senator Clay's remarks.

"Senator, that's not necessary! Let's try to stay calm here!"

The colonel chose this moment to pass the telex to General Eaker.

"Excuse me, General I thought you'd want to see this," The Colonel said.

General Eaker took the telex, nodded to the colonel who then left the room.

General Eaker read the telex, a broad smile spreading across his features and then he passed the document to General Spaatz.

General Spaatz grinned. "Curt Lemay!" He turned to the Senators. "The 305th Heavy Bombardment Group just landed in Prestwick."

"Well, that will increase your strength, won't it, General?" The first Senator asked.

"Yes...but the 305th is a case in point, Senator. Lemay bombardiers, navigators; his gunners... they were all transferred from the training schools to Lemay only two or three weeks before the group's departure from the United States." General Eaker was careful to emphasis his words. "They've had no training at all as integrated crew members, capable of operating with precision and interdependence. Daylight, precision bombardment requires *months* of intense crew training and coordination. Worse, Lemay was obviously unable to practice flying in formation until he arrived at the point of embarkation *last week*! Before that he simply didn't have any airplanes to fly formations with."

He lowered his voice. "All that training and experience will have to be acquired here - some of it in actual combat!"

"Are the other units here in similar condition?" the Senator from Texas asked.

General Spaatz turned to the chart. "We have six heavy Bombardment Groups here… two that have been operational for a month or so. It'll take twelve, maybe *fifteen*, groups to begin an effective strategic bombardment of German industry, groups that are fully trained and operational, instead… two of our more experienced groups were transferred to Torch, North Africa a few weeks back.

"Then… you're saying the training and experimental phase of the Eighth Air Force operation here in England… it's going to be much longer than you'd expected?" Senator Connally asked.

"Our original mission here was the strategic bombardment of German industry and military targets. We were to be supported by ground elements... not act in support of them," General Spaatz said. "It's pretty obvious that the Eighth Air Force Mission is being pushed aside in favor of a surface oriented military strategy." General Spaatz sat in a chair and placed his hands on its back. "Well, gentlemen if you've no further questions, they're expecting you at Grafton-Underwood this afternoon to observe formation practice down there. Your car and military escort are waiting outside."

Senator Thomas stood up. "General Spaatz, I just want to thank you. It's been a most enlightening session here this morning."

General shook hands with each Senator. "I hope we've helped you understand the situation here a little more fully."

Senator Thomas paused as the others filed out, led by General Spaatz.

"By the way, General Eaker, I notice your combat damage percentage has gone up from eleven per cent to thirty seven point one percent… in three months." He indicated the chart. "Does your present replacement flow cover that attrition?"

"No, Sir. Our replacement flow was set at twenty percent per month by the War Department in July. In actuality, it's rarely exceeded ten per cent per month," General Eaker said.

The Senator contemplated the chart for a few moments and nodded his head as if some inner understanding has just passed through his mind. He shook hands with General Eaker.

"Well... Thank you, General."

The Senator walked to the door and the General gazed after him, shook his head ruefully, then left the room too.

That afternoon at the Air Control Tower in Grafton England, a U.S.A.A.F. Colonel was gazing aloft through a set of field glasses when he suddenly lowered the field glasses, looked at the three Senators who were all standing on the outer bridge of the control tower and handed the glasses to the second Senator.

"They're beginning to form up now, Senator," he said.

The Senator took the glasses and peered upward at the developing formation.

"How many ships?" The first Senator asked.

"Twelve." The colonel was cautious. "We haven't worked out a standard formation quite yet. Since the flight crews are inexperienced, we've got to maintain a fairly loose grouping."

Senator Clay frowned at the colonel. "The British don't seem to share your enthusiasm for the mighty B-17, Colonel. It seems they're asking for consolidated B-24s instead."

"Well…Senator, I'm not in a position to criticize our British colleagues. I doubt that we could use their Lancasters effectively without knowing all the lore behind them. It's my understanding however that they used the Lend-Lease B-17s… well… that they just didn't use the equipment properly, that's all."

"Then I suppose the equipment *was* used properly over St. Lille last month?" He gazed at the colonel acquisitively. "More than forty of our free French brethren were killed and many wounded in less than ten minutes of misguided bombings by B-17s. Seems the bombs fell everywhere but on the targets."

"Well, Sir, precision bombardment is an attainable objective. But it does require a certain level of experience in order to keep collateral damage to a minimum," the colonel said.

"Yes, colonel, but that excuse is becoming a bit overused by now," Senator Clay said.

A USAAF captain merged from the interior of the Control Tower, offered his field glasses to the colonel and pointed into the distance.

"I don't think they see each other, Sir."

The colonel looked upward through the binoculars.

"Who is it?"

The captain looked upward also. "We don't know yet."

"He's much too wide on his form up turn."

One B-17 was flying in a straight, level flight while the other seemed to ascend in a manner that would bring it up directly under the other.

Senator Clay was angered that his developing argument has been interrupted. "What's wrong?" he asked.

The colonel ignored Clay. "Get him on the radio!"

"They're trying, Sir," the Captain said.

"I asked you what was wrong, Colonel?" Senator Clay demanded.

"That lower pilot… he's turned too. Damn!" The Colonel said. He turned to the Captain desperately. "Can't we do something?"

Two B-17s, one ascending up under the other in a manner that disallowed either pilot visual awareness of the other, brought the ships very close together.

Inside the cockpit of the ascending B-17, the pilot tapped intently on the radio dial instrument.

"You sure you got the damned thing on the right channel?"

The co-pilot adjusted the radio. "Yeah, Channel two." He looked at the pilot and gestured hopelessly. "Nothing."

The underside of the upper B-17 fuselage suddenly appeared just beyond the right cockpit window, catching the co-pilot's attention.

"Look out!" The co-pilot screamed.

The lower ship rose into the under belly of the upper ship, propellers striking skin and flying off. Parts of both aircraft started falling.

The face of the co-pilot in the lower B-17 was frozen in terror. Smoke and flames started rushing by the right cockpit windows and the starboard gunner hatch.

"Oh, my God." He crossed himself hastily. "I love you, mother."

The two B-17s suddenly exploded in a bright red ball of flame with sections of their fuselages flying in all directions. The sound of sirens could suddenly be heard in the background.

The colonel, numbed by the tragedy moved with a sense of urgency to get to the crash site. "Show the Senators to the lounge, Captain," He said.

Senator Clay was momentarily subdued. "I'll come with…

"*No!*" He shouted, and then tried to get himself under control. "No, Senator." He gestured in the direction of the accident. "If I had been watching, instead of listening to you, I might have been able to prevent that. Now… please… just go with the Captain quietly."

The colonel moved away hurriedly and the captain gestured the Senator to the descending stairway. "Gentlemen," he said.

He showed the Senators into the modest lounge area that has been especially equipped for them.

The captain motioned to a table holding coffee and cakes, obviously prepared for the Senators. "There's coffee over there. If you need anything, anything at all."

"Thank you, captain. Thank you very much," The second Senator said.

"The colonel will be along." The Senator nodded his understanding and the captain hurriedly left. The Senators took coffee. At first they were silent, then the shock started to wear off and the reality of the situation became painfully clear.

The Senator from Utah sat down wearily. "It's obvious to me that we've made an intractable error in not putting our Air Force on parity with the other branches of the military services." He took a sip of coffee. "I'm afraid we've left it far too long under the indirect influence of surface commanders who have little - if any - feel for the unique and absolutely vital requirements of the technology of airpower."

Senator Clay sat down. "Utter nonsense, Senators." He drank

some coffee. "I've always maintained that the so called theory of strategic bombardment was unworkable and unacceptable." He snickered. "You've been hoodwinked, gentlemen, by the sly cleverness of two persuasive Generals… *professional airmen.*"

The other two Senators looked at Senator Clay with distaste.

Senator Clay continued. "The results here speak for themselves. By the time they're through, if indeed we allow them to continue on with this disaster, they'll fill Flanders Field anew - with innocent French victims this time."

"Flanders Field indeed, Titus!" Senator Connally shouted. "The fields here in England, not even a hostile land, may not be large enough to hold our own dead - valiant young Americans who have died and will continue to die *needlessly* because you and the opposition you led in the United States Congress deprived them of the equipment and training they needed to survive." He glared at Senator Clay. "Furthermore, the English Channel may not hold the countless young soldiers who will most probably die in a massive invasion that might have been nothing more than a bloodless occupation if we had equipped the Eighth Air Force to do the mission it was created to do."

"How dare you speak to me in such a disparaging manner?" Senator Clay retorted.

"I shall do more than that, Sir! I shall strive to have you removed from your committee duties in the United States Senate. In my opinion, Sir, you're a disgrace to all free people everywhere! You've been too long caught up in your own political designs and schemes to support your friends in the Army and Navy who stuck to their outmoded strategy as a tradition instead of adapting to what is needed to address the threat of the 1940s." He took a deep breath. "You once asked America's mothers not to stain their hands with the blood of American youth by allowing the extension of the draft law. I suggest you try to wash the blood from your own hands, Titus! But ... I'm afraid, Sir, you shall find them to be permanently stained."

Senator Clay rose abruptly, glared at the two Senators for a moment and then walked out of the lounge in angry strides.

Two military ambulances came to a stop at the side entrance of a small, frame hospital structure. Several doctors and nurses emerged as the drivers themselves went to the back of the vehicle. One by one, the covered bodies of the dead airmen were removed from the ambulances and taken inside. Senator Clay stood and observed the tragic action unfolding in front of him. He closed his eyes as if trying to shut the grim scene from his mind. He thought to himself in a way he hadn't done in years. Had he failed to be an objective and unbiased representative of his country or a puppet of a few self serving generals and admirals? The mental answer he came up with was even more painful than the accusation of his fellow Senator inside. He could feel the fire in his belly extinguish and the cold fog of shame came over him. He had become the very type of bureaucrat that he loathed and had come to Washington to get rid of. He dropped his head as he realized that it was time for him to go home.

A FEW BRAVE MEN

Book II

SCHWEINFURT, PICCADILLY LILY AND THE BLACK BART EXPRESS

CHAPTER 36

In October 1942 in Prestwick, Scotland, Curt Lemay received written orders for the 305th from a USAAF Colonel, the Prestwick Operations officer. Several civilian, British and U.S. pilot types were seen at the long operations counter, signing in and out, and receiving instructions from junior operations personnel. In addition, several other pilot types mingled in the dimly lighted areas of the Ops complex, talking, and reviewing their paperwork.

The Colonel reviewed Lemay's orders with him. "…You'll be staging at Grafton - Underwood, Colonel. Join up with your ground echelon there too." He looked up at Lemay. "They'll move you on down to Chevelston in a few days."

"Will that be our permanent base?"

The Colonel shook his head in the affirmative.

"Soon as you're ready." The Colonel handed the last of the papers to Lemay. "It's all there." He paused. "You'll begin departure no later than 8:00 A.M."

"Right," Lemay said.

"Good luck, Colonel Lemay."

As Lemay turned to leave, he caught sight of Colonel Frank Armstrong, who was standing in a group.

"Shades of Pee Wee Reese," Lemay said, If it' isn't Frank Armstrong!"

They shook hands. "Been a long time, Curt," Armstrong said.

"I thought you'd taken the 97th after Gouselad, and brought it over?" Lemay said.

"Yeah. But the 97th's been transferred to *Torch*…North Africa!"

"And you?" Lemay asked.

"Training command in the U.S." Colonel Armstrong said. He shrugged. "Guess they figure my 'extensive' combat experience will be useful back there."

Lemay contemplated Armstrong's remark, a sudden thought coming to his mind. "Say, Frank, my men are green as gourds." He paused. "If I can manage to get them together, would you... would you talk to them? " He looked Armstrong in the eye "You've been in actual combat - been shot at. Tell 'em how it feels... what to expect."

"Well... I..."

"We go back a long way, Frank."

"I..." Colonel Armstrong said

"Good. I'll have them in the mess hall," Lemay said. He glanced at his watch. "Say in half an hour?"

Lemay began to walk away leaving the perplexed Armstrong gazing after him.

A few minutes later there was a meeting called. Colonel Armstrong began to address the 305th flight personnel, who were seated informally.

"... And those last minutes from the IP to the aiming point... that's when they really let you've it. Don't have to worry about their fighters bothering you though. Flak's too damned heavy. It's like a black cloud spread out all around you."

The 305th pilots and co-pilots listened intently as they smoked and drank coffee.

Colonel Armstrong continued. "We've used evasive turns all the way in to the aiming point."

Lemay looked surprised.

"It affords the ground fire less opportunity for a hit." Armstrong said.

"Frank, are you saying you actually zig into the target those last few minutes," Lemay asked

"Yeah, Curt. SOP is to turn every ten seconds - all the way in. They'll pulverize you otherwise."

"What's the loss rate, Colonel?" A young pilot asked.

"I can't give you that figure. However, battle damage has reached something like thirty-seven percent." Colonel Armstrong said.

"Per month?" The pilot asked.

"That's right."

A general rumble of surprised reaction was heard in the room.

Lemay, Preston and DeRussey walked toward their quarters on the base after the meeting with Armstrong, Two B-17s enshrouded in the habitual fog could be seen ghost-like in the distance. Lemay was obviously deep in thought.

"Something wrong, Colonel? Major Preston asked.

"You know even J. B. Montgomery...or Kilpatrick for that matter - best bombardiers we had in the old Second Bomb Group - they couldn't measure drift - get the Norden adjusted for an accurate salvo in ten seconds. It takes six or seven minutes of absolutely level flight." Lemay grinned as he glanced at the others. "Given that time, though, they could literally drop a bomb in a pickle barrel from twenty-five thousand feet." Lemay suddenly changed the subject. "Joe, report to me the minute the last ship fueled and ready for departure… no matter how late."

"Right, Colonel," Major Preston said.

Lemay turned to Colonel DeRussey. "John, what's the latest word on the crew that ditched off Gander?

"Got a new ship. Should have already left there. They've reached their quarters now - half tent, half frame structures."

"Bad piece of luck there - old Ben Fulkrod being on that ship. We sure as hell need him," Lemay said

Well, at least he didn't lose his equipment," Colonel DeRussey said.

"Fulkrod's mobile machine shop, He brought it all you know," Major Preston said.

They all laughed.

"Well… everybody on the flight line at 6:00 A.M." Lemay said.

Lemay turned in to his tent.

"Good night, Colonel," DeRussey said.

CHAPTER 37

Over the English Channel in November 1942, eighteen B-17's formed up in the Lemay eighteen ship *Lead High Combat Box* formation. Lemay was seated in the cockpit of the first aircraft with a radio microphone in hand, directing the ships into position.

"Number six, move in to your right," Lemay said.

Number six responded to Lemay's order quickly.

"That's it. Now, just hold that position. Remember those positions - the overall formation," Lemay said

Inside Captain Walker's B-17, Lemay's voice was heard over the intercom.

"Allow loose grouping now. We'll tighten it up as we get more experience flying it. We're going to practice it until you can fly it in your sleep!" Lemay said.

"Practice," Longmire said. He looked out the cockpit window disgustedly. "That's all we've done… eat… sleep and practice!" He turned to Walker. "The English broads - I don't even know what they *look* like!"

Walker grinned. "The old man knows what he's doing."

I don't know. This damned formation he's come up with. It isn't SOP over here. How do we know it'll work? And, I hear we're going to start practicing "BLIND" takeoffs… even when the weather's clear."

The conversation was interrupted by Lemay continuing transmission, "This is our first mission gentlemen. Even though it's only a diversionary tactic for the main strike force, we're going to fly it like a regular bomb run." He continued to speak into the hand held mic. "The way I figure it, the formation we're flying should give all eighteen aircraft a clear field of fire against enemy fighters, give us the necessary maneuverability, and an unobstructed bomb salvo over the target area. Good luck!"

Lemay climbed down from the turret, and took a position between the pilot and co-pilot.

"We're coming up on the French Coast line, Colonel," The pilot said.

"Three minutes to turning point," The navigator said.

"Keep your eyes open! They sure as hell know we're up here by now." Lemay said. He looked at the pilot. "I'm going observe the turn from the waist gunner's position."

The Pilot nodded

The 305th formation droned on to its 180 degree turn over occupied France. Walker and Longmire were both tense as they scan the sky around them. Suddenly, small, black flak bursts appear beyond the cockpit window.

Walker turned to Longmire. "Guess that makes us veterans. We've been shot at."

"Yeah."

Suddenly a flak burst shook the aircraft violently.

"Pilot to waist gunner! Any damage back there?"

"Don't see any. Damned close though." The waist gunner said.

"You can say that again!" Walker said.

Inside the lead B-17, the pilot, John DeRussey glanced at his watch.

"Let go home," DeRussey said.

"Think this outfit can make a hundred eighty degree turn?" The co-pilot asked

"We're about to find out," Colonel DeRussey said. "He spoke into the microphone. "Blue Sky Baker, Charlie… this is Blue Sky leader. Execute One Eddie Zebra right on command; repeat: One Eddie Zebra right on my command."

"Baker, Charlie… acknowledge."

The pilot of one of the B-17s, Captain Ron Miller responded to a previous radio command as he looked at the other B-17s to his left and then to his right.

"Blue Sky Baker to Blue Sky Leader… One Eddie Zebra right… on command," Captain Miller said.

In another B-17, the command pilot Captain Del Humphrey responded to the same radio command. Several B-17s were seen in formation beyond the cockpit window.

"Blue Sky Charlie to Blue Sky Lead... One Eddie Zebra right on command," Captain Humphrey said.

Colonel studied his wrist watch. "Six... five... four... three... two... one *execute*!"

The lead three B-17s of the 365th Squadron, now entered the 180 degree turn and the outside ship began to lose position rapidly. Lemay, was in the waist gunner position looking out and down on the turning formation.

"Where the hell you going down there, Charlie Three? If we had enemy fighters up here, you'd get your ass shot off," Lemay said. He shook his head resignedly.

Captain Humphrey gazed at his wingman, banked in a turn too steep and dangerously close.

"Look out Baker Six! You're too damned tight on your turn," Captain Humphrey said.

The B-17 responded and decreased its bank.

Captain Humphrey turned to the co-pilot. "Damn near clobbered us!"

Lemay gazed out on the debacle before him and simply shook his head. He left the waist gunner's position and emerged to stand between the pilots. Colonel Debussey gestured toward the control column, with a silent, questioning look at Lemay.

Lemay nodded vaguely. DeRussey eased out of the command seat as Lemay took over.

"Even if we *could* fly a perfect formation our bombing accuracy wouldn't be worth a damn," Lemay said.

"Evasive turns?" Colonel DeRussey asked.

"Yeah," Lemay said.

Colonel DeRussey frowned. "But, the alternative, Colonel...the increased element of risk..."

Lemay was firm. “It’s to be straight in - even minutes of level flight right in to the aiming point.” He thought for moment. “Boys up at *Pinetree* ought to know that too.”

The co-pilot, sensed growing tension between DeRussey and Lemay, and attempted to lighten the moment.

“You hear what happened when the Americans first moved in up there at High Wycombe?” The co-pilot asked

Both Lemay and DeRussey glanced at the co-pilot.

The co-pilot continued. “I understand that it was an exclusive girl’s school before the Eighth Air Force took it over. First night the staff officers moved into those old dormitory rooms, electric bells started going off all over the place. General Spaatz himself got up to investigate. Found every room had an electric bell button with an engraved card fastened to the wall below that read. “*Please ring bell twice should it become necessary to summon mistress.*”

Lemay grinned. “Well… we could ring a million bells out here I’m afraid, and get the same results. No experienced mistresses around,” he said as the waters of the English Channel below the 305th lead B-17 were noticed by Lemay and he relaxed in the pilot’s seat. “There had to be a change of tactics if they were to be effective and keep aircraft losses to a minimum,” he thought.

Eighty miles to the south of Lemay’s decoy mission, two groups flew in traditional formation approaching LeHarre, utilizing the evasive maneuvers that had become standard practice in the Bomber Command. The pilot of the lead bomber could see the German fighters peel off from their position two thousand feet higher than the B-17’s.

“Here they come!” The flight leader reported over the command channel. The ME-109’s made diving runs on the typical “V Type” formation. Despite the evasive maneuvers, the B-17s were easy targets. The voices of the gunners were loud and showed the fear that they felt.

“Bombardier to pilot, IP in thirty seconds,” came the call of the lead bombardier. “Heading will be 092 degrees from the IP.”

“Roger bombardier. IP in thirty with an outbound of zero niner two,” the pilot replied as he ducked when he saw the orange tracers heading towards his aircraft from his left wingman. “Number two, shoot at the god damned

German, not me!"

"Sorry, but the bastard came right between us," responded the pilot of number two. That was a problem of flying a formation where all aircraft were bunched up together at the same altitude.

"They got number six and twelve. Blew them out of the sky," came a radio call over the command net. "There goes two from the high squadron."

"IP, start your turn," announced the bombardier. Eight miles to target."

"Roger," replied the pilot as he made his turn. He straightened the aircraft on the assigned 092 degree course and started his evasive maneuvers. He looked out at the other aircraft on both sides. He yelled out to the bomber on his right, "Tighten it up or the fighters will eat us alive!"

Just then a German fighter put a burst of 20mm fire into the bird on the right. It started to smoke from both left side engines. It fell back from its slot due to loss of power. It fell out of formation only to be fatally attacked by two fighters.

The tail gunner reported three more bombers falling out of formation on fire. He also reported "Fighters are breaking off attack."

The pilot acknowledged, "Yeah, flak is starting ahead of us. Tighten it up so we hit the same target this time."

All the aircraft went up and down and side to side in a futile attempt to avoid the flak. Meanwhile, the bombardier desperately tried to get a steady point on the target through the Norden bombsight. He found it to be difficult. Add to the problems caused by the maneuvers was the turbulence caused by the flak.

"Bomb bay doors open," called out the bombardier. "Bombs away, closing Bomb bay doors." "Pilot to tail gunner," said the pilot over the intercom. "What's the bomb pattern look like." "Sir, it's all over the place, maybe a dozen bombs hit the target. The high squadron hit the wrong target."

The co-pilot saw flak exploding in front of the formation; the aircraft was jarred with tremendous force. It started to turn hard over on its right side. Why so hard a turn, he thought. Then he heard the pilot command "Abandon ship…bail out. Now!" Fear gripped him as he got out of his seat and followed the pilot to the open gunner's window to jump out.

"Why, what happened?" he again asked himself as one by one the crew jumped from the aircraft. Then he saw why. The right wing had been blown off between the number three and four engine. They only had one effective wing. He got to the opening and was being told by the pilot to jump. He started to climb through the opening when a force of white hot heat blew him away from the opening and everything went black.

The number four aircraft assumed the lead as the command ship exploded in a fireball caused by a direct hit. The pilot thought of the terror the crew must have felt before they died. First the loss of the outer half of the right wing, then the direct hit. At least six crewmen bailed out before they bought the farm.

"Okay, high and low squadrons form up on me," commanded the new lead aircraft. There are only fourteen of us left to get home." The new leader thought of the situation. Only fourteen B-17's out of 36 survived the mission, he thought with a sad attitude. Add to that, they only hit part of the target. Not much damage at that. Something had to change.

CHAPTER 38

A briefing officer at the High Wycombe conference room briefed wing and group commanders seated at the conference table, among them Colonel Lemay. The room was hot and stuffy, which made the tension even worse than usual.

"Technically phrased gentlemen, we're still in the *support* business."

"We've been ordered to concentrate our entire bombardment effort on the German submarine pens here at Brest," the staff officer said. He indicated the positions on the large wall map. "Lorrieent... St. Nazaire... and La Pallice. The U Boat operations from those bases are playing hell with the flow of supplies and equipment coming out of the South of England...South Hampton... Portsmouth ... Plymouth and moving along the sea lanes that supply the Allied invasion forces in North Africa." He turned away from the map and addressed the group directly. "When Eisenhower was given command down there, he apparently persuaded Marshall, Arnold and the War Department to put our strategic bomber offensive aside and concentrate on supporting his surface invasion."

"And that's the way it'll always be as long as we're subordinate to ground commanders," a wing commander said.

"I know, it's a familiar story," the staff officer said. "But, if the song writers are right, every cloud has a silver lining. We believe General Arnold may have been looking more toward that silver lining than the immediate cloud cover itself." He gazed around the group with a wry grin across his lips. "There have been no plans developed for the Heavy Bombardment Groups and equipment assigned to *Torch* after that operation is concluded! And, all of those airplanes and crews will still be in the *European Theater!* We could still prove the feasibility of high altitude, daylight precision bombardment."

"I don't know, Churchill's made it clear he's disenchanted with our efforts at daylight precision bombardment. Wants us to go to night saturation bombardment alongside the RAF," General Kuter said. "He's using some of the early high battle losses to support his position."

"Gentlemen, the Staff Artillery Officer is going to give you a general appraisal of the coastal defense batteries that surround these target areas," the staff officer said

The Staff Artillery Officer began to rise. General Kuter and Colonel Lemay, both carrying briefcases, emerged from the conference, and crossed through the clerical grouping as they made their way to the front of the structure.

"Curt, what's your feel for the 305th's combat readiness?" General Kuter asked.

"Well, we could be a top notch fighting force - in about four years!" Lemay said. He looked at Kuter and grinned. "Meanwhile, I guess we're about as combat ready as any of the other groups over here."

"This Group Stagger formation you've come up with... I'm thinking about making it standard throughout the wing. Should afford opportunity for perfect bombing results as well as group aggregation for defensive purposes," General Kutter said. He paused for a moment and thought as they continued to walk. "I understand you're in opposition to using evasive action during final target approach."

"In my opinion, it negates the entire concept of precision bombardment," Lemay said, "The Le Harre mission is a perfect example."

They reached the foyer, where they both paused. General Kuter extended his hand.

"Well, I'm putting your group on the combat ready list, Curt. Good luck."

"Thanks. The men will be glad to hear that."

General Kuter walked away and left the building. Lemay departed as well and quickly went to the command operations area. A staff Lieutenant

Colonel was seated at a desk behind a small counter arrangement. The Colonel stood up and handed Lemay a manila folder and stack of black and white photographs.

"Here are the strike photos and the strike records, Colonel."

Lemay took the material. "Thank you."

Lemay sat down at an empty desk and began to examine the records and the photographs. He pondered the records before him while the Lieutenant Colonel continued to be busily engaged with paperwork at his desk.

"Colonel," Lemay called.

The Colonel looked up, then got up and walked to the counter area where Lemay stood up, the strike records opened before him and a photograph in his hand.

The strike record here… mission number fourteen… 9 October. Flown against Lille."

"Yes, Sir?" the Colonel said.

"The record shows that a number of five hundred pound GPs were released over the target." Lemay indicated the relevant photograph. "The photos here account for only about half that number. Any idea where the others fell?"

"No, Colonel. The target damage assessments are all in the strike records there."

Lemay nodded his head, pushed the file materials across the counter, and then exited.

The staff officer gazed after him with puzzled annoyance.

Lemay lay in his bed, his hands clasped behind his head as he gazed up at the ceiling. He got out of the bed, went to the window and pulled the curtain closed, then flipped the lights on, crossed to a foot locker at the end of the bed, opened it and rummaged around until he located a large, hard bound military book.

Lemay slipped a sweater over his pajamas, secured a pencil and writing pad from his desk, then went back to the bed, propped himself up against the pillows and he opened the book. He looked down at the book before him titled: *Field Artillery: Ballistics* and began to make calculations on the pad. He gazed at a clock by the bedside that read ten P.M. The next time he looked it read three A.M. Lemay closed the book, laid the writing pad aside, and then laid back down against the pillows reflectively.

The next morning a Staff Sergeant rapidly approached Lemay's office door, a folded communiqué clasped in his hand. The Sergeant paused, knocked lightly, and then entered. Lemay was seated at his desk with Major Preston standing nearby.

The Sergeant handed Lemay a folded document "Just came down, Sir."

Lemay perused the document momentarily, then got from his seat and passed it to Major Preston.

"Get the staff, the Squadron Leaders and the Group Bombardment Officer in here," Lemay said.

"Yes, Sir," The staff sergeant said and left the office.

"St. Nazaire!" Major Preston said and waved the field order. "At least we're getting a standard three paragraph Field Order… with Strike information where it's supposed to be. Beats the six page narratives we got for our diversionary missions."

Lemay went to the window and looked outside. "I went up there and showed 'em how. Turned out, nobody on staff had ever been instructed in the preparation of a field order."

"Incredible," Major Preston said.

"Most of them up there, they're in the same boat we're in… brand new at the job," Lemay said. Their hearts are in the right place. They just don't know how to do the job. Civilian soldiers!"

Colonel DeRussey, Cohen, Fulkrod, Major Malec, the Group Bombardier, and the Squadron leaders, Humphrey, Miller and Dorsey entered the office. Major Preston passed the field order to DeRussey.

"Gentlemen, we're about to fly our first mission with a bomb load," Lemay said. He turned from the window his hands clasped behind his back.

"I've been doing some research... ballistics... and... I've made a decision. It may not be the most popular one around but we're going to do it anyway."

"Straight-in target approach?" Colonel DeRussey said.

"That's right," Lemay said. "Seven minutes... on autopilot!

"It'll be suicide, Colonel Lemay!" DeRussey said. "Colonel Armstrong made that clear up there at Prestwick! As well as the others over here who have flown combat missions."

Lemay spoke softly. "Frank Armstrong was an attack man; never assigned to a bombardment operation until he relieved Colonel Couseland in the Ninety-Seventh! Matter of fact, Couseland's the only real bombardment man they had over here so far." He looked back out the window. "We going to have to get our heads out of the clouds and realize what we're up against. I've got to make decisions. The American taxpayers pay me $372.00 a month to make these difficult decisions. That's a commander's job. If I pull in my horns when a tough decision has to be made, then I'm not worth a damn to anybody. And, I've got to live with the results of that decision, good, bad or indifferent!"

"I say if we're going pay the price for admission, then I think we ought to get results! Precision results! Recorded results! That's what daylight precision bombing's all about... destroy the military and industrial targets with a minimum of collateral damage to the civilian population and properties. Now, Malec and I both have examined the bombing records of the twenty-two missions that been flown over here so far! They show only about half of the bombs accounted for... not too many of those hitting the actual target. Those twenty-two missions flown by the other groups cost a lot of American lives and did very little damage. We can't win this war like we're going. Yes, I know that there are always losses in combat but we've an obligation to those who give their lives to this effort to make their sacrifice mean something."

Malec listened intently to Lemay, who continued.

"You just can't process the Norden bomb sight - figure drift and crank the necessary calculations into the Nordon in ten seconds."

Colonel DeRussey frowned. "We could lose the whole group, Colonel.

Lemay looked at DeRussey sharply, ignored the comment as he turned to Malec.

"Major Malec, I want all the bombardiers assembled in the briefing room at 1900 hours.

"Yes, Sir," Major Malec said.

"Ben, what are you going to have on the line in the morning?" Lemay asked.

"At least twenty airplanes, Colonel," Major Fulkrod said.

Lemay grinned. "I'll lay you odds that will be twice as many as the other groups will put up tomorrow. Glad we didn't lose you and your mobile machine shop back there at Gander, Ben."

"Thank you Sir. This St. Nazaire mission - nice way to celebrate your thirty-sixth birthday, Colonel… a day or so late but…"

Lemay thought for a moment. "I just hope a celebration's in order when we get back tomorrow." He glanced at the others. "By the way, gentlemen, I think it'd be best for me to break the news about the straight-in approach. Okay, let's get ready for tomorrow."

The officers saluted and walked out of the room as Lemay turned back to gaze somberly out the window.

CHAPTER 39

The Group Operations officer stood in front of the map of Europe that depicted St. Nazaire as the group target. He indicated the appropriate positions on the map to some of the 305th crews, who stood listening to him.

"Our approach to the target area has been carefully plotted to avoid as much coastal artillery fire as possible." The briefing officer said. "But you can expect the defenses around St. Nazaire to be intense… both ground fire and enemy fighters."

"Ten-shun!" an officer said.

The crews came to attention as Lemay entered, and strode up to the speakers position, unsmiling. He paused as the crews sat back down.

"I've been studying current 'evasive action' over the target strategy. Eighth Air Force strike photos made during evasive action over the targets so far reveal that the bomb sights were pointing everywhere *but* the target areas. They can't be pointing to a target if they're being destabilized by maneuvering and flak bursts."

The assembled crewmen were a study in tense excitement. Lemay turned to a prepared chart and removed the cover from it.

"Using accepted theories of ballistics, I figure three hundred seventy two rounds from a ground battery would have to he fired to hit a rapidly moving target at twenty five thousand feet distance." He turned away from the chart and faced the audience "That's a lot of rounds to get off… even for battle-experienced German ground batteries. In fact, evasive turns in target approach actually increase the probability of being hit and decreases bombing accuracy."

Lemay looked around the group, and then delivered his punch line.

"Gentlemen, we'll be going straight from the IP to the AP today!!"

The crews began to rustle about incredulously, looking at one another in disbelief,

Lemay went on "After the turn at the initial point, I'll be on auto until the bomb load has been solved. *Everyone will drop on the lead ship.* The bombardiers have all been briefed on this procedure. Any questions?

"Colonel… the people who've been over there tell us that would be suicide!" A young pilot said.

"Do *you* think it will be?"

"Well… I don't, know, Sir."

"Neither do they. They've never tried it," Lemay said

"Yes, Sir," The pilot said as he sat back down .

Lemay's voice rose. "We cried about our lack of equipment… training… the raw deal the Air Force has been handed!" The crew members were numb with shock. "Well… that's over. We're not going to use that crutch any longer! We came over here to do a job of strategic bombardment on German industrial and military targets… and… we're going to do it! You can forget about the English broads… the pubs! You're going to be practicing formation flying… precision bombing… blind takeoffs and navigation. We'll practice until you can do all of that in your sleep! Any questions?"

The crews remained silent.

"Ten-shun!" John DeRussey said.

The flight crews burst into a din of angry conversation as they began leaving the mess hall.

"And I was just beginning to believe that son knew what he was doing," Longmire said.

"Now I know why he wants us to forget English broads. We aren't going to live long enough to see any of them."

"Wonder where Old Iron Ass will be while we're flying "straight-in" to *hell*!"

Captain Ron Miller frowned at his two companions and said in a firm voice, "In the command seat of the lead aircraft!"

On November 23, 1942 at the Brampton Grange Complex, a stately British Castle transformed into a headquarters complex, a Bombardment Wing operation area was busy as usual. The walls were covered with aircraft scheduling boards, maps, squadron and group deployment charts and course projections to the day's target area.

The men were busily engaged in the collection and assimilation of strike information as it was received by radio and telephone. The urgency and tension surrounding today's mission was clearly evident with the level of activity and smoky atmosphere. A young Second Lieutenant was sitting at a desk receiving information over a telephone and hastily jotting it down.

The young Lieutenant rose from the desk, notes in hand, and walked quickly to a large deployment board where General Longfellow stood, along with his Chief of Staff.

A Staff Sergeant stood making chalk entries on the board which showed a 306th Heavy Bombardment Group column, a 91st. Heavy Bombardment Group "The Ragged Irregulars" column and a 305th Heavy Bombardment Group column. These columns revealed the total number of aircraft assigned to each squadron in each group… the number of aircraft operational within the unit and a column for the number of aircraft put up for the day strike along with the number of aborts.

The young Second Lieutenant stepped in front of the board and began reading off numbers to the waiting Staff Sergeant, who chalked in the information as it was called out.

General Longfellow and his chief-of-staff watched the result intently.

The young second lieutenant read from hisn'tes. "Ninety- first… ten up… six aborts." He paused and watched the information being recorded. "306th… eight up… four aborts."

General Longfellow frowned at the poor showing.

The lieutenant continued. "305th… Twenty up… six aborts."

The Staff Sergeant chalked in the figures "twenty" and "six" ,and then chalked in the total number of ships en route to the target from all the groups.

"Only twenty ships from all three Groups?" General Longfellow asked.

"That's what they're reporting, Sir," The lieutenant said.

General Longfellow frowned and shook his head in despair.

Lemay sat in the pilot's seat of the Lead B-17's, carefully listening to the roar of the engines. He had developed a sense for engine problems by the sound of the engine. In the navigator's area, the navigator was completing his navigation calculations.

"Navigator to group commander," The navigator said. "Five minutes to the IP, Colonel."

"High, Low Riders, this is Lead Rider One…" Lemay said.

Inside another B-17, Captain Don Miller was sitting in the command pilot's seat removing his service cap and putting on his flak helmet. As he did he looked inside his hat to see a photo of his wife and three kids. He had a sick feeling come over him thinking that he might never see them again. His personal emotions were suddenly replaced by cold fear that gripped every man on that mission. This was brought on by the voice of Lemay over his earphones.

"Keep your mind on your business. Now!" Lemay said over the command radio as he looked at the Group B-17s that were flying in the Combat Box formation. He could see the black puffs of anti aircraft fire begin to appear here and there. The flak was growing heavier beyond the cockpit window. The muffled flak burst explosions were heard over the droning roar of the engines. The B-17 started bouncing from the shock waves. Lemay knew the danger was just starting.

The Navigator monitored his wrist watch. "Thirty seconds to the IP Colonel."

The group began to turn. A large volume of flak could be seen about the entire formation.

"Seven minutes to target," The navigator said.

Lemay carefully trimmed the aircraft for the smoothest and most stable flight setting. Lemay carefully adjusted the trim of the aircraft to assist the bombardier and Norden Bombsight. Lemay reactivated the automatic pilot and then slowly removed his hands from the control column, the ship still bounced by flak shock waves but was steady.

Inside the bombardier's compartment of Lemay's B-17, the bombardier was intently cranks readings into the Norden bombsight while the group droned on to the target despite heavy flak bursts all around the aircraft.

Lemay was sweating out the long bomb run. The ship rocked violently by occasional shock waves. The co-pilot glanced toward the unflinching Lemay with obvious alarm written across his face. Lemay looked out the cockpit window at several B-17s amidst flak bursts. He shook head slightly in resignation of the danger. He tried to keep his mind focused on the enormous responsibilities as the lead aircraft and air mission commander to keep the fear that he had out of his head.

Captain Miller looked straight ahead almost in a trance as the bomb run continued. His sweaty hands were away from the control columns. The co-pilot also gazed straight ahead even as the ship was tossed by frequent shock waves. His face showed the unmistakable features of fear. Miller could see elements of the squadron through the cockpit window. All of them were being buffeted by flak shock waves.

Walker and Longmire were sweating out the bomb run when an inordinately violent shock wave buffeted the B-17. Beads of sweat appeared on Longmire's forehead as he momentarily closed his eyes to the violence. Walker glanced at him with some anxiety over his reactions. Both men felt sick with fear but they didn't let it consume them.

The bomb bay doors of Lemay's B-17 swung open. Major Malec worked feverishly to accomplish the final settings on the Norden… beads of sweat were dripping down his forehead even though it was below freezing in the nose section. Frost covered portions of the Plexiglas nose.

Lemay looked back across the left wing, then ahead as the flak burst violence grew worse and the co-pilot stared frozen straight ahead. "

"Stand by for bomb release," Major Malec said.

Lemay readied himself to resume control of the aircraft.

Major Malec crouched over the bombsight one hand raised - to no one in particular - as he prepared to trigger the bomb salvo.

"Bombs away!" Malec said jubilantly.

Bombs spilled through the open bomb bay doors and the ship heaved upward from the released bomb load. Then bombs began spilling from the bomb bays of the other B-17s. Inside the cockpit of Lemay's B-17, Lemay turned off the autopilot and regained control of the aircraft. He began to turn the B-17.

"Let's get the hell out of here!" He said.

The buffeting from flak shock waves continued.

"What did it look like, Malec?" Lemay asked

"We hit the target all right! I couldn't see very much – too much cloud cover!" Malec said.

A grin swept across Lemay's face momentarily as he surveyed the sky ahead.

"Not a cloud in the sky, Major. That was *flak*!" Lemay said

"Here they come! Fighters are climbing up on our flight!" The gunner said.

Lemay was tense now as the fighters began their attack, craned his neck to see how the other elements were faring.

"Fighter… nine o'clock!" The top turret gunner said.

"109…Closing at two o'clock!" The waist gunner said with a slight note of fear in his voice..

The top turret fifty caliber machine guns started their deafening, roaring chatter as they fired on the closing ME-109. The 109 flashed past the cockpit field of view – almost head-on through the formation. The waist gunner fired down on the 109 as it approached from two o'clock in almost simultaneous attack with the first fighter. Then 109 screamed across the gunner's field of view, the waist gunner attempting to follow through, but the aircraft was too fast.

Inside the cockpit of Captain Miller's B-17, he observed the action all around the formation.

"Stay on those bastards… shorten your bursts!" He said.

"We're hit, Captain! Number one!" The co-pilot said excitedly

Through the cockpit window, Miller could see black smoke billowing off the stricken left outboard engine.

"I'm shutting it down," Captain Miller said. He began to work with the prop and feathering controls. *"It won't feather."*

A distant speck, a ME-109 was closing in with lightening speed.

"Frontal Attack!" Lemay said. "High, Low Riders… this is Lead Rider One. Stay alert for frontal attacks. Looks like that's where they're going to be coming from! Pilot to Navigator — Stay on that 50 cal down there!

The co-pilot pointed ahead excitedly. "Colonel!"

Lemay observed the ME-109 in a frontal attack.

"Look at that son-of-a-bitch!" His eyes followed the lightning action "Straight in!"

"Waist gunner to pilot! He got Low Lead four! Whole left wing is breaking away."

The stricken B-17's wing broke away and began a rapid downward spiral.

"See any chutes?" Lemay asked.

"No Sir, nothing," The gunner said.

"High, Low Rider… this is Lead Rider One… stay in tight! Close up!" Lemay said. He glanced off to his left and saw a B-17 too close to the left wing of his aircraft. "Second element; get up in position."

The B-17 began to close into position.

"Here they come! Eleven o'clock!" The co-pilot said

The navigator began firing from the forward position.

A ME-109 closed head on and flashed across the flight path, passing just beneath the Lead Three B-17. The co-pilot looked out his window as the ship lurched violently from the impact of the bullets. He saw smoke and fire in the left inboard engine and quickly activated the engine extinguisher.

"He got number two - we've got a fire out there!" The co-pilot said

Captain Miller, glanced at his instrument panel, then "Pilot to crew! We've lost number one and number two…" His voice reflected the urgency. "We've got a fire! Bail out… repeat… bail out!"

The crewmen in Captain Miller's B-17, from the waist and radio compartment positions began to bail out .

The navigator and the bombardier in Miller's B-17 began to scramble to their escape positions. Suddenly the glass nose bubble disintegrated from the fighter's gun fire, bullets striking the navigator, killing him instantly and wounding the bombardier in the leg.

The waist gunner in Captain Humphrey's B-17 began firing at a rapidly moving ME-109, which began to roll over and down. Smoke started bellowing out from his engine. The waist gunner watched the stricken 109 and smiled.

"You got him! You hit the bastard!" the other waist gunner cheered.

The smoking ME-109 continued its downward spiral, and then suddenly exploded.

The waist gunners, in Captain Humphrey's B-17 cheered and slapped each other on the back. Captain Humphrey and his co-pilot grinned at each other momentarily then went back to the feverish search for other fighters..

"Nice going!" Humphrey said.

Some fifteen hundred feet away, Captain Miller struggled to control the stricken aircraft.

"Pilot to navigator—what's your condition down there?"

"The navigator, Captain; he's dead!"

"What about you?" Captain Miller asked.

"That…" He struggled to pull his shattered leg into a more comfortable position. "“That son-of-a-bitch hit me in the leg!"

"Bail out damn it!" Captain Miller shouted at the co-pilot.

"What about you?"

"I said bail out! That's an order!"

The co-pilot rose from his seat just as the ship lurched violently from a full burst of 20mm gunfire.

Captain Miller's B-17 exploded in a bright orange burst of flames.

Lemay's co-pilot having seen the explosion turned to Lemay. "Donnie Miller!! He just bought it!"

Lemay grimaced.

A ME-109 began to fly parallel flying parallel to the 305th but out of firing range.

"Come on in you son- of-a-bitch! Just come on in!" the waist gunner in Captain Walker's B-17 said.

Inside the cockpit of Walker's aircraft, the co-pilot Longmire watched the ME 109 closely. It was just taunting the formation but was hesitant to enter the overlapping fire of the combat box.

"Looks like *Old Iron Ass* knew what he was doing all the time!" Captain Walker said.

Longmire grinned. "Yeah, I'll never doubt him again."

The pilot of one of the ME-109 began to observe the 305th formation, and then suddenly peeled away, followed by a second ME.

"Lead Rider One… this is Low Rider One. They're breaking off the attack, Colonel. It looks like they've had enough for one day!"

Lemay's features reflected his exhaustion as he rubbed his hand across his eyes. "Roger Low Rider One. They'll look for stragglers. Stay closed up," he said.

The young Lieutenant headed towards General Longfellow, and handed him a communications sheet.

"The return tally, Sir," The lieutenant said.

General Longfellow perused the figures, a startled expression crossing his face.

"The 91st wiped out!?" The general said.

"Yes, Sir. The five ships they got over the target were all lost!"

"And the 305th?" General Longfellow asked.

"Two fighter attacks chewed them up but most are coming home." The lieutenant hesitated for a moment. "Lemay flew a "straight-in" approach to the target, General. He grinned. "Didn't lose a single ship to ground fire."

"I'll be damned!" General Longfellow said.

"Preliminary radio reports indicate they blasted the hell out of those sub pens!" The lieutenant said with a smile and a tone of pride.

"Straight in and didn't lose a single ship to ground fire!" The general said, smiling.

"That's right, Sir."

The general turned away and slowly walked towards the mission board contemplating what had happened in today's three heavy bombardment group operation. The established tactics of the past were not only ineffective, they were getting men killed, aircraft lost and producing negligible damage to the enemy. Curt Lemay had again provided the answer. First, the combat box formation and now the "straight-in" bomb run. The General knew that he had to make immediate tactic changes to follow the success of Lemay and advise Bomber Command of this latest development. He smiled as he thought, "Lemay deserves a commendation for what he's taught us. Perhaps he should be the Wing Commander instead of me."

CHAPTER 40

Inside the photographic dark room in Grafton-Underwood a large black and white photograph was being developed in a tray. Lemay and Major Preston looked at strike photos as they came out of the developer. The dark room technician stood behind them.

"Well, looks like we got most of our bomb load on the target," Lemay said. He glanced at Preston. "From what I see here, we didn't do much damage to the pens themselves." He looked back at the photos intently. "Those damned concrete walls must be fifteen or twenty feet thick!"

Colonel DeRussey entered the room. "They've finished the debriefing, Colonel. The crews are waiting." He looked at the photos in Lemay's hand. "How do they look?"

Lemay raised the photos. "Good!"

Colonel DeRussey paused a moment, thinking. "I… I guess I was wrong, Curt."

Lemay grinned. "Could have been the other way around." He waved the photos again. "What's important is that we got hits and recorded results. Now we can begin to improve..." He handed the strike photographs to the technician. "See that the intelligence people get these right away, Sergeant."

The lab technician took the photos. "Yes, Sir" he said with a smile. He knew that the group now would make a positive difference in the war effort.

Lemay, Preston and DeRussey left the room and proceeded to the briefing room.

The assembled flight crews were very tired but jubilant at the end of their first mission. They were gathered in the debriefing section waiting for their leader. They now had a feeling that with Lemay they stood a chance of surviving this insanity.

"Ten-Shun!" DeRussey said.

Lemay strode up to the speaker's position.

"Well… the strike photos look pretty damned good, gentlemen," Lemay said.

Cheers emanated from the tired crewmen.

Lemay continued. "It might also interest you to know that General Kuter has just informed me that the formation we've developed here has been made standard throughout the wing."

The assembled crewmen cheered loudly again. Lemay grew serious.

"I believe, when the results of today's mission have been evaluated, the "straight in" target approach will become SOP also. I'm starting a new procedure here today. We're going to assemble here the day after each mission and re-fly that mission. If any of you think the CO is a stupid son-of-a-bitch that will be the time to say so! No harm done. If you think what we're doing is wrong, then let us hear it and your thoughts on what ought to be done to correct that failure. Everybody's going to begin to understand why the 305th, and the Eighth Air Force, are here in Europe… what we're here for… and how best to get the job done. Any questions?"

What about fighter escort, Colonel? Are we going to get any?" A co-pilot in the back asked.

Like everything else, Lieutenant; it's on the way. We should have significant fighter presence by January, February at the latest," Lemay said.

"What's the status of our chin turrets, Colonel Lemay?" Captain Walker asked.

Replacement aircraft will come equipped with chin turrets after the first of the year, There has been a delay in the modification of our current equipment… mainly because of the bleed-off of our service groups to the North African invasion. There's hardly enough maintenance capability here now to repair battle damage, much less accomplish extensive modification. Any further questions?" He paused. "We're going to do this job over here, gentlemen, and we're going to do it *together!*"

The crews stood up proudly as Lemay left the room.

Lemay and Preston emerged from the debriefing area, and walked briskly along the hallway toward the 305th Office Complex deep in discussion about the problem in getting penetration of the cement sub pens.

Lemay was thoughtful and then said "I'm going start up a lead crew program, Joe. Crews picked and assembled from the best men we've got! Going to start bombing on those lead crews! Lead crew bombardiers and navigators… they're going to memorize the terrain and layout of every major target in Germany and will know them like they know the backs of their hands. Probably won't like it… but they're going to do it anyway." He looked at Preston. "Formations are going to start bombing on the lead crew."

Major Preston interrupted. "The staff and some of the crews are working up a little belated birthday celebration, Curt."

Lemay paused as they went into the headquarters area, his face becoming wrinkled in anguish. "Sorry… I've got some letters to write… twenty… as a matter of fact." He sighed. He stopped at his office door. "Sorry about the party."

Lemay walked toward his office as Major Preston looked after him. Preston smiled and shook his head resignedly. Lemay entered the office area, carrying his flight gear loosely, his hair disheveled and weariness written across his face. The Sergeant/Clerk stood up as Lemay entered the room.

"Names of the missing crew members been sent up yet?" Lemay asked.

The sergeant lifted a sheet from his desk. "Yes, Sir."

Lemay entered his office. "Pull their records and bring them in."

"Yes, Sir."

As Lemay deposited his flight gear on a conference table went to his desk and sat down, cupping his face in his hands momentarily.

The Sergeant entered with the records.

"I'd already begun to pull those, Colonel." He hesitated. "The mission, Sir, they said it went off okay." He indicated the stack of records. "Too… too bad about these." He deposited the records on Lemay's desk and Lemay nodded his head wearily.

"Is that all, Sir?"

"Yes, thanks.

The Sergeant left, closing the door after him.

Lemay reached for one of the records, opened it and gazed at its contents meditatively. It revealed the service record of Captain Donald G. Miller. Lemay gazed at the picture in the record jacket, his eyes misting over. Then he reached for stationary and pen and began to write.

Dear Mr. and Mrs. Miller:

It is with deep regret that I must inform you that your son is missing from today's action over enemy territory. I know there's very little I can say that will be of comfort to you in your sorrow. But I'm honored to have been his Commanding Officer. While history may never record his individual bravery and courage, they're nevertheless written in my heart forever. God Bless and comfort you.

Curtis E. Lemay
Colonel, Air Corps
Commanding Officer

When Lemay finished the letter, there were tears in his eyes.

CHAPTER 41

Coltrane was leaving the Intelligence Office of headquarters Eight Air Force at High Wycombe, England when he almost knocked over Colonel Curt Lemay.

"Excuse me! He said, then recognizing Lemay. My god, Curt, what are you doing over here? I heard that you were getting ready to go to the South Pacific."

"Good grief…Bart! It's great to see you again. Pacific? No, I cheated. I deployed the 305th here before they could redirect us. I really pissed off some Senators and Montgomery when I did. They had visions of using the 305th as cannon fodder. I screwed their plans by leaving two days early for England. Hell, our entire ground element and supply trains were either here or geared for here. What the hell are you doing? I thought you would have rotated back home. You sure did a great job from what I heard. My God, you're famous for your Black Bart missions. You can get any assignment that you want."

"No, I'm still here. My two-year commitment to the British isn't up until next month. Then I'm going to take you up on the offer to put me in a B-17."

Lemay looked at him in thought, "How many combat missions have you flown over here?"

"Well, the first year I flew 136 combat and this year only 82. We now have four B-25s. I have good crews that are carrying the load now. There's a lot of squadron paperwork and planning that keeps me down more and more. That's one reason I want to become one of your B-17 pilots. I just want to fly and leave the paperwork to you."

"You've to be kidding about the 218 missions. That's an incredible number of missions over enemy territory."

"No, that's a real number. Those are all actual combat missions flown over Norway, Denmark, France, Belgium, Spain and a few over Germany. We fly almost any day the weather lets us. Those resistance fighters and SOE spies must be supported. The mission and their lives depend on our delivering the goods," Bart said in summary.

Lemay shook his head. "I knew that you were flying a lot of high priority missions, but never that many. I see that you're a Lieutenant Colonel now. That much experience and that high of rank limits me where I can put you. But I'll find a place for you. Would you consider a staff position?"

"Staff? Actually, I belong in the air. I've never been good at admin type jobs. I'm thankful that the Brits are not big on paperwork. I'd take the job if I had your promise to get me a flying job within six months. Also, I'd better tell you off the record. I've been told that Churchill asked Roosevelt to make me a full Colonel when I leave next month. That may complicate things for you."

"Maybe not. I have an idea that I'm working on and there's something big coming. The B-29. It's designed to take the flight directly to the Japanese homeland. I may be going that direction next year. I can see where you could really be of help to me, especially if I get the B-29 command."

"Bart," Lemay said as he put his hand on his shoulder. "Use whatever pull you may have to get assigned to my staff. From there I'll get you into the air. This crash meeting may be very fortuitous for both of us. You're exactly what I need and need badly."

'That's music to my ears," Bart said with relief.

"Just one question," Lemay asked. "With your record and experience you could rotate home and sit out the rest of the war sitting on your ass at the Pentagon. So why do you want to stay on and fly here?"

Coltrane looked around and leaned closer to Lemay and said, "I've met a wonderful British lady and we plan to get married when we can. She's on active duty with the RAF working intelligence for the SOE. It's become an important position since Major Dalton was replaced by Lord Selborne last

February. It's complicated and it will take time to work out the details."

"Wait," Lemay said. "I remember seeing your picture in the *Times* at a charity event with a gorgeous woman. A wealthy blueblood as I recall. Is that the lady in your life?"

"Yes, but please don't tell anyone. It's tough enough and that bit of publicity would be very damaging to our plans."

"You have my word on the job and my silence," Lemay said. "Now don't go and get yourself shot up before you get over here with me."

"Thanks, Curt, this means a lot to me. See you in a couple of weeks. I'll contact the Prime Minister's office and General Arnold and make my request for a transfer to your staff. My second in command, Zak Middleton, is ready to take over. Black Bart operations are going very well, so my departure won't hurt anything. Can I bring my American crew with me? They wouldn't know what to do without Black Bart."

"Please bring them. They're welcome to join the 305th."

CHAPTER 42

The sound of hobnailed boots across a marble floor followed by a loud kick was heard just before Colonel Knoff cried out, "Colonel Knoff reports to the Reichsfuhrer, Heil Hitler!"

Reichsfuhrer raised his hand in the appropriate Nazi salute and looks carefully at the Gestapo Colonel before him. "Can I assume, Colonel, that your mission was successful?"

"Yes, Reichsfuhrer, the matter has been dealt with. However, an interesting development has come up that you may want to know about. It seems that a young lieutenant named Schultz was interrogating a recently captured resistance member. Lieutenant Schultz was most efficient in his efforts to obtain information about a supply drop by Black Bart. He says that they'll get a large amount of explosives, radios and ammunition. Approximately 1,500 Kilos of supplies," Knoff said pausing.

Hemmler became totally focused on the Colonel. "Go ahead, Colonel."

"With your permission, Sir," Knoff said as he unfolded a map.

"According to the individual, the drop will take place in far north Denmark. They've used this area many times before, as it's remote with few residents in the area and our closest troops are over ten kilometers away. It's in a large clearing and has excellent access by road. It offers the resistance force many ways to escape. They feel very comfortable in using this area and will do so just before dawn the day after tomorrow," Knoff continued.

Hemmler was still listening carefully and nodded for Knoff to continue.

"Lieutenant Schultz and I drove out to the location. It's perfect for an ambush to get the main core of the area resistance members and once and for all destroy Black Bart," Knoff explained.

"Yes, yes Colonel, go on. What's your plan?" Hemmler said impatiently.

"Sir, I took the liberty of having a machine gun platoon and two rifle platoons go out there and very carefully dig foxholes and machine gun nests here," pointing to a tree line on the north side of the clearing and on the east side of this road. "They'll undoubtedly use the road for vehicles to haul off the 1,500 kilos of explosives. It's probable that they'll also come through this area of trees on the west side and hide while awaiting Black Bart. The plan is simple. We wait until Black Bart drops the load. Then we radio the Luftwaffe at Alborg who will be waiting on strip alert for our call. As soon as we call them with the time and directions that Black Bart is headed, they'll launch and take up the picket line between England and Black Bart. They'll cover the area with a minimum of eight fighters. We'll launch every fighter and saturate the area so he can't get away. He cannot get away this time. Meanwhile, once the resistance has got to the supplies in the middle of the open field, Lieutenant Schultz will give the order to open fire and eliminate these bastards. They'll be in a crossfire from which there's no escape."

"Outstanding plan, Colonel. I must meet this exceptional Lieutenant Schultz," Hemmler said smiling.

"You're to return and see to the details. Take no chances. This is a very good opportunity to kill two birds with one stone. If you're successful, you and Lieutenant Schultz are to come back here and give me a detailed report. I may want to bring Schultz to Berlin."

"Yes, Reichsfuhrer, Heil Hitler," Colonel Knoff said as he clicked his heels, gave his perfunctory "Heil Hitler" and departed.

CHAPTER 43

The weather in Tempsford was starting to turn cold and damp. It was typical weather for late November and early December. Coltrane looked away from the Black Bart scheduling board and towards Zak Middleton. "Let's shift the new boys in 'Fancy Dreams' to the milk run near Bordeaux. I'll take the run to Denmark. I know the area and you can bet the Luftwaffe will be trying to get whoever flies the mission in their picket line trap. I'm not comfortable with the new guys taking on that hard of a mission just yet."

"Agreed. You know with the weather getting trashy, this could be your last mission with Black Bart," Middleton said as he handed Coltrane the latest weather forecast.

"It could be. Change of command is scheduled for 1300 hours on Saturday," Coltrane said with a tone of sorrow in his voice.

"It's high time we Brits get you Yanks out of here and add a little class to the operation," Zak said jokingly as he slapped Coltrane on the shoulder.

"You're damned right! Now let me take you out and corrupt you with alcohol and supper," Bart said in a joyful tone.

It was a little after 0600 hours the next morning when the Black Bart broke out of the overcast and the clear air some twenty miles west of the northern tip of Denmark. Captain Willard Sims was at the controls straining to see the coast line ahead. Sims had been chosen out of over two hundred volunteers to transfer from flying Lancaster and Wellington bombers to Black Bart. Willard would become the aircraft commander when Bart departed on Saturday. Today, his job was to learn as much as he could about northern

Denmark and the hazards involved in flying in the area, especially given the new tactics employed by the German Luftwaffe.

Sharp was trying to show his replacement how he had been navigating long range missions and at low altitude in hostile territory. It was quite difficult for his replacement to see everything because of the cramped quarters. Sharp was impressed with the new British GEE Navigation System but preferred to rely on his own navigation and use the GEE to confirm. "I have a go code from the reception committee," Sharp said as he adjusted his earphones. "Turn to 192 degrees. You're seven miles to the drop zone."

"Roger," Coltrane responded. "I have the controls," he told the co-pilot. "Start looking for a single white over red light. That will be our friends waiting."

Sims suddenly said "I have the lights, two miles."

"Roger, open bomb bay doors. Stand by to drop on my command, "Coltrane said calmly. Coltrane saw the large open area and mentally timed the drop. "Ready, drop!" he commanded. Sims hit the release switches one second apart.

"Cargo away," Sims reported. Then Royston reported four good chutes.

Coltrane made a hard right turn to head back to England when he heard screams and gunfire over his headset.

"It's a trap. They've us pinned down on two sides in a crossfire. We've been compromised. There's no hope for us. Let London know," said the nameless voice.

Coltrane made another turn to the north.

"Where are they shooting from?" asked Coltrane.

"They have machine gun nests in the north tree line and in the trees next to the road on the east side. There are troops on either side of the machine guns."

"Okay," Coltrane said. "Stay down and let me know how my first gun run works out."

"Do not come back. The fighters will be looking for you. You must escape now while you can. We're finished. Don't take the chance," said the voice of what must have been a British SOE agent.

Bart climbed up to three hundred feet to get a better look at the area and situation in detail. Then he descended to less than one hundred feet and turned east toward the north tree line. As he crossed the main road going to Skagen, he opened fire with all eight fifty caliber machine guns. He sent a continuous burst of rounds and tracers into the line of Germans, literally devastating the entire force on the north side of the clearing.

Suddenly, he was over water. He went out a half mile then turned south for a couple of miles while observing the area on the east side of the clearing then he made a descending turn back to the right and straightened out his course that would take him over the remaining German force that was partially firing on the still trapped resistance fighters and also trying to pull away from the incoming fire of Black Bart. This time, Bart used his rudder control to very slightly move the intense machine gun fire back and forth in a thirty foot path. That caught both those Germans still fighting and those trying to escape. Once again, the machine gun fire was devastating. The German force was totally destroyed. Only a half dozen could be seen staggering away from the firing position.

"Okay, get your supplies and get the hell out of there," Coltrane said.

"Thanks, Black Bart, you saved our bloody ass. We've a traitor in our group. We'll make contact with London as soon as we can find the bloody bastard and kill him. You must go now! The fighters must be getting close."

"Roger, we're out of here," Coltrane ended.

Coltrane was thinking to himself, "One good thing about the Germans, they always follow a plan and orders, not opportunity." He looked at his watch as he turned east back over the water. If they were going to come after Black Bart at the ambush site, they would already be here. That meant they were following orders by flying the airborne picket line. They'd be up there in force looking for them and burning up fuel. That gave Bart an idea. He turned northeast and got as low over the water as he felt safe. The heading took him to the far northeast end of Laeso Island. It took about eight minutes to fly the distance to the island.

"Okay, guys," he said over the intercom. This is what we're going to do. We're going to land at the German strip on Laeso Island. We'll go to the end of the runway and wait thirty five to forty minutes until the Germans start running low on fuel. Then we'll take off and hope we catch them in their staggered refuel plan. If they are, maybe we'll get lucky and sneak through. They've to be spread thin if they're."

Bart kept the aircraft at the lowest altitude possible. He landed at the vacant strip and turned the bird around and taxied back to the east end of the strip. He set the brakes and throttled back as far as he could without killing the engines. The crew looked out every window for the first sign of German troops from the local garrison or fighters.

After thirty minutes, Bart was getting uneasy about staying any longer and was concerned about his fuel remaining. So he said, "Time to go. Watch out for fighters. Any fighters, no matter how far away they are!"

The throttles were advanced and the bomber took off. Bart had gotten the plane no more than ten or fifteen feet off the ground when he raised the landing gear. He leveled off at thirty to forty feet, raised the flaps and then turned hard to the south to avoid being seen or heard by the German garrison. He flew about four miles before turning northwest to avoid the fighter base at Alborg. Eleven minutes later he was over open water in the Skagerrak Strait.

He turned and saw a cloud deck and climbed into it to avoid detection. He flew in the clouds for about forty minutes before breaking out into the clear air above the overcast. The warm sun felt good. "Sharp, give me a course for home," he said in a cheerful voice.

"Turn left to 205 degrees. You're 563 miles to your first scotch," Sharp said in a light and happy tone.

Precisely at 1300 hours on 13 December 1942, the drum major at the Cold Stream Guards Drum and Bugle Corps struck up a series of typical British military tunes. The sun was trying to show through to warm the cold audience who were present to watch what would otherwise be an informal occasion changing the command of a flying squadron from one officer to another. This was not such an occasion. Today, an American-led volunteer aviation unit would turn over its mission and aircraft to the host British forces. This unusual event was visited by numerous American and British officials including the Defense Minister himself, along with American General Hap Arnold and Colonel Curtis Lemay.

The normally low key change of command ceremony had been augmented to add appropriate pomp and ceremony befitting its honorable guests. After a short speech by the Defense Minister and General Arnold, who promoted Bart Coltrane to full Colonel, the Cold Stream Guard Drum and Bugle Corps passed back and forth in front of the remaining five members of the original six members of the American Black Bart unit and the twenty-eight new members who were in a formation directly behind them.

A British major in his dress uniform stood before the formation and read the general order that directed that Colonel Coltrane hand over the British pirate flag that had become the unit flag to Lieutenant Colonel Zak Middleton. The change of command was complete and the formation dismissed. The cold and shivering official guest, went into the Tempsford operations building for a reception of fine wine, caviar and champagne.

The Defense Minister came up to Coltrane and said, "I must run. The war you know. I do understand that you're staying with us to fight on." He looked at Major Annabel Beddows, who was standing by his side and remarked, "I can see why and wish you the best." Then he departed with most of the dignitaries.

Lemay walked up and said "That was very impressive. I hope that you don't expect the same ceremony when you get to that squadron at Chevelston. You'll be lucky if the First Sergeant greets you. I need you to train them for combat. They've flown eight terrible combat missions. I had to relieve the commander yesterday. The hand-picked replacement the Pentagon is sending over won't be here for three to five months. Until then, it's yours. Then I have a special operations problem for you to solve for me. Yes, you'll be flying too!"

"Thanks, Curt," Bart said. "That sounds wonderful to me. I'll check in on Monday morning, if that's okay."

"Fine with me," Lemay said turning his attention to Annabel. "What's your thoughts on all this?"

"I'm fine with it. There's a war on and we all have to do our bloody part. I wish things were different, but they're not. I accept that Bart is flying in harm's way. This is his duty and he loves it, almost as much as me," she said squeezing his arm. "It had better be 'almost as much as me,' " she said chuckling.

"Do you've any wedding plans yet?" Lemay asked.

"We've not set a date yet," she replied, "but maybe in the spring, depending on the war and what he's doing. I don't want to be a two-time war widow."

"I can't promise anything," Lemay said, "but I plan to have him on my staff after he cleans up that mess at Chelveston. He still wants to fly and I'll do what I can, but he's some experience and common sense that I badly need at the headquarters. The staff job I have for him still keeps him flying some, but not the day-to-day missions.

"That's great," she said. "Now we can set a date!"

CHAPTER 44

It was a foggy morning with low visibility and a damp cold temperature that went to the bone. The gate guard at RAF Chelveston handed the three military ID cards back to MSG Royston, who was driving the jeep taking himself, Colonel Coltrane and Lieutenant Colonel Sharp to their new assignment. Royston drove through the gate and went towards the squadron headquarters over a very rough and muddy road. The squadron area looked sloppy and rundown to Coltrane. It wasn't near as well maintained as Tempsford, and Tempsford was an older base. As they entered the ubiquitous Quonset hut that was the squadron headquarters, Coltrane noted how dark and drab the interior looked.

The First Sergeant was the first to see the new Commander enter and called the room to attention. A Major in a flight suit quickly came forward and reported, "Sir, Major Jack House, Squadron Ground Exec reporting, Sir."

Coltrane returned his salute and extended his hand. "Good to meet you. At ease, gentlemen," he said with relaxed authority.

Coltrane turned towards Sharp and Royston. "This is Lieutenant Colonel Sharp and First Sergeant Royston. They'll be joining us as well." Coltrane walked over to the old Squadron First Sergeant and shook his hand, "Top, I know that you've orders to High Wycombe, but I would ask that you delay your departure a week so the transition between you and First Sergeant Royston can go smoothly. Let's not disturb the men anymore than necessary," he said with a kind tone.

"Can do, Sir!"

Then he turned to Major House, "Since there are no flights today, everyone should be available. So would you set up a meeting with all aircrews and NCOs for 1400 hours?"

"Yes, Sir," he said as he looked at the two Squadron Clerks who were quietly watching the events before them. They grabbed their hats and coats and departed at a run.

"Now can you show us to the mess hall? I'm starved," Bart said with a smile.

"This way, Sir, we can slip in the back door to the Commander's table. The Mess Sergeant will bring us trays," House replied.

"Thanks, but I want to go through the line so I know what the crews are seeing and eating," Coltrane said. Then he followed House across the road to another Quonset hut which was the mess hall. As he entered, the room was called to attention.

Corporal Shapiro spilled hot coffee on his leg as he got up. "Damned officers, how many of these damned visitors are going to come see this hard luck bunch? We're nothing more than an amusement at a circus?" he said to another Corporal to his left. He looked up and saw a full Colonel and a Lieutenant Colonel. He turned to the other Corporal and asked, "Do you recognize either of them? The full bull has some decorations, so he's not our inbound commander. Why can't they give us a commander with some combat experience?"

The Corporal said quietly under his breath, "Shapiro, shut up. That's Black Bart himself."

"You're shitting me," Shapiro said.

There was a hushed murmur of chatter going throughout the mess hall as word spread about the identity of their visitor.

Shapiro looked up at Coltrane then down to his meal tray. "Black Bart, now that's what this unit needs. Somebody with real combat experience and huge set of balls. Too bad he's only visiting. Who's the half Colonel with him?" Shapiro said as he ate the beef stew. The guy next to him just shrugged not knowing.

Coltrane went to the chow line and grabbed a tray. This caught the mess Sergeant by surprise. "Sir, if you'll sit down, I'll get your tray for you."

"Thanks, but I'll handle this one myself." Coltrane then looked at the

Mess Sergeant and pointed to the serving table which had numerous patches of spilled stew and other meal items." Sergeant, the men might appreciate your efforts more if the serving line didn't look like the latrine floor after a Saturday night beer bash!" The salad wasn't properly drained after washing. It's standing in an inch of water. That shouldn't happen, should it?" Coltrane said.

"No Sir, it will be corrected," the embarrassed Sergeant said.

Coltrane then took his tray to the commander's table. He looked around at the condition of the mess hall. Coltrane and was amazed at how young they were. Some couldn't be old enough to shave, but soon would be killing Germans at 25,000 feet or being killed.

After lunch, he went to the Mess Sergeant. "Sergeant, the quality of the meals is to get better and quick. Find a good scrounger and let's get him wheeling and dealing for steaks and anything else you may need to make some great meals for these guys. You've one week to bring up the quality and atmosphere or you can go cook for the infantry," Coltrane said, then left before the Mess Sergeant could respond. Then stopped, looked up then back to the Mess Sergeant who was still in shock. "Get some white paint and more lights. This is a cave and not a place to eat."

Coltrane entered the headquarters. "First Sergeant, I assume that you've a scrounger in the squadron. Get with him and have him help the Mess Sergeant get some real food for the men. He needs some white paint and more lights as well. He looked up then at the old First Sergeant and the incoming First Sergeant Yank Royston. "Get enough paint and lights to brighten this place as well." Then he left for the briefing room…another Quonset hut!

Major House overheard some off the wall comments about the new commander and turned to the men seated and standing along the arched walls. "Whoever said that the new commander is a Pentagon warrior has no idea who this is. For those of you who have your heads in a rectal defilade, Colonel Bart Coltrane is better known as Black Bart." There was silence in the room.

Precisely at 1400 hours Colonel Coltrane entered the operations briefing room. "At ease, take your seats. I'm Colonel Samuel Barton Coltrane, your new Commander. Joining me is Lieutenant Colonel Kelly Sharp and First Sergeant Yank Royston. Our mission is to make you combat ready and an effective combat element of the 305 Bombardment Group. So far, your first eight missions have been less than adequate, in fact, dismal. My job is to change that. You'll fly your assigned position in the "combat box" and focus on bombing the target or following the lead ship if you're a part of a larger mission. Did anyone not understand what I just said?"

"Obviously you haven't flown combat in the Eighth Air Force or have gone against flak," came an unidentified voice from the crowd.

Major House got up and stepped in front of Coltrane. "Both Colonel Coltrane and Lieutenant Colonel Sharp have been flying for the RAF for the last two years. They've both flown over two hundred combat missions over enemy territory. They've flown against flak and anti aircraft over Norway, Denmark, France, Belgium and Germany. They flew these missions at altitudes less than five hundred feet, not at a safer 25,000 feet. They're also credited with two ME-109 kills and they did it from a B-25. Now, anyone here have any questions about their combat qualifications?"

One young Captain stood up and asked, "Sir, welcome to hell. I do have a question about what you've said." Coltrane nodded and the Captain continued, "Sir, how do we avoid flak on the bomb run if we maintain straight and level flight?"

"Captain," Coltrane said, "that's a damned good question. First, the short answer is that you don't. We, or should I say the British, have learned that the gunners can't tell if you're going up, down, right or left from the ground. They aim for the flight and fire as many rounds as they can at your altitude. Moving or jinking only throws your bombardiers off target and doesn't improve your chances of survival. That means we have to come back again and again until we reduce the target to rubble. The distance from the IP to targets has been shortened as much as possible. That will reduce your time of flak vulnerability. During those few minutes, you must focus on steadying up on course, tighten your formulation so your bomb pattern will be effective and concentrate on placing your bomb load exactly where it belongs. Look, these are not guys on the ground aiming at a specific aircraft like they were shooting with a deer rifle. They're shooting at the group and hoping for a kill. It's a function of luck and numerical probability. Before and after the bomb run, it's vital that you confine your evasive maneuvers so as not to open up critical openings in the combat box."

The box works and gives you and the planes around you the best chance of getting home when the fighters attack. It's that simple! Are there any questions on the bomb run or combat box?" he asked as he looked at the men. "Okay, tomorrow we'll fly a mission and see if there's any improvement. It should be a milk run, but it will give us both flak and fighters to deal with. Once I feel that we're ready, we'll be tasked with much more important missions. I'll be flying tail end Charlie tomorrow to see how well you fly and bomb the target. Colonel Sharp will be flying as the navigator for the lead ship. There will be a three day pass to London for the crew that has the best bomb pattern. Aircraft Commanders who violate the two new rules about jinking on bomb run or breaking the combat box will have their orders appointing them as aircraft commanders revoked, demoted to co-pilot and transferred out of the unit. No exceptions," Bart said with bold and commanding voice. "Dismissed!"

CHAPTER 45

In January, 1943, an American military staff car - its bumper flags flying the stars of a Major General, was parked in front of the Casablanca conference site. Inside, Prime Minister Churchill and General Ira C. Eaker were seated at a linen covered dining table in the small, ornate room. The décor was opulent and reflected its North African culture. The soup course had obviously just been served. A uniformed servant stood by, waiting.

"We were led to believe in Washington last January that you'd be making heavy delivery of bombs on German targets months ago, Churchill said as he began to eat his soup. "Yet America has been in the war for more than a year now, General, and you've failed to drop a single bomb on Germany by your daylight methods."

"Surely you realize, Mr. Prime Minister, that the bomber offensive set forth in Rainbow 5 has been gradually altered by our combined chiefs themselves," General Eaker said. "We simply hadn't counted on a heavy bomber build up in the Pacific or the diversion of heavy bomb groups for the North African campaign." He gazed at the Prime Minister, who continued with his soup quietly. "The Eighth Air Force has suffered severe and unexpected shortages of equipment and trained manpower because of those shifts in grand strategy."

"But, General, given that, you've still failed to prove your high altitude daylight precision bombardment theory," Churchill said. He stopped eating his soup. "Personally, I deeply regret that we've put so much effort and material into it!" Churchill gestured with his soup spoon. "I shall always believe that if you Americans had concentrated on night bombing along with our own RAF, we would have succeeded in getting a far larger delivery of bombs over Germany by this time. And… we could have gradually worked up to a reasonable degree of accuracy with the scientific night radar methods we're developing. That, of course, is what I intend to recommend to the combined chiefs and to Mr. Roosevelt during the conference here." Mr. Churchill went back to his soup.

General Eaker frowned. "And that's why General Arnold requested this meeting, Sir." The general leaned forward to press his point. "Mr. Prime Minister, we feel that indiscriminate bombardment only arouses the anger of the helpless civilian populations in the targeted area. Your own country is perhaps the greatest example of that. The brutal and indiscriminate night bombardment of London inflicted little damage on British war production. Yet, the Londoners, indeed all of Britain, became fiercely united against the Germans."

The Prime Minister had stopped sipping his soup now, his spoon poised in mid-air.

General Eaker continued. "The national morale and cohesiveness rose to a level rarely paralleled in human history. It was, in your *own* words, "their finest hour. "Furthermore, if the combined chiefs alter their grand strategy once again in this regard, it would take months to re-train and re-equip the Eighth Air Force Heavy bombardment groups. I'm afraid our future effectively would simply dissolve into a meaningless morass!"

The Prime Minister was impressed. "Even if I were inclined to reconsider my position, General, I still remain quite skeptical of your ability to accomplish meaningful results with daylight precision bombardment."

We're close to it, Mr. Prime Minister. Within the next three months we'll have begun to receive many additional heavy bomb groups," General Eaker said. Our crews coming out of the training command schools will be better trained. The group commanders, particularly Colonel Curt Lemay of the 305th, are developing a formation and bombing strategy that's beginning to produce a marked improvement in our efficiency and performance. *Daylight Precision Bombardment is a proven concept, Mr. Prime Minister!* It's just that we've had to build an Air Force, train it and fight it *all at the same time*! If we in America had organized our Air Force as a separate and autonomous branch of the military services… as you people did with the RAF back in the twenties, then our status here today might be quite a different story. The bomber offensive we'd have been capable of mounting would have already dealt Hitler's industrial output a severe and crippling blow." General Baker leaned forward now. "I suggest, Sir, that the RAF continue its night radar offensive while the Eighth Air Force continues to concentrate its efforts on day light bombardment That way, we'll have an around-the-clock Bomber offensive against the German fatherland!"

The Prime Minister's imagination had been captured. "I'm forgetful that your administrative command is indeed quite different from our own." Churchill paused for a moment to consider Eaker's remarks. "You advance a powerful argument, General Eaker." He began to eat his soup again. "Prepare your case for presentation to the combined chiefs of staff at tomorrow's conference, General." He paused. "I shall give the matter further thought.

General Eaker took a deep breath. "Thank you, Mr. Prime Minister."

"Your soup, General. It's cold. Shall I have a warm one brought in for you?" the Prime Minister asked.

General Eaker didn't care about the soup. "No, Sir, its fine… just fine."

"Well, whatever the case now, we shall soon have your mighty B-29 super bomber over here, We've heard some rather remarkable reports about the machines."

Eddy Allen sat in the flight commander's position of a B-29, which was parked on the Renton Ramp early one morning in February, 1943, and a Boeing engineer, Davis, sat in the co-pilot position. The engines were all running idle.

Eddy Allen looked out over his left shoulder, and watched the left wing engine props turning at idle RPM and then Davis looked out over his right shoulder and saw the right wing engine props turning at idle RPM. Both looked for anything unusual or out of place.

Eddy Allen glanced at Davis. "Let's roll!"

Davis responded with a thumbs up gesture as he lifted the radio microphone and began a radio transmission.

"Renton Mobile Control… this is Boeing two niner. We're proceeding to takeoff position."

"Roger Boeing two niner. We've got you - loud and clear! You're cleared for takeoff."

The huge aircraft began to move out. The Superfortress turned on to the runway at takeoff position, and final engine checks began. The pilots glanced at one another, and then Eddy Allen pushed the throttles forward. The aircraft began to respond, hurtling down the runway, lifting off gracefully and flying in a twenty degree climb, with the B-25 chase plane catching up to observe the test flight.

Several Boeing executives and a few engineers were seen, grouped around the mobile radio transmitter that sat on a table in front of the large van. An engineer was seated before the transmitter, listening to every word that came out of the speaker as if it was a person. The others were all gazing upward at the B-29 as it gained altitude.

"Renton Mobile… this is Boeing two niner. We've entered the test area. Test procedures briefed for five thousand feet are beginning. Stand by," Eddy Allen said in a usual calm voice.

"Roger, Renton Mobile standing by."

The flight engineer's face assumed a look of apprehension when he looked at the instrument panel. He tapped a temperature gauge for the number three engine as if it were stuck in position and therefore not registering properly. The engineer turned to glance in the direction of the pilot.

"Eddy, we're beginning to get excessive temperature on number three. It's… it's coming up pretty fast! Damned fast!"

Eddy Allen looked toward the flight engineer, with serious concern on his face.

The right scanner's body stiffened noticeably as he reported, "I've got smoke trailing number three!"

A thin contrail of smoke had begun to emanate from the number three engine nacelle. The flight engineer continued to watch the temperature gauge intently.

"Eddy, we'd better cut number three—immediately!"

Allen adjusted the flight controls for the procedure. "Cut number three!" Allen commanded

"We've got a fire in number three!" The flight engineer said.

"Feather that prop… hit the fire extinguisher!" Eddy Allen said.

"Renton Control… this is Boeing two niner," Eddy Allen said. "We've got a fire on board… number three engine. I'm returning to base immediately."

"Boeing two niner, we read you. We're instituting emergency landing procedures here," replied the engineer at the radio.

"I've got bursts of flame trailing number three," the scanner said.

Eddy Allen looked at the flight engineer. "What about the extinguishers?"

"They're functioning," the flight engineer said.

"Right scanner position?" Eddy Allen asked. "What are your conditions back there?"

"The fire is severe and the flames are trailing past the blister," the right scanner said.

Davis looked out the cockpit window and then glanced toward the radio operator. "We're keyed into the engineering monitor?" He asked.

"Right."

"The oil cell behind number three engine is evidently on fire," Davis said. He turned to Allen. "We need to check the position of those fire extinguishers relative to the oil cells on all four engines. The main magnesium wing spar runs just behind the lubricating oil cells… fire's probably ignited the magnesium."

"The extinguishers are expended," the flight engineer said with an elevated voice of fear.

"Right Scanner… what's your condition back there now?" Eddy Allen asked.

The right scanner's vision was totally obscured by smoke racing past the side blister.

"The dense smoke and flame made seeing the fire almost impossible. "I can't see the wing at all," the right scanner said.

"Renton Control… we're on final… we'll require immediate emergency equipment procedures at the runway."

The B-29 began to approach the runway in the distance, its number three engine smoking badly. The mobile van and the men standing between it watched the approaching B-29, still in the distance. The group of men gazed mutely toward the approaching B-29 as it neared the runway.

Davis continued to watch the number three engine area intently. "*There she goes!*" he suddenly yelled.

Eddy Allen attempted to correct for the sudden lurch to the right, and then, suddenly the aircraft spun clockwise.

"We're going in!" he said.

At Renton Control Tower, the flight controllers saw a giant fireball suddenly erupt in the distance, mushrooming upward. The dismal wail of sirens pierced the silence.

A telephone rang at the reception desk in General Arnold's office in the Pentagon. The master sergeant seated the reception desk reached for the telephone.

"General Arnold's office," the Sergeant said. He paused and listened for a moment." "Yes Sir… one moment please."

General Arnold was seated at his desk, busily absorbed in work.

"General Arnold, the President of Boeing Aircraft is on the line, Sir," the Sergeant said.

General Arnold reached for the phone. "Hello," he said and paused. "Hey PG good to hear from you. How's it going out there?"

General Arnold's features grew taut as he leaned forward, as if a sudden weight had descended on him. "When?"

General Arnold listened for several moments and the horror of what he was hearing registered on his face.

"All of them?" He listened again. "Thank you, PG. I'll get back with you."

General Arnold flipped the intercom switch.

"Yes, Sir."

"See if you can get the President on the line. It's urgent," General Arnold said.

"Yes, Sir," the Sergeant said.

General Arnold wiped his face with his hand in incredible disbelief at what he'd just heard as he waited

"The President will be on the line momentarily, Sir," the Sergeant said.

General Arnold waited tensely, and then the President picked up the phone.

"Mr. President," he said.

The President responded.

"I'm afraid I have some bad news," General Arnold said. "The B-29 prototype crashed this morning. It hit a packing plant out near Renton mile or so short of the runway." He paused. "No, Sir - there were no survivors." He was silent again. "Yes, Sir - the engineering staff was on board." He listened. "I'll be there in half an hour, Sir."

General Arnold replaced the telephone in its cradle on the intercom, then simply buried his face in his hands. Then he took one hand away from his face and depressed the intercom button and said, "Get my car and driver out front immediately."

CHAPTER 46

Coltrane looked over at the outside air temperature gauge in front of the co-pilot. It was slightly less than forty below zero at 28,000 feet. It didn't get any warmer in July than now in February 1943. It gave him a shiver to think about it. Then a real shiver came over him when the top gun turret called out "Fighters at 9 o'clock – same altitude!" Bart looked to his left but didn't initially see them. "There they're," he thought to himself. He looked around at the squadron formation. It was in a tight combat box. The past eight missions had shown them that the combat box really worked. They had only lost four men to hostile fire and no aircraft. The bombing accuracy had steadily improved to become the best in the 305th Group. Not bad improvement for the forty five days that he had the squadron. This would be a real test today. They were going after the marshalling yards and dry docks at Antwerp. The fighters would be merciless and the flak heavy enough to walk on.

"IP in three minutes," Sharp said over the intercom. "Course will be 073 degrees."

"Roger, watch for fighters at our 9 o'clock headed for the low squadron," Bart said calmly. "the sneaky bastards may hit them first and catch us from behind."

Flak dots came up in front of them. The fighters were confirming the proper altitude for the gunners on the ground. "No amateurs," Coltrane thought. "Well neither are we."

"IP, turn to 073 on my command," called our Sharp. "Now, turn. Target eight miles."

Inter aircraft chatter was increasing due to the high number of German fighters attacking the two squadrons. Fear was in their voices, but not panic. The sound of machine gun firing could be heard in the background as they called out the incoming German fighters.

"Fighters breaking off," came the cry as the Luftwaffe was getting out of the way for the flak barrage that was about to start.

Coltrane could see the first burst of flak ahead of the two groups of bombers. It got heavier and heavier as they approached the targets. He looked up and to the left and saw the ME-109's orbiting as they waited for the bombers to get out of the killing zone of the anti aircraft fire.

"Bombardier to pilot, I'm ready. Target in sight," said the bombardier.

"Roger, it's all yours," Bart said as he reached down to the switches on the lower control stand and engaged the autopilot. In the middle of the shallow right turn, a flak burst sent a piece of shrapnel through the co-pilot's instrument panel. It barely missed the co-pilot and fell to the floor just behind him.

The autopilot was now slaved to the Norden bombsight that gave the airplane its steering commands to take it to the target.

"One minute to release," came the report.

There were constant explosions around the aircraft tossing it up and down like a cork in a lake.

"They got the 'Purple Plane' ", said the right waist gunner. "Direct hit!"

Coltrane shook his head. Suddenly he felt a hard hit to the control yoke. An alarm went off indicating a fire. The bomber yawed to the left. He looked out his window and saw the left outboard engine on fire. They'd been hit!

"Chop power and feather number one, and pull the fire extinguisher on the son-of-a-bitch," Coltrane said in a strained commanding voice.

The bombardier called out, "Give me some right peddle for ten seconds."

Coltrane pushed the right peddle which controlled the rudder. "How is that?"

"Great, just hold it a few seconds more. "Bombs away. That should delay the trains for a few days."

Coltrane was trying to keep control of the B-17 as it started to keep yawing to the left due to unequal power on the right side. He increased the left inboard engine to as much as it could take without blowing a cylinder better known as a "jug." He reduced the right outboard engine slightly to further reduce the yaw. The plane became more stable but at a slower speed. He knew that he would have to fall back. "Bandito, this is Black Bart. Take the lead, we're hit and on three engines."

"Roger, Black Bart, Bandito has the lead," came the voice over the radio. "Execute right turn, now."

The right turn gave Coltrane the chance to turn into his good engines and cross under the protection of the high squadron and end up on the right side of the squadron once it had made the slow right turn in formation. In the middle of the shallow right turn, a burst of flak sent a piece of shrapnel through the pilot's instrument panel just above the AC Volt meter. It barely missed Bart's face lodging in the top of the cockpit just behind him. Bart tried to ignore the close call and focus on his engine instruments. He noticed that the RPM needle on the struggling left engine was starting to fluctuate slightly. He knew the additional strain was too much and he would have to reduce the power some or lose the engine entirely. That would definitely slow him down to a point where he would no longer be able to keep up. His aircraft would fall behind the protection of formation become a sitting duck for the fighters. He just had to fight off the fighters as he limped back over the North Sea towards England. The Germans would certainly go after any crippled aircraft like Black Bart.

The top turret called out, "Here they come. They smell blood in the water. Come on, you bastards, come and get us. We still have a big sting waiting for you!"

Sharp called out over the intercom, "Here comes the calvary to the rescue!"

Bart looked out and saw British fighters engaging the Germans. They would keep them off long enough to escape. "They had cheated death once again," he thought. He then turned his attention to the condition of the bomber as it limped home. He looked at what was left of the engine and far tip of the wing or where the last three foot of wing tip should have been. The engine was slightly hanging downward; Coltrane assumed from the heat of the fire. That would slow them down some but otherwise of no importance... he hoped.

Bart adjusted the engine controls to give them the best fuel rate while trying to keep up with the formation. He focused on the engine instruments as he set the right two engines manifold pressure to twenty-eight inches and the propeller RPM to 1850. The left engine had to carry the larger load due to the loss of the other engine. He reduced the manifold to 29.5 inches and 1900 RPM. This was as much of a load that he felt the engine could sustain for the trip home. That gave them a sustained speed of 130 MPH instead of the usual 155 MPH. Luckily the flight home was seemingly uneventful after that, but they were not able to keep up with the squadron. They fell behind a little but now that the formation was clear of fighters Bandito could reduce formation speed to accommodate the three damaged aircraft struggling back. He would make it home tonight after all.

As the Black Bart came to a stop at its parking position and the three working engines shut down, a staff car drove up. Bart knew that must be Lemay or someone higher. So he got out quickly and went over to the car. Lemay rolled down his window and said, "Get in, Bart."

Coltrane got in the car only to find Lemay and the new Bombardment Division Commander. Lemay introduced Coltrane and immediately went into the reason for his visit. "Bart, we're getting ready to take the battle to the enemy war machine itself. On the 27th of January we had a great attack against Wilhelmshaven. It was only the first and you did great on that mission. If you can stay alive for ten more days, I want your squadron to spearhead the attack on Nordenham. After today's mission, you certainly deserve it. Reports from the air recon boys indicate that the rail yards no longer exist."

"It'll take a month to repair and rebuild. We could have done better on the sub pens, however. That's not your problem, yet!"

"Yet?" Coltrane said.

"Well, your replacement is on his way over. He should be ready to take over soon after the Nordenham mission. I still have a position for you on my staff, or have you forgotten? I'm sure Annabel will remember."

Bart hung his head for a second or two then looked at Lemay. "I guess that I got caught up in the squadron and forgot that this was temporary. I'm just *summer help* here," he said. "I'll be ready to join you whenever you say, Sir."

"Actually, the Division Commander here wants you to be his operations officer. It means a brigadiers star for you and you'd be working out of London until the Division is officially formed in the summer. Then you'll move to an outline airfield like Grafton-Underwood. I can't offer you a star or that level of a staff position. It's a great career move, Bart," Lemay said.

Bart shook his head then looked at the three-star general and said, "Sir, the offer is tempting and probably what I want, but my head is swimming with the last mission and getting ready for the St. Nazaire. Could I have forty-eight hours to collect my thoughts and give you my decision, Sir?"

"Sure, Colonel. Here's my direct phone number, call me by the end of the week. I do realize how overpowering all of this is after this mission. I'll be waiting for your call," the General said.

"Thank you, Sir," Bart said as he got out of the car. He stood there for a minute and watched the staff car drive off. Sharp came up behind him and asked "Was that Lemay?" Coltrane just nodded as he turned and got into the jeep with Sharp. Coltrane put his foot on the dashboard and said, "I need a fucking drink."

CHAPTER 47

It had been two days since Lemay and the new air division commander had discussed the operations job and Bart was torn between two emotions. The staff job with Lemay, or the operations job and a brigadier's star at air division headquarters in London. Bart pondered, "That would allow him to be with Annabel all the time and be in a safe job so they could get married. The problem was, Lemay needed him very badly for some special operations project. He owed Curt. He could not overlook what Lemay had done for him and what might be ahead. "Lemay was just too good of a man and a leader to be let down," he thought. "I guess that I have to put the greater good of many and Curt Lemay ahead of himself," he decided. "Oh, well," he thought, "I have until tomorrow to make a final decision."

His concentration was broken by Kelly Sharp. "Boss, your Supreme Commander just called and she needs for you to meet her at the Rattskeller at 1500 hours today. She said that it was extremely important that you be there and on time.

"From the sound of things you're already married," he said, teasing Bart. "Things here are in good shape and I can handle the store if anything comes up. Why don't you catch the 1205 train so you won't be late and get your ass in big time trouble."

"Thanks, Kelly. She wouldn't have called unless it was damned important, Coltrane replied. Besides, I need the time to think over that job offer. The train ride will give me the opportunity to think through the matter without being disturbed or distracted."

By the time it took Coltrane to get to the Rattskeller, he had made up his mind. He would stay with Lemay. He could still get married, but would only see Annabel on a regular basis between whatever projects or missions Lemay might have for him. This was best, especially given the turn in the war against the Germans. They now had the aviation resources to conduct a proper bombing campaign against the German war industry.

As he walked into the Rattskeller, Reggie came out from behind the bar and gave him a big hug and said, "That terrible woman who took you away from me is in your usual booth with a couple of civilian gentlemen."

He walked back to the last booth and saw Annabel. She got up and gave him a long and passionate kiss. "Welcome, dear, to the conspiracy." Then she pointed to Curt Lemay and Hap Arnold who were sitting with their backs to him in civilian clothes.

"My sweet cowboy," I want you to give what these gentlemen have to say serious consideration. I don't know what the details are, but the overall idea puts me at the altar on 3 June of this year. I'm going to be there, I hope that you can make it," she said with sarcastic humor. "Love, I must go do my duty for God and King. So you guys work out the details. Cheerio," she said as she kissed him goodbye.

Bart sat down across from the two men not having a clue what was going on with Annabel or the two senior officers.

Lemay was the first to speak. "Bart, this meeting never happened… agreed?"

"Yes Sir, I understand," Bart responded.

First of all, both of us want you to take the operations job at the new air division. We're the ones that got the general to ask you. He's absolutely no idea about what we're going to discuss. Sorry too for getting Annabel involved, but it was the best way to get you here without attracting the attention of others. All she knows is that we're trying to get you a staff position here in London. Beyond that, she knows nothing. She's a strong woman that knows what she wants and that's you…you alive. To that end, she'll do whatever it takes. She told me in no uncertain terms that if I didn't get you out of high risk missions she would pick up the phone and call her friend, Mr. Churchill, and get it done through him. Well, she doesn't have to make the call. You're headed to London as Deputy Chief of Staff: Operations of the new bombardment division. You do have to make the call to the general accepting the position.

"Now, let's talk about the rationale behind all of this. You need to sit back and listen to what General Arnold has to say about the larger picture. It's the future of strategic air power here, in the Pacific and the future Air Force," Lemay said as he sat back and nodded to Arnold.

General Arnold casually looked around to ensure nobody was listening. Then he started. "Bart, strategic bombing is winning this war. We're now equipped with enough B-17's and B-24's to take the war to the Fatherland. You've seen firsthand since you got here in 1940 the vast improvement in aircraft and joint air/ground operations. You flew a mission two days ago that proves that we can systematically destroy the enemy's capability to produce weapons of war and his will to fight a losing war. It's going to take another eighteen to twenty-four months to destroy his industry and support the ground invasion. The outcome is clear and our results from strategic bombing have made the powers in Washington true believers in aviation. You've been a key part of that success in your Black Bart missions and now in B-17 bombings."

"While we're here bombing the enemy night and day, our Army and Marine ground pounders are marching up the islands of the western Pacific. The Japanese are not only creative and resourceful, they're fanatical in their war efforts. They too must be bombed into submission. Unfortunately, the B-17 cannot do the job.

"We do have a plane in the works that can do the job. "The B-29." It will have the range and capability to destroy their industry and war machine. It will be late this year before it can be put into operation. Curt here will be taking on that mission in a few months. That fact is only known by a handful of senior officials. There's another project that's even larger than that. It's a means to bring the war with Japan to a decisive conclusion. I can't say anything more than that at this time, sorry! If you look at the enormity of the size of the Army Air Force on a global scale, it's enormous and getting larger as well as becoming responsible for the long-term defense of our country. I'm talking beyond the current war."

"Curt and I both feel strongly that after the war we'll have other smaller conflicts to deal with as well, as a larger threat. Russia and China are both becoming very strong economically and most of all militarily. We must look beyond the current conflict towards keeping the global peace and the protection of our country from the threat posed by these powers. There are very favorable discussions and planning going on towards the establishment of a separate branch of service for the Army Air Force.

Curt will tell you about new aircraft that are on the drawing boards that will amaze you. Strategic bombing is just in its infancy as you'll see in the next few years. Air power is an essential part of our nation's defense. Curt and I want you to be a part of that future. Your posting to the new division is just a step, a very short step at that. You'll do exactly what was set forth by the new commander. We want you to get the unit fully organized operationally between now and when it officially is activated in July. It will also be your job to assist the 801st Bomb Group (Carpetbaggers)to get operational at Harrington by September. They're the U.S. equivalent of your old SOE missions. In early August you'll receive orders assigning you to a special interservice coordination office supporting Project Matterhorn. That's the code name for the deployment of the new B-29's to India. From there, Curt will bomb the hell out of Japan. You'll officially be working for me, but occasionally you'll be secretly working for Curt. He needs someone that knows the plan and can help him prepare for the air war in the Pacific. It's a job for someone like you who has the reputation and rank to get things done. That's why we want you to take the operations job. That will give you the promotion to Brigadier General. You'll need the horsepower to deal with the various people, companies, government agencies and foreign governments. Especially with Leslie Groves. Is all of this starting to make sense to you?" Arnold asked in conclusion.

"Actually, yes, Sir. I can clearly see the program now and in the future," Coltrane said in a serious tone. "Who is Groves?"

The General continued, ignoring the question, "Very well, then. You'll fly the next bombing mission into Germany, then be reassigned. We can't afford to lose you in combat. You're the key to the endless coordination of so many critical projects. Are you on board with us?" General Arnold asked.

"It's hard to say no to something that big and important. You can count on me, Sir," Coltrane said still dazed from the General's explanation. 'Looks like I'll need a little flexibility to get married. She's a socialite and a part of the British aristocracy. I have nightmares about the magnitude of the wedding itself." Both men laughed. Then Bart looked over at Curt and said "Since you got me into this mess, would you be my best man?"

"I'd be honored," Lemay said, "But I'm scheduled to be in Washington and Wichita, Kansas in June. Perhaps General Arnold will do it for you. It sure can't hurt the social standing to have an American four-star General as your best man."

"Sure, I will. I'd be delighted to be a part of your wedding," Arnold responded.

"That's assuming he's still alive," Lemay said. "He's been pushing too hard. He's already had one heart attack."

"I'm fine, Curt," the General retorted. "Now, I need something to eat besides the damned British fish and chips."

"Sir, I highly recommend this place. I lived here before assignment to Chelveston. The food is great!" Bart said, as he waved to Reggie for menus.

CHAPTER 48

"Bombs away!" was the cry from the Black Bart bombardier, squatting over the Norden bomb site in the nose of the B-17. Bart breathed a sigh of relief as he switched off the autopilot slaved to the bomb sight. He took control of the aircraft and looked for the lead squadron to make its outbound course taking them back to England. The lead started his turn to the right as expected. He then went on the intercom and asked the tail gunner to give him a report on how well the squadron had done hitting their assigned target, which were the railway yard and the docks at Nordenham, Germany. He leaned back into his seat and looked at how well the squadron had maintained the combat box and listening to the report on how they had devastated the target. He was happy as well as proud of the progress the squadron had made the past few months. He mentally fumbled for today's date then remembered it was the first of March, his birthday. "This mission was a great birthday present," he thought.

"Looks like Viceroy 22 was damaged more than reported as their bombs hit closer to 2nd Air Division's target than ours. Everyone else did great despite the flak," came the voice of the tail gunner who was getting ready for the returning German fighters.

"Think Viceroy 22 can make it home?" Coltrane asked.

"I doubt it, Colonel." "He's badly hit by flak and the fighters also did him a job on the way in. He's lost his left inboard engine and the left outboard is smoking as well. It's sinking below the Box," was the sadly spoken report.

"Keep an eye on him. I can see the ME-109's starting down on us," Coltrane said. "So far we've only lost three of the fifty-five that we started with.

It would be great if that was all that we lost on his last combat mission over Germany. I hope our fighters get here soon."

"I've got two ME's on the port side headed straight for us," said the left waist gunner.

"Roger, turrets take a crack at them," ordered Coltrane. The vibrations from the three sets of fifty caliber machine guns were suddenly offset by hits from the German fighters. "Give me a damage report!"

The engineer reported back quickly. "They got Segar in the leg, but he'll make it. Not much damage. It'll keep the metal shop boys up late tonight, but that's all."

The wounded gunner came up on the intercom. "Eat your heart out! I got my ticket back home. This'll get me sent home for sure," he said as the engineer placed a tourniquet on his badly wounded leg. Segar was smiling, knowing he was homeward bound. The injection of morphine given by the engineer added to his happy attitude.

"Bandits, 12 o'clock," came the cry of the top turret gunner. "No, wait, those are our Little Friends. Go get them nasty Huns!"

Coltrane relaxed and signaled for the co-pilot to take over the flying duties. The strike force of B-17 bombers were headed back to their home bases. "Not a bad strike into Germany," Coltrane thought.

Silence came over the B-17 as the four engines were turned off. Coltrane remained in his seat and reflected on his many combat missions. For him, combat was to only be a memory. He was now headed for staff positions for the rest of the war. He finally got up and climbed out of the access door to a waiting First Sergeant Royston. "Sir, hop in the jeep. You've a meeting at 1700 hours at General Eisenhower's new headquarters at Bushey Park in Teddington. You've to sign over command to Colonel Capeheart who is waiting in your office. I'm to pass on to you that Major Beddows will meet you at Bushey Park."

"What the fuck is going on?" Coltrane said.

"They've moved your schedule up a few weeks, you're about to become a one-star. Sir," Royston said and then added, "Sir, if you can get me transferred to your staff, I would really appreciate it. I'd sure hate to go through this damned war with anyone else but you."

"Pack your bags. I'll fix it at headquarters. Find a good replacement so Capeheart isn't left in a lurch."

"Done, Sir. I have your dress uniform ready as requested. Your bags are packed and I'll have you there with time to spare," a happy Royston said.

Bart was standing in the main salon of the huge house that was being renovated in prelude to its becoming the headquarters in the fall for General Dwight David Eisenhower. He was the unannounced selection of the Supreme Commander of Allied Forces Europe. Annabel came in with Sir Hugh Dalton, Curt Lemay and two other general officers. Only moments later came General Eisenhower and his entourage. Also with him was Air Marshal Leigh-Mallory, the Commander of all Allied Air Forces Europe and Major General Ray Baker.

Coltrane came to attention and saluted as Ike came up to him. After returning his salute, Ike said "I have wanted to meet you for some time. I'm impressed with your development of the Black Bart operation and other combat achievements. President Roosevelt asked me to personally conduct this ceremony." He nodded to a Lieutenant Colonel who came to attention and commanded, "ATTENTION TO ORDERS!" At those words all present came to attention as the Adjutant read the first of two General Orders. Coltrane was awarded the Distinguished Flying Cross with two oak leaf clusters, the Silver Star and two Bronze Stars for his numerous missions behind enemy lines.

Then the second General Order was read, "By order of the President of the United States with concurrence of the United States Senate, Samuel Barton Coltrane is promoted to Brigadier General United States Army."

"Congratulations, Bart," Ike said after he pinned the stars on his uniform. "I was wondering if you could spend a couple of days with a study group that Lieutenant General Frederick Morgan and Major General Ray Barker are heading up. Your experience and observations would be of great assistance to them."

"Yes Sir, I'd be honored to help them if I can," Coltrane responded.

"Excellent, General Baker's office will contact you tomorrow to make all the arrangements," Ike said as he again shook Coltrane's hand and left at a fast pace.

The group became active again and congratulations given before departing as well.

Lemay came up to him. Before he could say anything, Coltrane quietly whispered into his ear, "What's the deal with Morgan and Baker?"

Lemay got closer and replied, "'OVERLORD!' They're designing the invasion of Europe. They've a very long list of questions that you can best answer for them. Your experience will be incredibly important to them and the plan. After that, it's off to the Air Bombardment Division Headquarters with you. We'll miss you in the group, but you can do a lot of good in the ops job there. I'm still looking at September for your transfer to the other job that Hap mentioned. Things are starting to really heat up in the areas where your help is needed. I still can't tell you any more than that," he concluded. He saw Annabel and motioned her over. "I won't be able to be at your wedding, but all the best," he said. "If Hap doesn't have a heart attack, he'll be with you then. He's actually looking forward to it. Annabel, until we meet again, good luck." Then Lemay gave Annabel a kiss on the cheek and departed.

A very happy Bart Coltrane asked, "Where are we going for supper?"

"Love, we're meeting Elizabeth and Philip at the Ritz. It's time for you to get involved in the wedding plans," she said as they left the salon.

CHAPTER 49

It was almost midnight when Annabel and Bart entered Annabel's London home. It was typical of the other expensive homes on Braton Street in London's very stylish Mayfair area. It was the address of wealth and political prominence. The American Embassy was just a stone's throw from the four-floor residence. They went into the library and stood before the fireplace, warming themselves after a cold walk from supper at the Claridge Hotel. Bart went over to an antique serving table and poured a fine Napoleon cognac into two brandy snifters. He handed one to Annabel as he put his arm around her. Neither said anything at first but then she asked, "I assume that the 3rd of June is acceptable."

"It certainly is as long as you show up," he said as he hugged her with his arm. "What kind of wedding do you want? A big or a small wedding? Here, or up country?" he asked.

"I'm expected to have a highly visible wedding. However, given the hardships made by the war, we might be able to keep it a little smaller than usual. Perhaps we could use the church at Temple Mount instead of Westminster Abby. We could keep it to 200 to 250 people, maybe," Annabel said in a matter of fact tone.

Bart was shocked, but came back with a question, "If we used Westminster, how many would attend?"

'Oh," she said lifting her head and eyes upward to the ceiling, 'at least 500 or so, and the Archbishop would insist on conducting the ceremony. He's an old family friend and helps me with the charities. Besides, my social obligation you're a Brigadier General and that requires a little pomp and circumstance as well."

Bart turned his head slightly and rolled his eyes. "So much for a quiet wedding at a small English countryside church," he thought.

She thought for a moment then said, "Let me talk with a few people on what is required and appropriate. I definitely want Elizabeth and her boyfriend Philip Mountbatten involved. Philip is in the Royal Navy doing his part for the war effort and a really nice guy, as you saw tonight. Elizabeth writes to him every day. She intends to marry him even if her parents continue to object. Her father calls him 'The Hun.' He's really a great chap and is totally in love with Elizabeth.

"Elizabeth always helps me with my charity work. That's unusual for most eighteen year old girls," she continued.

Bart was listening closely to Annabel's description of her friends and things that she wanted to have at the wedding. He looked at her and decided to show interest by asking her a question. "Philip is in the Navy, so can he get away for the wedding?"

Sure he can, especially since Elizabeth's father is King George the Sixth. This has got to be somewhat overpowering to you. Don't worry, dear, it will all work out. I'm sorry, but I'm obligated to certain formalities. Please be patient and don't worry about a thing."

Bart smiled sheepishly, "I should have known that you would be involved with the Royal Family. We were with them for two hours and there was no mention of royalty or her father being the King. She doesn't act like royalty or what I thought royalty would act like. She's very down to earth like you," Bart said shaking his head. "We'll do everything proper. I'm ready for anything that you want to do. Just tell me where and when I'm to be at any function. This could be fun," he said in a happy tone as his hand slid down her back to her butt. She jumped when he pinched it.

Bart went over to the overstuffed leather sofa and sat down. "We need to talk about what we're going to do after the war. I only have nine more years in the service to qualify for my retirement. Lemay and Arnold are looking to me to help them with the post war Army air corps reorganization."

"Can you get out after the war?" she asked.

"Sure, but flying is all that I know. I have to make a living for us," he responded. "But, I'm open to new ideas."

"Is there any type of civilian flying or business that you would like to pursue?"

Bart became quiet and thoughtful. "Well, there's going to be a great demand for air freight after the war. Here in England, as well as Europe, Africa and in the India-Southeast Asia area. But that takes a lot of money. But it's something that we could do together," he said.

She smiled. "Yes, it would be wonderful to build something like that together. How much money would it take to start and operate the air freight company?"

Coltrane thought for minute and took his finger and wrote some imaginary numbers on the top of the coffee table. He mentally came up with his answer, then turned to Annabel and said, "If we bought war surplus Douglass C-54 and C-47's that are not going to the military or will be excess at the end of the war, we could probably cover the markets for about $7,500,000 US dollars. I wonder if we can get a loan for that amount?"

Annabel smiled and got up and went over to Bart and extended her hand and said, "We have a deal, partner. We'll pay cash."

Coltrane smiled, "I forgot that you do have some money in the bank. This will work for us and it will be fun. Now why don't we go upstairs and discuss the matter in bed."

CHAPTER 50

At Wright Patterson Army Air Force Base in Dayton, Ohio, an olive drab C-47 pulled in and turned broadside to the Transit Terminal. The passenger door of the C-47 opened and the portable ladder dropped to deplaning position. Colonel Erik Nelson stepped down, briefcase in hand, and proceeded directly to a waiting staff car. The driver of the vehicle spoke to the Colonel before closing the rear door of the staff car after the Colonel entered the vehicle.

"The Base Commandant wondered if you'd mind stopping by before going on over to the B-29 Office, Colonel Nelson, Sir?" The driver asked.

Colonel Nelson looked up at the driver from the rear set and smiled. "Of course not, I'm honored that he'd remember me."

The driver grinned knowingly, "Oh, he remembers you alright, Sir."

The driver closed the door, got into the vehicle himself and drove away.

A few moment later, Colonel Nelson entered the typical military office, only to be met halfway across the room by the Commandant himself - Major General Echols.

"Erik! Good to see you again," General Echols said. They shook hands. "I hope you didn't mind the driver bringing you by."

"Not at all, General," Colonel Nelson said. He gazed at the General's stars. "I believe it was 'Captain' Echols the last time I saw you."

The General clasped Colonel Nelson's shoulder. "It's been a long time."

Colonel Nelson's eyes caught sight of a very large black and white, ornately framed photograph which hung behind the General's desk. It was a scene of six early day Army aviators posed around an ancient biplane. Lowell Thomas was seen in their midst. Erik Nelson was one of those aviators. At the very bottom of the photograph were the following words:

The First Round-The-World Flight

USAAC 1924

Colonel Nelson, gazed at the picture, a half smile playing across his lips. "I see you keep old memorabilia hanging around, too," he said.

General Echols turned back from the picture to look at Colonel Nelson. "It was a historic achievement." He gestured Colonel Nelson to a chair.

"It would've been easier in a B-17!" Colonel Nelson said.

The General seated himself across from Nelson.

"There might not have been any B-17s, Erik—perhaps not even an air corps as we know it, if it hadn't been for pioneers like you, and the others, who fought so hard to expand the frontiers of military aviation. Hell, General, some of our own people were holding out for support type aircraft and battleships."

"Well… it's still a troubled frontier," Colonel Nelson said. "You've heard, I'm sure, that the President ordered the B-29 into full production yesterday… without the benefit of test flight experience."

General Echols nodded. "He had no alternative. Without the B-29, we'll lose the Pacific War."

"Exactly," Colonel Nelson said. He thought for a moment. "But it'll be a problem laden program, and if we fail… well those frontiers we worked so hard to establish may be in jeopardy again."

"What's the game plan, Erik?" General Echols asked. "How are they going to handle the engineering changes that normally flow out of test flight data?"

"Engineering changes resulting from the initial test flights of the individual airplanes will be referred to a committee. They'll decide whether the change should be incorporated on the production lines or as an engineering modification to be installed after the ships are completed," Colonel Nelson said.

General whistled. "The potential for disaster—it's staggering! Why, even on the B.-17 program, continuing engineering changes were an almost insurmountable problem and we tested that airplane for *years* before going into full production with it."

Nelson nodded in agreement.

General Echols continued after a moment of contemplative silence. "They told us you'd been appointed Hap's number one trouble shooter with authority to *obliterate* red tape, military politics or anything else that gets in the way of the program."

Colonel Nelson laughed. "I'm afraid the obliteration of red tape and military politics might he an unrealistic undertaking."

General Echols smiled. "Well, Erik, Captain Agather has all of the information you need from his office ready and organized: projections, production curves, concentrations of skills, production capacities at the various plants—everything!"

Colonel stood up. "Then, perhaps I'd better not keep the Captain waiting.

General Echols went to his desk intercom.

"You'll like Vic Agather, Erik. He's efficient to the point and dedicated to the B-29 program itself." General Echols spoke into the intercom. "Have Colonel Nelson's car brought around, please."

"Yes, Sir, right away, Sir."

"What's his background?" Colonel Nelson said.

"ROTC and flight training… Harvard, I believe… investment and merger experience on Wall Street, called to active duty and assigned to head up the B-29 materials, manpower and machine tools allocation group here at Wright Pat a couple of years ago," He extended his hand. "I know you're pressed for time, Erik, but we'd be honored to have you for dinner this evening if you can swing it."

Colonel Nelson shook the General's hand. "Thank you, I'll touch base with you later."

"Right. Let me know if you need anything… anything at all. The entire base is at your disposal."

Erik Nelson nodded, smiled, and turned to leave, then paused thoughtfully. "There's one thing: I d like to take a look at Captain Agather's service file if… if it's not too inconvenient for you."

General Echols was momentarily puzzled. "Of course not. I'll have it brought over here right away."

Colonel Nelson opened the door. "Thank you."

The two men saluted each other as Nelson turned and left, closing the door behind him.

A tray that once held sandwiches and hot coffee, the cups now empty and disarranged, sat on a corner of the office desk. Captain Agather and a weary Colonel Nelson stood before a large map of the United States. A conference type table piled high with manuals and statistical documents were all disarranged and cluttered from having been handled extensively.

"I think that about does it, Colonel Nelson. I think it's pretty clear to everyone that we've got some real problems with the R3350," Captain Agather said. "If problems arise at the modification centers, then you'd probably want to take people from the Wichita production lines." He pointed to the appropriate area on the map… to help out."

"The flight crews will be reporting in to Great Bend," Colonel Nelson said. He indicated the relevant map areas. "Pratt here and Salina over here and lastly Walker over here."

"Right, Colonel, and that's where we propose to install the engineering modification kits that will be sent out from Renton and Wichita initially," Agather said.

"The actual flight crews will be installing the kits themselves?" Colonel Nelson said.

"That's the way it's planned, Sir. Hopefully, it'll allow the crews to familiarize themselves with the aircraft from the moment they begin reporting in," Captain Agather said.

"I don't know… but I guess it's risky *any* way we go."

Colonel Nelson crossed to the conference table, seated himself there, and wearily, thumbed idly through a manual as his mind attempted to comprehend the scope of the briefing that has just been completed.

Captain Agather watched the Colonel contemplatively, then went to the conference table and sat down, and then spoke in a solicitous tone.

"Colonel Nelson, my wife and I have a small apartment near the base here, I know she'd love to have you for dinner this evening… and I think it might he relaxing for you, too," Agather said.

Colonel Nelson looked at Agather for a moment. "Why, that's very thoughtful of you, Captain. You're sure your wife wouldn't mind?"

Captain Agather said, "Absolutely certain, Colonel, I'll call her right away. What time shall I tell her? Well, I've got a matter to discuss with the Commandant. What do you say to seven-thirty? Is that all right?"

Captain Agather stood up and replied. "Of course, seven-thirty, it's then."

CHAPTER 51

A lone B-24 Liberator flew westward toward Reykjavik, Iceland in the predawn hours of May 3, 1943. The bomber had been converted by the Army transport command for passenger service. The crew was experienced in the VIP type mission that they were on. This was their sixth transatlantic trip in this aircraft in the past two months. Tonight was different. One of the engines was not running as smoothly as it should. Both the pilot and co-pilot were straining to listen to the throbbing number four for a clue as to what was malfunctioning. The night masked the small stream of fuel that was racing across the lower side of the engine nacelle and becoming a mist as it crossed the lower side of the right wing. The pilot was listening closely for any sign of what would tell them what was wrong as the co-pilot made very slight changes in the propeller pitch and RPM. The co-pilot was becoming frustrated as he could not get the prop pitch to stay synchronized with the other three engines.

The co-pilot was eyeing the tachometer and said "still dropping…" The pilot replied, "How about the carburetor heat?" The co-pilot adjusted the carburetor heat to the maximum and waited a moment to observe the results, then said, "Nothing," The pilot shook his head and said in a dejected voice "Better feather it." Then he pressed the radio transmit button, "Reykjavik Tower, this is Air Transport Command two-nine-zero…over."

In the passenger cabin behind the two pilots, Lt. Gen. Frank M. Andrews was busily engaged in paperwork, not aware of the problem with the engine. An aide was sitting across from the General. As the engine was cut, the General glances out through the side window, perplexed. The General watched the prop coming to a standstill. Then he resumed his work.

The pilot's face brightened as Reykjavik Tower responded. "ATC two nine zero, Reykjavik control, over" came the voice over the radio.

The pilot lifts his microphone and replied, "Reykjavik Tower, we're approximately fifty miles southeast of Reykjavik Field, on a heading of three-four-zero, inbound from Prestwick, Scotland. We've just feathered number four engine. The condition is stable, but request "straight-in" approach, over." The Reykjavik Tower operator quickly responded to the serious situation. "ATC two-niner-zero, you're cleared for "straight-in" approach to runway three one. Descend to five thousand feet, maintain present heading. A flight of B-17s will pass above you at fifteen to seventeen thousand feet in approximately ten minutes. That's the only traffic reporting at the present time, over."

"Roger, Reykjavik Tower, runway three one. We'll require mechanics on an emergency basis. We've got Frank Andrews, Commanding General, United States Forces, European theater on board, en route to Washington, D.C.," informed the pilot.

Reykjavik Tower operator acknowledged, "Uh…Roger two-niner-zero. Stand by for verification."

The pilot calmly replied, "Roger Reykjavik Tower." The pilot began rising from his seat, speaking to the co-pilot. "I'd better tell the General what's going on. It's going to be tough getting mechanics on the line this early in the morning." The co-pilot nodded, assuming control of the aircraft.

The pilot entered the cabin bending down to speak to the General. "General Andrews, we've been unable to resolve the problem on number four. I felt it advisable to feather it." "What's our position?" asked General Andrews. "Sir, we're about twenty minutes southeast of Reykjavik, Iceland now, and cleared for a "straight-in." I've asked them to have mechanics standing by," answered the pilot.

"Thank you," Andrews stated, then paused thoughtfully and said "Stay on them for those mechanics. It's imperative that we get into Washington tonight. I'm scheduled with the Joint Chiefs at 0900 in the morning."

"Yes, Sir, I understand, Sir," the pilot responded.

A USAAF staff car parked on a ramp adjacent to the main runway. A Brigadier General stood alongside the staff car as the ATC B-24 pulled up, turning around to its parking area as directed by an Air Force ramp person. The number four prop was feathered on the huge aircraft. The left rear passenger door opened and General Andrews and his aide emerged and descended the portable stairs. The Brigadier General walked to the stairs to greet them. General Norwood extended his hand and said, "General Andrews."

General Andrews, shaking hands warmly, said "Bret, nice to see you again. How's the ferry business?" General Norwood said, "Booming!" Just refueled twelve B-17s and sent them on their way to Prestwick." The party then began to walk to the waiting staff car. General Andrews looked at the young Brigadier General and aide. "We're going to snow you under with B-17s passing through here before the summer's over." The driver held the car door open as General Andrews and Norwood entered the staff car. The aide then entered the front seat area. The Generals settled into the rear of the Staff car. The sound of engaging gears distracted the General as the vehicle began moving out.

General Norwood looked at Andrews and asked, "Speaking of B-17s, just how is the bomber offensive coming along?"

"Still bogged down in support operations, Bret," Andrews said. "The submarine menace has absorbed most of General Baker's Eight Air Force effort. He paused introspectively, as he glanced at Norwood ,and said "It's all had its effect upstairs."

General Norwood responded quickly, "What the hell did the combined chiefs expect?" "You can't penetrate reinforced concrete walls fifteen feet thick, no matter if you bomb from nineteen or nine thousand feet!"

General Andrews gazed out the car window for a moment and said, "I'm still convinced we could bring Germany to her knees with daylight precision bombardment. We're getting some of the old Second Bombardment men over there now." He glanced back at Norwood. "Curt Lemay for one. Those men built their entire careers around bombardment. It's beginning to pay off. Losses are decreasing, and there's significant improvement in our bombing accuracy."

General Norwood said with a slight edge of sarcasm, "But the build up for the surface invasion, it's still going on?"

General Andrews said, "Yes. Operation Bolero's in full swing. Stalin's putting intense pressure on the Allies to pull off an invasion of the European continent, even as early as this summer. He desperately wants relief from the German advances along his Western front."

General Norwood responded, "He should realize that a successful bomber offensive would give him that relief. With the German's industrial capability destroyed, they sure as hell couldn't continue supporting troops on the Russian front!"

General Andrews began to grin tolerantly and said, "Well, things haven't changed much from the early days, Bret. It's still a battle for resources... budget...concept. General Arnold's bucking some pretty stiff opposition to the bomber offensive top side."

General Norwood looked stunned and said, "I thought all of that would change when Titus Clay retired."

General Andrews looked at Norwood then back at the passing aircraft then said with concern. "If we can just manage to get significant numbers of airplanes and crews over there before the winter months close down our ferry routes." General Norwood then respectfully said, "You know, every officer in the United States Air Force felt a sense of pride and personal achievement when they named you commander of all U.S. Forces in Europe last month, General Andrews. We felt we at last had an airman in a key field command. We're hearing rumors that you'll soon be named the Supreme Allied Commander."

"British, Free French, Russia, America, all under a unified theater command?" stated the incredulous General Andrews. "It staggers the imagination. Anyway, I don't think it would be me," he said. "My money's on Eisenhower getting selected."

The Staff car pulled up in front of General Norwood's Quarters, a typical quonset hut type structure that had become the mainstay of the military. The Generals and the aide alit, the driver holding the door for the Generals as they entered. The pilot stood in front of the faulty engine on the ATC B-24 as the mechanic snapped the cowling in place. The mechanic then climbed down from the scaffold, pulled it back from the engine, then, gestured to the co-pilot to start the engine. Two additional maintenance personnel were watching with the pilot and mechanic, one with a fire extinguisher ready to extinguish any fire. The co-pilot actuated the engine starter, and the starter whined loudly. The mechanic watches the power plant roar to life and smiled. The co-pilot smiled broadly as he applied throttle to the number four engine, intently watching the gauges as he did so. Presently, the mechanic entered the cockpit, gazing at the gauges also. The mechanic and the co-pilot glanced at each, both nodding affirmatively. The mechanic continued to watch the engine instruments as he said to the co-pilot, "Can't figure what was wrong. Carburetor fuel adjustment wasn't that far off."

The co-pilot said "What about the carburetor heat?" The mechanic replied, "Nothing wrong with it." The mechanic shook his head perplexedly. The co-pilot then said "Well, she's purring like a kitten now." Meanwhile, unseen by anyone was the underneath section of number four engine where a rivulet of fuel was being blown back along the bottom wing surface, turning into vapor in the prop wash.

The mechanic waved to the man with the fire extinguisher and his companion as they secured the fire extinguisher, then crossed to a service truck nearby, oblivious to the fuel leak. General Andrews was walking back and forth as he dictated. The aide and a clerk typist were taking shorthand and the typist transcribing, was frantically transcribing. "With longer range fighter cover, our heavy bombers could make deeper penetrations into the heart of the German industrial sector, with less battle damage and casualty. The continuing development of wing tanks, and the P-51 power problem, therefore, should be a matter of first priority."

General Norwood entered the room, interrupting the General. "The plane is ready, General," General Norwood reported.

General Andrews nodded his understanding as he handed the last shorthand notes to the typist. "It'll only take a moment, Sir," the aide said.

The ATC B-24 was waiting with its engines at idle, awaiting its passenger. At the rear entrance to the ATC B-24 as General Andrews, Norwood and the aide entered, General Andrews turned to General Norwood and stated "Well, Bret, sorry to descend on you like this," as they shook hands. "Thanks for everything," he said.

"Have a good flight, General," Norwood said, grinning wryly, "I … uh…hope you're able to deal with that Washington morass successfully."

General Andrews nodded and grinned, then entered the aircraft followed by the aide. The ATC B-24 powered-up and turned away without anyone noticing the fuel leak. The ATC B-24 then lifted off, a fog of engine fuel streaming out behind the number four engine, not noticed by the two pilots.

General Norwood gazed at the ATC B-24 in the distance, tensing as he suddenly spotted the fuel vapor trail. General Norwood ran to his staff car hurriedly, speaking to the driver even as he entered. "Control tower…step on it!" The staff car moved swiftly away. The co-pilot cursed as the number four engine surged, its irregular throb catching the pilot's attention as well. "What the hell? It's that damned number four again!" The co-pilot looked out the side window toward the ailing engine only to see the engine in flames. "We're on fire!"

The pilot then commanded, "Feather it! Hit the fire extinguishers! Reykjavik Tower, we're turning back, we have an emergency!" General Norwood hurriedly entered the control tower operations area. The control tower operator glanced up and said in an excited voice ,"They're turning back, General, some kind of emergency." General Norwood commanded, "Call up the emergency vehicles!"

"Yes, Sir", replied the operator.

General Andrews tightened his safety belt calmly and gazed out at the ailing engine. He knew this was not a simple problem. They were in peril. The pilots were frantically making cockpit adjustments relative to the emergency. The co-pilot glanced up, frozen as he screamed, "Look out! There's a mountain dead ahead!"

General Norwood watched helplessly as the ATC B-24 struck the mountain, exploding in a ball of flame. He turned his head in despair. The control tower operator became silent, looking at General Norwood, the tragedy obvious in his gaze.

A somber mood was over General Eaker's office at High Wycombe, eleven hundred miles away. General Eaker stood and gazed out a large window in the office complex. An aide enters, walking briskly to a radio, addressing

General Eaker even as he went to turn the radio on. "It's coming in now, Sir. We've patched it in directly from the BBC." General Eaker said, without turning from the window, "Thank you."

"Good Evening, everybody. This is Lowell Thomas broadcasting from upstate New York. Well, there's tragedy in the news tonight for the United States Army Air Force…the second time in less than a week! Lieutenant General Frank M. Andrews is dead…killed in a plane crash in Iceland during the early morning hours. Only five days ago, Major General Robert E. Olds died in a sanitarium in Arizona from a rare heart disease. General Andrews was considered the odds- on favorite to become Supreme Commander of the European Theater of War. A horse cavalryman turned aviator, General Andrews was the early day air corps' most powerful crusader for the four-engine bomber and the Mitchell-Douhet theory of strategic bombardment. A military spokesman today said the supreme European command will probably go to a regular Army general, naming General George Marshall and General Dwight Eisenhower as possibilities. Elsewhere on the news front, the United States Coal Industry has ... "

The aide snapped the radio off. General Eaker wearily spoke, "It's hard to imagine the Air Force without Frank Andrews. Billy Mitchell… Frank Andrews…Bob Olds…we wouldn't have four-engine bombers if it hadn't been for their professional insight…their courage to fight for what they believed in." After a long pause, he continued, "Order the flags at half-mast throughout the command."

"Yes, Sir," the aide replied and exited.

CHAPTER 52

It was over two hours before the wedding was to start, but Bart was to arrive early to meet with the Archbishop and other church officials concerning every aspect of the ceremony. Bart really didn't have a clue how popular his bride-to-be was in England. Her charity events for children and the war veterans were known and respected throughout the British Empire. Her wealth was enormous. She was one of the wealthiest members of the empire, but you would never know it to look at her dress, car, and casual day-to-day activities. "She may be a 'Blue Blood,' Bart thought, but she's as common in life as the people of England and West Texas."

When the taxi pulled up to the side door of Westminster Abby, he could see two dozen onlookers and press standing near the main entrance. "This is going to be a three-ring circus," he thought. As he got out, a middle-aged man in a terrible fitting brown coat and pants approached him. He saw the sudden uneasiness of the General and quickly said in a deep cockney accent, "General, I'm Harbone with the *Times*."

"Could you spare a bit of time with me?" he asked.

Coltrane did not trust the press, but for some reason took a liking to this one. "Sure," he said smiling. "What can I do for you?"

"Looks like your wedding is going to be a bloody circus," he said jokingly.

"My sentiments exactly," Coltrane replied as the two laughed together.

"How does it feel to be marrying one of England's finest flowers?"

"For an old West Texas crop duster, it's a dream come true." She gives me a warmth inside that could melt the Arctic ice cap. She's intelligent and is a real partner in every aspect," Coltrane said.

"That's quite a mouth full, mate," the reporter said, then asked "What is a crop duster?"

Bart smiled and replied, "Out in West Texas where I come from, we grow miles and miles of cotton. The cotton fields go as far as the eye can see. Cotton has an enemy called the boll weevil, which must be killed or you lose the crop. Given the vast area, we use an old World War I aircraft to spray the insecticide on the cotton. We fly about five feet off the ground and spray a couple of thousand acres per day. I used to be one of those crop dusters. Not a glamorous job, but I did get to fly and it paid fairly well."

"Fascinating," he said as he wrote down his remarks. "Will you and the Duchess be relocating to West Texas after the war?"

"No, we'll be staying here in London. I love it here and she intends to continue her charity work."

"Since you're an American general, I assumed that you would be relocating."

"Our home will be in London and I'll go where the Army sends me until I retire in a couple of years. There's still a war on," Coltrane said.

The reporter looked at the General for a moment then continued, "It's impressive to have Princess Elizabeth as the Maid of Honor. There are rumors that the King was to be present, but decided not to come, since Philip Mountbatten is a part of the wedding party. There's a reported conflict between the King and young Mountbatten.

Coltrane saw the trap and responded, "If you would read your own paper, you would know his Highness has been down with the influenza for over a week. As far as any problem between them, I haven't been told of any. I do believe that the story is substantially blown out of proportion. Besides, the King isn't likely to be at the wedding of a commoner like me."

The reporter almost broke out in laughter. "Commoner, you say. Brigadier General "Black Bart" Coltrane. You came to the aid of Great Britain in our darkest hour before the U.S. entered the war and flew over 200 missions over enemy territory. I seriously doubt the British people would ever consider you a simple commoner. A British hero, maybe. But never a commoner. Thanks for your time, General, and all the best in your marriage. Cheerio."

Bart went inside the Abby and was struck speechless by the beauty and majesty of this incredible church. The ornate detail on the high columns and walls were almost overshadowed by the woodwork, flags and stained glass windows. He felt very humbled by this magnificent structure. A young priest saw Coltrane and offered to take him to the Archbishop, who was waiting for him. The head of the Church of England talked with Coltrane and discussed the procedure again with him. He took him to the cathedral and pointed out aspects of the formal wedding as it would happen and what he would do. Then they returned to the office. Bart was ushered to a nicely appointed waiting and dressing room to wait for the ceremony to start. Fifteen minutes before the service, General Arnold arrived. He was very tired and did not look well. Bart thanked him for doing him the honor, but would not be offended if he wanted to go rest instead. The General said "no" with a decisive voice. "This is important," he said. "It's important for you individually, as well as the United States. This is an important event for both countries."

Bart had not considered the political impact of his wedding, but quickly understood the situation. He could hear the massive pipes of the organ begin to play. The young priest returned and escorted them to the rear of the cathedral and placed them into the proper place in the procession. "It was time," Bart thought. He was about to marry a woman that absolutely warmed his heart and made his knees like Jell-O. He truly loved Annabel and looked forward to the rest of his life with her.

The trumpeters sounded the opening notes to "Trumpets Volunteer" followed by the magnificent pipe organ, as the wedding procession started down the aisle. Bart suddenly had weak knees and butterflies in his stomach. "Combat wasn't as bad as this," he thought.

CHAPTER 53

Lemay was in his private quarters in Elveden Hall going over paperwork. Lemay sat there with his pipe in his mouth, as he sat behind a desk in an ornate but obviously private apartment room in the Elveden Castle. Tireless and formally attired, he was reading Helen's letter.

My dearest Curt, Father stays glued to the radio and busily updates his maps, one for missions flown by the 305th and now one for the Third Division! Janie sends her love – all of us do. Good night my dearest....All my love, Helen.

There's an urgent knock at Lemay's door. Lemay looked up. "Yes?"

The door opened and two MPs shove a small, gardener type civilian into Lemay's room ahead of them. The civilian stood meekly, uncomfortably. The taller MP reported, "Colonel...we...uh...we just found this creep skulking around the grounds outside."

"Well, who are you?" Lemay asked. "My name is Guinness, Sir," the man said meekly. Lemay gazes at the man a long, incredulous moment, then, "You're..you're not the Earl of Iveigh," Lemay asked, pointing with his pipe stem. "Yes, Sir," the man said as he gained his composure. Awe stricken, Lemay then said as he rose to his feet, "Then you own this...uh...this structure."

"Yes, Sir," the Earl said. "When the Air Force personnel moved in, I moved into the groom's cottage down the way. I...I only wanted to look at the shrubbery on the north portico, General. You see, we've some rose plants there...they've developed a fungus."

Lemay commanded the big MP, "Send the Sergeant of the Guard in here, immediately!" The startled MP responded and left the room. 'Yes, Sir." Lemay extended his hand. "I'm sorry about all of this, Sir. I'm Curt Lemay, the Commanding Officer here."

The Earl saluted and said "Yes, I know, Sir."

"Would you…uh…like to look around while you're up here?" he gestured toward a large picture frame on the wall draped with a sheet. "We've tried to take care of the place…covered the paintings." Lemay looked back at the Earl sympathetically. "It must mean a great deal to you."

"Oh, yes, but we're only too happy to have it being used as it is," the Earl replied.

The Sergeant of the Guard entered with the MP Lieutenant who was officer of the Guard. Lemay said, incisively, "Sergeant...this is the Earl of Iveigh. I want every MP here to recognize him on sight! Do you understand?"

Both the Lieutenant and Sergeant both responded timidly, "Ye…yes, Sir!"

"See to it, Lieutenant!" Lemay commanded. Then Lemay turned to the Earl and said "feel free to call me anytime…for any reason."

The Earl was moved by the Colonel and was genuinely appreciative. "Why…thank you, Colonel. That's very kind of you. I shall be no bother however…no bother at all."

"It's no bother, Sir," Lemay said in a soft voice. The Earl and the Guards exited and Lemay gazed after them, grinning, shaking his head resignedly.

The next morning the guard was on the entrance gate to the castle grounds and came to attention as a staff car sweeps through, its bumper flags bearing two stars, rippling in the air flow. The staff car came to a halt as General Eaker and his aide alit, striding brusquely up the steps, disappearing inside. They walked down the hall to Lemay's office which was once the library of the ancient complex.

Centuries-old paintings hung along the walls in this thoroughly typical English castle atmosphere. One couldn't help but be impressed with the tradition and culture of the castle. Lemay met Eaker and the aide, shaking hands with them. "General Eaker, good to have you here, Sir," Lemay said. General Eaker concluded the salutation.

"Curt."

General Eaker removed his cap and placed it on a side table, then moved to a large military wall map, pausing there, clasping his hands behind his back as he speaks to Lemay. "Curt, the pressing question up at Bomber Command these days is the rate of our operations and the ability of daylight bombing formations to make the necessary penetrations into the heart of the Reich."

Eaker turned to the map, indicating general areas of the European land mass. "Since the combined chief's operation 'point-blank' directive in June made the date for the cross channel invasion of Europe contingent on our gaining aerial supremacy over Germany, the destruction of the German air force and the factories and installations supporting it, our rate and range problems have suddenly become very acute. "

General Eaker turned from the map, paced a few steps as he spoke, his hands clasped behind his back, then turned and crossed back to the wall map. "But if we throw our available forces into that battle recklessly, our strength will deteriorate before we've been able to accomplish that point-blank directive. On the other hand, if we try to conserve our forces in the interest of building them up, waiting until we've reached full operational strength three or four months down the line, or waiting for our longer range fighter planes, which we likely won't have until the end of the earlier either, then the enemy gets a much desired break from our daylight bombing."

Eaker was pacing and gesturing with his hands as he emphasized his words. "Intelligence sources indicate we've already begun to cause massive diversions of the German labor force. They're relocating their industry. We've interrupted their synthetic rubber production and their airframe production. Production of fighter planes has fallen behind schedule. They're pulling fighter groups out of North Africa and the eastern front in order to strengthen their western front. They're definitely on the defensive. Any time we give them for retrenchment now would be to their advantage, not ours," Eaker said loudly for emphasis. Lemay nodded his understanding as he looked at Eaker, then back to the map. General Eaker turned to the map again indicating the relevant area. "You're familiar with Operation 'Juggler', the long-range coordinated attack planned against the Messerschmitt factories here at Regensburg and Weiner Newstadt?"

Lemay replies, "Yes, Sir! That operation of course was to have followed the bombing of the Ploesti oil refineries here in Rumania. We've changed those plans up a bit. For good reasons, I believe. We've put together a plan for a simultaneous attack against Regensburg... and Schweinfurt, here, where the bulk of German's ball bearing industry is located. Since the Third Division is equipped with the latest B-17s, bigger tanks and longer range, you'll lead that mission, Colonel. The Third Division will bypass Schweinfurt, hit Regensburg, then go on out across the Alps to North Africa. You'll refuel and reload bombs there, then hit an additional target on the way back."

Lemay answered in a curious voice, "A shuttle mission?"

General Eaker continued, "That's right. The First Division will follow ten minutes behind. They'll hit Schweinfurt and return to base here. You'll have standard fighter escort as far as they can go. You'll, of course, pull up the German fighters as you go through. The First Division, ten minutes behind, will go through relatively free because you'll have already taken the fight going in. They'll have bombed Schweinfurt before the German fighters can refuel and get back in the air. They'll pick up standard fighter escort on the way out."

Lemay gazed thoughtfully at the map, then said, "Three targets with an effective loss rate of one! And, deeper penetration into Germany. You do know the First Division has a new Operations officer? Bart Coltrane has finally left the theater and is now in Washington. The new guy is just getting started. But they should be okay, since Bart set it up from the beginning."

"That's the idea, Colonel," replied General Eaker.

Lemay pondered a map for a long moment, then said, "Timing…that will be the critical factor…and, the variable weather conditions at both ends of the routing." Lemay paused as he contemplated the areas on the map, then turning to General Eaker, said, "Not to speak of the German fighter defenses deployed around the area. If they've reinforced their western fighter belt, successful penetration would depend on the effectiveness of our own fighter escrow. Without it, our losses going in could be, uh…significant."

General Eaker slowly walked to the side table for his cap, then looked at Lemay and said "You'll have to go down to North Africa, Colonel. Make the necessary arrangements through General's Spaatz and Norstad down there.

Fred Anderson will get the mission details down to you as soon as possible." Eaker paused, turned to Lemay, grinning, "Speaking of Fred, Colonel, I was unaware he was the one who alerted you to get the hell out of Syracuse before they shipped you off to the Pacific!"

Lemay, chuckling, said "In the nick of time!"

General Eaker was smiling and trying not to laugh, "I heard about it when Fred got over here last month to take over Bomber Command." General Eaker paused reflectively, then turned to Lemay, "Well…we're both glad you made it. Your lead crew concept…it's made a lot of difference in our bombing efficiency. I'm afraid we've taken too much advantage of that good situation from time to time….but, we've had little alternative. We're getting more bombs on the target, and that's what it's all about!"

Lemay was grinning tolerantly and softly replied "We ran out of lead crews a couple of times back in the 305th. Finally, we had to increase the training program." Lemay paused thoughtfully, then said, "General Eaker, there's a question in the back of my mind – been there every since we learned about the point-blank directive."

"What's that, Colonel?" General Eaker said. Lemay stated, "If the Eighth Air Force <u>is</u> successful in destroying the German air force, there wouldn't be <u>any</u> effective resistance left to keep us from an almost routine and systematic destruction of the German industrial apparatus," Lemay said, posing a rhetorical question. "Why the cross channel invasion? German industry would inevitably collapse under daylight bombardment. The German army would be immobilized. Only an occupational force would be required in that event."

General Eaker smiled faintly, "Colonel, there isn't a field grade officer in the entire Eighth Air Force who doesn't ponder that same question, pretty damned often." General Eaker and the aide shook hands with Lemay and crossed to the massive wooden doors and into the hallway. General Eaker paused, turned back to Lemay, "Oh, by the way, Curt…I've got a young Lieutenant Colonel on staff…Bernie Lay. He'll be taking over an air group pretty soon. Needs some combat missions under his belt. Can you find a place for him on the Regensburg mission?"

"I'll have Kissner find a slot for him. That mission will change his mind about wanting a group", Lemay said smiling.

General Eaker said, "He was a professional writer in his civilian life before the war – maybe you can find some use for him in that way." General Eaker and his aide then exited the building.

Lemay gazed after them momentarily, then crossed to gaze thoughtfully at the wall map and contemplated the map, the weight of the grim task ahead reflecting in his features.

It was very early morning on August 17, 1943 at the 100th Bomb Group Briefing Room – located at the Thorpe Abbotts airfield. There was a black cloth covering a huge aerial wall map which covered today's mission.. The 100th air crews were quickly taking their seats for the briefing. The 100th Bomb Group Intelligence officer strode to the platform and pulled the cloth cover from the screen. A hush fell over the air crews as the red string stretched across the map, revealing both the target and the North African destination. The Intelligence officer indicated the relevant area on the map, using a short wooden pointer to pinpoint the position, then started his briefing. "Your primary is Regensburg! Your aiming point is the center of the Messerschmitt ME-109G aircraft and engine assembly shops there."

He then moved a few steps into the center of the speaker's area, the pointer held in both hands as he continued speaking. "This is the most vital target we've ever gone after. If you destroy it, you destroy thirty percent of the Luftwaffe's single engine fighter production. You fellows know what that means to you personally."

Lieutenant Colonel Bernie Lay, who was sitting in the first row, had a sick feeling in his stomach and turned pale. The Intelligence officer stepped back to the map, thrusting the pointer dramatically at a position in North Africa. "Telergma," he said loudly. "That's where you'll land. General

Norstad's down there with the Twelfth. They've got a depot set up for the North African Campaign. They'll have spare parts…mechanics…everything you'll need."

The Intelligence officer turned to still another hand-marked map that revealed the weather fronts along the related areas. "The latest forecast indicates the weather over the target area will be excellent," he said as he turned to the crews. "However, conditions here may tend to get a little murky before 'start' time." He turned back to a board containing the vital statistics of the mission. "Takeoff time is 0600…."

The Operations Office of the 100th Bombardment Group Heavy was very busy on the morning of August 17, 1943. Colonel Lay entered the operations office and walked through the crowded room to the besieged Operations officer. A Squadron Leader recognized Colonel Lay and called out, "Colonel Lay!" Lay sees the young Squadron Leader and worked his way through the crowd.

"Good morning, Captain," Lay said as he shook his hand. "Looks like we've a big one for today."

The Captain nodded his head and agreed. The Squadron Leader asked, "You going with us on this one or….?"

"Yes, if there's a slot for me to fill in," Colonel Lay said.

The Squadron Leader turned to the Operations officer and said "Who've you got Colonel Lay listed with?"

The Operations officer perused the list and replied, "Uh…Lieutenant Rogers – low squadron."

The Squadron Leader thought about the situation and called out, "Sir, why don't you put him up with us in high squadron….co-pilot with Murphy. They've flown together before." The Operations officer looked at the Squadron Leader then at Colonel Lay.

"That will put you in the 'Tail End Charlie' element of a fifteen mile long parade, Colonel."

Colonel Lay, grinning, replied, "Well…I'm not exactly a candidate for a purple heart, but I guess I'll take my chances with Captain Murphy."

The Operations officer erased and re-entered Lay's name and said "You got it, Sir." Lay went out on the flight line to the "Piccadilly Lily," a 100th Bomb Group B-17, it's nose art dimly visible through the skiffs of early morning English fog. The ship sat squat and sinister. The crew sat quietly, tensely, under the right wing. Captain Murphy, Colonel Lay, the navigator and the bombardier were sitting on the tarmac discussing procedures. The top turret gunner was laying nearby with his head on his parachute pack. The right waist gunner was seen at the gunnery opening, performing a last minute check on the huge 50 caliber machine gun assembly. Despite the light chatter between everyone, there was an atmosphere of high tension. A jeep pulled up by the nose of the "Piccadilly Lily," coming to a halt as the driver peered searchingly through the fog. The driver called out, "Captain Murphy...

"Yeah," Murphy yelled back.

The driver reported, "The start has been postponed... hour and a half, Sir."

"Thanks," Captain Murphy said.

Captain Murphy rose off the tarmac and crossed to the airplane, beginning still another visual check of the ship, compelled by his building anxiety. "This was a big mission deep inside Germany. The target was one of the most heavily protected by anti aircraft and fighters," he thought. "There would be heavy losses for sure." Once again he had a sick feeling in his stomach. Fear was creeping back out of Lay's sub conscience.

The navigator scanned the limited visibility and said to Lay, "This stuff must reach on up there for Bomber Command to postpone the start."

Colonel Lay quipped, "Funny thing. A year ago today, August 17, I was behind a desk up at High Wycombe. We got twelve B-17s off to bomb Rouen. It was the Eighth's <u>first</u> mission. He looked at the others, grinning wryly, then continued. "Those twelve Forts represented a maximum effort back then. We're putting thirty times that number of heavies in the air this morning!"

The bombardier said dryly, "Some fucking birthday celebration!"

"Yeah, it sure is," Colonel Lay said.

The navigator looked over at Lay and asked, "Your first mission, Colonel?"

Colonel Lay shook his head, "No, my fifth... In the last ten days!"

The crew became quiet, each person caught up in his own thoughts. Presently, Lay rose, crossed to the tail assembly where Captain Murphy was continuing his visual check.

"Captain Murphy? Colonel Lay calls out.

"Yeah" came a short reply.

"Anything I can do?" the Colonel asked.

"No…no Colonel. Thanks anyway. I….I was just giving Lily the once over," Murphy said nervously as he scanned the overcast. "Forming up could get a little rough in this overcast."

Back at Lemay's operation complex at Elveden Hall, Lemay and several members of his staff gathered around him as they contemplated the pending mission. Major Preston, Captain Fulkrod, the Weather Officer, the Intelligence officer, and the Anti aircraft Officer are all looking at the Mission Board or out the window at the fog. Lemay was dressed in basic combat flight gear. Colonel Kissner quickly moved from a data-gathering area to Lemay. "We're about out of time, Curt," Colonel Kissner said. "We've either got to scrub – or go."

Major Preston added, "The division…it could go on the gauges, Colonel."

Lemay was pondering the situation for a long moment, then said to the Weather Officer, "Is it going to get any better out there?"

"No, Sir," replied the Third Division Weather Officer. Lemay looked down in thought. After a moment, he turned to Kissner and said, "Tell 'em to crank up!" Kissner turned to cross back to the data area.

Lemay turned to Fulkrod and put his hand on Fulkrod's shoulder. "Ben, you've done a helluva job! It looks like we're starting out with a full complement of airplanes from every group in the division. You keep this up and Orville Anderson's liable to make you a general too!" They all laughed, but the laugh was hollow and tense. Lemay shook hands with Preston, Fulkrod, nodded at the others, then turned to leave.

While still watching Lemay, Major Preston said "It would've been nice if they could've kept schedule. Things could get a little shaky."

Fulkrod said, "Yeah, but you can't win 'em all." Colonel Dawson walked from the tail empennage toward the right front wing, pausing at the open waist gunner's position. Colonel Dawson, the Group Commander looked over at the Sergeant and asked, "Sergeant, you got those smoke grenades all set?"

The gunner replied, "Yes, Sir. All I gotta do is ignite them and toss them in the hopper…just like you and Colonel Lemay showed me."

The Group Commander smiled and replied, "Good!"

The Group Commander walked on toward the forward end of the aircraft just as Lemay's staff car pulls up through the fog. The Group Commander met Lemay. "Colonel…we're ready to roll."

Lemay nodded and they entered the aircraft through the lower nose hatch, hoisting themselves up into the ship itself. The Group Commander settled into the cockpit with Lemay taking a standing position between the flight deck seats. Lemay busied himself plugging in the communication microphone and putting on his parachute. The Group Commander, seated in the pilot seat said to the co-pilot, "Check list?"

The co-pilot responded "we've completed the preliminary checklist, Sir!"

The Group Commander, reading his checklist, commanded "Prepare to start engines. Master switches… "

The co-pilot, activating the switches, responded, "Master switches on."

The pilot then said, "Battery switches and inverters."

"On and checked," came the reply. The pilot peers out the cockpit window. The pilot read the next item on the checklist. "Ready on One," he said. The left outboard engine prop began to rotate as the engine coughed to life, belching smoke, then a red tongue of flame.

The inboard prop began rotating as that engine also roars to life. In the next parking slot, a jeep emerged through the fog, coming to a stop in front of Captain Murphy's B-17, the "Piccadilly Lily." Two large amber lanterns located on the rear of the jeep glowed eerily through the fog. The Air Officer in the right front seat spoke to the aircraft commander with a hand held radio microphone, "Captain Murphy?"

Captain Murphy raised his oxygen mask containing his radio microphone closer to his lips and replied, "Murphy here."

The Air Officer lifted his mike and pushed the transmit button. "We'll lead you out to the runway."

Captain Murphy pushed his intercom and said, "This is it!" He started the cockpit procedure as he talked to the squadron, "Crank up and trail out on us."

Colonel Lay peered out of the right cockpit window and reported, "Ready on three!" The engine prop rotated as the engine roars to life. Lemay and Murphy looked out the cockpit at the jeep as Murphy applied throttle, easing the ship out on to the taxi ramp. The jeep could be seen with its glowing amber lights leading the lumbering B-17 down the taxi strip. The jeep moved slowly through the fog with the "Piccadilly Lily" just behind the jeep. Then another B-17 emerged through the swirling fog... followed by still another.

Once they were at the end of the runway and all the aircraft were ready to go, the final checklist items were checked carefully. The pilot called out the next item, "Tail wheel... "

The co-pilot replied, "Locked."

"Gyro…"

"On."

"Generators…"

"On."

"Okay, we're as ready as we can be," the pilot said nervously.

The Control Tower was watched by the pilots as a green spot light was aimed at the waiting B-17s on the runway. Then it was time to go face death at 27,000 feet. Lemay's B-17 began its takeoff roll, then another B-17 rolled up for takeoff with a third B-17 moving in behind it. Lemay's B-17 lifted off and flew into the fog. The next B-17 began its takeoff roll, then another B-17 and another.

Lemay depressed his intercom button, "Start the smoke lamps. Pilot to waist gunner. Hit that smoke lamp, Sergeant."

The waist gunner pulled the yellow smoke grenade igniters and tossed them into the hopper attached to the outer fuselage of the B-17. The two trailing ships spotted the yellow trail of smoke and moved in to form up on the lead B-17. The co-pilot scanned upward and ahead of the aircraft. His fear had made his hands sweat.

Lemay transmitted on the radio, "Blue Swallow Seven…this is Blue Swallow Able. Report when you're tacked on."

"Blue Swallow Able…this is Blue Swallow Baker. Formation complete."

Blue Swallow Able…this is Blue Swallow Charley….all Charley elements formed up."

Zebra Group Leader called Able on this check in, "Blue Swallow Able…this is Blue Swallow Zebra. All Zebra elements in position," he said while leaning forward to look out through the windscreen.

Zebra Group Leader's voice was heard by the others, "Looks like a swarm of angry locusts from back here!"

Lemay was glancing at his wrist watch when he heard the comment and smiled. Mentally, he noted that they were ten minutes behind schedule, then he radioed, "Lemay to tail gunner... Any sign of the fighter escort back there?"

The tail gunner responded, "Negative, Sir."

Lemay looked over at the pilot and said "The First Division…it's probably still on the ground too."

CHAPTER 54

Back in the operations area at High Wycombe, General Fred Anderson was standing adjacent to the ops area along with the Bomber Command Weather Officer, Intelligence officer and his Chief of Staff. All were observing the data being posted on the various control boards in the operations area.

The Operations officer went over to General Anderson and reported, "Lemay's all formed up, General."

General Anderson asked, "Any word on the First Division?"

The Operations officer lowered his head slightly and said "They're still reporting insufficient visibility, General."

General Anderson cried out, "Dammit!" in exasperation. "How did Lemay get off?"

The Bomber Command Chief of Staff stiffened up to answer. "On the gauges, Sir. SOP with the Third. All takeoffs, no matter what the visibility... They're accomplished with the pilot's seat let down and him on the gauges. The co-pilot watches outside and keeps him from running off the runway. Lemay's standing orders. He did the same thing when he ran the 305th."

"What about the fighters?" General Anderson asked.

The Operations officer responded, "Three squadrons off so far, General." General Anderson shook his head, "Not even ten percent. Well....we can forget about timing. We've lost it! Fighter escort too, probably." General Anderson turned to the Weather Officer and asked, "What about the First...how long before it'll be clear enough for them to start?"

"Hour and a half maybe," replied a sheepish Weather Officer.

"And the weather over the target?" the General asked.

"Excellent, General," replied the Weather Officer.

"Is there any damned chance of it holding a few more days?"

"No, Sir," said the Weather Officer. "North Africa either. Same front moving across both areas. Could be a week or more before it breaks again."

General Anderson, his hands clasped behind his back, paced back and forth, weighing the situation that obviously had gone awry. Then he remarked gingerly, "Well…we've waited nearly a month for these conditions. Tell Lemay his condition is 'Go!'"

The Operations officer nodded to the Control Officer who sat at the radio console.

General Anderson uttered almost inaudibly "God go with you, Curt."

Lemay hit his mike button, "Blue Swallow Zebra…this is Blue Swallow Able. Any sign of our fighter escort back there?"

"Blue Swallow Able…this is Blue Swallow Zebra. Negative. Only thing we got behind us are the twelve replacement ships. They're starting to turn back to home base now."

The navigator completed a calculation and then calls out, "Navigator to pilot"….we're crossing the Dutch Coast…on course, Colonel."

"Blue Swallow Seven….this is Blue Swallow Able. We're probably beginning to register on RDF down there. Their western defense belt fighters will be up any minute now," Lemay said as he looked out the window. "Blue Swallow Seven leaders…keep a close check on your elements. Keep them tucked in. The bad guys will be here soon." Lemay continued, "Without fighter escort, we'll have to rely on our own guns! Good luck!"

In the "Piccadilly Lily" Colonel Lay and Captain Murphy exchanged anxious glances. Colonel Lay makes restless, last minute adjustments to his oxygen mask. "Why am I here? I should have taken a desk job, but no, I had to be a combat leader," he thought to himself.

Lemay walked to the rear compartment. He looked out of the right waist gunner's position at the low squadron. They weren't in close formation! Lemay radioed in very stern tones, "Low Able Squadron – get those damned elements in closer!"

Murphy's B-17 with two additional B-17s formed up on it and moved closer in formation. Murphy and Lay scanned their respective sectors beyond the cockpit window. Presently, Murphy pointed off to his left, where bursts of flak were beginning to appear. Lay nodded his awareness of the beginning flak. Lay, as he looks at his wrist watch, and noticed that it read 10:25. They were still behind schedule. Murphy and Lay continued searching the sky ahead.

Suddenly, a gunner yelled out, "Fighters…two o'clock low!"

All attention was directed to the German fighters who were climbing rapidly. The ME-109 made a swift 180 degree turn, then headed straight toward the low squadron. The ME-109 flashed over the top of the group at an incredibly fast closure speed. The chatter of machine guns, both from the fighter and the B-17s, filled the headset above the roar of the engines. The B-17 in the right rear of the formation began smoking from its right outboard engine. The ME-109 broke away in a half roll, after it shot a short burst at the Lily. No hits. The right waist gun and the lower ball turret gun of Murphy's Fortress fired at the departing ME-109 without any hits.

Lay looked out at the B-17s on their right side. The right outboard engine of the B-17 was still smoking. Murphy pointed out an ME-109 far ahead, making a sharp 180 degree and closing head-on toward the B-17s. The ME-109 breaks away from the attack in a half-roll, as the left B-17 in the three-plane formation began smoking from the left inboard. Murphy and Lay watched the ME-109 as it passed by on the left side. The left waist gunner tracked the ME-109 with his fire. Suddenly there's a cry from the waist gunner "Got him!" The 109 spun downward on fire.

Lay looked up to his right and sees a B-17 as it rolled out, smoking as it bellies up on its downward plunge. He felt sick inside. He asked himself, "Did I know any of them?"

Murphy saw the expression on Lay's face and knew what he was thinking. "Colonel, just remember this when you start scheduling missions. There will be death. That's combat. Just make every death count."

Lay looked over at Murphy and said, "That fact is etched into my mind - the hard way."

Then they saw still another B-17 beginning its crippled descent, crew members bailing out in the midst of the formation. A B-17 in the high group exploded. The remains of the B-17 were floating in fiery balls to the ground below, some debris just missing the aircraft.

Lay said, in grim astonishment, "That was Rogers…the ship I was assigned to!" Murphy, sweat coursing down from his forehead onto his oxygen mask, gazed at Lay for a concerned moment, then gestured for Colonel Lay to take control of the B-17, obviously intending to distract Lay from the effect of the B-17 explosion.

The Zebra Group Leader was making a radio call, "Blue Swallow Zebra…this is Zebra Leader…I'm going to pull us in closer to that group up ahead. Fill up those holes – close up on me." Lay and Murphy looked out through the windscreen where a lone B-17 was seen by the two pilots, then another moved up from the left and closed on the first ship, even as a third B-17 eased in, closing from the right, just as a German fighter swept up on a deflecting attack.

Lemay listened to the intercom transmission. An unidentified aircraft commander said to his gunner, "Lead 'em!"

Another voice was heard, "Shorten your bursts – we've got a long way to go!"

A second voice reported, "Fighters coming up – three o'clock low."

A third voice in an excited tone said, "109s – nine o'clock low!"

A fourth voice as heard over machine gun fire, "Two whole squadrons of those Bastards! Climbing up…seven o'clock low!"

From another voice came, "Looks like two squadrons over here… twelve 109s…uh…eleven 109s….climbing up on our right."

Back in the Operations Center at Bomber Command, General Anderson and members of bomber command Staff had gathered in the operations area as before, except General Eaker had now joined the group.

They all watched the operations data report systems intently. The Command Intelligence officer was on the telephone. He hung up the telephone, made a final note, then crosses to General Eaker and Anderson.

The Intelligence officer reported to General Anderson, "They passed over Eupen at 10:41, General. They've encountered heavy fighter resistance all the way in from the Dutch coast." The single seat boys are using aerial bombs – wing rockets – you name it."

General Eaker looked grim when he asked, "Any estimate on their losses yet?"

"No number yet, Sir…apparently heavy though. Um...uh… intelligence sources are reporting many of their fighters are using belly tanks."

General Eaker gave that some thought before saying, "That means they'll have had fighter resistance all the way in to the target then."

"Yes, Sir." General Anderson, glancing at his wrist watch, said, "They should be approaching the IP."

From the rear of the fifteen mile long flight of B-17s, elements of the Third Division moved inexorably through the embattled stratosphere. The sky was full of bright lines of tracers, smoke trails from damaged or exploded aircraft from both sides. Lay saw another B-17 with one engine feathered and another smoking. The waist gunners and the tail gunners were bailing out. The aircraft slipped under Lay's B-17 in a tight, descending turn, obviously heading in. Zebra Group Leader's B-17 was starting to trail smoke from an engine. The Zebra Group leader fought the controls, trying to maintain position and level flight, while his crew fought to keep the fighters from finishing off their plane. The crew of Zebra Leader saw a fighter rolling up and out from a pass at a lower echelon, its 20mm cannon fire raking their B-17 in a deflecting fire on its way out of the upward roll. The radio operator was looking forward from aft of the waist gunner's position. Suddenly, he's slammed to the deck of the B-17, screaming. The right waist gunner continued firing at the ME-109, tracking its upward spiral. The ME-109 passed over and above the Zebra Leader's B-17 in the inverted portion of the upper arch of its roll. Suddenly, it disintegrated in a brilliant burst of orange flame. The waist gunners were trying to help the stricken radio man whose screams could be heard above the top and tail turret gun firing, intermingled with the throbbing engine roar.

The radio man was incoherent and screaming, "My god! My legs! Do something!"

The radio man's legs had both been virtually amputated by a 20mm cannon shell from the ME-109. Once again, there was a ME-109 coming head on toward the Zebra Leader's B-17.

The Zebra Group Leader and his co-pilot both ducked instinctively from the oncoming fire of the ME-109. The Plexiglas nose cone exploded with a shattering rush of air after having been pierced by a 20mm cannon shell. The bombardier was struck, knocking him backwards. The navigator struggled to pull the wounded bombardier away from the screaming rush of air through the shattered nose cone. The co-pilot gazed apprehensively out to his right, where he saw an engine smoking profusely. The Zebra Group Leader and his co-pilot saw numerous smoking B-17s in front of them.

The co-pilot turned to the Group Leader, terror registering in his voice. "Let's get the hell outta here!"

The Zebra Group Leader angrily said "Hell, No! Feather that prop! Help me fly this damned airplane!"

In Lemay's aircraft, the navigator, completed a calculation, then said "Navigator to pilot…Thirty-seconds to IP." Lemay nodded from his position behind the two pilots. Lemay could look forward through the cockpit window where puffs of flak were beginning to appear amidst the other elements of the lead group. He knew it was about to get real rough.

Lemay said to the two pilots, "That should relieve fighter attacks," gesturing toward the flak. Lemay turned to the aft side cockpit window to observe the group after its turn on the IP. Lemay looked at the pilot as he gazed at the instruments apprehensively during the bomb run, his hands clasping his legs as the autopilot flew the aircraft which itself vibrated from the flak shock waves that were increasing in intensity. The bombardier raises his hand in a climaxing gesture, then excitedly reports to the crew, "Bombs away!" Bombs begin to tumble from the bomb bay doors. The other bombers also started their bomb drops.

The Regensburg anti aircraft batteries firing at the B-17s were having an effect on the planes of the Third Division above. The shockwaves alone could damage a B-17 or even bring it down. The anti aircraft battery itself was struck by the shockwaves of bombs bursting nearby, its occupants sent flying through the air grotesquely. The war could go both ways. The rectangular conflagration that was the ME-109 G Messerschmitt factory at Regensburg was struck by the massive bomb load. Civilian areas around the factory were unmolested.

Colonel Lay twisted his head to see the bombed area. Colonel Lay said to the pilot, "Perfect pattern!"

In awe, Murphy said, "We saturated the whole damned factory area!" The factory along the river in Regensburg, was now a rectangular area of devastation.

Above Regensburg, the combat continued. Lay knew then that the key German industrial cities like Hamburg, Brussels, Frankfurt, Bremen, Vegasack, Marienburg, and Wilhelmshaven would soon become rubble under the hands of the Eighth Army Air Force. It was only a matter of time before they would not have the capability to wage war and would be forced to surrender.

Later, at the Reich Chancellery in Berlin, a black and white photo of the Regensburg Messerschmitt factory in smoking ruins and was being looked at by Hitler and his staff. Adolph Hitler and Albert Speer gazed at the photo which was in Hitler's hand. Hitler laid the photograph on the map table before him, turned to cross slowly to a table in the center of the Reich Chancellery Office area bearing a large scale model of the cultural center planned for Post War Berlin. He stood gazing at the layout for a long moment, then, still gazing at the scale model, spoke as if his mind were detached from the present and roaming the distant future, remarked, "Albert…I want the Triumphal Arch larger," as he touched the model Arch on the table.

A very dismayed Speer said, "But Mien Fuhrer!"

Hitler, undaunted and still gazing nostalgically at the model arch continued, "Our Armies will one day march through the arch in glorious commemoration of the Third Reich's victories."

Speer, walking over to Hitler's side, spoke softly and patiently , "If the daylight bombing continues, Mien Fuehrer, all shall soon be lost! Already, I've diverted nearly half a million workers from the labor force in the relocation of our plants…but…." He then gestured to the photograph… "Disbursement may not hold the solution now. The Regensburg raid reached deeper into our interior than ever before. The bombing itself was a masterpiece of precision. We must increase our fighter resistance…it's our only hope!"

Hitler crossed to gaze out the Reich Chancellery window. "No, Albert. Our only hope lies in the allies going through with the invasion they're planning."

Albert Speer exclaimed, "Invasion?"

Hitler abruptly turned from the window, suddenly speaking with enraged frustration. "YOU are the Minister of War Production and Armament, Minister Speer! You take care of that!" Hitler said, turning back to the window, his features set grimly. "Leave strategy to me!"

CHAPTER 55

Helen Lemay was smartly dressed in her Red Cross uniform as she walked rapidly toward a ward at the end of the hall of the large Griles General Hospital. She carried a folder of medical files and notes as she approached the ward door. Robert stepped away from a hall window as Helen approached. "Why, Robert!" Helen said in a surprised tone. "How are you?"

"I'm fine…just fine. I knew you'd be up here this morning. I've been waiting for you," Robert said smiling.

Helen smiled as well and said "I'm glad, Robert."

"I…I just wanted you to know…I…uh…I went home…saw my folks," he said.

"That's wonderful, Robert," Helen said excitedly.

Robert was finding it difficult to hold his emotions in check as he told Helen his story. "I went to church with them. Wasn't like I thought it would be. No one hardly even looked at me."

Helen's hand grabbed Robert's forearm in a reassuring gesture. "The doctors tell me your surgery's coming along nicely."

"Yeah, well thanks"…Robert replied, looking at Helen with warm respect. "You know what I mean."

"Yes, Robert, I know what you mean.

Helen looked down the hallway and saw a patient peering out through the small door window as he turned to the others. The patient cried out with excitement "Here she comes!" The patient hurriedly joined the others in the ward as they anxiously waited for Helen. As Helen entered, she says "Good morning, everybody," and crossed to the speaker's podium at the front of the ward, pausing to gaze at an object there, puzzled. A patient holds up a *Saturday*

Evening Post, opened to an article entitled "I Saw Regensburg Destroyed."

"What's this?" she asked.

The swarthy one quickly volunteered, "A story about the General, Miz Lemay!" Another patient joined in "Yeah, it was a mission report! War Department gave it to the Post with special permission to print it."

A third patient also joined the other voices, "It's a helluva…I'm sorry Miz Lemay…it's a whale of a story! They lost twenty-four airplanes, but he sure blasted that Messerschmitt factory!"

The swarthy one loudly and proudly added, "He was right there in the lead airplane, you know." Colonel Lay said there were sometimes sixty parachutes in the air at one time."

Helen sank into a nearby chair, trying to scan the article and assimilate the excited remarks from the ward patients all at the same time. "Greatest air battle so far, Miz Lemay! Will you send it to the General? We'd like him to autograph for us."

Helen, deeply moved, replied almost in tears, "Of course. He'd be honored."

The telephone rang at the Maitland house, momentarily frustrating Mr. Maitland's desire to catch the end of the Lowell Thomas broadcast from London.

"I'll get it, Father," Helen announced.

Mr. Maitland turned the console radio off as Helen picked up the phone. "The Maitland Residence," she said. "This is Helen Lemay!" Helen tensed, inadvertently dropping her handbag to the floor. Janie and Mrs. Maitland emerged from the kitchen area, both looking at the ashen Helen intently. "Yes, General," she dreaded that this might be the call telling her of Curt's death. Janie crossed to her mother as Mrs. Maitland simply gazed at Helen, obviously fearing the worst, and Mr. Maitland, his features tensed also. Helen was biting her lip, about to cry and laugh…all at the same time. "Yes… yes, I'm alright. Thank you, General."

Janie said apprehensively, "What's wrong, Mommy?" "It's Daddy, darling," she said, stooping to clasp Janie to her breast. "He... he'll be in Washington tomorrow."

"Oh, Mommy! That's Mrs. Marple next door... Said she didn't think I had a Daddy!"

Helen, laughing through tears, said, "She was only joking, darling. After all, he's been away a long time you know."

Janie smugly said, "Anyway, she'll know now, won't she Mommy?"

"Yes, dear. Now she'll know," Helen said smiling.

It was a sunny day in Washington, which was a rare sight for November. An ATC C-54 pulled into a parking ramp, braking and turning broadside to the crowd just outside the transit passenger terminal. Helen Lemay was gazing at the aircraft expectantly. Air Force personnel were pushing the steps up to the aircraft hatch. One of the attendants ascended to open the hatch itself. She noticed several reporters and photographers as they gathered at the foot of the steps. They became very animated as Lemay, Zemke, Nye and Robinson emerged, in that order. Photographer's flash bulbs began to pop. The four officers paused at the photographers' request. Lemay crossed to Helen, gathering her in his arms.

Helen was embracing Lemay, kissing him, embracing him again. "Oh Curt, my darling…my dearest darling…"

A battery of photographers detached themselves from the interviews at the foot of the aircraft and crossed over to Lemay. As Lemay looked up, a photographer said, "Once more, General." Lemay was smiling, obligingly bending to kiss Helen again,."Of course." Presently, General Lemay guided Helen to a waiting staff car. A photographer said musingly, "Old Iron Ass!" Another photographer said, grinning, "Looks pretty soft to me!"

The first photographer replied, "Yeah, betcha the German's won't agree. He has done a job on them."

Helen and Lemay settled into the back seat of the limousine. Helen surveyed the interior of the staff car. "Pretty sumptuous, General. What's it all about?"

Lemay looked at Helen, a little embarrassed, and said, "General Eaker felt some of us ought to come home... Tell the people what it's really like…"

Helen was serious now, "For how long, darling?"

"Maybe a month, Lemay said. General Arnold's people have the itinerary worked out. Packed schedule, I understand. I have to go out to his office this afternoon. Then they're giving us a two-day leave before it all begins." Lemay put his arm around Helen and hugged her.

Late that afternoon, Lemay returned from his meeting with General Arnold. The Maitlands and Helen were ready to have a cocktail and hear about the war from Curt. Helen crossed the room with the tray to her father and Lemay, both standing near the wall map, engaged in casual conversation. Lemay was telling Mr. Maitland his view, "Their head-on attacks hurt us the most…that and the lack of long range fighter cover." Lemay paused, took a cocktail from the tray, tasted it then nodded appreciatively to Helen. Mr. Maitland took a cocktail also, waiting eagerly for Lemay to continue.

Janie sat on the edge of a living room chair, fidgeting, obviously wishing Lemay would wind the conversation down for a moment. Mrs. Maitland crocheted on the sofa, glancing at her husband and smiling slightly as they took a cocktail from the tray. Lemay gestured appropriately with his free hand. "The Luftwaffe single seat fighters fly parallel the formations until they're five or six kilometers ahead, then turn and attack in swarms, elements of four, head-on!" Mr. Maitland said, "Pretty rapid closure rate!"

Lemay nodded. "They commence firing at about nine hundred yards out, and…"

Janie could restrain herself no longer, and slipped down from the chair and crossed to her father, interrupting the conversation. "Daddy..." Lemay glanced down at Janie, then tried to continue…"and get away by flying…"

Janie was persistent, urgently saying, "Daddy…" Lemay was becoming a little disconcerted but continued anyway, "flat over the bomber formation." He looked down at Janie, smiling tolerantly. "Yes, Janie."

Janie said in a sheepish tone, "I want you to sit on the front porch with me, Daddy."

Lemay was completely taken aback, "but, Janie, its cold out there!"

Janie conclusively said, "I'll get your hat and overcoat." Janie left the room to secure the articles of clothing. She wasn't going to be put off any longer. Lemay looks over to Helen, bewildered. "Buy….but why" Helen was smiling indulgently, waiting until Janie was out of earshot, then, softly said,

"She wants Mrs. Marple to see you," as she glanced at her watch. "She'll be coming home any minute now."

"Mrs. Marple?" Lemay asked.

Helen then said, "She uh…." She caught herself, deciding it best not to disclose all of the story. "She's just proud of you darling."

Lemay took his cap and overcoat from Janie, and put them on carefully, deliberately. Then turned to Janie and asked, "How do I look?"

Janie smiled proudly and said "Fine! Just fine, Daddy." Lemay and Janie crossed to the front door as Helen watched them leave.

Janie and Lemay were sitting on the front porch, the cold, evening shadows lengthening. Janie was looking intently toward the sidewalk at the end of the block. Janie saw Mrs. Marple coming around the corner of the block, a small bag of groceries in her arm. She was a prim, middle-aged woman. Janie went to the porch railing, gazed at the approaching Mrs. Marple, then turned to Lemay. She said casually, "Well, I see Mrs. Marple coming home from work." Lemay took the cue, timing his response to Mrs. Marple's passing the Maitland's front gate, then rising with an air of old world charm, bowing and touching his hand to his cap, all of which was a bit exaggerated.

"Good evening, Mrs. Marple," Lemay said. "How nice to see you!" Mrs. Marple glanced at the General, then did a mild double take as she recognizes him.

Mrs. Marple became overwhelmed. "Why, General…General Lemay! Oh my! It's…it's nice to have you here in Cleveland. We've read so much about you, you know."

Lemay bowed slightly again and said, "Why thank you, Mrs. Marple… thank you."

Mrs. Marple began to walk on, her day suddenly brighter. "Well… uh…good evening, General."

Lemay, still with the Old World charm said, "And the same to you, ma'am." Lemay turned to Janie, grinning broadly. "How was that?" Janie broke into bright laughter as she climbed into the General's lap, hugging him happily, "I love you, Daddy!"

A FEW BRAVE MEN
Book III

"THE B-29"

THE ROAD TO TOKYO GOES THROUGH CHINA

CHAPTER 56

President Roosevelt grinned and was obviously pleased by General Arnold's report. "Chiang Kai-shek has already begun construction on the advance refueling bases in the Chengtu area, you know. They've made real progress there...thousands of coolies are doing the job by hand!"

General Arnold said, "Yes Sir."

President Roosevelt continued, "Any slip-up on our commitment to begin B-29 operations in China by mid-March would adversely – and critically – affect our relationship with Chiang." The President, chuckled reflectively, then continued. "He's never been too happy with our decision to defeat Germany before turning our efforts to the Japs anyway. Expressed those resentments rather forcefully at the Cairo Conference you remember."

General Arnold grinned as he remembered. "Yes Sir."

President Roosevelt looked at Arnold and said, "Our commitment on the B-29 effort to begin in March there in China seemed to allay his resentment to some degree. We just can't afford any slip-ups, you know."

General Arnold was uneasy when he answered, "Yes, Mr. President. I...uh...understand that." Roosevelt caught Arnold's uneasiness, and became suspicious himself.

President Roosevelt eyed Arnold with growing concern and asked in a firm tone, "How many B-29s do we actually have operational?"

General Arnold regained his composure and replied, "The ships are being flown from the factories out to the Kansas training area. As you remember, Mr. President, we were to accomplish the modification there. Uh...none of those airplanes are operational at this point."

"None?" Roosevelt asked, somewhat startled.

"The…the modification kits…they got mixed up in shipment. They can't identify which particular aircraft they're designated for. I've got Erik Nelson and his people out there in Pratt, Salina, Great Bend and Walker trying to unscramble the mess right now," answered Arnold.

"How many B-29s are involved in all?" asked the President.

"One hundred and thirty so far, Sir," was the reply.

President Roosevelt became angry and said, "Why that's every damned ship that's come off the assembly lines so far! They're not doing us any good sitting out there on the ground in Kansas, you know!"

"Yes, Sir."

President Roosevelt calmed a little and said, "Look Hap, you tell Erik Nelson I don't care what he's to do! I want those airplanes operational! There's no percentage in the B-29 crews reporting in to continue training in B-17! Most of them are already proficient in 17s anyway. You tell Nelson he's absolute authority to do whatever he's to – except countermand anything connected with the Manhattan Project! Make sure he understands <u>that</u>, Hap!"

General Arnold acknowledged by saying to the President, "Yes, Mr. President. He already understands that, Sir."

It was a very cold day even for November, 1943 in Pratt, Kansas, the focal point of Hap Arnold and the President's concern. Captain Agather wiped his hands with a shop rag, lifted himself up to a standing position, momentarily surveying the work he and the two enlisted men have been engaged in. The two enlisted men continued working on the system.

"We'll run another check as soon as you get it buttoned up," Captain Agather said. He moved to the B-29 exit hatch and climbed down to the ramp and went over to the maintenance lieutenant, who was frustrated with the engine modification procedure.

The lieutenant noticed Agather coming over and said, "You know,

Captain, I believe it would be easier to change the whole damned engine than it would be just to get through that screwed-up cowling design!"

Captain Agather pondered the situation for a moment, then asked, "How long do you figure it'd take to change out a complete engine?"

The lieutenant was taken off guard by Agather's response.

"I was just kidding, Sir. It's just that it's harder to gain access to the power plant itself than it's to accomplish the engineering changes once we're in there."

A jeep pulled up alongside Agather and the maintenance lieutenant. The driver saluted and said "Captain Agather, Colonel Nelson wants to see you…right away, Sir." Captain Agather nodded as the jeep drove away. Captain Agather looked back to the maintenance lieutenant, "I wasn't kidding, lieutenant. It just might be easier to change the entire engine unit. The new engines they're shipping out of the Chrysler-Dodge factory in Chicago already have those modifications incorporated. Why not divert part of the manufacturer's flow here to Pratt…and…send the replaced engines back to the factory. They've got more time to make modifications than we've."

The lieutenant was beginning to grin and said, "Well…I guess if we had those new engine yokes from Babcock up in Erie, we…we'd be in business. That's what they're designed for…engine replacement in the field."

Captain Agather told the officer while climbing into his jeep, "I'll see what can be done." In the meantime, you'd better work out a relief schedule for your men, Lieutenant…every half-hour or so. They're getting too cold to be efficient."

"Yes, Sir," replied the lieutenant as he gazed after Captain Agather, who drove off in the jeep, then shook his head in bewilderment as he turned back to the scaffolding.

As Agather entered the engineering modification office, Colonel Nelson was seated behind a battered old metal desk talking on the telephone. The Pratt, Kansas office was a temporary and hastily-arranged office area.

In an angry tone, Colonel Nelson said to whoever was on the other end of the phone call, "That's right! They're to be taken right off the assembly lines and flown up here this afternoon. They're not to take time for toothbrushes or goodbyes...Just get them out to the taxi ramp! Look, Mr. Schaffer, I'm not insensitive to your problems down there, but I can't give you a week to restructure your assembly line operation. I've got to have those assemblers up here this afternoon."

Captain Agather entered the office, shuddered against the outside cold as he closed the door behind him. Nelson looked up at Agather, motioned him to a chair. Colonel Nelson continued his phone call. "Right. Transportation arrangements have already been made. Thank you. Goodbye." He hung up the phone and turned to Agather. "Well, Vic…I've just got us four hundred and fifty assemblers. I want you to go down to Boeing in Wichita this afternoon with every available transport we can scare up, and start hand-picking them right off their assembly lines down there!"

Captain Agather was momentarily stunned by the magnitude of the undertaking. "Well…that will help! At least we'll get experienced modification people, that way." Agather paused, having collected his scattered thoughts. "Colonel, those engine change yokes the Babcock people are making for us up in Erie…" Colonel Nelson asked, "The field replacement devices?"

Captain Agather responded, "Right. What's the delivery status, Sir?"

Colonel Nelson rummaged through a stack of papers on the desk, finding the letter he wanted. "I believe they're ready for shipment, at least some of them. Yeah…looks like they're ready to begin shipments according to this."

"Sir, I need as many of 'em as I can get," pleaded Agather. "Tomorrow morning would be great if I can get them! That is, assuming that Boeing Wichita will consent to letting me have all the new R3350s they've got in stock down there...and that they'll start trucking them up here this afternoon!"

Colonel Nelson began to smile broadly. "Well…old Schaffer will cry a lot, but I think we can work something out. The only problem is, we'll have all of our transports tied up pulling those assemblers out…and regular shipment from Erie would take too long. What airlines service the Erie-Pittsburgh area?"

"Well…American for one I think," said Captain Agather. "I'll check it out."

"How's the kit situation coming along, son?" Nelson asked.

"We're still trying to find some kind of pattern to the problem. Once those assemblers get up here, we'll have a better chance I think," Captain Agather answered as he rubbed his tired eyes.

Colonel Nelson looked at Agather, "You know, of course, they're forecasting subfreezing temperatures for the next week or more. That will cause you some real problems out there, Vic. The engine heating problems are bad enough…without this. We…we just needed more time…time to assimilate and work out all of this unpredictable data. By the way, son, a Major General stopped by here a few minutes ago….said he was pressing charges against you…insubordination I believe."

Captain Agather swallowed nervously, "I'm….I'm sorry Colonel Nelson. It's just that there's been a steady stream of those spit and polish field graders…all trying to establish a reputation for themselves by suddenly coming up with a comprehensive solution to the B-29 problems. They consume a lot of time!"

Colonel Nelson, with a smile playing at the corners of his mouth, said "He had a theory alright! Totally impractical…impossible in fact! I… uh…discussed the matter briefly with General Arnold. He's got a command vacancy up in Greenland. Seems to think the Major General is just what he's been looking for to fill that slot. He'll have plenty of time to cool off up there!" Colonel Nelson seated himself at his desk, still chuckling. "You'll have your engine yokes, Victor, by eight o'clock in the morning. You can make plans accordingly."

"Thank you, Sir," Agather said, greatly relieved.

Colonel Nelson gazed after the departing Captain for a moment, then reached for the telephone.

High above Pittsburgh an American Airlines airplane was transporting an Army three-star general who occupied a window seat, his wife seated next to him. They finished their coffee and sandwiches. A stewardess bent down to them and asked, "Would you like me to take your tray, General."

"Yes, thank you," the General said as he glanced at his watch. "Have we made up the delay out of Chicago, stewardess?"

The stewardess politely responded, "I'm sure we've General Coslow, but I'll ask the Captain."

Mrs. Coslow smiled at the stewardess and said, "General Coslow is the guest of honor at a War Department staff party in Washington this evening. The General served in the War Department before the war, you know."

Just forward of General Coslow was the cockpit of American Flight #271. Captain Reeves was Flight Captain of Flight #271. He glanced toward the co-pilot with incredulity. "Engine yokes!"

Pittsburgh control operator radioed, "American two-seven-one, this is Pittsburgh control, do you copy?"

The stewardess opened the cockpit door and peered into the cockpit, just as Captain Reeves began the responsive transmission.

"American two-seven-one, we read you Pittsburgh control," responded Captain Reeves.

The Pittsburgh control operator's voice was heard over Captain Reeves and the co-pilot's headsets. "American two-seven-one – please advise time of course change and your new heading."

"Roger, Pittsburgh control," responded Captain Reeves.

The stewardess bent over and asked, "Captain, the General's still worried about getting in to Washington on time tonight. He…uh…doesn't seem to be too fond of airplanes anyway," she said smiling.

Captain Reeves shook his head and said "We've just been diverted to Erie…emergency cargo for the Air Corps, Patty. I guess the best thing to do is just level with the General. Tell him we're acting on orders issued under the authority of President Roosevelt and General Arnold."

The co-pilot grinned as he turned from his calculator and told the pilot, "The new course is three-four-zero."

Captain Reeves picked up his microphone and called out, "Pittsburgh control, American two-seven-one. We're coming left to course heading three-four-zero…descending to ten thousand feet."

The perplexed stewardess gazed at the pilots momentarily, then turned from the cockpit door, closing it behind her. General Coslow looked up to observe the approaching stewardess. The stewardess bent down and addressed the General. "General, we've had a change of plans...we...we're going in to Erie instead of Washington, D.C." The General sat in stunned silence for a moment then began to rise from his seat, erupting, "You tell the Captain I'm coming up there to the cockpit personally to find out just what the hell is going on! He damned well better have some good reasoning behind that decision."

"Now, now, Amos...," Mrs. Coslow said in a calming voice.

The stewardess played her trump card and said, "I believe the order was issued on the authority of General Arnold. We've been diverted to Erie to pick up an emergency cargo for the Air Corps." The general sank slowly back onto his seat, seething. "We should've court martialed that son-of-a-bitch when we nailed Billy Mitchell!"

"Amos!" Mrs. Coslow said.

A C-54 pulled into a parking ramp at Smokey Hill Army Air Force Base in Salina, Kansas. It was met by a staff car and several officers. As the aircraft came to a halt, a USAAF Technical Service Command Colonel stepped from the Staff car, approached the C-54 and stood waiting as the steps were pushed up to the exit hatch near the cockpit. General Arnold stepped from the aircraft, followed by Major General Bennett E. Meyers, along with an aide. Colonel Stephenson met General Arnold at the foot of the steps.

"Welcome to Smokey Hill, General Arnold...General Meyers. I'm Colonel Stephenson. The CO's not on the base at the moment. As a matter of fact, the control tower just notified us a few minutes ago that you were on the way in, Sir."

General Arnold smiled and shook the Colonel's hand. "Thought we'd come down and watch the B-29 departures this afternoon. How many are you going to get off, Colonel Stephenson?" Arnold asked.

Colonel Stephenson said cautiously, "None, I'm afraid, Sir. At least not this afternoon anyway."

General Arnold was completely shocked and said, "What do you mean?" A steely edge crept into his tone as he replied, "I thought you people had the modification problems under control here!"

"It isn't just the modification kit mix up, General," Stephenson replied. "We've got a severe shortage of replacement parts for the engineering changes that have been ordered. Colonel Nelson's been working night and day on that kit mix up. He took several hundred assemblers up there to Pratt from the Wichita Plant assembly lines a few days ago."

General Arnold looked at the Colonel and said with an icy tone, "But all our airplanes…they're still on the ground? Here, Pratt and Great Bend?"

Colonel Stephenson replied, "Yes, Sir." The party went to the waiting staff car without further words.

Colonel Stephenson was standing before several charts dealing with engineering changes and modification progress on the B-29.

General Arnold stood by him, his hands folded behind his back. He's unsmiling as he listened to Colonel Stephenson. General Bennett and the aide stood beside General Arnold. Several Technical Service command staff officers listened to Colonel Stephenson. Colonel C. S. "Bill" Irvine was one of them.

Colonel Stephenson, with a pointer in hand, turned from the charts to General Arnold and explained, "So you see, General Arnold…each airplane has accumulated a hundred or more engineering changes. All of that was to be accomplished <u>after</u> the ships had come off the assembly line at the factory, were test flown and then delivered to us here. Not only do we've a shortage of spare parts to accomplish the engineering changes themselves, but as you already know, those damned modification kits were shipped from Renton without identification."

General Arnold stood silent for a few minutes, then, speaking with a quiet and deadly edge to his voice said, "What you're saying is you've got several thousand engineering changes…without the necessary parts…and… the modification kits, and you still don't know where they hell they go! Is that it, Colonel?"

Colonel Stephenson responded, "Essentially…uh…."

"What kind of operation are you running here, anyway? Why haven't you coordinated these problems with the Boeing people…the modification centers…the bases, Colonel? If I have to, I'll come down here and run the damned place myself," Arnold said.

Colonel Stephenson said "General…I…."

General Arnold interrupted by saying, "Have you had enough B-29s operational for close coordinated crew training?" Colonel Stephenson looked at him and said, "Uh…no, Sir. They've only been able to get in about two hours per crew, Sir. We've…uh…been using B-17s."

General Arnold, whose anger was monumental at this point exclaimed, "Damn!" He then paused to collect himself and seething said, "Let me clarify the situation for you, gentlemen: President Roosevelt and Winston Churchill made an agreement with Chiang Kai-shek at the Cairo Conference to start B-29 bombing missions against Japan, out of China, no later than March fifteen! The Chinese have placed top priority on the preparation of the necessary landing strips over there. The Generalissimo is an important ally, if not our MOST important, at the moment!"

General Arnold crossed to the window and gazed out for a few seconds, his hands still clasped behind his back. Then he turned to the stunned Colonel and said, "You've got three weeks to get those airplanes in the air…all of them! No excuses accepted! Bennett, you stay on here. You've the authority to use my name in any way you deem necessary…whatever it takes to get this mess coordinated!"

General Meyers responded, "Understood, Sir."

General Arnold looked at Meyers and ordered, "Make a list of the shortages. Contact every factory in the United States that's involved. Have those parts sent in here by plane. TOMORROW!" General Meyers nodded his understanding.

General Arnold went to the exit, the aide following. "I'm going over to Pratt. I'll review the modification problem with Eric Nelson over there." As he started through the door, he turned back and said, "I want to see that list of shortages…bring it over to Pratt…by zero nine hundred….IN THE MORNING!" He then abruptly exited with the aide following closely.

"Colonel Irvine, you're temporarily assigned as my deputy, effective immediately," said Meyers. "Right, General," Irvine said without comment.

General Meyers turned to Stephenson and said, "Colonel, you get that shortage list compiled…even if you people have to work all night!

Colonel Stephenson felt like a man on whom the sky has just fallen. "Yes, sir."

Over at Pratt Field, several mechanics busily worked on the B-29 engines. General Arnold, his aide, Colonel Nelson and a Pratt staff officer approached the front of the aircraft. Captain Agather was pouring over a large set of airframe blue prints spread out across a mechanic's work table that stood near the nose section of the B-29. A USAAF Captain and a First Lieutenant poured over the blue prints with Captain Agather, all of them in grease-soiled clothing.

General Arnold said to Nelson, "You've got the flight crews working too?"

"Yes, General…full time, as of today. I…I uh know where you're with the President in this matter, Hap. We <u>all</u> know your neck is on the line. No one's getting much sleep around here anymore. There's no lack of effort around here,. We know how important this product is to the big picture, Sir."

General Arnold gazed at the effort going on around the B-29, his tension seeming to ease somewhat with Nelson's reassuring awareness of the critical nature of the situation. Colonel Nelson looked at Arnold and continued, "<u>All</u> flight crews here at Pratt will be reporting to Captain Agather as they come in from their training flights today, and…until further notice… same thing over at Great Bend and Salina."

General Arnold said, "Well, Eric…it's a hell of a situation," as he gazed up at the B-29. "The most advanced bomber the world has ever known…just sitting there…like wounded birds. The outcome of the war in the Pacific may well hinge on these birds you know."

Colonel Nelson looked at him and said, "Yes…well it's…it's…just a matter of finding a pattern to the problem, General. Once we do, then it'll only be a matter of days."

General Arnold asked, "They're still working on a correction for the engine heating problems?" Colonel Nelson replied, "Working on it, yes. A solution? No." The group crossed to a new engine being made ready to hoist up into a replacement position.

Colonel Nelson continued pointing to the appropriate cylinder on the engine and said, "The top rear cylinders have a tendency to overheat – simply because we can't get enough airflow back there to them. When they get hot, they're likely to warp a valve and swallow it." He glanced at Arnold. "The results are: engine fire!"

"What do you think, Eric?" Arnold asked.

Colonel Nelson said, "Well, it's…it's really a design problem, General. Nobody's ever built twin radials before. Of course, it's too late to change the basic design now. Captain Agather, the Wright engineers, they've developed some engineering changes that are helping. But the basic problem still exists. And…it's going to be a costly problem. At least until we can accumulate enough actual flight experience to determine the performance parameters and develop flight procedures around them."

General Arnold gazed at Nelson for a moment, then said "You..uh… expect the operational losses to be heavy?"

Colonel Nelson nodded and said, "The possibility exists."

General Arnold thought for a moment then said, "I'd like to talk with confidentiality, Erik."

Colonel Nelson nodded. "We can go up to the Base Commandant's office." General Arnold and Colonel Nelson then went to the office and removed their overcoats and caps.

General Arnold looked into Nelson's eyes and said in a very low but serious voice, "Everybody's wanting the B-29s, Erik," he said, as he crossed to a wall map of the world. "Chennault insists they be assigned to his Fourteenth Air Force in China. Nimitz wants B-29 wings placed in his Pacific Command. Stratemeyer…he seems to think they'd been promised to him! He even wrote me a letter to that effect. And…of course, there's Mountbatten in the China-Burma-India theater…and MacArthur in the south…powerful commanders, accustomed to getting what they want!"

Colonel Nelson shook his head and said "Sounds like the B-17 hiatus all over again, General. We had to supply field commanders all over the world with B-17s before we could get around to supplying our own training command and the Eighth air force with Fortresses. By that time, the combined chiefs had already begun planning surface invasions of North Africa and Europe."

General Arnold quickly responded, "But…we've proven the theory of strategic bombardment over there. There's nothing to stop us now from a continuing and systematic destruction of the German industrial apparatus."

"But there'll still be an invasion?" Nelson asked.

General Arnold contemplatively thought about his reply then said, "If…if we can concentrate the B-29s into a single, massive striking force against Japan alone…I believe we can achieve victory in the Pacific without the necessity of invading the Japanese homeland."

"An invasion of Japan…that'd be a long and bloody campaign by anybody's reckoning," Nelson said dejectedly.

General Arnold looked at Nelson and said, "The President has tentatively approved a proposal to organize the B-29s into a separate air force, to be placed under the direct authority of the Joint Chiefs of Staff…with the commanding general of the Army Air Force as its executive agent."

Colonel Nelson reacted almost as astonished as if he'd been told the air force had become a separate entity itself, he said, "Why…that…that's make you the chief of an independent air force. That's getting pretty damned close to Billy Mitchell's dream."

A smiling General Arnold replied, "It's under consideration by the Joint Chiefs. The War Department's working on the details of the plan. The British…they'll have to approve. Part of the projected operation…now code named MATTERHORN…it'll be based in their area of responsibility. We've got K. B. Wolfe out in Calcutta, now, supervising the construction of four operational bases in that general area."

Amazed, Colonel Nelson said, "India?"

General Arnold responded with "Yes. We can get almost unlimited supplies of fuel into that area…by running a pipeline from here down to the Calcutta area. Since the Burma Road is vulnerable to Japanese attack, and until we can get the Ledo Road open, the plan is to airlift fuel to forward areas in Chengtu, storing it there until we've got enough stockpiled for a mission.

"General, you mean you're going to have B-29s flying their own fuel over the Hump, off-loading and then returning to their bases in India for more?" Nelson asked in surprise.

General Arnold looked at Nelson and explained, "One B-29, making four or five flights over the Hump will stockpile enough fuel for one Superfortress to fly a mission out of Chengtu…against the Japanese home islands. It's the only method we can come up with, at least the only one that will come anywhere close to meeting the timetable set up by Roosevelt, Churchill and Chiang…until we can take Formosa…or some of the Marianas chain." General Arnold crossed to a window, gazed out wearily, his hands behind his back. "Roosevelt's damned discouraged with the B-29," Arnold said as he turned to Eric. "The entire U.S. Army Air Force is under the gun on this one, Eric. Unless we turn the B-29 around…and damned quick!...the cause of strategic bombardment will be set back twenty years…not to speak of the hundreds of thousands of Allied lives that will be expended in a surface invasion of Japan!"

General Arnold walked to the desk, seated himself on the edge, speaking to Colonel Nelson persuasively. "I want you and your team to go on out to India with the 58th Bombardment Wing. Set up shop out there. Get the local factories in a cooperative arrangement. Modify those damned engines until they'll perform properly."

Colonel Nelson grinned wryly and responded, "Fair size task, General."

General Arnold gazed at Nelson and said "You were the first man to fly around the world, Erik. Everyone thought that was impossible! I need you to pull off another miracle, just one more!"

"Well…I…I guess you don't leave any options," Nelson said.

CHAPTER 57

McGregor realized that April 5, 1944 was a big day. Finally B-29s were deploying overseas for combat. He steered his B-29 onto the runway, pausing at the end of the runway for one last check of the engine instruments prior to takeoff. He heard the control tower give him permission to depart. McGregor applied the throttle. The massive aircraft began to roll forward, and finally lifted off.

Thirty-eight hours later, Captain McGregor looked out at the moonlit and windswept Libyan Desert near Marada…traces of a native village seen in the distance. It looked barren and lonely and silent, unlike the sound of his aircraft engines. Bob Ragland was working with his navigator's calipers as he measured the dead reckoning distance from Pratt, Kansas through Gander, Marrakech and the present position over Libya on the night of April 7, 1944. Ragland shook his head, incredulous at the distance traveled. McGregor then looked over at the flight engineer, who gazed intently at the gauges before him. The flight engineer was closely watching the four engine temperature gauges, now registering nearly 300° centigrade…with 300° clearly marked as the extreme danger level.

The engineer shook his head then called the pilot on the intercom, "Cylinder head temp, Mac…it's still climbing."

Captain McGregor looked over at the engineer and asked, "Any adjustment left on the cowl flaps?"

The engineer shook his head negatively and said "No, they're squeezed open as far as they'll go."

Captain McGregor looked thoughtful and asked, "Want to try climbing up to a cooler layer of air?"

The engineer, without taking his eyes off the temperature, said "Negative. Liable to blow a cylinder head or warp a valve any minute as it is."

The co-pilot glanced out the window apprehensively and said, "That's all we need, an engine fire over North Africa…at night!"

Captain McGregor looked out his window and said to whoever was listening, "Probably do just as well to stay at this altitude, anyway. Don't seem to have much lift."

The radioman added, "I keep seeing that B-29 wreck at the end of the runway back in Marrakech?" That's what happened to 'em. Somebody said they just couldn't get off…no lift."

The co-pilot thought for a minute as he looked at the desert then commented, "Good thing we're going up to England. These babies just aren't built to operate in hot, humid climates!"

"England…through Cairo, Egypt," McGregor said flippantly.

The co-pilot said, "That's the way I figure it, going up through the back door. I figure they'll shoot us up there out of Cairo…tonight. Keep the German's from knowing about us that way."

Captain McGregor said in a resigned tone, "We're not going anywhere tonight. The way these engines are running, I figure the plugs are fouled from all that heat. Probably have to be changed in Cairo. That will take a couple of days at least."

The radioman said confidentially, "Well…it ain't going to be England anyway, Captain. India…that's where we're going! I talked to a radioman back in Marrakech. He picked up a distress broadcast from a 58th Bomb Group B-29. Went in somewhere between Karachi and Calcutta. That's where they were headed…Calcutta."

Captain McGregor, perplexed, asked, "You trying to start another rumor?"

The radioman said, "Hell, no, Captain. I'm just telling you that we're headed for India…somewhere up around Calcutta!"

Captain McGregor said, "Well, we'll get our final destination in Cairo." He then turned to the navigator and said "What's our ETA, Bob?"

Ragland glanced at hisn'tes and said "0710 hours Cairo time."

Captain McGregor glanced at his watch and added, "Little over two hours." Then, he turned to the crew chief and said, "Harry, you get on those plugs the minute we land at Payne Field, understand?"

Harry said in a tired tone, "Gotcha, Cap'n."

Almost two hours later, as the sun shone brightly into the faces of the pilot and co-pilot, McGregor responded to the Cairo Tower operator who directed them to start the approach and to descend to 4,000 feet. He pushed the intercom button, "Pilot to crew, prepare for let down and landing. Report when prepared for landing."

The massive B-29 landed and parked in the military area of the airport. The crew immediately got to work on the aircraft engines before they could shower, sleep and see the sights of Egypt. It would be the 9th of April before the plane was ready for the next leg of their journey. Today would be a free day for the crew to enjoy the sights of Cairo and Egypt.

Miller was reading from a guidebook when he told the group what he had found. "Says here a young prince stopped to rest in the shadow of the Sphinx. As he slept, the Sphinx spoke to him, promising him Egypt's throne if he would remove the sand that had piled up around the statute. The Prince, Thutomouse IV, did clear the sand and indeed became King of Egypt – THIRTY FOUR CENTURIES AGO! Get this…and at that time.. the Sphinx was already ELEVEN HUNDRED YEARS OLD!!!"

Captain McGregor was overwhelmed by the magnitude of the Egyptian culture. "Four thousand, five hundred years…"

A camel driver came up to McGregor and interrupted his concentration, "A thousand pardons, Captain," the toothless camel driver asked McGregor. "Picture? On the camel? You leave address…I send to your home in America."

McGregor nods affirmatively and says, "Why not?" The camel got to its knees, allowing McGregor to mount. The camel driver snapped the shot. McGregor dismounted and Miller climbed on the camel. McGregor handed his address to the driver. Strange…our routing...highly secret…but...they'll know where we've been when they get these pictures!"

Haggarty was grinning and replied, "Yeah!"

The camel driver gazed at McGregor with an ancient wisdom. His leathery face broke into a knowing smile. "The Gods will smile upon you, Captain."

McGregor catches the driver's look, pondered it for a moment, and then left with the others, leaving the camel driver gazing after them.

The Sheppard Hotel dining area was beautiful. There was a vast array of military types from all over the world, some with their women – all dining in this sumptuous surrounding. A beautiful Egyptian belly dancer swirled and swayed to the twanging of oriental musical instruments. McGregor, Haggerty, Ragland and Miller were all seated at a select table, cocktail glasses before them. Ragland glanced at McGregor who watched the dancer intently. "Like the camel driver said…the Gods will smile upon us." Captain McGregor grinned, "Gotta admit it, it beats the infantry alright!"

McGregor looked ahead at the short runway ahead of him at Chakulia, India and was amazed that the runway was not fully completed. Indian laborers were painstakingly placing stones in the runway, still under construction, at the far end. Long lines of laborers were carrying stones, mixing a primitive mortar, some pressing the stones in place. He could see several other B-29s on the ramp of this steaming jungle facility. He throttled back to get as slow on final approach as he could in this hot atmosphere without stalling out. He would put the bird down at the end and shut it down fast before he went off the far end where the workers were still working. The heat made the high density altitude of the air difficult to keep the B-29 airborne. A jeep with a "Follow Me" sign led them to their parking spot. McGregor's ground crew gathered around the jeep and a small flatbed and watched a B-29 pull in.

Haggerty cried out over the intercom, "Our ground crew! Wonder how long they've been here!" McGregor shut down the four engines and a tired flight crew headed to the exits to get back on good old ground. The flight crew dropped from the nose hatch as they were met by the ground crew.

A crew chief was grinning at McGregor and said, "You guys are five days late, Captain."

Captain McGregor replied in a tired voice, “Yeah…had to change all the plugs in Cairo…and again in Karachi.”

The ground crew chief gestured to the other 29s “Pretty much the same with all the others.”

Captain McGregor asked, “Problems?”

The ground crewman said with emphasis, “Problems?! One disappeared over the Arabian Sea…one went in at Marrakech…five between here and Karachi.”

The co-pilot added, “Yeah. We saw the remains of that one in Marrakech.”

Captain McGregor asked “Where do we sleep?”

The ground crewman gestured to a row of tents right by the hard stand, “You're looking at it.”

Captain McGregor, crestfallen, said “Not exactly the Waldorf, is it?”

The ground crewman said matter of fact tone, “Food's worse!” They went to the rear of the aircraft where baggage was being passed from the rear compartments. The ground crewman talked as they walked, “They just carved this damned thing out of the jungle a couple of months ago, Captain. They laid a pipeline in here from Kiunglia. No need for gasoline right now, though. Grounded…all of ‘em.”

Captain McGregor nodded and said, “Engine heating?” The small truck had approached the area where baggage was being passed down. The ground crewman began loading the baggage, McGregor helping as they continued talking.

“Yeah…among other things. Can't hardly get the damned things in the air. Then when they do, bang! Engine detonations! General Arnold's trouble shooters…they're out here from the States. Bent over backwards trying to figure out what the hell to do.”

The ground crewman motioned McGregor to a jeep where he was driven to a large tent. McGregor and the ground crewman entered the large tent which served as the headquarters tent for Chakulia Field. Many of the personnel were at work, stripped to the waist and still perspiring form the unbearable heat. A radio was blaring out an all-American jazz piece. Captain

McGregor was astonished, "Jazz…over here?"

The ground crewman smiled as he said, "Tokyo Rose…direct from Tokyo. Best jazz station in the Far East…that's if you can put up with her propaganda bull! That's how we knew you were five days late!"

Captain McGregor turned and looked at the crew chief. Astonished, he said, "You mean…"

The ground crewman was enjoying McGregor's naive amazement. "Name and tail number! Read 'em over the air about an hour ago! She does it with every arrival so far." Then she tells us all we've been sent out here to fight with unsafe airplanes…and that we'll all be killed in them! Operations…it's right through here, Sir."

McGregor nodded and went into the secondary tent area. Upon entering, he was surprised at the crude mission boards and maps hastily put up on the walls. There was a beehive of activity as the men went about their duties. A captain came over to him and introduced himself as the assistant operations and scheduling officer. He briefed McGregor on what to expect in the future and how the missions would be scheduled and flown in the command. As he left operations, McGregor had a real bad feeling.

CHAPTER 58

President Roosevelt sat in his wheelchair in the Old Cabinet Room at the White House. A screening of 16mm footage of the construction of the related airfields in China was in progress. Hundreds of coolies were seen carrying stones, carefully placing and packing the stones into a hard surface. They watched a giant roller being pulled by at lest a hundred coolies. The President asked, "And which base is this, Hap?"

General Arnold answered, "Peng Shan. It's the last of the four B-29 bases under construction in the Chengtu area."

President Roosevelt looked over at General Arnold and General George Marshall…both were watching the film intently. President Roosevelt took his cigarette holder out of his mouth and pointed to the screen. "All built by hand! Why…it's almost like watching the building of the Pyramids."

General Marshall responded, "Certainly as primitive!"

President Roosevelt asked, "When will they be in service, Hap?" "Within the month, Mr. President," General Arnold replied. The film concluded and the screen went to black. The room lights came up as General Arnold rose and crossed to a wall map featuring East Asia temporarily fastened to the wall for this particular conference. He pointed to the related areas on the map. "All four groups of the Fifty-Eighth bomb wing are on location in the Calcutta area now. They'll stock- pile gasoline in the four forward staging areas around Chengtu, Pengshal, Kinglia Kwanghan, and Heinching." He then continued, "That uh….that effort's been delayed, however..heating problems with the R3350 engines."

President Roosevelt asked, "Engine problems?" But I thought we had all of that resolved, Hap!" General Arnold said, "We're working on it, Mr. President. General Wolfe's assured me that he'll start hauling gasoline and supplies over the Hump well before the end of the month."

President Roosevelt turned to Marshall and asked, "The language for the Twentieth Air Force Charter, has it all been worked out, General Marshall?"

General Marshall replied, "Yes, Mr. President." The Twentieth Strategic Air Force has been created and officially placed under the authority of the Joint Chiefs themselves, with General Arnold as its executive agent. General Hansell will act as his Chief of Staff. Admiral King provided the final definitive language to the JSSC people that established Hap in that position."

President Roosevelt seemed astonished. "Ernie? Agreed!" His grin broadened. "Remarkable. The Navy supporting the Air Force! Your arguments for the independent of the Twentieth Air Force have apparently been more persuasive than any of us thought, Hap."

General Arnold responded while grinning, "I've tried, Mr. President."

President Roosevelt turned serious and said "We're all aware of the economic, logistical and operational problems inherent in the Matterhorn plan, Hap. Of course the objective justifies the risk…getting our B-29s within striking range of the Japanese Home islands. But…I want every B-29 in the Fifty Eighth Bombardment Wing over the Japanese home islands the day Nimitz begins the Marianas invasion..." the President said, glancing at Marshall questioningly.

General Marshall nodded and replied, "June fifteenth."

President Roosevelt said with a firm voice, "That's just two months off, Hap. I…I'm not going to tolerate any excuses on this one."

General Marshall got up and crossed to stand at the map with General Arnold and pointed to the related areas on the map. General Marshall looked at Arnold, then turned to the President and said, "With the Japanese amassing supplies and equipment up here in the bend of the Yellow River, it's pretty obvious they're getting ready to advance against Chennault's bases down here at Kweilin and Linchow. All of the Hump tonnage the Air Transport Command can manage will be required to reinforce Stilwell's Army…and Chennault's Fourteenth Air Force. They've got to hold East China at any cost! Your boys are going to be on their own. They'll simply have to supply their forward base there in the Chengtu area for their early missions against the home islands."

General Arnold nodding his understanding replied, "Of course, Sir. General Stratmeyer has already apprised us of the Air Transport Command limitations, General Marshall."

President Roosevelt became serious again, "There are several strategic and political advantages to be gained in staging a successful B-29 mission against the home islands on the exact date of the Marianas invasion…not the least of which is making the Japanese aware they're already vulnerable to Twentieth Air Force strategic bombardment with our B-29s operating out of India, even without the Marianas! Otherwise, they might increase their commitment of forces to defend the Marianas Chain to prevent the building of our B-29 bases there."

"I understand all of that, Mr. President," said Arnold.

President Roosevelt continued, "And…another thing. Operation Overlord…the long awaited invasion of Europe…it's currently scheduled for early June. A significant B-29 effort against Japan on that date would be highly desirable. The reasons are obvious."

General Arnold again responded, "I understand, Mr. President."

President Roosevelt looked at the two Generals and said, "I…uh… think it's best to keep the Twentieth Air Force…and the unique nature of its command system. That all ought to be kept under wraps until the June Fifteenth mission over Japan. Chiang Kai-shek's going to be damned unhappy that the B-29s weren't put under Chennault's command!"

General Marshall responded, "Of course, that would have been a disaster, Mr. President. Chennault and the Generalissimo are totally committed to a "China first" policy."

President Roosevelt wearily said, "I know, General Marshall…I know. It's been the same with Douglas MacArthur and the Philippines. The rest of the global war can go to hell until the Philippines have been retaken!"

"I understand, Mr. President. I have General Coltrane standing by outside should you have any specific questions. He's been in India and knows firsthand what the problems are," General Arnold said.

"Bring him in. I've always wanted to meet him. He's had one hell of a career. I value his opinion," the President ordered.

Coltrane marched in and rendered a salute. Roosevelt nodded and extended his hand to meet him.

"A real pleasure to meet you after all the years, Black Bart," the President said in admiration. "Now take a seat and give me some short and hopefully sweet answers to tough questions."

"Yes, Sir," he said as he sat in a straight back chair almost in front of the President.

"What do you see as the biggest problem that we've in our India operation?" Roosevelt asked.

"Short term will be logistics and fuel to forward bases," Coltrane replied without hesitation. The President then turned to Coltrane and said, "Now, tell me about the other supply and fuel problems."

Coltrane resumed his briefing. "The other supply problems will resolve themselves in time. The fuel over the Hump is something that can only be done by air for now. I think that greater aviation assets other than B-29s should be added to relieve the situation to some degree. As long as we must fly out of China, we'll have this problem, Sir," he paused then continued.

"The supply chain has no flexibility due to the standing operating procedures set forth by General Wolf's headquarters. It's not a matter of quantity, - it's priority and distribution. Critical engine parts arrive at the port, but they're handled essentially the same as the general supplies. That adds a couple of weeks to the delivery of the critical parts and equipment."

The President interjected," Do you've a solution, General?"

Arnold looked shocked at the response. "Yes, Sir. I'd suggest that the critical parts be identified at port and flown directly to the destination airfield by civilian contract air freight, Sir," Coltrane said then paused again for questions.

Arnold thought quietly then said, "That would be an excellent way to resolve the problem."

The President then asked, "Are there any air freight companies over there that can do the job?"

"Yes, Sir. There's one in the area that can do the job, but is about to go out of business. I can get the freight company a bridge loan out of London to turn it around so it can do the job, if the President directs, Sir," Bart said with confidence.

"Who would make that kind of financial risk in that part of the world during war time?" asked the President.

"One of my wife's companies will undertake the risk, Sir, but it constitutes some conflict of interest on my part, and you must approve such a conflict, Sir. But the bottom line is that it can start direct shipments within ten days if you and General Arnold approve the plan, warts and all," Coltrane finished in a softer tone.

"Conflict of interest, hell, Bart, if we maintained a strict ruling on conflicts the war industry would stop by sundown. Yours is negligible at the most. You're hereby directed to proceed to India via London and establish the new air supply system immediately. Hap, you send General Wolf the appropriate directives implementing Coltrane's plan," the President said in his formal voice before smiling and nodding for Bart to continue.

Coltrane continued, "Maintenance and ongoing B-29 modifications will continue for a long time. That can't be quickly changed. Weather over Japan will always be a problem for high altitude bombing especially given the very high altitude winds. A significant problem will be the chain of command. Everyone wants control or at least priority over the B-29 strike capability. The sooner we can base out of the Marianas Islands, the better performance will become, Sir," Coltrane said with conviction.

The President looked at Arnold. "He sure doesn't pull any punches. Bart, I understand that you sneaked out on a reconnaissance flight over Japan. Is that true?"

"Yes, Sir, I needed to get a first hand feel for what the situation was and what problems our bombers would encounter. I couldn't find out behind a desk," Bart said.

"So your points were based upon actual experience?" Roosevelt asked.

"Yes, Sir," Coltrane replied.

You may consider this a direct order from the Commander-in-Chief.

Stay out of aircraft going into combat! Your experience and judgment is far too valuable to lose in combat. Do you and General Arnold understand?" the President directed.

Both men nodded and said, "Yes, Sir" together.

"Do you think that bombardment will eventually do enough destruction to get the Japs to surrender?" Roosevelt asked.

"Sir, air power is the only way that we can reduce their capability to wage war, reduce their will to fight and avoid an invasion of their homeland. The invasion will cost millions of US and Japanese lives. Air bombardment is the key, Sir," Coltrane said with conviction.

"Very well put, Bart, and you're right," said the President. "Will the B-29 do the job for us?"

"Yes, Sir. It's the best that we've today."

"Today," said the President. "I interpret that to mean that you're looking ahead to the replacement aircraft. I have been told that you've been spending some time with Ted Hall at Convair. So what do you think of the B-36?"

"Sir, my read is that it's an essential weapon that can deter any Russian strategic or global conflicts. It's great range and altitude capability, as well as the ability to drop up to 72,000 pounds of ordnance. However, it's slow, it can't refuel in the air, and the potential fuel and hydraulic leaks are even more of a limitation to its capability. There are a series of design problems that must be resolved before we start construction," Coltrane said looking at Arnold to see if he had said too much or was too frank.

"So, you see the Russians as a post-war problem for global security?"

"Yes, Sir," Bart replied.

"So do I, General. Now what are your thoughts on Boeing's Model 424?" the President said as he watched Coltrane's reaction. "Yes, Bart, I know that you've been talking with George Schairer at Boeing. I have my own spies out there as well," he said smiling very broadly.

"Sir, that's the future and the answer," Coltrane said sheepishly. "What they're working on is an all jet intercontinental bombing platform that will keep the global peace. If they can conquer some design problems, the aircraft will fly higher, faster and longer than the B-36. It can be the next generation platform for 'Silver Plate' and that nuclear capability is what is needed to deter the Russians. If it's developed and placed into a special mission bomb wing whose mission is to be on constant alert for enemy attack, we can keep the peace, Sir."

"We, I assume means in a new separate air force?" he asked.

"Yes, Sir," Coltrane replied.

"You make a very good case for service separation and strategic bombing capability. You seem to know an awful lot about everything we're doing today and tomorrow. For the sake of the country, stay out of combat. You know too much classified information to be killed – or worse – captured." Then the President looked at Arnold and continued. "Hap, I see why you brought him to this meeting. He's a good and convincing proponent for air power. He also is insightful into our problems in the Pacific. Keep up the good work, Bart."

The President looked tired and weak. He motioned to the aide to come over to wheel him out of the room. Then he turned to Arnold and Coltrane. "Gentlemen, you'll have to excuse me, I'm not up to snuff right now. Good day."

The two Generals left the room. As they exited the oval office, Arnold held Bart by the arm. "That was excellent! You did well on every subject. You've made my job to sell air power a lot easier." He paused, turned his head toward Coltrane then continued, "So you don't think much of the B-36?"

"I think the B-36 can be a great aircraft. It's limitations and flaws, but it's going to be a stop gap answer to our long range objective, Sir. But it will give us the platform we need to get to the all jet Boeing 424. There's our future," Coltrane said.

"You've obviously done a lot of study into the two aircraft. More than I have seen before. Now let's find ways to end the war in the Pacific before the body count gets too high," Arnold said as he walked away.

Eight thousand forty miles east of the White House was the headquarters building of the XX Bomber Command in Kragapur, India. The headquarters was originally built as a prison compound, but in early 1944 it was the headquarters of Brigadier General Kenneth B. Wolfe, Commanding Officer of the XX Bomber Command. The staff officers of the XX Bomber Command were a very dejected and frustrated group of men. The operations officer walked briskly along the hallway, turning into General Wolfe's office. He carried a teletype message tightly in his hand. He handed Wolfe the teletype message. "This just came in from Washington, General," said the operations officer.

As General Wolfe read the message, an angry scowl began to cross his features, just before he exclaimed a rhetorical question in angry astonishment.

"Shakedown Mission!"

A daylight precision mission against the Japs!

With every damned B-29 in the command still undergoing engine modification?"

Wolfe rose, crossed to a large wall map of Asia where sectors of B-29 radius of operations were scaled in: one from Formosa reaching the lower portion of Kyushu, one of Chengtu and reaching Kyushu, one from Guam. Then he looked at the same type of radii extending down to the Dutch East Indies from Calcutta and another one from Ceylon. Wolfe gazed at the map a moment before he replied, "Any word from Stilwell's engineers?"

The operations officer said "No, General. Nothing!"

General Wolfe punched the Chengtu area with his finger in an angry gesture, "We sure as hell can't stockpile gasoline in our forward bases if they aren't operational yet, now can we?" The operations officer, startled, responded sheepishly, "Uh…no. No, Sir."

General Wolfe turned from the map and crossed to the window, gazing out pensively. General Wolfe said to the operations officer, "Our crews haven't had <u>any</u> training. We're just barely able to crawl…and they call on us to do a…a hundred yard dash!"

CHAPTER 59

Back in Cleveland, Ohio, the paper boy on his bike threw the morning paper. Mr. Maitland opened the door, taking the paper and the morning mail inside and slowly walked to the breakfast room reading the headlines. Helen and her mother were at the breakfast table drinking coffee. Mr. Maitland seated himself, becoming absorbed in the morning paper. Helen opened the morning mail.

Suddenly, Mr. Maitland cried out, "The second time!"

"The second time for what, dear?" asked Mrs. Maitland.

Mr. Maitland responded quickly, "Curt's outfit's bombed Berlin!" Four divisions flew the mission this time, nearly four hundred B-17s!"

Helen stiffened as she grasped an unfolded letter in her hand. Suddenly, she gasped – a terrified sound. "Oh! Oh, God! No…." Helen dropped the sheet to the table, rushing to the hall telephone.

Mr. Maitland reached for the object, raising it to read its contents. He rose to follow the terrified Helen, reading the piece of letter stationery where words cut from newsprint had been pasted across its surface. He read:

YOU NOT FEEL SECURE YOUR DAUGHTER JANIE IS ALRIGHT!

SHE BE HELD UNTIL YOUR HUSBAND STOPS BOMBING GERMANS!

Mr. Maitland lowered the sheet, crossed to the hallway where Helen was waiting – frantic – for a response to her call. Mr. Maitland came over to be with her. Helen, after having waited for what seemed forever for the person to come to the phone, said, "Mrs. Holmbey…is…is Janie there?" Several blocks away was the private school facility that Janie Lemay attended. Its manicured yards and well kept building bespeaking its stature in the community.

Mrs. Holmbey, the headmistress of the school responded to the frantic Helen Lemay. "Why yes, Mrs. Lemay....I saw her just a few minutes ago. Mrs. Lemay! What's wrong?"

Helen told her of the threatening letter.

"Yes! I'll go find her! Right now! Of course...I'll stay right with her," Holmbey said in a frightened and urgent tone. Mrs. Holmbey went to Janie Lemay's classroom, her eyes searching the area where twelve or so children were in the midst of a crayon sketching session. The young female teacher glances up at Mrs. Holmbey ,questioningly. Mrs. Holmbey now stood in the middle of the room, her anxiety turning to a frantic question. Mrs. Holmbey asked with a quiver in her voice, "Janie Lemay! Where is Janie Lemay?"

The teacher replied in a shocked tone, "Why she..." Mrs. Holmbey asked again, "Where is Janie?" Just then Janie entered the classroom, startled to hear her name.

Janie said shyly, "I'm here, Mrs. Holmbey."

Mrs. Holmbey asked, still frantic, "Where have you been?"

Janie was startled now. "I just went to the bathroom. What's the matter?"

Mrs. Holmbey showed some relief, "Your Mother...she's coming after you! We'll get your coat."

Janie, became a bit skeptical. "But...I can get it, Mrs. Holmbey."

Mrs. Holmbey reassured her and said to the concerned girl, "Well... I'll just walk along with you. You don't mind that, do you?"

Janie gazed at the distraught headmistress and said, "Is something wrong, Mrs. Holmbey?"

Mrs. Holmbey replied softly, "No....nothing's wrong...at least not now, dear." They left the classroom and headed for her office.

Janie was sitting in a chair, her coat on and her lunch box in her lap, obviously baffled by the events, when Helen Lemay entered, going to Janie and gathering her in her arms, vastly relieved. Mrs. Holmbey worked quietly at her desk, then got up to join Helen and Janie.

"What's the matter, Mommy? You're all upset! And Mrs. Holmbey.... she's been acting funny too!"

Helen was smiling and crying at the same time, "It's nothing… nothing really. I just wanted you at home with me this afternoon…that's all."

Janie said to her mother, "Sure. Now I know what's the matter with you. You just miss Daddy, don't you?"

"Perhaps," Helen said as she was preparing to leave. Thank you, Mrs. Holmbey." Mrs. Holmbey said, "It was nothing," as Helen and Janie left for home.

Three hours later, two FBI Agents alit from their vehicle, one checking his notes to affirm the correct address as they entered the front gate and walked to the door of the clapboard house. One of the agents rapped on the door. The door is opened by a frowzy middle aged, recluse lady. The first agent asked ,"Mrs. Hilderbrand?" The woman responded, "Yes…" The agent displayed his credentials, "FBI…" The woman opened the door wider and asked the agents to enter. The agents stepped into the living room, eyeing the surroundings carefully. One of the agents crossed to a table where several newspapers had been out – extracts having been pasted on several sheets of stationery – the same as that received by Helen Lemay. The agents looked at one another, then the first agent gestured to the notes, "You…uh….been sending these other to other people too?"

Mrs. Hilderbrand, her facial expressions obviously those of one who is mentally ill, "Everybody that's bombing Germans! It...it's not right to bomb Germans! I tell the President if they don't stop!"

The second FBI agent, very patiently and tolerantly gathered up the prepared notes, "You mustn't do this anymore, Mrs. Hilderbrand. Do you understand?"

Mrs. Hilderbrand nodded, dumbly, mutely. The agents exit the home leaving the woman staring vacantly after them. A few minutes later, halfway across Cleveland, the agents stood in the hallway, hats in hand, Helen and her parents listening to them. The first agent, apologetically stated, "She's harmless. She's been a mental patient at a local hospital here from time to time. No record of any violence. Anyway, there's nothing we can do until she does something."

"Does something? You mean, you'll have to wait until Janie's been kidnapped before you can do anything?" Helen responded with concern.

The second agent added calmly, "I'm sorry, Mrs. Lemay. And, I'm sorry the news people got a hold of this. That kind of publicity could give some real nut ideas."

Mrs. Maitland looked at Helen and said, "Colonel Wynn called from Montgomery again this morning, Helen. He wants you and Janie to come down there."

The first agent asked, "Colonel Wynn?"

Helen looked at the agent and said, "The Commanding Officer... Gunter Field...in Montgomery."

The agent smiled and responded, "Perhaps a military base would be a safer place for you right now. You'd be on the base there at Gunter Field? Then...I would advise it...at least for awhile."

Helen gazed back at the agent as she replied, "Alright...if that's what you advise."

The agent apologetically answered, "As I say...we're sorry. There just isn't anything we can do at this point. Your husband, the General, he's doing a tremendous job over there, Mrs. Lemay. Perhaps it will all be over soon."

Helen said, "Thank you, you've been most kind." The agents left the Maitland house.

CHAPTER 60

The atmosphere was tense at USAAF airfields in England as the ground crews and emergency vehicles waited nervously as several B-17s approached the field. General Lemay was on the hardstand next to his staff car, waiting with a small group of officers almost surrounding it. Colonel Ted Berrington's B-17 pulled in, its engines turning up in a final roar before fading to silence as the throttles were cut. Berrington dropped from the nose hatch, his hair disheveled and tired but jubilant as he went over to Lemay.

Lemay said, "How was Berlin, Colonel?" Berrington was grinning as he addressed General Lemay.

"It was hot and heavy, General!"

Lemay, still poker-faced, asked, "What were the bombing results?"

Berrington paused, then continued, 'Well, Sir, we got good concentration on the primary target."

The Earkner Bell Bearing Works was your target?" Lemay asked in confirmation.

Berrington nodded and said, "That's right, Sir."

Lemay asked without a pause or acknowledgement to Berrington. "What about their fighter resistance?"

Berrington looked at Lemay without any smile or joy, "Heavy... damned heavy, General. Our long range fighter boys...they did a helluva job, General. German fighter losses were extremely heavy."

Lemay and Berrington got into the staff car, the driver closing the door and entering the front seat. The vehicle drove off quickly to the headquarters.

Just outside of the photographic lab at Harrington Field, Lemay and others waited impatiently. The door opened and a technician handed Lemay freshly processed glossy photos. He held them up to the light. Berrington who was at his side, and the lab technician also strained to see the bomb damage photos. Lemay was obviously pleased when he turned to Berrington and said, "Well, I'd say the Earkner Bearing Works in Berlin will have a little trouble opening up in the morning. We're finally doing a job over here, Colonel... thanks to you and the other crews."

Berrington, overwhelmed with the totally uncustomary compliment from Lemay said, "Why...why, thank you, General."

Lemay, still eyeing the photos, said, "What we need now is time...just a little more time to finish the job."

Lieutenant General Tooey Spaatz's staff car moved swiftly up the drive of the Supreme allied Headquarters, its bumper flags rippling in the air flow. The vehicle came to a halt in front of the imposing building that's the Supreme Headquarters itself. The driver opened the door for General Spaatz, who exited and crossed brusquely to the entrance. A high ranking aide exited Eisenhower's inner office, closed the huge paneled oak door behind him and spoke to the MPs stationed on either said of the door saying, "See that they're not disturbed. I'd advise you not to get too close to the door either." The MPs nodded and grinned.

General Spaatz was greeted by Eisenhower and told to be seated. General Spaatz was seated before Eisenhower's desk. Huge wall maps, paintings and other accouterments made the surroundings typically English, typically palatial.

Spaatz said, "But General Eisenhower, the Eighth and Fifteenth Strategic Air Forces here in Europe <u>must</u> be allowed to make their maximum contribution to eventual victory, not merely assist in an early invasion of Normandy! Quite frankly, given six months of uninterrupted concentration on Germany's industry, the Eighth and Fifteenth Strategic Air Forces could achieve victory….a victory that would make the invasion of Europe more of an occupational effort."

General Eisenhower rose from his desk, crossed to the window. "That's an opinion, General Spaatz!" Eisenhower said, gazing out reflectively. "Not one that's widely held either." He then turned to Spaatz, speaking quietly, persuasively, "General, I believe it's imperative that the Eighth and Fifteenth Air Forces be directed to soften up German ground forces and inhibit their movement of equipment and troops to the Normandy beaches. The transportation and communications systems leading to the Normandy area must be neutralized before the invasion. General Arnold himself has endorsed that plan."

Spaatz became really irritated with Eisenhower's typical ground commander's appraisal of the situation. "To divert the Eighth and Fifteenth Air Forces to the interdiction of the Normandy Beach area now would only be a specious appearance of support, General Eisenhower. Sounds like a typical, half-baked British idea. It would be the greatest disservice we could possibly do!"

General Eisenhower, losing his own control for a moment, said "Disservice! General, how in the hell can you call the interdiction of the Normandy Beaches…the invasion site itself…a disservice?"

Spaatz became aggressive in his position with Ike. "General, we now have sixty…SIXTY…heavy bomber groups here in Britain…with thirty-two groups of long range fighters. We can put twelve hundred B-17s over a single target or diversified targets anywhere in Germany at will! Furthermore, the practicality of strategic daylight precision bombardment has been proven! We're – at last – in reach of our goal of completing the destruction of the German air force…and…pressing on to the destruction of the primary industrial targets. To divert that capability now, from the mission we're trained to accomplish, will have the final effect of prolonging the war!"

General Eisenhower turned and looked directly at Spaatz and said, "Tooey, I made it clear when I assumed Supreme Allied Command here in Europe last month that there would be NO invasion unless the German air force had been destroyed first. Both the U.S. and Britain agree to that! "

Spaatz said sternly, "General, the German Air Force is NOT IN FRANCE! Not in the...the Normandy Beach area! THE GERMAN AIR FORCE IS DEPLOYED ALONG THE WESTERN FRONT OF THE GERMAN HOMELAND!"

Spaatz calmed down a little and with a great deal of effort said, "And... every strategic mission we fly over the German frontier draws up fighter elements that are subsequently decimated by our own long range fighters! Now you're asking me to divert our heavy bombers and long range fighters to the interdiction of the Normandy invasion site...two months before the invasion itself is scheduled...to commit the strategic air forces to supporting roles for that invasion."

Eisenhower became thoughtful and was somewhat persuaded by Spaatz's argument, uncertain of the concept himself. He says, "Only to soften up the ground forces...inhibit movement of troops..." Spaatz looked at Ike and knew it was time to press the issue. "General, whatever damage we'd be able to do to the transportation systems and bridges in the Normandy area now could easily be repaired before the invasion! It's still two and a half months down the road."

General Eisenhower angered now that his judgment has been called into question, said, "I might remind you, General Spaatz, that all U.S. Strategic Air Forces in Europe have been placed under the direction of the Supreme Allied Commander...under my direction in other words. I have been perfectly willing to avoid terms and language that might startle anyone, but I must have full power to determine missions and priorities...for all forces... without having to negotiate in the heat of battle! The INTERDICTION of the Normandy area has been made A MATTER OF HIGH PRIORITY for the strategic air forces, General Spaatz, and it will continue to be so!"

Spaatz pulled back slightly and looked down momentarily, sighing and resigned to the inevitable, "Well...we spent the first year over here trying to knock out the German submarine pens before the Combined Chiefs finally realized that was a misdirected effort!" He said, rising to leave, "Looks like we'll spend the rest of our time knocking out buzz bomb factories and interdicting the Normandy invasion site!" He started to leave, then turned back to Eisenhower, "But maybe…just maybe…when that damned invasion has been carried out…when they actually have ground forces in Europe!...Maybe we can get on with the strategic bombardment of German war production… synthetic oil refineries…bearings...aircraft industries. If they don't have oil… war production…they're not going to be able to do a hell of a lot of defending over there." Spaatz looked at Ike, grinned and said, "At least we ought to be able to keep 'em from kicking your asses off the continent once you're there!"

General Eisenhower was now grinning too, "Tooey…I'm in sympathy with your position. I…I want your support. I'd rather have it willingly…not begrudgingly."

Spaatz quickly added, "Then let me have a crack at the synthetic oil industry…before we're diverted to the transportation priority."

General Eisenhower asked openly, "When??"

Spaatz said, "First available weather," as he crossed to a wall map. "Their entire synthetic petroleum industry is concentrated here in the Ruhr, General…and here in the Ploesti area. General Eaker's Fifteenth Air Force has played hell with that, leaving the Ruhr as their main source of petroleum products," he said, looking at the General squarely. "Those plants are vulnerable. We can get to them and knock them out with minimum losses to our air forces."

Eisenhower gazed at the map, then crossed slowly back to the window gazing out for a long while, then said to Spaatz, "Alright…alright Tooey. Go after it! He then turned to Spaatz and spoke with clear firmness, "But… just remember one thing: the interdiction of the Normandy area will remain a strategic Air Force priority. The invasion of Europe has become the first priority of both Britain and the United States. It's my job as Supreme Allied Commander to see that it's carried out successfully. I intend to do that, General Spaatz…at any cost!"

Spaatz was grinning when he replied, "Understood, General. I…I guess we'd better stick together in this damned war, General, or we'll end up under a British commander.

General Eisenhower said, shaking his head, 'We came a lot closer to that than you can possibly imagine, General Spaatz!"

Spaatz crossed to a side table, secured his hat and shook Ike's hand then left. Eisenhower smiled after he left, then crossed to his desk, and resumed his work.

CHAPTER 61

It was May 12, 1944, and once again the aircrews gathered into the group briefing room. The black curtain over the mission map could not conceal that the day's target obviously was the Ruhr. Flight crews were smoking and chatting idly as they awaited the briefing. An aide called out, "TEN-SHUN!" General Doolittle, Commanding General, Eighth Air Force." General Doolittle strode to the briefing platform, followed by General Lemay. General Doolittle ordered, "Seats." Then, using a pointer to indicate target position on the map, "Your target today is the synthetic oil refineries here in the Ruhr…I.G. Farben…the Leuna works…" Then Doolittle turned back to the crews, "These targets are the most vital elements of the entire German war production machine! Everything we've done up to this point has been prologue to this type of strategic mission. If we destroy their oil refineries in the Ruhr…we'll have struck a paralyzing blow to the Germans' ability to continue the war. I believe the Third Division is one of the most efficient groups of men and machines the United States Army Air Force has produced to date. You're qualified…to the man…for the mission ahead. Good luck! I only wish I were going with you." Then Doolittle turned to Lemay, "Curt."

Lemay said, "I can't add much to that, Gentlemen. Colonel Berrington is going to lead the Division. You're in good hands so...best of luck to all of you." Doolittle and Lemay exited, as the room quickly and proudly snapped to attention. Then the crews began moving to the exit also. An hour later, Lemay's staff car with Doolittle, Lemay and Colonel Berrington pulled up to the hard stand. They got out with Berrington preparing to enter the B-17 parked at the hard stand with its engines already at idle. Lemay said, "Good luck, Ted." He then gripped Berrington's forearm in a brief gesture, "Put them outta the petroleum business over there."

Berrington grinned and said, "I'll see to it, General." He quickly walked to the B-17, entering through the nose hatch, as Lemay and Doolittle watched the aircraft.

Doolittle found himself standing outside the car watching Berrington's B-17 lift off, another following closely behind. You could see he missed flying with his men. Then they went to Lemay's office at Elveden Hall, and Lemay and Doolittle went inside as the staff was busy with the beginning of an important strike mission.

Lemay asked Doolittle, "Coffee?"

Doolittle nodded affirmatively as General Lemay poured, handing the cup to Doolittle who settled into a nearby chair, followed by Lemay. Doolittle sat his cup aside. He looked concerned, then looked up at Lemay and said, "Curt, General Arnold's been asking some questions around…wanting to know who could best handle the B-29s…the Twentieth Air Force…out in India.

"I thought Kenneth Wolfe had that command," Lemay said with a question in his tone.

Doolittle began, "KB's a production man, you know. A damned good one too. But that program needs an innovator…a bombardment professional with an eye for the impossible!" Doolittle paused, gauging Lemay's reaction before going on then, "General Eaker and I both recommended you, Curt."

Lemay responded in a surprised tone, "From what I've heard, that program's in deep trouble."

"You're right, Doolittle said, "If anyone can pull it out, it'd be you. The whole program...It's gotten off to a bad start."

Lemay leaned back in contemplation, "That's an understatement." Bart Coltrane briefed me on what he saw out there. It wasn't pretty."

Doolittle continued, "Arnold hasn't made a decision yet. I…"

A knock at the door interrupted the conversation. An aide peered in. The aide said, "Mission reports are coming in, General." Lemay and Doolittle rose, walked to the door, and down the hall. The operations officer, Colonel

Preston, approached Lemay, scanning some hastily scribbled notes. Preston said with concerns, "Sir, there's been heavy fighter resistance all the way in. Our own fighter boys have been able to keep them away from the bomber formations so far. They're apparently still headed for the primary."

Lemay looked over to the weather officer, "Weather holding over the primary?"

The weather officer nodded at reports, "So far, general. Two tenths cloud cover maybe, so far so good."

At 24,000 feet over Germany, the air battle was as rough as it had ever been on any previous missions flown by Colonel Ted Berrington. He knew the "Fatherland" would go all out to protect the Ruhr and its valuable industry and resources. Today, the Luftwaffe was living up to his expectations. Berrington controlled the aircraft with great difficulty due to the flak shock waves bouncing it violently. If it wasn't the Luftwaffe, it was the flak. "This was definitely going to be the roughest yet," he thought.

The navigator's voice caught Berrington by surprise as his concentration had been outside until then. "Navigator to pilot…one minute to the IP, Colonel." Berrington glanced up and out to his left, then acknowledged on the intercom.

Berrington said, to no one in particular, "If those fighter boys can just keep 'em off another minute or two." Berrington watched a P-51 peel after a ME-109 that pulled up from a fighter encounter below that prevented a head-on attack on the formation below. The P-51 fell in behind the 109. The 109 weaved and twisted, but the P-51 stayed on its tail, firing sporadic bursts from its wing guns. The ME-109 dove sharply to the right, then exploded in a bright ball of fire. The ME-109 went down, the P-51 peeling away to join the ongoing fight below…Berrington could see the general area of the target. He knew the flak would be more intensive just before and just after they unloaded on the target. The bombardier, raising his hand, then reported, "Bombs away." Berrington began to turn away from the target, as planned.

Berrington was concerned about the formation not staying in tight for mutual protection. "Everybody stay tucked in now. They're going to follow us out. Let's keep a tight formation."

An extremely excited gunner yelled into the intercom, "Two bandits at nine o'clock broke through the fighter screen!"

Berrington looked up and out to his left. Berrington said in a calm and deliberate voice, "Alright…stay calm..get on 'em!"

A voice from another plane said, "Look out, Ted! He's going to ram you!"

Berrington tensed, looking frantically to see which way the attack was coming from.

Suddenly Rosenberg screamed, barely in time to push the control column to a vertical dive position. Rosenberg ducked as he yelled, "Look out!" as a twin engine Messerschmitt dove into Berrington's B-17, colliding at the upper mid section – both aircraft exploding. The debris of Berrington's bomber was sifting downward onto the other aircraft below. The flight crew in the other B-17s watched the grim scene silently.

The somber voice of the pilot of Berrington's wingman said, "I'm pulling up to lead position. The rest of the lead element tack in on me. Let's go home."

At the Eleveden Hall Operations room on May 12, 1944, Preston hung up the phone, obviously shaken, and walked slowly to Lemay. Preston reported, "Sir, they've hit the target. They're on the way back."

Lemay sensing something was wrong, waited, looking Preston in the eye.

Preston continued, softly, "Ted bought the farm, it…rammed by a twin engine job."

Lemay stood quietly for a moment struggling to control his emotions, although that inner-struggle is but barely perceptible in his features. "Other losses?" Preston continued, "Pretty light apparently. They're reporting the German fighter losses to be extremely heavy." Presently Lemay turned to leave the room and as he did, said, "Preston, I…I want to see the strike photos when they're available." Preston nodded, gazing after the departing General.

CHAPTER 62

At the Berghof Obersalzberg, Germany on May 23, 1944, Herman Goering's voice was heard as he talked with Albert Speer. "You must <u>not</u> go through with this madness, Speer."

War Production Minister Speer, Reich Marshall Goering, General Keitel and General Adolph Galland were gathered with four German industrialists who stood nearby in a separate grouping, while several high ranking German officers came and went along the entrance as Goering and the others talk. Goering was angry and was admonishing Speer. Goering exclaimed, "The Fuhrer…his burden is already great enough without this!"

Speer quietly and resolutely replied, "It's time he knows the unvarnished truth, Herr Goering. The Luftwaffe is finished…and…so are we. It's simply a matter of time. The end is inevitable! Already Berlin is a mass of rubble. And now the oil refineries."

Goering looked at Speer, "That's treason, Minister Speer!" Speer nodded, and unperturbed said "It's fact, Herr Goering."

A frustrated Goering was eyeing General Adolph Galland ominously, "This is your doing, Galland. You're the one who told me enemy long range fighters were shot down over Achaean, hundreds of miles further than they reportedly could penetrate!"

General Adolph Galland responded, "But Sir…I asked you to go see for yourself."

Goering said, "Why go? I knew they weren't there! You've betrayed me Galland. "

The Commanding General of the Luftwaffe fighter forces quickly responded, "and you've betrayed ME!"

General Galland stated, "I have betrayed no one, Herr Goering... least of all you! I have cut training flights to one hour per week to conserve on precious petroleum. I have held our fighters down except where our most vital war production was under attack. Held them down to keep them from being destroyed by the Eighth Air Forces, long range P-51s, and the damnable P-47! But I cannot perform the impossible, Herr Goering! We've suffered grievous losses. We're unable to prevent the daylight bombing of our industries any longer."

A German general and his aide emerged from the salon, and walked by the Speer group to exit the Berghof. The aide announced, "Gentlemen... the Fuhrer will see you now."

Goering said to Speer in one last desperate attempt, "You must not do this!" The group and the German business men entered the salon, Speer entering last. The German business men entered the salon, but remained near the door as Speer, Goering, Kietel and Galland greet the Fuhrer. Adolph Hitler rose from the small, ornate table where he had been working to shake hands with Speer who then nodded to the business men. They grouped in front of Hitler's as Speer refreshed the Fuhrer's memory as to their identity.

Speer said, "Mein Fuhrer...Herr Krauch, the director of our chemical industry."

Hitler, in a pleasant and informal voice, "Herr Krauch..." Speer said, "Herr Pleiger, Reich commissioner for coal and our synthetic fuel plants." Hitler nods and uttered a polite "Herr Pleiger..." Speer then introduced, "Herr Butefisch, the head of the Leuna Works."

Hitler looked cautiously at the man, "Herr Butefisch, I understand the Leuna Works were heavily damaged in the May twelve bombing."

Butfisch responded, "Yes, Mein Fuhrer... our plant is out of operation. It will take some time to repair it."

Hitler softly spoke, "That's too bad. Our tanks benefit greatly from your plant's synthetic fuel output."

Butefisch said apologetically, "I'm sorry, Mein Fuhrer."

Lastly, Speer introduced, "And Herr Fischer, Mein Fuhrer, the chairman of the board of I. G. Farben."

Hitler, in an upbeat voice, "Ah, yes, it's good to see you again, Herr Fischer." Hitler paced a few steps, his hands behind his back, then turned to the group. "Gentlemen…I have asked you here along with Reich Marshall Goering, Field Marshall Keitel, and General Galland hoping we might reach some understanding as to where we really stand in terms of synthetic petroleum production."

Goering quickly added, "Mein Fuhrer…we've nearly eighteen months of reserves on hand!"

Hitler momentarily ignored the Reich Marshall, "Herr Speer…"

Speer looked at Hitler and responded, in a confident tone, "Our immediate sources of supply have been interrupted – production temporarily cut by at least thirty percent, Mein Fuhrer. Two or three more raids of the May twelve magnitude against our fuel refineries could drastically restrict our source of supply. Such damage would require months to repair."

"Herr Fischer, do you agree with Minister Speer?" Hitler asked.

"Most certainly, Mein Fuhrer, Fischer replied. "The I.G. Farben synthetic fuel facilities were heavily damaged May twelve. Production has been interrupted severely. It's a most difficult situation…Mein Fuhrer!"

Hitler reassuringly said to Fischer, "You'll manage somehow."

Herr Pleiger then reported, "Our coal pressurization facility has been shut down for extensive repairs, Mein Fuhrer! Without our process, there's no synthetic fuel production!"

General Keitel anxiously placated Hitler, "We've been through worse crises."

"We were foolish in building our synthetic production plants so closely together in the Ruhr. Now, with South Africa and the Ploesti fields in Rumania cut off, our only source of petroleum supply is our synthetic plants here in our own Ruhr." Hitler paused, then posed the hypothetical question, "If the Eighth Air Force bombers were diverted to other objectives…the interdiction of an invasion site for instance..Would you have enough time to relocate some elements of our fuel production?"

"Perhaps," Speer said. "It would depend on how long that time might be." Hitler tossed his hair to the side as he said, "Two or three months?"

Speer lowered his head slightly and replied, "I do not think so Mein Fuhrer."

Reich Marshall Goering said in a false air of confidence, "Perhaps it could be done!"

Keitel said, in an attempt to satisfy the Fuhrer, "We shall be able to bridge the gap with our reserves. Look how many difficult situations have we already survived in the past, Mein Fuhrer? We shall survive this one too."

Hitler, was unimpressed with Goering's and Keitel's obsequities. "In my view, the fuel, Buna rubber, and nitrogen plants represent a particularly sensitive point for the conduct of the war, since a great magnitude of vital materials for armaments are being manufactured in such a small number of plants. Our only hope lies in the chance that the Allied Air Force command is as scatterbrained as our own…and their bombers will be diverted to other targets before they destroy our plants altogether. Otherwise…we…we may be faced with a particularly grim set of options." Hitler crossed back to his desk, oblivious to the presence of the others who now begin to exit quietly before Hitler's temper flared.

CHAPTER 63

One of the other B-29s was flying close enough to see McGregor's B-29, now named the "Monsoon Minnie." The nose art had five camels painted in a neat row above. "Monsoon Minnie." The two were on a fuel ferry flight across the Himalaya's, better known as "Hump" to a staging base in China. The Hump was the name given by Allied pilots in the China Burma India Theater of Operations ("CBI") to the eastern end of the Himalayan Mountains over which they flew from India to China to resupply the flying Tigers and B-29 operations of the XX Bomber Command. The region was noted for high mountain ranges and huge parallel gorges. Allied pilots began flying cargo resupply missions over the Hump in April 1942, after the Japanese blocked the Burma Road. To maintain an uninterrupted supply to China of strategic materials and fuel the U.S., Chinese, and British forces developed an air bridge to support the critical combat needs of the Allied Forces and especially the XX Bomber Command. The 22,000 and 29,000 foot elevation of the mountain range, along with cloud-masked mountain tops, high winds and bad icing conditions made the trip over the Hump difficult and dangerous.

McGregor and the co-pilot were both working to keep control of the ship in the mountain turbulence. They were keeping a close watch ahead for any number of unpredicted problems. Experience had taught them that there would be something that would go wrong along these flights. It always did! McGregor glanced out and down to his left. He saw the jutting peaks of the snow-capped Himalaya's. It was a cold sight to him. It made him appreciate the warm cockpit of the B-29. He didn't want to end up on one of those cold mountains as others had. McGregor worriedly glanced toward the flight engineer and asked, "Is the cylinder head temperature still holding?"

The flight engineer looked at the engine temperature gauges and replied, "Yes, Sir. Those last engine mods have helped a lot. But they still need more improvements."

McGregor glanced at the fuel gauges, apprehensively. They were getting down to low levels. "Ragland," McGregor called out, "We still on course? Be a hell of a place to get lost or run out of fuel!"

Ragland said, "Plenty of others have already gone down out of fuel. We're right on course, though. Chaklulia ETA…uh..." He paused as he made a quick calculation, then he answered… "Forty-three minutes."

McGregor nodded, his anxieties monetarily eased as his eyes scanned his instruments.

The Monsoon Minnie's ground crew chief and the base artist await the arrival of the Monsoon Minnie at her hard stand. The ground crew scrambled around the aircraft as it pulled in slowly, guided by the crew chief's hand signals, then braking to a stop. Its engines ran up then became silent as the throttles were cut. The ground crew placed the wheel chocks behind and in front of the huge tires.

McGregor and the flight deck crew begin climbing down the nose hatch ladder. The crew chief asked, "How'd it go, Sir?"

McGregor took his hat off and wiped the sweat off his forehead and told the chief, "No problems. Still don't have cruise control down pat, though. Fuel on the return leg gets a little scarce."

The crew chief smiled, "Well, if my calculations are right, you've ferried enough gasoline over the Hump in these six trips to supply one B-29 for one mission out of Chengtu," the crew chief said as gestured toward the nose, where the artist was beginning to sketch in a sixth camel.

McGregor said in a disgusted manner, "We're nothing but a damned trucking outfit!" McGregor and the flight crew crossed to a waiting personnel vehicle. The Monsoon Minnie's flight crew drove the personnel carrier up to the crew tent and McGregor's crew got out and headed for a vat that held Cokes that had been cooled only by the tepid water in the vat itself.

Captain Keller came over from the adjacent tent, wearing only khaki shorts. He said to McGregor, "You guys run into any Jap fighters?"

McGregor said, "No, thank goodness. The Himalayan peaks are enough without Jap fighters too." "Zekes jumped us this morning," Keller said as he got a Coke.

McGregor was astonished. "Where?"

Keller looked at him, as he opened the Coke. "Just before we started over the eastern edge of the Hump."

McGregor exclaimed, "Damn! I thought Chennault's fighters had that route pretty well secured.

McGregor's co-pilot replied sarcastically, "If we don't plow into a Himalayan peak with a sick engine…the damned Japs are going to get us!" McGregor opened his Coke, the hot fluid spewing in a brown shower from the bottle. "Yeah!"

"Keller saw a Servel refrigerator up in Calcutta. It was a nice compact kerosene model," Ragland said, as he pointed to Keller. Keller nodded and quietly answered "Yeah? Why didn't you buy it?" McGregor asked.

Keller was reluctant to reveal all he'd done in Calcutta and said "Well...I'd…spent all my dough by then."

Haggerty asked, "How much?" Keller said, "Dunno!" Ragland chimed in, "We could take up a collection and buy that damned thing!"

The Calcutta shop looked dirty from the outside to McGregor as he gingerly made his way through the crowded street to the shop. The small Servel refrigerator was in the window on display. McGregor looked through the store window as he entered and began a crafty bargaining session with the Indian shopkeeper for the Servel. McGregor gestured toward the refrigerator, then offered a number of folded bills. The shopkeeper shook his head in an emphatic, negative response. McGregor added bills. The shopkeeper was still unimpressed. McGregor made his final offer – taking the last of the American money from his pocket. The shopkeeper was unrelenting. McGregor turned to leave. The shopkeeper's face broke into a broad, cordial smile as he crossed to the window to secure the refrigerator for McGregor. McGregor realized he had been taken, tossed the bills on the counter angrily.

The railway train compartment on the Calcutta to Kharagpur train was hot. McGregor looked at the British English newspaper on the seat. It was dated June 4, 1944. McGregor sat in the train compartment crowded with Indian commuters whose personal hygiene obviously left something to be desired. He explores their facial expressions as they looked at McGregor with no small amount of skeptical amusement. McGregor was highly uncomfortable.

The Indian railway commuter train pulled into the Kharagpur Station. McGregor alit from the coach, as many Indians moved to and fro and went by him... all eyeing McGregor as they passed. McGregor made his way to the station agent. McGregor said to the agent, "I'd like you to hold something here at the station for me, as he pointed to towards the baggage car where the Servel was being unloaded, "I'll go out to the base and get a jeep." McGregor, pointed at his watch and said "I'll be back in…uh..half an hour." The Indian station agent only stared, obviously unable to speak any English at all. McGregor still pointed to the refrigerator, "You…uh…you hold… hold…here." Still no response. "Look…" he was beginning to talk with his hands. You keep…I come back." "Hold! You hold!" folding his arms if carrying a load. The station agent's face breaks into a delighted grin as he gazed at the Servel, believing McGregor is giving it to him. He bows profusely as he started to move away. McGregor was dismayed. He was grabbing the Indian and restraining his departure. "NO! Not giving it to you, dammit! I want you to hold it here for me!" A graying and cultured Indian gentlemen, having witnessed the interchange, now communicated McGregor's wishes to the Indian railway agent. The cultured Indian spoke in the appropriate Indian language and dialect to the agent. "The Captain wishes you to hold the article here…indicating the Servel…in safe-keeping until he returns for it." The agent was grinning sheepishly as he restated his understanding. The Agent again spoke in the proper dialect, "Tell him I'm sorry, I misunderstood. I shall put the box in my freight room. It'll be safe there until he returns." The cultured Indian turned to McGregor, "He says your box will be stored in his freight room. It'll be safe there." Everyone bowed to each other…two or three times. McGregor departed for the airfield.

As McGregor walked up to the Monsoon Minnie, there was much activity around the Minnie – crews loading bombs, ammo, etc. McGregor asked, "What's going on?"

The crew chief replied to the Captain, "Looks like the first mission, Cap'n. They just told us to get 'em ready!"

In the crew briefing hut at Chakulia Airfield, just before daybreak on June 5, 1944 the atmosphere was tense. A voice in the back of the hut called, "TEN-SHUN!" The crews rose as Harmon mounts the platform turning to the assembled crews of the 40th Bomb Group. Harmon states, "At ease," as he quickly then starts again. "Gentlemen, this it the day we've all waited for!" The crews were hushed and expectant with this news. Harmon continues, dramatically, "Today we're dropping the first bombs from a B-29… the weapon that will eventually bring the Japanese to surrender. Do a good job, and good luck!" Harmon departed and the crews rose to attention, then sat down as the operations officer began the briefing by tearing the cover from the tactical wall map.

The operations officer dramatically said, "Your target…pointing to the place on the map…the Makasen railroad yards at Bangkok, Siam!"

The crew vented their disappointment loud and long. McGregor and Keller were seated together, looking at each other in disbelief. McGregor asked, "What the hell's in Bangkok worth hitting?"

"Damned if I know!" replied Keller.

The operations officer paused to allow the talking to stop. "This is a shakedown mission gentlemen…a high altitude, daylight precision bombardment exercise…ordered by General Arnold himself. You'll fly in the usual four-plane diamond formation…."

Keller was speaking to McGregor as the briefing officer continued, "That will be interesting! Have you ever flown formation in a B-29?"

McGregor said disgustingly, "Once…last month. So far it's been single ship fuel runs over the Hump."

The intelligence officer briefed the crews on the enemy fighter forces and anti aircraft batteries defending the target. This was the first combat mission so the briefing was much more detailed than usual. The intelligence officer then turned serious as he covered what the crews were to do should they get shot down. "Now, if you go down in the area to the north and east of the target proceed up the rivers avoiding the Japanese at all costs. The local natives are generally friendly but may turn you in for the reward. If you're in the Vietnam area, you'll be in better hands. The Viet Minh will help you get back to friendly lines. The crews exited the briefing hut somewhat more quietly than usual, shaking their heads. Keller and McGregor emerged, side by side without saying anything.

Keller turned to follow his crew and then turned back to McGregor momentarily. "You sure that Indian is taking care of that ice box?"

McGregor grinned and said, "Yeah!"

Keller was boastful as he said, 'I've got a quart of Haig & Haig. I've had it ever since I left the States. We'll celebrate tonight with our own ice cubes!"

McGregor continued to his crew carrier, grinning at Keller's remarks. The sun made its first signs of daybreak on January 4, 1944 at Chakulia Field. The Monsoon Minnie turned at the end of the runway. The pilot of the B-29 just ahead of McGregor advanced the four throttles and the big B-29 rolled down the runway and lifted off amidst the dust of a previous takeoff. The Monsoon Minnie taxied into place, ready to taxi onto the runway. There was an earth-shattering explosion. McGregor looked at the co-pilot, "What was that?!"

The co-pilot pointed off to his right. There was a red ball of fire followed by a pall of black smoke rising into the sky. McGregor craned to see, "Someone must have lost an engine on takeoff and went in!" The co-pilot replied "Looks like it! Fourth ship up…bombs and gasoline must have exploded all at the same time." He glanced toward the tower, "There's the green light!"

McGregor nodded and applied throttles and the Monsoon Minnie turned into takeoff position, then McGregor released the brakes and the

Minnie began to roll out.

The co-pilot eyed McGregor apprehensively as he held the mammoth ship on the runway deliberately – waiting to gather as much speed as possible before rotating the ship for liftoff. The co-pilot glanced from the speed indicator to Mac "One twenty…one twenty-five…one thirty"…glancing at the runway's end. The co-pilot said cautiously "Better start to fly!"

McGregor, unperturbed, applied gentle pressure to the yoke. The Minnie, as she lifted off, passed through the pall of smoke from the crash site. McGregor gave the wheels-up signal and then glanced off to his left at the crash site.

The co-pilot asked as he saw the shock on McGregor's face. "What's wrong, Mac?"

McGregor didn't answer for a long while then he responded quietly, "You say it was the fourth ship up?"

The co-pilot said unconcerned, "Yeah."

McGregor sadly told him "That had to be Keller. He was four ahead of us."

The co-pilot closed his eyes to the reality and a tear came to McGregor's eyes.

CHAPTER 64

In the War room at the Pentagon in Washington, D.C., General Arnold and two USAAF Colonels stood gazing at a large ceiling to floor wall map of the Far East. General Hansell entered the room reading a lengthy teletype message in hand. General Hansell started telling the group what was on the report without looking up. "Looks like ninety-eight B-29s got off to Bangkok out of a projected hundred and twelve. Twenty-one of those aborted before reaching the target. Several ships tacked on to the wrong elements... attempts to fly formation were abandoned...most of 'em uh...going in singly."

General Arnold shook his head in dismay, as Hansell continued.

"Looks like seventy-seven ships actually bombed the target. The weather deteriorated so some had to bomb by <u>radar</u> in a seven-tenths cloud cover. They probably bombed everything but the target." Indications are they made repeated passes in their attempts to line up on the target itself...at different altitudes! General Arnold exploded, "DAMN! Any collisions?"

General Hansell looked up and said, "Guess not, Sir."

General Arnold, exasperated, said "Sounds like a Keystone Cops movie!"

General Hansell looked back down and continued, "On the return – thirty ships landed outside the command...the usual engine over-heating problems, faulty fuel transfer systems...and...looks like a lot of 'em simply ran out of fuel."

General Arnold puts his hands on his hips and walked over to Hansell "How many have we lost?"

"Five...so far," General Hansell replied as he went to the map – indicating the related areas as he read them out... "One crash reported up near Kungming…another near Calcutta. They're reporting…uh….three ditched in…in the Bay of Bengal."

General Arnold started to become angry. "What about Jap fighter resistance and is there any estimate on target damage?"

General Hansell responded softly, "Probably minimal. No mention of it here." General Hansell then added, "Uh…:Wolfe claimed he can only get fifty planes up for the mission against Japan itself and that will have to be moved to the early part of July."

General Arnold burst out angrily, "Fifty planes! July! What kind of war is he fighting? Is he even fighting the same enemy?"

General Hansell, afraid of what the next items would bring out of Arnold, cautiously said, "He…claims the Bangkok mission kept him from increasing his stockpile of gasoline up in the forward areas."

One of the General's aides spoke up, "He's got some real problems out there, General." The colonel paused to judge the General's reactions and then added, "Stilwell exercised his Theater Command authority yesterday to divert all the Hump tonnage to his Chinese Army…and to Chennault."

General Hansell looked up and said, "Chiang Kai-shek even ordered the B-29 gasoline stockpile up at Chengtu turned over to Chennault's fighters. General Stilwell balked at that one."

General Arnold dejectedly told the group, "Chiang has absolutely no global outlook at all! His only thought is, 'Aid to China.' That's all he could say when I met with him and his people in January. He simply brushed all other important matters aside, obviously believing POWER could force the impossible." He pointed to Mao's position up north on the map before continuing. "Even if we're able to save him from the Japanese, Mao Tse-tung's revolution up in the north will bring Chiang down eventually."

The colonel said in a plea, "Sir. They've got some real problems with the Japanese out there, General." The Japs are coming down from the Yellow River up here in a major offensive against Stilwell and Chennault. Intel says thirty divisions or more!"

"I've got to have that B-29 mission against Japan June fifteenth," Arnold said. The President simply won't hear any excuses! General Arnold paced for a few moments with his hands behind his back. "Inform General Wolfe I expect a seventy plane mission to be flown against the Imperial Steel Works at Yawta…June fifteen!

General Hansell quickly interjected, "General Arnold, as things stand now, that'd be impossible. Fuel stocks are so low even the transports are having to waiting in the forward areas for gas to return to India." General Arnold paused contemplatively, then said, "Assign the Second and Third Air Transport Squadrons to TWENTIETH Bomber Command. Wolfe is to increase the number of B-29 fuel ferrying flights over the Hump to the absolute maximum…nothing withstanding! Put the 312th Fighter Group on limited fuel ration."

The Colonel said "But, General…they're assigned to the Calcutta area to defend the B-29s there!"

General Arnold looked at him without saying anything, and abruptly left the room. The two Colonels and General Hansell glanced at each other skeptically.

It was June 7, 1944 when the captain ripped a teletype message from one of the banks of teletype machines at the 58th Bomb Wing Headquarters in Kharagpur, India. A colonel stood beside him and read the message as it printed. The colonel was grinning when he said, "I'd better stand a long way from General Wolfe when I hand 'em that."

A few minutes later the colonel knocked on the door then entered, handing General Wolfe the message. The colonel only said, "General Arnold's office."

General Wolfe read the message, then jumped up from his desk, his anger monumental, "What the hell do they think this is our here?!" Those boys in the overstuffed chairs up there must be nuts! Get the staff in here right away!"

CHAPTER 65

First Sergeant Royston drove the jeep slowly over the rain-rutted dirt road leading to a small airstrip near the Village of Barakpur some sixteen miles north of the Calcutta dock area. After a particularly hard bump, Royston muttered something under his breath.

Brigadier General Coltrane was riding in the passenger seat and Coltrane's aide-de-camp in the rear seat. The bump kept the aide airborne more than seated. Coltrane looked over to Yank Royston and said, "I take it you're not impressed with the Indian road infrastructure." Sir, we're a small jeep that can't deal with these monster ruts and bumps made by a loaded deuce and a half truck will break an axle for sure," Royston staid as he held onto the steering wheel as his ass left the seat.

"I'm sure we can get a road crew and rock brought in if we need to work out of here," Coltrane said as he grabbed the seat to keep from being launched out of the vehicle. Suddenly, the jeep came out of the heavy forest and into the wide open area of the Barakpur Airfield. Bart saw several small buildings scattered on either side of the rock and gravel runway. There was one larger building that resembled a hangar. He pointed to it and Royston turned towards it. The road was partially rocked and somewhat smoother. They pulled to the near side of the hangar opening. Inside there was an old German Junkers JU-52/3M with its three engine cowlings off being serviced behind what was an American Douglas DC-2 which was a vintage transport from the mid 1930's. It had been replaced in the U.S. Army Aviation fleet with the larger and more powerful C-47, the military version of the DC-3. He got out of the jeep and looked around and saw another DC-2 and JU-52 parked close by. There was an assortment of other foreign aircraft parked around the airfield. From what Bart could see, most were one step from being abandoned. Some were missing propellers or engines, even wings. "Quite a state of disrepair," Coltrane thought to himself. The aide stopped a passing mechanic and asked where the office was. The Indian mechanic looked at the U.S. Lieutenant with some skepticism, but pointed to a door on the far side of the hanger. The group walked over to the office, carefully noting as much as possible about the facilities and runway. Bart knocked twice on the door jamb of the open door to the office and called out, "Mr. Majumder?"

"Yes," called out a voice from a room off of the office. Then a man in a World War I flight suit came out of the room and into the light. He was a remarkably fit man for his apparent age. His almost snow-white hair and leathery face made him look older than he probably was. "I'm Majumder," he said with authority. "You must be the Yank General the government office called me about," the man said in perfect British-accented English.

Bart extended his hand, "I'm Brigadier General Bart Coltrane, Mr. Majumder. I'd like to talk to you for a few minutes if you can spare the time."

Majumder looked cautiously at Coltrane then asked, "When I was last in London back in 1940, there was a Yank pilot flying for the RAF behind the German lines. As I recall, they called the bloody bloke Black Bart. Any connection, General?"

Coltrane was somewhat taken back and embarrassed by the obvious question. "Sir, this is First Sergeant Yank Royston. He and I flew those missions. I guess you could say I'm Black Bart."

The heretofore dignified Indian pilot became quite animated, "Black Bart! He cried out as he grabbed Coltrane by the shoulders and gave him a bear hug. Then he turned to Royston and shook his hand so hard that Royston thought the hand would be crushed. "Not the grip of an old man," thought Royston.

"Please come with me, gentlemen," said the Indian pilot. He took them into a back office behind his more austere and disheveled office he normally worked out of. The back room was paneled and decorated in the traditional British style. There was a fine cherry wood conference table and chairs in the back center of the room. On the far wall was a full bar complete with mirrors and three dozen bottles of liquor. It could have been any bar near Piccadilly Square. The barstools were padded armchairs with heavy wood legs. They were unique in that each barstool had its own set of aircraft safety belts as ornaments.

"What can I get for you chaps?" asked Majumder. "Surely it isn't too early for you blokes."

Royston and the aide got quiet and looked away for a moment. Bart looked at his watch and said, "Well it's after 1700 hours in Washington, and I'm here on their business. So scotch for me," Then Coltrane looked at the other two, "What's your pleasure?"

A very happy Majumder filled the order and walked to the table with the drinks on a silver serving tray. He motioned for everyone to take a seat. He lifted his glass in toast and said "To the King!" The others raised their glasses and toasted as well.

"Royston here was born in England," Coltrane said. He came over to the states as a kid and later joined the U.S. forces. I can't help but ask your background. You're Indian, but you've a hard British accent and have this British style bar in deepest India. Do you mind explaining to a curious Yank?"

Bloody well, right, old chap," said Majumder. I was born near Bangalore to parents who had a great deal of wealth and were politically popular here and in London. I went to school near London and later was selected to attend Sandhurst. I flew SOPS in the Great War over France. I got shot down but was rescued before the bloody Bosch could get me. I loved England and its culture, but my dying dad told me my fame and fortune was in India. He bloody well was right, you know. I couldn't live in London, so I brought London to India. This is an actual bar that was destroyed by a Zeppelin bomb. I packed it up and sent it here. It's my part of Heaven on Earth. I got back and started the air freight business and was doing well until the bloody Japs went into China. They bloody well made a cock-up of my routes into China. That was a majority of my business. So I'm closing down and moving back to London. I still have my inheritance and property near Bangalore and in Sussex as well. I don't need the grief or the financial loss over time. But that's me. What can I do for you?" Majumder asked as he poured another round.

"Did I hear you say that you were flying those old planes into China?" asked Coltrane.

"Certainly, old chap. I went into the western area every week with one to three flights," he said in a matter of fact tone.

"Didn't the Japs attack you?" Bart asked.

"No they didn't want any political problems with shooting down unarmed Indian cargo planes carrying civilian cargo and not war supplies. Besides, they fly much higher than we do. We can't fly very high with a full load of cargo in these old crates. We fly from here or wherever the cargo is picked up at and fly to Doom-Dooma in far-eastern China near the mountains. We refuel there and snake through the mountains into China. We can go as far as Chengdu, Chaklia or Kungming. If we run short on fuel, we stop at this out of the way point near Zhongdian, ran by a bunch of Chinese traders or some say, bandits. They'll sell fuel to anyone, even the Japs if they've cash. Nowadays, I think that they would just kill the Japs and take their plane and money. They've hurt their trade a lot."

"You spoke about a financial loss if you continued. Is it solely because of the loss of business, or are there other reasons?" asked Coltrane.

Majumder thought for a moment, then sipped his drink before answering. "It's the loss of the China market to be sure, but you add to that the high maintenance and fuel costs of those four birds out there that have a financial foot to my groin. I have one DC-2 and one Junker that will fly. The other two are parts birds for the flying aircraft. I need money for repair parts, fuel, pay crews and the like. With fewer contracts, the funds just are not there to justify staying in business. I would love to have a contract or two with your government hauling cargo, but you have your own support aircraft. So bottom line, as you Yanks put it, we close and sell off the assets," the Indian pilot said as he quickly finished off the scotch in his glass. "Besides I want to retire."

Bart said with a soft tone, "I'm sorry." He waited a moment, then asked, "How much money would it take to turn this around and get all four birds flying? How much do you want to sell the whole operation?" The

Indian knew a loaded question when he heard it. He thought for a moment then replied, "General, those aircraft may be old and junk, but they're worth something. So is the business itself. I wouldn't take less than 280 thousand pounds sterling. As far as putting it all back in the air, I'd say forty-thousand Sterling for parts and another forty to fifty thousand for operating funds."

Coltrane leaned back in his chair and took a big gulp of scotch and motioned with his finger for more. Majumder was more than glad to accommodate the request. "What about the pilots, crews and other personnel; will they stay on for a new owner?"

Majumder could see where Coltrane was going. He would make a great deal. It was truly a deal of a lifetime with the U.S. government funding. "Of course they would stay. Good jobs are hard to find these days with the bloody war going on."

Coltrane looked at him for a moment then turned to Royston and his aide, "Would you give us a couple of minutes alone. Royston, you and the Lieutenant go look at the maintenance operations for me."

Yes, Sir," they said in unison and departed.

Bart looked at the crafty Indian and smiled, "I could see dollar marks in your eyes a few moments ago. You know what I want in general," he said pausing. Let's get down to making a deal. The U.S. government isn't involved. It's sanctioned a private British concern to enter into an agreement with you, however. Majumder was suddenly confused. Had he misread the American? "Here is the proposition," Coltrane said in a measured business tone. You'll be given a non-recourse loan from a British company for one hundred thousand pounds for repairs and operational cost. The lender will pay you 300,000 pounds for an option to buy your entire company and its operations two days after the Japanese surrender for ten pounds Sterling. You will agree to continue management of the company and will retain all profits during the period prior to the British company exercising its option to buy for the ten pounds. The U.S. Army Air Force will enter into a commercial air freight contract with you to carry priority cargo to its bases in India and China. You'll only charge the Army the standard rate that you're currently charging local clients; you'll not disclose to anyone what the cargo is and where it goes. That one item will get your contract cancelled on the spot. When the aircraft takes off with our cargo, there will be two Army Air Force Guards on board who know the route to China. If your pilots try to divert for any reason, the guards will shoot and kill the pilot. I assume the co-pilot will remember the correct course. The Army will make Avgas available to you at commercial rates should you not be able to get it from the civilian source. Needless to say, you'll lose some money buying from the Army, so keep your fuel supplier happy. When you're called for a shipment, you'll immediately do whatever it takes to get that cargo to its destination. Army aviation cargo has absolute priority. That's the deal. Are you interested?" Coltrane said as he picked up his glass and finished the scotch.

The Indian air freight company owner sat there in silence remembering all of the terms and conditions. "Where is the trap or the hooker," he thought. "That's a very nice offer, General. I can't find fault with it."

"You won't, Coltrane said. "It's designed to give you what you want and what the buyers want plus encourage you to stay on and run it until after the war. All you've to do is deliver the cargo and keep the operation and cargo a secret. Do you accept the offer?"

The Indian pilot looked at Coltrane and said, "Care for another scotch…partner?" "Very good, but I'm not a partner only a facilitator," Coltrane replied smiling.

"Let me have your bank information and I'll have the 100,000 pounds wired to your account tomorrow. The option agreement will be ready in two or three days, then you'll get the 300,000 pounds option money. And there's one other condition," Bart said. Majumder stiffened in anticipation of a killer deal term. "You'll agree to fix that damned road coming in here," Bart said almost laughing.

"I'll personally get my shovel and get to work," Majumder said as he poured yet another scotch for the two of them.

CHAPTER 66

It was a beautiful June day in Washington. There was an informal gathering of senior Pentagon personnel in the office of General Arnold. He was honoring General Lemay for his successes in Europe by pinning a Distinguished Flying Cross on an olive drab tunic already festooned with several rows of colorful service ribbons. General Hansell and other USAAF officers were smiling and shaking Lemay's hand with pride and admiration.

General Arnold stepped back in next to Lemay and said, "Congratulations, Curt." The others excused themselves and left Arnold and Lemay alone.

"Thank you," said Lemay.

General Arnold walked towards his clerk, then turned to face Lemay, his hands behind his back. "Curt, I'm going to give it to you short and sweet. Our B-29 program has been a debacle so far. It's dangerously close to collapse. And it isn't just the problems with the airplanes themselves, either. Chiang Kai-shek, Chennault, Stilwell, even Mountbatten, they're all escalating the problems we're having. Added to that is the air logistics problem. Thank God Bart Coltrane was directed by the President to get there and organize an air logistics operation to support the critical parts issue. It could be the bridge from our standard support system to the individual units that we need." Arnold paced, his hands still behind his back and said, "That should help some. But we need more."

General Arnold looked at Lemay and in a serious tone announced, "I've relieved Kenneth Wolfe of the command out there and promoted him, in fact, and brought him back to material command here in the States. That's really his field anyway. We need a professional bombardment man running the Twentieth Strategic Air Force…a man with combat experience. You were highly recommended for the job." Arnold was now leaning back against his desk. "Curt, if we can unleash the full B-29 potential against the Japanese home islands in time, we may be able to avoid an invasion. Even the most conservative estimate places Allied losses in such an invasion at a half million lives…troops…not counting Japanese civilian losses which would be even greater. There are other considerations, too," Arnold said, looking at Lemay with the serious gravity of the situation. "The future of the United States strategic bombardment…it's growth and peacekeeping role in the troubled aftermath of the war…all of that, Curt, will be affected by the success…or failure…of the B-29. You'll be on your own…answering to this office ONLY. Even your target list and priorities will be prepared and authorized by the Joint Chiefs and issued through this office."

Lemay interrupted, "What about missions, General? I'll obviously need to fly quite a few of them."

General Arnold smiled and continued, "I'd anticipated your desires along those lines, Curt," he said, holding up one finger. "We…we're authorizing one….just ONE!"

Lemay argued, "A field commander ought to lead missions – especially those that involve the initiation of previous untried procedures."

General Arnold, in a raised voice said, "ONE, Curt. That's final. Unless there's something else. I have Bart Coltrane waiting outside. He's doing a great job, even better than we hoped. He got that ragtag air freight operation going to get you the parts quickly, but we need much more. That's why he's here and I have to tell him about Zak Middleton. He got shot down and was badly injured."

General Arnold hit the button on his intercom system, "Send in General Coltrane," he said with authority. Seconds passed before the door to General Arnold's office opened and Brigadier General Bart Coltrane marched into the office and formally reported to General Arnold. Arnold returned his salute and extended his hand. "Welcome back to the States, Bart." Take a seat. I wanted to let you know about Zak Middleton," he said, as he saw the sudden expression on Bart's face.

"Zak was on a Black Bart mission over eastern France when two ME-109's caught him in crossfire. He was able to fight them off with one kill and one probable before he went down. An American unit cut him out of his plane. The others were killed. He was badly wounded, but he's alive and doing well in England. He'll probably be out for the rest of the war. They're going to retire him medically with full pay. He should recover enough to fly, but not for the military. He turned down a desk job so SOE decided to pin a medal on his ass and put him out to pasture. You may want to stop by and see him on your way to India or China."

"Wow," said Bart. "Retirement. That's not going to set well with him. He's all action, and sitting on the sideline will kill him."

"Well, perhaps he can land a civilian pilot job in a few months," Arnold said in a positive tone. Both generals got up and saluted General Arnold and left the room.

Lemay looked at Bart and asked, "Hungry? We can grab a bite downstairs in the Flag Officer's Mess before we head out."

"Sure, I've never eaten there," Bart responded. As they entered, the facility was busy and crowded. They looked for a couple of open chairs when a voice said, "General, these two seats are not taken."

Lemay turned to see where the voice came from. It was a middle-aged man in civilian clothes wearing round glasses. They immediately sat down. Lemay was quick to thank the gentleman. "We appreciate your generosity, Sir. I don't think we've had the pleasure. I'm Curtis Lemay and this is Bart Coltrane," he said in a congenial tone as he extended his hand.

"Good to meet you, fellas. I'm Harry Truman," he said in a midwest country accent.

"Senator Truman?" asked Bart.

"That's what they tell me, but I've asked for a recount since I got here," Truman said in a dry tone. "You two are not unfamiliar to me. Lemay, you're bombing the Germans back to the Stone Age, and young Coltrane was flying behind the lines before the war started," Truman said as he looked at each man as he spoke.

Actually, Senator, I'm operating B-29's out of India and China now,"

Lemay corrected.

"Well, there you have it. It just proves what's going on in this damned war that we in the Congress don't always hear about," Truman said in frustration. "How about you two bring me up to speed while we eat."

Lemay saw a chance to get another true believer in strategic bombing, and he took it. Between bites, he and Coltrane gave the Senator a thumbnail history of bombardment in Germany and Japan.

After almost an hour, Truman looked at his watch. "Gentlemen, this has been wonderful. I never knew one-tenth of what you told me. I can see your point about the need for a separate aviation branch. It would be difficult to make such a drastic reorganization during the war, but afterwards would be a good time. When we scale down to a peacetime posture, that would be an excellent time. I'll chat with my cohorts in the Senate about it. I do ask a favor of you two. Each time you come through Washington, stop by my office and keep me updated. It helps to know all the facts when you're in voting on important issues," said the Senator as he stood up and extended his hand. "Best of luck to both of you. I appreciate the job that you're doing," he said, then walked out of the room at a brisk stride.

It was late in the afternoon and, as usual, it was hot as Coltrane, his aide-de-camp and First Sergeant Royston entered the old hospital. The Sergeant behind the desk quickly stood to attention as the American General approached. "Afternoon, Sergeant, could you direct me to Lieutenant Colonel Zak Middleton's room?" Coltrane asked.

"This way, Sir," he responded and marched to the far left wing where Zak was seated in a wheelchair looking out the window seeing nothing, but in a full stare out into the trees. The Sergeant knocked on the open door and reported, "Sir, you have visitors!"

'Very well, who are they?" responded a very dejected man.

In a loud booming voice, Bart said, "The son of a bitch that's going to kick your ass out of that wheelchair!"

At the first sound of Bart's voice, Middleton's attitude and facial expression made a sudden, positive change. "Bart!" he called out as he spun the wheelchair around to see Coltrane and Yank Royston. He tried to get up, but just quite couldn't muster the muscle control to do it.

Sit down, you bum!" Bart cried out. "Save your energy for the nurses."

Zak lowered his head slightly and said in a low tone, "Nurses here look like gorillas and were trained by the Gestapo. Be careful when you leave. They're known to roll soldiers for beer money." "Yank, so good of you to come too," he said reaching out to shake his hand. Your mere presence has shortened my recovery time."

"Good to see you, Sir. You look a lot better than I expected for someone who went through what you did," Yank said.

"So good of you to say so, old boy. I appreciate that. Sometimes I think that I'm all washed up and life is nothing more than checkers in Hyde Park. But the fact is, I'll have a full recovery. It will just take some time. The sawbones told me I could fly again in time. Now that was good news. The bad news is they're promoting me to full Colonel and putting me on the bloody retirement list. I haven't a bloody clue what I'll do with myself after I get well. Ghastly thought, being retired," he said in mock sadness.

"I need to talk to you for a moment in private. Before they go, could you tell us how the buggers got you," Bart asked.

"Actually, it's quite simple. I had my head up my ass. We'd just made the drop to the French Resistance and I started a turn back towards home. I let myself get too high and the bloody ack-ack hit me with a couple of rounds in the aft section. I pushed the nose down to get in the trees when a line of tracers came from the right. I knew it had to be a ME-109. I chopped power and turned directly into him and hit him with a long burst of 50 cal as he flew by. That was all of Mr. Gerry. Then I started taking hits from the high left. Another ME-109! I had problems with my right engine but it held for a while. I saw him coming down from my 10:00 o'clock high position maybe a mile away. I could see he was very fast and heading down to get me on the inbound pass. So I pulled one of your tricks and chopped power again and turned into him in a climb.. As I passed upward, I hit him with a full stream of fire. I obviously hit the bloody bastard, but he got away. I started looking around to see what condition I was in and the aircraft status. Everyone was dead. I had been hit twice, but for some reason, I didn't feel any pain until then. The right engine crapped out and I could feel the plane shake and break up. So I made a crash landing in the cow pasture in front of me. I hit a drainage ditch which took everything behind the cockpit off. The nose section with me in it bounced twice before hitting a hedge row head on. The next thing that I knew I was here. I have been out for three days. The quacks here have done a marvelous job fixing me up. Full recovery is their prognosis," Zak finished with a flare in his voice.

"Unbelievable!" Yank said. "It's beyond a miracle that you made it at all."

"Yes, yes, Royston my good man, but remember, the one confirmed and one probable as well," Zak said and everyone broke out laughing.

"Okay guys, please give me a minute or two with this old war hero," Bart said with emphasis.

"See you, Colonel," Royston said as he left. "Now," Bart said with clear intent. What I'm about to tell you is only known by me, Annabel and our attorneys and accountants, so keep a tight lip on this or some very nice people will get their feelings hurt and my ass in big-time trouble. Can I have your word as to secrecy?"

"You know you do, Bart," Zak said emotion welling up in him. I'm leaving the service at the end of the war. I'm not following Hap and Lemay in their post-war effort to get a separate branch for aviation. What they need from me will be done before I leave. I won't leave them hanging out to dry on this.

"Enough said. Annabel and I are going to start an air freight service out of Heathrow before Christmas. I plan a second hub in Genoa shortly after that. It's in Allied hands and secure now. Third hub will be in Hong Kong with a fourth in Manila. We've contracts for six C-54 and twenty five C-47's. Half are ready or will be ready for pickup 1 December. The war production board has agreed to the civilian release since the U.S. and British governments will obviously be our main client, as long as the war is going. The war here as you can see will be over in a year maybe sooner. "We can expand as fast as the market allows us. Annabel is financing, so we've plenty of available funds. Annabel and I want you to join us when you get out of here."

"Bart, thanks, but I don't need your pity," Zak said sourly.

Bart suddenly moved his face to within eight inches of Zak's and said in a very harsh but quiet voice, "and I don't need a chief pilot and general manager with a bad fucking attitude! The offer is real and I don't want to hear a negative reply. The doctors told me that you would be on your feet and out of here in a month. You'll need another month to fully recover. At that point, you're no longer limited, including flying. I want you to get with Annabel when you're up to it and start putting the pieces together for me. I'll meet with Sharp and Royston tonight and tell them of my plans. They'll be offered jobs as well. Sharp will be your operations manager. Royston will be in charge of maintenance. Accounting and legal is covered by Annabel's people. I'm stealing a cargo sales hot shot named Tommy Adkins and the best cargo manager in the business from BOAC. With the defeat of Germany within sight, I can get early releases from Washington on any combat pilot, mechanic or otherwise that have been over here in combat for over six months. I think we can even get a few Brits to join the venture. Do you get the picture?"

Zak was awestruck. He could only nod.

I'm leaving for India and China tomorrow to find a solution for Lemay involving his aviation support. I'll be gone three maybe four months. When I get back, I expect you and Annabel to have everything ready to go. On 1 December, I want to have a meeting with everyone that you have. I expect to be flying cargo here in the U.K. by Christmas and out of Manila by the first of March or sooner. Now can poor pitiful you get the job done or do I have to find someone else?" Coltrane finished in a slightly softer tone than he started.

Zak looked at Bart for a moment then said, "Go eat fish heads and rice. We'll be ready for you when you get back."

CHAPTER 67

Colonel Nelson stood on the Chakulia parking ramp watching several mechanics work on an engine on a B-29. The scaffolding was pulled up alongside the engine so he could climb up and look inside the engine cowling. Then he went down to get out of the mechanic's way. Just as he got back to the tarmac, Captain Agather and Mark Maidell drove up in a jeep and came up to Colonel Nelson. Colonel Nelson, looked at Agather hopefully, "Well, how'd it go, Victor?"

Captain Agather said, "I talked to the people at Hindustani Aircraft factory in Bangalore. They tell me it will take a year…maybe!"

Colonel Nelson said, "How about the Army engine overhaul plant up in Calcutta?"

Agather shook his head and said, "We looked at it on the way back this morning. We shut it down, Colonel."

"Shut it down!" exclaimed Colonel Nelson.

Captain Agather looked at the Colonel as he regained his composure, then continued, "That's right. Their overhauls were terrible. Those damned engines weren't even holding up ten hours! After looking at the operation up there, I understand why."

"Well…Victor! What are we going to do?" asked Colonel Nelson.

Agather's eyes had fallen on a large pair of metal shears lying on a steel bench at the foot of the nearby scaffolding. He went over to the bench, picked up the shears contemplatively, looked at the cowling flaps then at the shears. Agather climbed up to the cowling flaps, studied his intended procedure momentarily and then neatly trimmed the long cowl flap with the shears, the excess metal falling to the scaffold flooring with a metallic clanging. Agather, in the fashion of one who has completed a daring act, grinned down on Nelson and Maidell. Captain Agather smiled and announced, "Re-manufactured cowl flaps," as he held up the shears triumphantly. "We just need to issue every crew chief a suitable pair of tin shears."

The Colonel smiled broadly as he gave Agather a double thumbs up.

It was a hot and humid day for September in Chengtu when a B-29 pulled in, its engines cut and its props wind milling to a stop. The flight crew disembarked. A jeep pulled up, driven by a USAAF Captain. The captain driving the jeep yelled out to the pilot, "Colonel Blanchard wants to see you, Captain, right away!" The captain piled into the jeep which headed off to the forward base headquarters. Colonel "Butch" Blanchard's forward office area at Chengdu got on September 8, 1944, official communication that shocked all that saw it before it was given to be the pilot.

The B-29 captain hurriedly entered the hut, went to Colonel Blanchard and said "Colonel."

Colonel Blanchard handed the captain an official document and watched the pilot for his reaction. The captain was carefully reading the document, then gave an astonished exclamation, "Lemay!" he cried out.

Colonel Blanchard said in a firm tone, "That's right," Captain Corbett. Washington gave him permission to fly one mission."

Captain Ira Corbett, the B-29 Captain argued, "But Colonel, there's Jap fighters up there in Anshan! We'll be flying over enemy held territory most of the way to Manchuria."

Colonel Blanchard looked at the pilot with concern and said, "That's why he selected this mission. They figured he could get a good look at their fighter tactics and their anti-aircraft defense systems."

Captain Corbett still tried to argue the point, "I've got a four-gun top turret Colonel! No room for an extra passenger." Colonel Blanchard stood up to his full six-foot three-inch height and spoke sternly to the young pilot, "The General understands. And…he's been briefed on all emergency procedures. When you're the formation commander, you always take along an extra pilot anyway. You're not to abort the take-off, Captain…nor the en route flight! You'll bomb the PRIMARY target…and…return General Lemay…safely. "

Captain Corbett said, in resignation, "Thanks, Colonel. I'll be sure the airplane understands all that…Sir. Is that all, Sir?" The angry captain exited and Colonel Blanchard grinned. Captain Corbett and his flight engineer walked brusquely toward their B-29. Drums of gasoline had been rolled up alongside the ship and crews were below and on the wing, busy refueling the B-29. Captain Corbett, still angry said, "I don't like it, Dick… not one damned bit. I've heard about Lemay."

The flight officer replied, "He's made some significant changes up at Bomber Command, Ira. We needed 'em."

Captain Corbett sarcastically argued back, "Tell that to Wolfe's staff. Old Iron Ass has already sent half of 'em packing…and he's only been out here ten days! Calls it reorganization!"

"Look Ira…we've had problems..no secret. Extra cautious measures won't cut it. The man knows what he's doing," argued the engineer.

Captain Corbett continued his ranting and raving, "He's a great pilot…great navigator and obviously a damned good combat commander… I'll give you all that! But I don't want to be physically close to him any longer than necessary. Major Generals can be damned dangerous animals.

The flight engineer became irritated and responded in a hard voice and attitude toward the pilot. "Not if you know your job…and you know your job, Ira. We've got nothing to worry about."

The Captain approached the crew, motioning for them to gather around for a preflight briefing. Five hours later, Corbett's B-29 was in the combat airspace over Manchuria. Lemay was at the navigator's table, comparing charts with visual topography below, the navigator relaxed, enthusiastic as he worked with Lemay who peered through the drift sight occasionally.

A worried Captain Corbett exchanged wary glances with the co-pilot. Lemay turned to the engineer's flight panel. The flight engineer was totally relaxed as he went over the panel with Lemay, pointing to the cylinder head temp gauges as he talked.

The navigator reported over the intercom, "One minute to IP, Captain Corbett." Corbett nodded.

Lemay looked at the navigator and said, "I want you to observe the bomb patterns through the drift sight, Captain."

The navigator responded with a smile, "Yes, Sir."

As the bomb run neared the critical point, the flak bursts grew heavier, bouncing the B-29 violently. Lemay saw a B-29 in the formation, turning away in a gentle evasive turning then back toward Lemay's B-29. Lemay observed the evasive action, frowning, then gazed out and ahead of the formation. Lemay saw tiny dots in the distance ahead of the approach formation. Lemay pointed to the Jap fighters then looked at the co-pilot.

The co-pilot nodded and replied, "They just stay up there General. They fly what appears to be aerobatics and then come in when we leave the target. They've never made more than one pass at us in their attacks. Suddenly a violent explosion rocked the B-29. The co-pilot calmly said, "Flak bursts! Must have exploded under us."

The radioman called out over the intercom, "I'm hit!" The left waist gunner was the next crew to call out a problem from the flak burst.

"Left waist to pilot! "CFC's been hit Cap'n."

Lemay used his mobile radio/intercom mic, "Central fire control… General Lemay…hang on back there…I'll be back there as soon as the Jap fighters have pressed their attack."

The bombardier cried out, "Bombs away!"

Corbett began the post-bomb run turn. A formation of Japanese fighters above and to the left of the B-29 was seen by Corbett. He knew that the fighters' approach would be to slide behind the formation before they turned to press the attack.

Lemay gazed at the Japanese fighters, watching every move they made. Lemay was amazed as he watched the Jap zeros maneuver, "What the hell are they doing? They've turned the wrong way! They'll never catch up!"

Corbett concentrated on his controls and formation position. He looks around to see what Lemay is doing. Only Lemay's parachute was seen where it had been. Captain Corbett said to the flight engineer "Where the hell is the General?"

The flight engineer looked at Corbett and said, "Grabbed a first aid kit and took off!"

An aggravated Captain Corbett shook his head and said, "The son of a bitch didn't take his damned chute!"

The flight engineer responded in an attempt to calm the pilot, "There's an extra one in the back. He'll be alright!"

Captain Corbett almost yelled into the intercom, "Pilot to waist gunner – the General back there?"

Waist gunner replied, "Haven't seen him!"

The navigator said to the pilot that he had checked the radar officer before he went back. "He's still in the tube."

Captain Corbett disgustingly replied, "Damn! If we lose a Plexiglas bubble back there, the depressurization will propel him through that tube like a fucking bullet!"

The flight engineer grinned wryly and said, "It wouldn't dare!"

Captain Corbett grinned too and calmed a bit, "Will he be okay?"

Navigator…uh…piece of flak lodged in his flak vest…that's all."

Lemay emerged from the transfer tube, dropped down by the CFC who held both hands up in pain. The CFC was startled by the General's presence. "I'm alright, General. My hands…they're just numb. Damned flak hit the hand grips…that's all, General, uh, Sir."

Lemay grinned, patted the gunner on the back and moved on toward the aft end of the aircraft.

Captain Corbett frowned as he observed an instrument on the panel before him. "Cabin pressure. It's dropping." They all looked around the cabin. The co-pilot was pointing upward and over the navigator's area, "There they're…flak holes." Captain Corbett called out to the flight engineer, "Set the turbo pressure higher. That oughta keep the cabin pressure up."

Presently, Lemay emerged into the cockpit, noticed the turbo pressure the first thing. Lemay said to Corbett, "Your turbo pressure…it's too high, Captain."

A nervous Captain Corbett told Lemay, "Well, Sir, we ran outta cheese sandwiches!"

Lemay asked, "Sandwiches?"

Captain Corbett pointed meekly to the flak holes "Generally use 'em to stuff up flak holes!"

Lemay was not amused. The co-pilot, having witnessed the interchange, grinned as he turned back to his work, his attention immediately attracted by the B-29 in formation on their right. It was heading toward them for an inevitable collision. The co-pilot yelled out, "Look out!"

"What the hell?" said Lemay, with a hint of anger.

The B-29 recovered, flew straight for a few seconds then turned right in a sweeping turn that carried it rapidly away from Corbett's B-29 – a signal light blinked from a light deck window.

Lemay asked, "Can you read it?"

The co-pilot said shaking his head, "Negative, Sir, something about dysentery."

Lemay just closed his eyes at the utter incredulousness of it all. Then he said, "Get on the radio! Find out what the hell's going on!"

Captain Corbett said quickly, "Can't general. Not allowed to break radio silence until we've crossed the Yellow River. Orders from Bomber Command, Sir"

Lemay could only stare…dumbfounded.

All of the 58th Wing Group commanders were assembled along with the Wing Staff offices awaiting General Lemay. Colonel Nelson, Captain Agather and Mark Maideil were a part of this group. The conference room itself was typical of the forward areas – wall maps, aircraft data posters and technical data. Lemay entered like a bull. "Gentlemen, one of the first things I want you to understand – breaking combat formation is a COURT MARTIAL OFFENSE!"

Lemay continued, "Butch…one of your men broke formation on the Anshan Mission! Damn near creamed us. Medical reports showed the pilot had been weakened by a long siege of dysentery. The co-pilot...the co-pilot mind you…took it on himself to break formation in order to land at a field he figured would be closer in. Jap fighters could've cornered 'em up there alone!

The field could have been overrun with Japs! He risked the lives of his crew and his plane! And what kind of medical officers have we got out here who'll let a sick man fly a mission?" Another thing. "This business of radio silence. Hell! The Japs know where you're. YOU'VE JUST DROPPED BOMBS ON 'EM." I'm not going to press the issue this time, but there'd better be no repeats."

"Understood, General," responded Colonel Blanchard. Lemay looked at Blanchard, "I'm grounding the entire 58th wing temporarily!" I'm going to bring in some specialists on TDY from the Eighth Air Force. We're setting up a training school down at Budhkundi…a ten or fifteen day refresher course on pilotage – synchronous navigation – visual and radar – formation and bombing practice. Every crew over here is going to graduate from Budhkundi Tech or be transferred out! Group commanders will select six lead crews from your outfits. Use the best men you've got to make up those crews. Have 'em report up here to the operation officer. He'll take it from there. But I'll tell you this much – they're going to learn this theater and the targets in it until they can fly to 'em and bomb 'em…with precision results, with their eyes closed! Colonel Irvine..I want all the maintenance people in one pool. If a crew has finished work on their ship…they'll move on and help the next crew. No maintenance crew…repeat…no maintenance crew will be allowed to sit on their butts as long as there's any repair work to be done on a B-29 anywhere in the command. "

"Yes, Sir," said Irvine.

Lemay continued with emphasis "And while you're at it…I want eighty hours a month…up time! Beginning now! I won't be asking any question how you did it…just DO IT! Scrounge…browbeat…politic…even steal if you've to – but give me eighty hours a month operational time on each ship!

Irvine answered, "Right, General. I've developed a plan. I'll be submitting it within the next day or so."

Lemay looked around the room, "Colonel Nelson, how are you coming with the engine modification?"

Colonel Nelson responded, "We're going to be able to handle it… within the command, General."

Lemay continued, "I've advised Washington not to send any more B-29s out here without those modifications already installed. You think you got the heating problem under control?"

Colonel Nelson looked up at the General and said, "Not really. It'll continue to be a problem…but…I think if we teach the crews proper cruise control…then I think we'll probably be able to work around the problem."

Lemay sharply directed a question to Nelson, "What's being done to overcome the problem permanently?"

"Sir, we've developed a fuel injection system in the top dead center. It'll solve the detonation problem once and for all. Same system the Germans developed in the thirties for the 109 and the engines for their Tiger tanks."

"What about economy?" asked Lemay.

Nelson looked at Agather, obviously intending him to answer. "Fuel injection will have a marked improvement on fuel economy, General Lemay, Captain Agather quickly stood up and responded.

Lemay then asked Agather, "When will it be standardized?"

"Sir, all ships after the first of the year should come equipped fuel injection systems."

Lemay then continued, "I noticed a problem we've got while I was out at Grand Island. Bomb bay doors…open with a jack screw system…slows the airplane by fifteen to twenty miles per hour. The Norden's already been set before the bomb bay doors open. That speed deviation throws the bombing aim off. Those doors should operate pneumatically, opening in a couple of seconds or so."

"We'll get on it, General," Captain Agather said and sat down.

Lemay then said to everyone in a big booming voice, "I'm ordering the discontinuance of the double crew system, effectively immediately. There'll be ONE crew for each ship. The system was a waste of trained flight crews! Gentlemen, we're at a point over here where we're either going to do our jobs or be replaced. It's that simple. Nothing personal. From here on there's no such word as impossible out here! Challenge maybe…but not impossible? Erase the word 'impossible' from your memory."

Lemay left the briefing abruptly and was followed by the Chief of

Staff. Lemay and the Chief of Staff went to Lemay's office. Lemay told the Chief of Staff, "I'm going out to Ceylon this morning, and visit the CBI theater Commander there. Keep after things here. I'll be back tomorrow. As they reached the office door and paused there momentarily, the Chief of Staff eyes Lemay's shoes, his tie and all in a tongue in cheek manner. "What are you looking at?" Lemay asks.

The Chief of Staff smiled. "Just making sure your shoes are shined and your tie is straight…that's all, Sir. You're going to be in pretty classy company. Mountbatten's quarters in Maharaja's palace out there in Ceylon, you know. And something else, General, I'll lay you two to one he's going to try to make you use the 29s to support his operations out here!"

Lemay arrived at the Maharaja's Palace in Ceylon, which is the headquarters of British Admiral Mountbatten, Commander of the China Burma India Theater. Admiral Mountbatten, in full uniform, was seated at one end of the huge, ornate dining table, Lemay at the other. The room was covered with oriental rugs, suspended from the ceiling and pulled back and forth by four servants to create a cooling breeze around the dining table. Four costumed Ceylonese servants stood at "the ready," Lemay and Mountbatten were just finishing dessert.

"What are the mechanical difficulties with your Super Fortress? Have your engineer's resolved them?" asked Mountbatten.

Lemay said politely, "The B-29 is a technologically advanced weapon, Sir. It was pressed into service before it was fully ready. A certain amount of debugging was to be expected."

A servant brought a large teak wood box of cigars, opening the lid and proffering the box to Lemay. Lemay took a cigar and bit the end off before the servant can produce the silver shears to be used for that purpose. The servant gazed at Lemay incredulously as Lemay reached for one of the ornate silver candlesticks, tilted it forward and lit his cigar from it.

Mountbatten smiled faintly as the servant offered him the cigar box. Mountbatten took a cigar. The servant produced the shears and Mountbatten neatly trimmed the butt from the cigar itself. The servant then produced a long stemmed device which flamed on the end and lit the Admiral's cigar. Lemay watched the procedure through a cloud of smoke. Mountbatten then said, "General, I'm preparing to take Akyab Island…amphibians landing in the northern and eastern sectors. It's all a part of our drive north, of course. We're not certain just how many Japanese troops are on the island or what they've out there."

Lemay listened as he enjoyed the very good cigar.

Mountbatten continued, "I've had plans drawn up to include pre-invasion, saturation bombing by your B-29s…three days before I land the Allied troops there."

Lemay replied, "That doesn't quite meet my mission out here, Admiral Mountbatten. Anyway, there isn't anybody on Akyab."

"How did you arrive at that conclusion, General?" Mountbatten asked.

Lemay matter of factly stated, "I've been looking for some Jap targets down here to run some practice missions on. My intelligence people showed me that island. There might have been a company there at one time, but nobody's out there now.

Mountbatten said, "I think there are!"

Lemay firmly responded, "I can't use my bombers on an operation like that. I've got to follow out the directives that have been ordered by the Joint Chiefs."

Mountbatten, equally as firm as Lemay, stated, "General Lemay, I don't think you understand. I'm the supreme commander of all Allied efforts in the China-Burma-India theater. The conduct of war out here is my responsibility."

"Yes, I understand all of that, Admiral Mountbatten," says Lemay. "If there were heavy concentrations of troops on the island, I could perhaps fly a practice bombing mission there…but even that would have to fit a strategic high altitude, precision exercise." Lemay rose from the table, as did Mountbatten. They gazed at each other for a long moment, and then Lemay walked over to Mountbatten, offered his hand in a manner that concluded the matter. "I'm sorry, Sir," Lemay says. "Thank you for an excellent dinner…

and a great cigar."

Mountbatten shook Lemay's hand, silently.

"Good day, Sir," Lemay said and left.

Mountbatten gazed perplexedly after him.

Bart Coltrane was starting to sweat in the hot and humid atmosphere at Barakpur, India Airfield. He opened the side cockpit window of the C-47 as he shut down the two engines. After shutting off the master power switch, he got up and went to the rear cargo door. The crew chief had already opened the big door and put the metal steps in place. As he climbed down, he heard the voice of Colin Majumder say, "My God, a General doesn't have his own pilot? Did you get in trouble and have your pilot taken away from you?"

Coltrane started laughing even before he finished getting down. "Yeah, I must have pissed Vinegar Joe off real bad." He shook the Indian pilot's hand warmly. "Great to see you again, Colin. You've been doing a great job, far beyond my expectations."

"Thanks, General. The money is a great incentive." Majumder then pointed his thumb at the Indian pilot standing next to him, "This is Shashi, one of the best pilots that I have ever flown with."

Bart looked the man in the eyes as he shook his hand. "My thanks for keeping this operation going in spite of Colin."

The humor caught Shashi off guard and he fumbled his verbal reply, then he got his wits back and said, "The honor is all mine. Your combat reputation has proceeds you, sir. I'm honored to fly with your operation here at Acacia."

Bart looked back at Colin and asked, "Where are you off to today?"

Shashi and I are going to make a supply run to Kunming with these two new C-47s you got us. What are you doing over here? I thought you were in Washington."

"Actually, General Lemay asked me to look into the downed pilot situation in Indochina. We're not getting our downed aircrews out of Vietnam.

We see them go down with good chutes but they just don't get out. Either the Japs are getting them or the Viet Minh are not following through with the agreement they made with us a couple year's back in exchange for arms."

Majumder looked at Shashi then back to Coltrane. "I could give you my opinion, but I'm too far removed to be of any significant value to you." He looked up into the clear sky then into Coltrane's eyes. "If I know you, you'll want the hard, cold facts. Can you spare three or four days to get the truth?"

Bart quickly replied, "A week if it's necessary to get an accurate understanding of the situation."

Very bloody well then…you fly the other C-47 instead of Shashi to Kunming. From there we'll go and see some friends of mine that are really doing some damage to the Japs in Vietnam," said Colin with conviction. "You can find out for yourself the answers. We'll fly the supplies to Kunming, then we'll fly some supplies to a place just north of Vietnam and you can talk to my friends. They're the best people to tell you the facts."

Coltrane looked puzzled, "Who are you taking me to meet?"

"My friend is Nguyen Sinh Cung. You'll also meet a couple of his friends, Giap and Dong. They'll give you the answers that you seek," replied Majumder.

"What kind of supplies are we delivering to them?" Coltrane asked.

"Mainly rice with some medical supplies and ammunition," he said softly. "They send me whatever money they've and I get them what supplies I can buy for them. I personally pay for the flight time and gas. I respect the job that they're doing against the Japs with almost no money and bloody little outside support. That's all that I'm going to tell you. The rest will become very apparent once you get there."

Coltrane saw a deep respect and admiration in the words Majumder spoke. "Good! Now when do we leave for Kunming?"

"Now! We fly there and offload the stuff for the Army and load up the Viet Minh supplies before sunset. We lift off from Kunming at 0330 hours. That puts us there at dawn before the Jap air patrols start flying. "Think you can keep up with me flying through the mountains?" Colin asked in a joking tone.

"I'll try," Coltrane said as he slapped Majumder on his shoulder. "Let's go. I want to see how you get through the Himalaya Mountains."

The first beams of sunlight were starting to appear in the Eastern sky as the two cargo aircraft started to circle around a dirt road in a Chinese valley.

Bart was following behind Majumder and listening to his narrative about the landing field which was nothing more than a road. "You can see the road is clear of any obstacles and is quite smooth. They keep it well maintained just for our deliveries. It's a remote area of China some twenty miles north of the Vietnam border. They're safe here from Japs and patrols, but they do have two Jap air patrols a day. They're very predictable. One after breakfast and one after lunch. The Japs aren't too aggressive in the area. They're constantly looking for the Viet Minh resistance fighters. The Viet Minh are taking a heavy toll of the Japs near Hanoi and much further south," Majumder paused as he focused his attention to the power and propeller settings as he leveled out at 1,500 feet above the ground below. Then he continued. "We'll land to the north on the road. Set down as soon as you can as you only have 4,700 feet before the hills at the end. That should be more than enough room for a pilot flying a desk," he said poking fun at Coltrane. "When you get to the end, just follow the people on the ground. They'll help you go between those hills into the protected area."

Bart could see what he was talking about. He noticed a canyon area at the north end of the road. It was about 3,000 feet by 2,500 feet in area with jungle surrounding the open area. Coltrane followed Majumder, a mile behind. The landing was smooth. Coltrane seized the opportunity to take a jab at Colin Majumder. "Don't you wish Barakpur was this well maintained?" There was no reply.

As Bart taxied the C-47 to the end of the road, he saw the other C-47 literally disappear into the jungle. A man in black pajamas started to direct Coltrane to a specific part of the road that went between two hills covered in trees and vines. He only had a few feet of clearance one either side of the wing tips. Slowly he moved forward in the direction of the man in black with an old rifle slung over his shoulder. Suddenly, he was in the open area of the valley. He was directed to an area where the jungle reached out over the top of the cargo plane. It would be almost impossible to be seen from the air. He shut down the two engines and went to the rear. His crew chief, a young Indian lad of no more than twenty years, already had the aluminum steps in place so Bart could get down.

There were at least thirty armed Viet Minh surrounding the aircraft when he got down. He stretched the stiffness out of his body while he waited for Colin to come to his rescue. Bart could see that most of the attention was on what was in the aircraft and not on him. That was a relief.

Colin gently worked his way through the crowd along with three other men who were older and obviously in charge.

Colin stood between Coltrane and the three gentlemen and started the introductions. "Brigadier General Bart Coltrane, may I introduce my good friends, Nguyen Sinh Cung, Vo Nguyen Giap and Pham Van Dong of the League for the Independence of Vietnam, which is also known as the Viet Minh."

Coltrane stood at attention and with a very slight polite bow, extended his hand and said, "It's my honor to meet such distinguished warriors for freedom. Your efforts against the Japanese are commendable."

The three men did not immediately react or reply to Coltrane's comments. Then the short, younger man asked, "General, why are you here?"

Stunned by the direct question, Coltrane knew he was speaking to a front line soldier who had no time for platitudes. "I'm here to find out what has happened to our downed flight crews," Coltrane stated bluntly.

The older man with the graying mustache and goatee responded, "Some are here awaiting transport out. We've no way to transport them to friendly Chinese bases. We had an arrangement with the OSS to send them back on supply planes. There hasn't been a supply plane from the Americans in almost a year. The last plane had two thousand rounds of ammunition to go with the old pre-World War I surplus rifles. Junk at best! No food, medicine, radios, and enough modern rifles and machine guns to fight the enemy. Can you explain why the delay and why we're given these old obsolete guns and a handful of ammunition?"

Coltrane looked the leader in the eye and replied, "I'm at a loss for an explanation, Sir. I'm not aware of the details of your arrangement with the OSS. I do not represent them. I represent the United States Army Air Force and General Curtis Lemay, Commander of the XX Air Force. It's obvious that your efforts and needs have not been made known to the Army Air Force and General Lemay. Perhaps, this would be a good time for you to tell me exactly what your objectives and critical needs are. I'll do what I can to resolve the impasse and get what you need."

Nguyen Sinh Cung smiled and said, "It's said that a picture is worth a thousand words. Walk with me and see for yourself, General." The man started for the tree line followed by the others. As he walked, he motioned to the men standing around whom immediately went to the two aircraft to unload them.

Coltrane looked at the leader and the other two and asked, "What association do you've with the resistance leader known as Ho Chi Minh?"

Nguyen Sinh Cung, the man with the goatee, smiled and said, "I'm Ho Chi Minh. I took the name for protection while I was exiled to France. I'm the one your OSS called Agent 19."

Coltrane saw something in the man's eyes that spoke of integrity and intelligence. He had come to the right man to get a clear picture of the war in Indochina.

"General, we're a people that have endured countless attempts by outsiders to conquer this land. The latest invader is the Japanese. They too will be repelled as all others have been."

It may take time and blood, but in the end we shall endure until victory is achieved. Your western world, Europe and the Japanese think in months and years. We don't think in these terms. We look at the long term no matter how long it takes. This is our home and we're prepared to fight to the death, no matter how long it takes. This is a large country with a diversity of climate and terrain. It's home to us. For you, it's a mountainous jungle with endless rice paddies and oppressive heat. Vietnam is a very difficult area to fight in for outsiders. We employ a completely different form of combat. We use the land and millions of people to our advantage. We choose to use the unconventional form of warfare. The peaceful rice farmer you see tending his rice fields by day is a warrior by night that ambushes your patrols and bombs your bases. The aggressor doesn't know who the enemy is and can't arbitrarily kill everyone they see. Your own morals and world opinion would never allow such slaughter. We've tens of thousands watching the enemy's every move and report it to us within a few hours or less. We've agents working for the Japanese in all of their offices and facilities so we know everything that they're planning. Our intelligence gathering capability is very extensive. So you're in a quandary as to how to fight us." He looked at the very interested Coltrane. "Please don't be offended by my use of the term 'you'. It's meant to reflect all outsiders, not you or your country individually."

Coltrane nodded and continued to walk by this astute leader known as Ho Chi Minh. Ho could see that he had Coltrane's interest and attention. He would not lose this opportunity to educate this American general.

"This area inside the protective hills is our training and supply base. We call it Happy Valley," Ho continued. "We're outside the normal Japanese areas of military influence and domination. We see air patrols a couple of times a day. Our primitive communication system alerts us when they take off from Hanoi and what direction they're headed. We're able to hide until they're gone. The valley is perfect for us. It's only twenty miles to the border. We can be safe from the Japanese here. The surrounding mountains cannot be scaled by a significant military force. We've automatic weapons on top to fight off any attempts. We've a nice stream going through Happy Valley for water and fish.

"It's an excellent headquarters for planning and training. We train over a thousand Viet Minh every month. They're then deployed to various parts of the country to establish individual cells of four to eight men. Each cell is trained by those who are trained here on political philosophy, community development and guerrilla warfare. The military planning and execution is directed by Vo Nguyen Giap here," he said pointing to the short man walking next to Majumder. "On any given day or night he execute anywhere from four to ten attacks on the Japanese or French."

Coltrane reacted to the mention of the French. "But the French are on our side."

"They're ruthless colonists. They take and take and give back nothing," said Dong.

"So true," Ho said. "The French are only a friend until we eliminate the Japs then they'll resume their conquest for all of our resources. The French cannot be trusted."

They had walked well into the trees. They had come upon what appeared to be a dispensary or makeshift hospital. There were twenty or thirty men lying on mats with serious wounds. Medical personnel were applying crude medical treatments to the suffering soldiers. Coltrane was horrified.

Ho pointed to the men and their individual maladies. "This man has gangrene and we've no medicine to treat him with. We'll give him a natural painkiller to make him comfortable until he dies. This man needs surgery to be saved. We've so little for our people. The medicine that you and this black market thief brought in today will be of enormous help, but it will only go so far. We need more." Ho had affectionately put his arm around Majumder's neck. "If it wasn't for this wartime profiteer, we would be in real trouble. He takes the very few dollars that we can get and supplies us with what he can. Our hearts and loyalty to Colin is without limit. He's our only outside help. Your promised support has been almost non-existent," Ho said in despair. They walked over to a group of soldiers squatting around a small fire cooking rice

Ho reached down and picked up one of the weapons and handed it to Coltrane. "Do you recognize this weapon?"

Coltrane took the weapon and looked at it then answered, "Yes, it's a British Enfield musket from 1857." Then he pointed to a small stack of British Enfield rifles that predate World War I. "I recognize that old Enfield No. 4 rifle as well. Don't tell me this is what you're fighting the Japs with."

"Unfortunately, these are our main weapons. Most of them were supplied by your OSS. We also have twenty or so Lewis machine guns from World War I as well. We take the more modern weapons from the Japanese we kill, but that's not enough. We need a large volume of modern weapons and lots of ammunition if we're to be effective against our mutual enemy," Ho said as he watched Coltrane's facial reaction. He saw the expression of a man shocked and dismayed at the revelation.

Bart looked at the military mastermind of the Viet Minh, Vo Nguyen Giap and asked, "How do you fight the Japs with these antiques?"

The genial man smiled and said, "We seldom rely on the guns. We watch the enemy and learn his weakness, then attack swiftly and disappear. The habits and standing procedures of an organized army is always its worst enemy. They're predictable in everything they do. That gives our guerrilla force an advantage and we exploit it to the fullest. The Japanese have a ridged chain of command and attack procedures that makes them vulnerable to our type of hit and run attacks."

Coltrane shook his head in amazement, "How many units do you've in the field attacking the Japs?"

Giap looked at Bart and said proudly, "We've over five thousand operational cells from here to the southern tip of Vietnam. We hope to have three times that number in the field by the end of 1945. Our nationwide recruiting is going very well. In addition to the trained strike cells we've over 380,000 trained troops ready to fight. All we need are guns, ammunition and explosives."

Coltrane looked at him and nodded in acknowledgement. Then he turned to Ho Chi Minh, "Sir, you said that there were some downed airmen here. Could I take them back with me?"

"Yes, you brought supplies and you've learned firsthand what we're doing for the war effort. Now you know what we need to defeat the Japanese. Can I assume that you'll make your superiors aware of our situation and efforts?"

"Yes, Sir, you can count on my reporting this through my chain of command to the President. You can also count on additional supplies from the U.S. Army Air Force operating out of India and China," Coltrane said with confidence.

Ho pointed to another area of the jungle. As he got closer they could see U.S. Army aircrews huddled together and laying on mats. They came to attention as Ho approached. Then a Lieutenant Colonel saw Coltrane and saluted. "Sir, Colonel Danforth reports to the General."

"At ease, gentlemen," Coltrane replied. "Can I give you men a lift back home?"

There was a chorus of cheers from the group.

"How have you been treated?" asked Coltrane.

"Sir, it's been very rough, but we've been treated as well as can be expected. They just don't have anything. They can't take care of their own people, much less our guys."

Coltrane turned to Ho and Majumder and asked, "Can we take those eight really bad soldiers back to Kunming for medical treatment? I think our medical staff there can save them and get them back to you ready to carry on the fight for your homeland."

There was no immediate answer from Ho. He stared into Coltrane's eyes for a few seconds. Then he reached out and grabbed Bart by his shoulders and said, "We've a new friend and ally."

Bart turned to the Army Lieutenant Colonel and instructed him to put his sick and wounded on board the aircraft then put the Viet Minh casualties on board as well.

"Sir, this has been a real eye opener. I'm sure that the President and General Lemay will ensure that additional supplies of food, ammunition, medicine and other useful equipment will be forthcoming," Coltrane said with authority. Ho looked at Coltrane and extended his hand and said, "Thank you, General, I shall count on your support. Have a safe flight back."

Just after the two C-47 took off, Coltrane looked at the very rough terrain and made a radio call to Majumder. "You know Colin, I'd hate to be in a war against those three. I don't think that we could win a war in these conditions against them."

Majumder replied, "Strange, Giap said that he would hate to be in a war against you and others like you."

There was silence as they flew to Kunming.

CHAPTER 68

Late in September 1944, Lemay was visiting Chengtu. Lemay, Blanchard, an aide and Captain Agather were inspecting the bomb bay doors on a B-29 as they sprung open, obviously activated by a pneumatically controlled device. Just as the doors closed and reopened the second time, a jeep pulled up, driven by a USAAF colonel.

The colonel said to Lemay, "General Stilwell's on his way down here, General Lemay.

Lemay nodded, as he asked, "How's the fuel coming along?"

The Colonel replied, "Two Squadrons from the 40th left, General. Should have it wrapped up in an hour."

Lemay turned back to the bomb bay action, addressing Agather. "Good work, Captain," Lemay began to cross to the front of the B-29, the others following Agather alongside.

Lemay continued to talk to Agather, "You people need to step up to the cruise control training. A crew burning seventy-six hundred gallons over the Hump can sure as hell learn something from a crew that's making the same trip on sixty-one hundred gallons."

Agather said, "We'll keep on it, General."

Stilwell's staff car arrived on the scene. General Stilwell got out and walked over to Lemay. He wore his World War I flat-brimmed campaign hat.

Lemay smiled and shook Stilwell's hand. "General Stilwell, Colonel Blanchard, Captain Wells. Stilwell shook hands all around.

General Stilwell started the conversation. "They told me you'd been out at headquarters, General. Sorry I missed you."

Lemay said, "Just a courtesy call, General. "I stopped by on the way back from Ceylon."

General Stilwell responded by saying, "Well I heard you were up here in the Chengtu Valley. Thought I'd stop by."

Lemay looked at Stilwell and smiled, "I'll have the mission off in about an hour, General. Why don't we have dinner?"

General Stilwell grinned, "Well Chennault thinks your B-29 boys are freighting in some pretty exotic food supplies over the Hump, Lemay. Dinner might be a pleasant surprise."

"Lemay turned to the aide and said, "See if they can put something together in the way of dinner up at the Officers Club, Captain."

Captain Wells replied to Lemay, "Sir, I can tell you, General, there's nothing here in the entire Chengtu Valley but "C" rations!"

Lemay said "Well then, suppose you could scrounge up a bottle of booze?"

Captain Wells smiled, "I'll try."

Lemay shook his head. "Meanwhile, General, how about a look at our B-29s. They're fueling up for a mission up north. Be leaving in a couple of hours." As they walked along the flight line, the crew assembled in front of the B-29, all observing the Generals.

A Sergeant grinned in admiration for the two Generals whose reputation has garnered their pseudonym, "Vinegar Joe and Iron Ass!"

Lemay and Stilwell sat alone at a corner table in the crude tent which was jokingly referred to as the "Officers Club." Lemay lit his pipe, smiled and said "Sir..The word is my boys are living pretty high on the hog here in the forward area."

General Stilwell said stiffly, "Chennault and I don't agree on many things, Lemay. But…one thing we do agree on, the B-29s ought to start paying their way out here immediately or they should be removed from China altogether."

Lemay cautiously responded, "We've a potentially potent weapon in the B-29, General, once we get all the bugs out of the operation. It seems to me that the potential justifies some extraordinary measures and consideration."

General Stilwell, in a stronger tone, said, "Look, Lemay, the tonnage we were able to fly in over the Hump was already strained to the maximum before these damned forward staging bases for your B-29s were built up here in the Chengtu Valley. I had to take engineering battalions from the Ledo Road construction to build them. The Ledo Road might have helped increase our flow of supplies, one of the most critical problems we've got out here. That and the Generalissimo."

"Chiang?" Lemay asked.

General Stilwell stated, "Crooked as a dog's hind leg! That's why we've never allowed Land-Lease materials coming into the theater to fall into his hands. Management of those resources is just another headache placed on my Command because of the 'Generalissimo.' Getting along with that son-of-a-bitch is a pretty heavy load for an old country boy! And…Roosevelt seems to think I ought to love the corrupt bastard!"

Lemay grinned as he said, "Well, I believe we've the potential to end the war with the strategic bombardment of the Japanese home islands once we've mastered our B-29 weapons systems. And I think we're making significant progress there."

General Stilwell shook his head, "Sounds like the propaganda Spaatz and Eaker generated over in Europe. I seem to remember they were going to bring Germany to her knees without an invasion."

"Could have done it too, given a few more months," Lemay said. "You see, General, we had finally reached a strength proportionate to the magnitude of the task. That's been the perennial problem confronting the strategic air arm in this country."

General Stilwell stiffly asked, "Then…why didn't they bring Germany down?"

"Eisenhower pulled us off the strategic mission at its most critical time!" Lemay responded, as he leaned forward a bit, his body English emphasized his point. "General Stilwell, I feel that the destruction of Japan's ability to wage war lays within the B-29 command…not operating out of these forward areas, however. I don't believe General Arnold himself ever thought this would work. But I believe we can reach a strength commensurate with the magnitude of the task…and…I believe the B-29 will ultimately be the potent weapon with which Japan will be defeated."

General Stilwell leaned back in his chair. "Lemay, I've heard all that bullshit before, to the point that it becomes wearing. I never believed Billy Mitchell was anything but a publicity seeking mystic and his strategic doctrine a bunch of horse manure. Not much has happened in this war to change my frame of mind. Certainly not the B-29! Japan is a formidable enemy…fanatic in its religious tendencies and ruthless in warfare. Japan will never capitulate, not until the last rice paddy has filled with the blood of her last soldiers. It'll take an army to do that…and a damned big one."

Lemay pondered Stilwell, realizing it's futile to argue the matter any further.

CHAPTER 69

A formation of B-29s was flying near Singapore en route to their target. McGregor was flying the Monsoon Millie when the ship bounced occasionally from flak shock waves. McGregor said to the co-pilot, "Intelligence officer was right. The flak was going to be heavy!"

The bombardier followed the target approach through his bombsight. The bombardier suddenly called out, "Something's wrong. We're way off target!"

The radio operator almost simultaneously called McGregor, "It's the lead ship, Captain. It's a bad run. They're going out in a one-eighty. Going to make a different approach."

The left waist gunner on the intercom called out, "Waist gunner to Pilot…I can see Jap fighters taking off down there, Captain. Lots of them."

McGregor said to no one in particular, "Figures. Guess they'll be arriving about the time we finish the bomb run." McGregor looked over on several Jap fighters, and lined up to engage them. The lead Japanese fighter pilot was obviously climbing as fast as he could to reach his prey.

Meanwhile, the formation flew past the target and made a slow 280 degree teardrop turn back on a course to the target. The bombardier flipped the toggle switch that opened the bomb bay doors. He was ready this time, he hoped!

The opening of the bomb bay doors added to the nervousness of the crew. It was different this time for some reason. McGregor struggled to maintain control of the aircraft, which was violently tossed by the increased flak shock waves and the strong high altitude winds. McGregor was closely watching the lead element release its bombs.

McGregor said to the co-pilot, "There they go." The bombs systematically dropped out of the bomb bay. McGregor watched the lead element intently. As McGregor was watching the lead element, the flak shock waves were still bouncing the aircraft. To no one in particular, McGregor said "Take the turn! Let's get the hell outta here!"

The bombardier called out, "Bomb bays closed." McGregor began the turn.

The co-pilot looked up at a Japanese fighter that was in a turning dive toward McGregor's B-29. He became more nervous than usual. The Jap had a good position on their B-29. It could be shot down in the next few seconds.

The right waist gunner said to the pilot, "We got a Zeke! Eleven o'clock!"

McGregor glanced off to his left, still busy with the control yoke. The Japanese aircraft streaked toward them, belly up and diving, but it seemed to miss the B-29 by only a few hundred feet. The lower turret of McGregor's B-29 fired on the enemy. A trail of bullet holes suddenly appeared across the right wing, striking the outboard engine and went across the wing and up the main fuselage just behind McGregor. The bullets tore big holes in the fuselage. The pressurized air in the cabin condensed from sudden depressurization, causing instant fog in the cockpit.

McGregor ordered, "Get those oxygen masks on everybody!" Pilot to crew…we've been hit up here! Report all damage!"

The navigator was shaken and clutched his thigh area. "I'm hit!"

The radio operator had blood on the right side of his face. "The bastard hit me too."

McGregor calmly said, "Hang in there, we'll take care of you as soon as these damned fighters clear out!" McGregor could hear the incessant gun fire from a turret a above and behind him. McGregor ordered, "Get off that gun trigger! Fire in bursts!"

The left waist gunner's voice was heard over the intercom, "Left waist gunner to pilot – Captain, Horneyia had that turret!"

McGregor remarked, "Well, tell him to quit firing steady – shorten the bursts!"

The left waist gunner cried out, shocked, "I…I can't Captain. He's gone!" The side blister was blown, the seat belt straps of the absent gunner trailed through the blister, flailing wildly in the slipstream.

McGregor said over the intercom, "What do you mean?"

The left waist gunner responded, "His blister blew. He must've taken the gun sight with him. He had control of the turret".

McGregor ordered, "Hit his switch – take control of that turret!" The gunner did and the firing ceased.

Tail gunner to Pilot…"I see him! Chute's open!" The tail gunner was leaning forward slightly as they looked down at the parachute. "They're making a pass at him! The damned Japs are shooting at the parachute!" McGregor's facial features reflected the tragedy of the right waist gunner's plight.

The flight engineer was tense as he gazed at the engineer's flight panel. "Captain…we're losing oil pressure on number four! Must've hit the oil tank behind the engine."

McGregor said to the co-pilot, "Weinberg and the RO…they going to make it?" The co-pilot nodded, moving back to the wounded men.

McGregor looked around, then upward. He saw a large hole in the top of the bird cage directly above his seat. Then he sees a large dent in the amour plate only scant inches above McGregor's head. McGregor said to nobody in particular, "Twenty millimeter must've exploded right above my head!"

The engineer reported, "There goes the oil pressure on number four!"

"Feather it!" McGregor ordered. The engineer activated the prop pitch controls to actuate feathering of the propeller but nothing happened. He said, "No dice! I'm shutting her down!"

McGregor looked out to his left. The engine was trailing smoke. He looked at the engine as the prop began running away…He could hear its inertial scream rising above the other noise. McGregor tensed as the engineer continued working with the prop controls. McGregor announced, "The prop's running away!" He watched the propeller tachometer as the needle pegs. McGregor hit the alarm button registering a first alarm, "Pilot to crew. Prepare to abandon the aircraft. We've got a runaway prop on number four!

McGregor then turned to the flight Engineer and said, "Be prepared to hit the fire extinguisher!"

The crew members, mid-ship, hurriedly adjusted their chutes as they took emergency stations. They awaited the dreaded command to abandon ship. They had just seen what the Japs did to parachutes.

McGregor grimaced as the prop's shrill scream increased. McGregor said to the co-pilot, indicating Weinberg and the RO, "See that they get their chutes on!" While looking out at the engine, he noticed it was already red hot around the hub! McGregor made a radio call to the flight leader, "Red Dog Leader, this is Red Dog Eight. We've got a runaway prop here. We're dropping out of formation…preparing to abandon the aircraft."

"Roger, Red Dog Eight. We're marking your position. Good luck," replied Red Dog Leader.

Suddenly the prop, now a piercing scream, began to vibrate the ship excessively. McGregor struggled to maintain control. The red hot runaway prop suddenly tilted slightly then separated from the smoking engine, whirring up and above, spinning over the wing. "There she goes!" McGregor said to the engineer. "Hit the extinguishers!"

The engineer activated the fire extinguisher on number four.

McGregor gazed at the engine for a few moments and then went on the intercom, "Pilot to crew. We've lost the prop on number four. Then he paused, gazing apprehensively at the afflicted engine. "We may be alright…if we don't get a fire."

The co-pilot said to McGregor as he gestured to the RO and the navigator, "They're alright, Mac. Need attention as soon as possible." Weinberg was wincing from the pain in his hip, "Captain, there's a small landing strip just inland. Chart shows it's held by the British."

McGregor looked over to the co-pilot, "What do you think?" The co-pilot replied, "Might be our best bet."

McGregor called out on the intercom, "Pilot to crew. We're going to try to make it to a field just inside Burma. We're probably going to be alright but stay on your toes."

The British airfield just inside Burma had a sign in front of the tent that read: 865th RAF - Fighter Wing – Headquarters. A Sergeant hurried into the tent. The wing commander was startled as the Sergeant entered and saluted.

The Sergeant said in an excited voice, "Just got a radio blip, Colonel. We have a crippled B-29 on the way in, Sir."

The Colonel reached for his cap, "Damn! They can't land here. They'll have every Jap in the countryside in for afternoon tea."

The Sergeant and the Colonel exited the tent hurriedly. The English Colonel's vehicle pulled up to the Monsoon Millie, and the Colonel got out, just as McGregor dropped to the ground from the nose hatch. The colonel said to McGregor, "I say old fellow, you simply can't land here you know." The Nips have fighter bases less than eighty kilometers north…and troops just ten kilometers up the range there."

McGregor was angered with the RAF Colonel's bluntness. "I have landed here, Colonel. And I've got wounded on board. They need medical attention."

The Colonel walked to a position slightly in front of the aircraft, suddenly seeing the blackened engineer nacelle for the first time. The Colonel, turning back to McGregor. "I say! You do have a problem don't you?" The Colonel went to his vehicle, reaching for the radio. "Base headquarters, Colonel Simpson here. Send an emergency vehicle out right away. Better send a medic along."

At the 40th Heavy Bombardment Group Headquarters in Chakulia, India, a captain entered Colonel Jake Harmon's office, grinning broadly. He handed Harmon a teletype. Harmon also began to grin. Harmon was laughing now, 'So the good RAF Colonel wasn't too happy, eh?" handing the message sheet back to the Captain. "Guess we'd better get an engine out there right away.

"Yes, Sir," the Captain said smiling.

At the RAF Fighter Base in Burma a few days later, on the number four engine of McGregor's B-29, the maintenance crew was snapping the cowling back in place.

McGregor's crew chief entered the RAF Colonel's office and walked over to McGregor, who stood talking with the RAF Colonel. The crew chief said, "She's all ready, Captain."

McGregor turned to leave. "I'll ride out with you."

The RAF Colonel said in typical British subtlety, "Sorry we couldn't be more hospitable, Captain. We do have a war to fight here, you know." The RAF colonel continued, "I'd appreciate you're passing the word to your commandant…no more landings here. It does put us in a pretty pickle you know!"

McGregor saluted half derisively, and then he left. The Colonel gazed after him momentarily, then sat back at his desk and resumed his work.

McGregor ran the engines to full power for takeoff. "Hang on, we're going to thank the British as we leave. He releases the brakes and the B-29 gained speed quickly. As he became airborne, he let the aircraft draft over the tent area. The B-29 passed over the tents in a thunderous, cyclonic roar, and the tremendous prop wash leveled the tents in a domino-like effect as the B-29 swept over them. The RAF colonel made his way out of his demolished headquarters, gazing after the departing B-29. The RAF Colonel, bewildered and simply said, "I say!"

A cold north wind was blowing an early snow shower through the streets of Washington when General Arnold and Colonel Wild Bill Donovan entered the Oval Office.

"Good morning, gentlemen," the President said in an unusually joyful voice. Please take your seats. Can I offer you some hot coffee on this cold morning?"

"That would be nice, sir," Arnold replied. He then looked at the President's steward and said, "Black, please," Colonel Donovan nodded in the order.

"What news do you have for me today?" the President asked as he turned away from watching the snow fall to look at the two visitors.

General Arnold started the conversation by holding up a six page report then packing it on the desk. "Sir, Curt Lemay sent Bart Coltrane to Southern China to find out why we were not getting many of our downed pilots out of Indochina. As you know, Colonel Donovan's representative made an agreement in the last days of 1941 with the leaders of the Vietnam Resistance Movement called the Viet Minh to destabilize the Japanese and get our downed pilots out. The project officer was working under very difficult limitations but did get some supplies to the Viet Minh. Not nearly enough or timely but what he could. One of his difficulties was a way of delivering the supplies to the very remote area that the Viet Minh were based. The availability of modern weapons was initially a factor in 1941 and early 1942. As time went on, the weapons became available, but he couldn't get them flown in on a timely basis. This lack of perceived American support resulted in what we thought was a change in attitude on the part of the Viet Minh. But it was not in reality. The Viet Minh have been very effective against the Japs despite the acute lack of modern weapons and supplies."

Colonel Donovan then added, "The project officer is one of my best men and has done well given the limitations. We need to get the supply chain fully operational and support the Viet Minh. That may now be possible, thanks to Coltrane."

Arnold resumed his observations. "Coltrane flew a couple of those old freight aircraft full of rice, supplies and arms into the Viet Minh a couple of weeks ago. He was taken there and introduced to the leaders by Colin Majumder who runs the Acacia Air Freight Company. Unknown to us, he's been privately supporting the Viet Minh as best as he could. They would send him meager funds and Majumder would buy what he could and fly the supplies to a secret training base just outside Vietnam in China.

"Neither Colonel Donovan nor I were aware of this link to the Viet Minh. This could be a real breakthrough in many ways. Coltrane has made friends with Ho Chi Minh, General Giap and Phan Van Dong, and 'the Big Three'. He got over twenty aircrews out as well. Bart has written this very detailed report to General Lemay who has forwarded to us.

"His report boils down to the following points:

"1. There should be a weekly flight from Kunming to the Viet

Minh, supplying them with mostly rice and medical supplies, along with arms, ammo and medicine, and bringing back downed air crews.

"He indicates that the Japanese have taken most of the rice and other food items resulting in a local food shortage in the Hanoi area. It's becoming a serious problem. They need medical supplies to handle the sick and wounded.

"2. Modern weapons are badly needed to augment the existing British Enfield rifles and muskets."

"Muskets," the President said loudly.

"Yes, Sir, that was all that was available back in early 1942 when we started supplying them," Donovan replied.

"Go on, Hap," the President said with irritation.

"They need 100,000 rifles and automatic weapons. Coltrane suggests that be the limit at this time. According to him, that would be enough to employ against the Japs but not enough to be a factor to the British or French after the war. He's concerned about the Viet Minh's long-term objectives. The Japs have found out the hard way how difficult it's to fight in that hostile terrain and climate, a guerilla type action. He thinks the British and French would not be able to win if challenged by the Viet Minh. Coltrane thinks the Communist long term objectives could be adverse to our interests. Therefore, we need to be supportive so we can get our downed aircrews out, but not arm a possible future enemy force.

"3. It's imperative that Colonel Donovan get Major Patti in to work face to face with Ho Chi Minh and his leadership. Coltrane will be glad to take him in and arrange the meeting.

"What are your instructions, Mr. President?" General Arnold asked in conclusion.

"Bart sure does get around, doesn't he? I trust his judgment in matters like this," the President said, then continued. "I assume that you two both concur."

"Yes, Sir," the two visitors said in unison.

"Very well, the President said, "Make it happen."

CHAPTER 70

"Damn, it's cold," Bart thought as he got out of the taxi that he and Annabel flagged down in front of the Ritz Hotel for the short ride to the Connaught Hotel in the Mayfair district of London. He helped Annabel out and then walked quickly inside. The hotel general manager was there to greet them and escort the couple to the ballroom where the annual St. Dwynwen's Day gala was to be held. Traditionally, Annabel and her family hosted the charity event to raise money for disabled veterans from World War I. Princess Elizabeth and her boyfriend, Navy Lieutenant Phillip Mountbatten were already there, checking out every detail of the services for their friend and event chairwoman Annabel Beddows Coltrane. The four greeted each other and headed to form the official receiving line. They only had a few minutes before the master of ceremony, the Earl of Gloucestor, formally directed the two Beefeater Guards to open the doors. The official guests represented the social elite of Great Britain and various officials from ambassadors to captains of industry. This year, the Prime Minister was not leading the dignitaries, due to a virus. Churchill was an institution at this charity gala, so his absence was deeply missed.

The line moved quickly as usual until the arrival of Field Martial Montgomery and General Eisenhower. There was spontaneous applause as they arrived and joined the line of dignitaries. Montgomery led the military delegation. When he was formally introduced to the chairperson, he made the perfunctory greetings. He turned slightly to the left and gestured to the other military officers and said, "Duchess, I hope that you don't mind my bringing these other chaps that seem to be passing through London en route to Berlin." There was immediate laughter and polite applause.

"The honor is all mine and welcome, gentlemen," she said with the grace and dignity of a queen.

Montgomery then said, "Annabel, dear, this is General Dwight Eisenhower and his Chief of Staff, Major General Bedell Smith. You, of course know my good friend, Sir Hugh Dalton and his American colleague, Colonel Bill Donovan."

"Thank you Monty, I have had the pleasure to meet everyone in your party except Colonel Donovan," she said.

Eisenhower moved just past Annabel with a flowing move to just in front of Bart. "Colonel Donovan is here to have a chat with one of America's finest young generals," he said with his eyes fixed on Bart's, as he shook his hand. "Bart, the President sends his warmest regards and compliments on the work that you've been doing. According to the President, you've been able to mix oil and water on several sensitive programs. I was very favorably impressed with what he had to say. Besides forbidding me to recruit you for my senior staff, he asked me to arrange a private meeting between you and Colonel Donovan tonight, if you have time."

"Of course, Sir, give me a few minutes to finish the receiving line and I'm all yours," Bart said, still in shock from the accolades offered by Eisenhower. Then he motioned for the hotel manager who was observing from behind the line. He quietly asked him to find a private room for General Eisenhower and party so they could have a short meeting. He also asked that a bottle of the hotel's best scotch and cognac be made available to them.

It took Coltrane almost ten minutes to complete the formalities and arrive at the private room. When he went in, Eisenhower was just finishing off a snifter of cognac as he headed to the door with Bedell Smith. Ike shook his hand and said, "I'm leaving you to the mercy of these wolves." Then he departed.

Bart looked around the room and saw that there was only Dalton, Donovan and another man. It suddenly dawned on him that this was "Mr. X," the OSS man that he dropped into Norway. Dalton got up and handed Bart a snifter and poured an inch of cognac into the glass. Then he looked at the two OSS agents sitting there smiling like the cat that ate the canary.

Then he added another inch. "Bart," Dalton said with some caution in his voice, "I believe that you've met both of these gentlemen in the past." Colonel Donovan needs no introduction, but the other chap…"

"Yes, Mr. X," Coltrane said as he interrupted Dalton and approached the man.

Mr. X got up smiling and extended his hand, "My name is Sears. Avery Sears. I'm a Colonel in the Army attached to the OSS. That was some ride you gave me to Norway. I understand that you did over 220 drops like that one…and you're still alive…amazing," he said in a warm tone of admiration. "Thanks to you our mission was very successful. We kept the Germans from getting some very critical resources and we got the underground fully operational."

Colonel Donovan leaned back on the overstuffed leather chair and put his hands behind his head while gazing at the crystal chandelier almost above him and softly interjected, "What are your plans for after the war, General? I understand that you're getting out!"

Coltrane was caught off guard by that little known fact. "Yes, Sir, that's correct. I didn't know that had become general knowledge."

Donovan smiled, "Actually, it hadn't. We, or should I say, our British counterparts here, came across your plans sort of indirectly. They saw where a newly formed company named Acacia Air Freight had been formed in the U.K. to engage in domestic and international air freight business. The name on the application was Annabel Beddows Coltrane. About the same time we and the FBI became aware of a rather large purchase of the civilian version of the Douglas C-47 and C-54 transports. Well, as you can imagine it didn't take us long to figure out the plan. Our discrete inquiries on both sides of the Atlantic painted a clearer picture. You'll be leaving at some point after the war to take over the expansion of the fledgling air freight business. Initially, your operations will start out of Heathrow, servicing the U.K. and most of Western Europe. You'll also start a smaller operation out of Hong Kong, servicing Kunming, Shanghai, Yokohama and Manila. You plan to expand to regional hubs in Genoa, Italy, Gibraltar and make Manila a hub for the Philippines area. How am I doing so far?" Donovan asked in a patronizing fashion, then continued, "You had originally planned to service south and central Africa, India and Southeast Asia before you decided that was too much capital to risk on a startup business." Donovan stared at a motionless and expressionless Coltrane. "You've already recruited a bunch of your old crew and couple of Dalton's boys as well." Your wife and her chartered accountants and solicitors have examined every aspect that you presented and found the plan reasonable." He started laughing. "Reasonable, in accounting talk means a probable success." Your plan is excellent, General. Your only hang-up is the fact that you really don't want to leave your friends in the military hanging on a limb when you leave. Admirable, but unnecessary. You want to see strategic bombardment become a separate branch of the service and the employment of new weapons and aircraft to deter aggression on the United States. Both are inevitable whether you're active duty or not. You've been very instrumental in that area. Time will see both of your goals become reality. 'Your heart is in the right place and so is your civilian future," Donovan said as he watched for Bart to think on that statement and react.

Bart did react as anticipated and asked, "You said that my heart was in the right place as a civilian. What do you mean by that, Colonel?"

"You don't have to be in the military and wear a uniform to be of service to the President and the United States of America," Donovan's voice softly said with hard conviction. "The air freight business that you're planning can be of enormous benefit and service to our country as well as our British friend here," he said slapping Dalton on the back as he stood up. "As General Eisenhower said earlier, the plan that Dalton and I are going to propose has both the President's and Sir Winston's approval and support."

"What the fuck is going on here?" Coltrane said in a burst of anger. "My new wife and I came up with a plan where she and I could build a "mom and pop" business together. It was to be something that two people in love could do together and have fun doing it. Lord knows we aren't doing it for the money. Her estate and assorted businesses income is many times more than we can ever spend. Money isn't a factor, only the ability to do something together. Nothing more! You got into my personal life and want to turn a fun and loving venture into something else."

Dalton raised his hand gesturing for peace and the floor. Coltrane became quiet but totally focused on Dalton. "Bart, you haven't heard the proposal yet so why the anger?" Dalton asked.

Coltrane said nothing but nodded as if to tell them to proceed. Then he went over to the table and freshened his drink before taking a seat at the table. Dalton and Donovan took seats at the table with drinks in hand.

"First of all, your wife makes no secret of this venture and everything we know is pretty much public information. You don't buy that many and type of aircraft without the government knowing and being involved. There's a war on. We do respect your intent and objectives. It's not our plan to change your plan, only to expand it to accommodate a serious intelligence need that both of our countries have for the future. Let's take another approach to this, if you'll permit," Dalton said as he looked for an approving nod from Bart.

"You've already hired Zak Middleton to run the company while you're off being an active duty officer until the end of the war. He'll open the main office at Heathrow and sales offices in about ten places in the U.K. Sharp and Royston have applications in for release. I'm sure you'll get them approved through your connections in Washington. You'll hire British and American combat pilots as they become available. As the war ends, you'll open sales offices in the larger European cities and start service there. You plan to make Genoa and Gibraltar hubs for your 600 mile coverage area. The same can be said for your south Pacific hub out of Hong Kong. These plans are economically practical and very viable. You plan to continue your active duty service until the war is over and you've accomplished some specific objectives that you've promised Hap Arnold and Curt Lemay. So far, this is great for everyone. This keeps you active duty for the end of the war plus eighteen to twenty-four months. Then you two love birds will expand and develop the company as the market demands. All of this is fine with me and Donovan. What we want you to do is add a south and central Africa hub, and India-Burma-Thailand hub and expand your south Pacific hub. Not only with the 600 mile feeder routes, but more long haul routes as well. The OSS or friends of the OSS will enter into a long term contract with Acacia that will provide an annual retainer equal to your operating budget for the expanded system. Donovan will also get you all the experienced combat pilots and crews that you'll need. You or Zak will interview them, and select the ones you want. You fly all of your normal commercial flights as planned. You charge your new primary contractor a standard rate. You can't lose money. The only requirement, or string as we say, is that the pilots' sent to Africa, India and south Pacific hubs will be our trained agents… and our missions take priority over other commercial missions. That should seldom be the case, but if a conflict presents itself, our mission goes first. Yes, we're conducting substantial intelligence operations, but it will be done very discretely. That's a must for your operation and ours as well. If our operations and cover are compromised, it defeats our long term objectives. We'll have a 'contractor's representative' like Avery at each hub to coordinate our needs with your local manager. We're putting our best men in these locations. Avery Sears at your main office at Heathrow, Pete Cyr in Hong Kong, Archimedes Patti working Vietnam, John Webster in India and Mr. Drake and another of our chaps in Africa." Dalton paused to let it all sink in and get a reaction from Bart. Bart remained silent and motionless so Sears went on.

"Every effort will be made to help you complete your obligations to Hap and Lemay as fast as possible cutting that eighteen to twenty-four months down smartly. They cannot know about our arrangement. Nobody can, for obvious security reasons." He concluded by pouring more cognac into his snifter and looked eye to eye with Coltrane for an answer. Coltrane said nothing but broke the stare with Dalton. He took a long drink from the snifter and looked back over the room and the occupants. Just then the door opened and Annabel walked in and went over to the chair next to Bart's and sat down.

"My feet are killing me" she said. Besides standing for so long, I need medical attention on both feet. Monty, may be a great field general, but he can't dance worth a crap." Everyone laughed and sipped the cognac.

Dalton was still awaiting an answer from Bart.

Annabel broke the silence. "From the silence and tense air, I take it my cowboy hasn't agreed yet."

That caught Bart's attention. His head snapped toward her. "You know the proposal then? Yes. Churchill and this mutt double-teamed me in Winnie's office yesterday." It sounded like it would fit in with our overall plans and it was an important intelligence operation. I told them that it would be up to you. Besides it will get you out of the service and its dangers, and back into the cockpit mistress you love so much. You'll be flying again and that will make you happy. So I'll put up with the 'other mistress' if you want to take their proposal."

Bart smiled and looked over to Sears and said, "Zak starts opening the office at Heathrow in March. When can you start?"

CHAPTER 71

It was a lovely fall afternoon at Gunter Field. The base theater had been opened for a special viewing of a new Fox Movietone newsreel for Helen and Janie Lemay. Helen and Janie were ushered to their seats in the theater by Colonel Wynn, his Chief of Staff and the base entertainment officer. Colonel Wynn said to Helen, "When Captain Rutherford told me about this newsreel, I figured you'd like a private screening."

Helen smiled, unaware of what she's about to see. Both she and Janie seated themselves along with the officers. The house lights went down, and the familiar Movietone film introduction and music were seen and heard. The film switched to an air-to-surface cut of Guam, then the following title appeared, superimposed over a B-29 pulling in toward the camera. The headlines printed over the B-29 said, "LEMAY TAKES OVER IN THE MARIANAS." Lemay dropped from the nose hatch of the B-29, obviously having flown it in, and, cigar clamped in his mouth, went over to a group of officers who have been waiting for his arrival, General Hansell, his chief of staff and an aide. More enlisted men and officers were gathered as spectators..

The voice of the famous Lowell Thomas started the narration. "Cigar-chewing General Curtis Emerson Lemay arrived on Guam to take command of the Twenty-First Strategic Air Forces there. Lemay replaced General Hansell, seen here with his staff."

Both Janie and Helen grinned broadly.

Lowell Thomas continued, "B-29s wrecked havoc over the Japanese home islands beginning late last year." Lemay was still seen in the film, talking casually with the welcoming group of officers.

Lowell Thomas voice continued, "Lemay's arrival on Guam to assume command of the B-29 bomb wings already operational there signals stepped-up strategic missions against Japan with the precision and efficiency that have made the Iron General known from Berlin to Tokyo!" The film showed selected scenes of B-29 activities on the Marianas while Lowell Thomas continued, "Lemay now commands the most potentially destructive force on earth. How long can Japan withstand the relentless bombardment that promises to be infinitely greater than the Eighth Air Force has rained down on the German homeland?" The screen went black – the house lights came up.

Colonel Wynn said "Well, Janie…how about that?"

Janie replied in an innocent and serious tone, "I just want to know when my daddy's coming home." Helen brushed Janie's cheek with her lips, emotional but smiling.

CHAPTER 72

Bart Coltrane gently touched the big B-29 down on the North Field of the island of Tinian, the home of the XXI Bomber Command. He was flying one of four new replacement aircraft joining the air war against Japan.

As he got out of the aircraft, the Commanding General's staff car drove up. The young Army captain riding in the back got out and came up to Bart. "Sir, General Lemay sends his compliments and requests that you join him at the headquarters."

"Very well," Bart said and looked at his aide-de-camp Lieutenant Ford and First Sergeant Royston. "Grab my gear and take it to the BOQ then meet me at General Lemay's office. First Sergeant, go get a drink or two and meet me at General Lemay's office at 0800 hours tomorrow." Then he got into the car.

"Bart!" Lemay said in a tone almost a yell. "How did you get in the pilot seat of a B-29?"

"They were short a pilot for the ferry mission here, so I took advantage of the situation. Good for you. The Chief of Staff would call the MPs on me if I even got close to one. Come in here and let's talk." Lemay looked at a Master Sergeant standing by the door to his office. "Nobody disturbs us. You understand?"

"Yes Sir, nobody disturbs you," he replied as he closed the door.

"Sit down, Bart. You came at a bad time. I'm falling on my face out here. The results are dismal at best. I'm not hurting the Japs and the Navy is pointing out our ongoing failures to anyone who will listen. Strategic bombardment is looking real weak just when we need a strong second act after Europe. I'm searching for an answer and not finding a damned thing."

Bart remained silent and listened as Lemay recounted his problems from the high winds, equipment maintenance, ongoing engine problems and no concentrated bomb strikes on the critical war plants in Japan. Then he sat down and looked at Bart. "I'm surprised they left me in command."

"What am I overlooking or missing, Bart?" he asked.

"Well, this is an interesting set of problems. Here's a possible solution but it's risky and won't be favorably looked upon by the world community, and the hand- wringing liberals in Washington," he said, pausing to get Lemay's reaction. "Curt, you're trying to pinpoint bomb the main industrial plants that do little more than assemble a final product. You need to go to the source of the parts. Hit the civilian population and the buildings that surround the plants. There's the source of the parts and the backbone of the Japanese industrial capability. It's not the main plants, it's the small shops around them that make the parts for the plants. Let me ask you a question. What is the main composition of the structures around the plant and for that matter all of Japan?" he asked as he got up and walked to the wall map.

Lemay looked puzzled at first, then replied, "Wood, paper and other non-metal materials."

"Right, highly flammable structures!" Bart said in a strong voice.

"Look at this," Bart said. "If you flew at low altitude at night and used incendiary bombs like you did in Germany. You could destroy large areas around the plants which would halt production and terrorize the population. It might even break their will. Use the wind to spread the fire. You don't have to be in formation to be effective. Just set up your flights where they drop their loads in a solid five mile line a mile upwind of your target area. The wind will carry the fire and destruction across your target. You would have the same effect as Dresden. Fly low altitude at night when they can't scramble fighters or effectively use anti-aircraft fire. String out your flights so you keep them up all night fighting fires all over the area."

"Washington and the flight crews will think I'm crazy. The world will think me worse than Hitler. But you're right, it will do the job," Lemay said as he pondered what he had just been told. "Thanks. You may have saved strategic bombardment, hundreds of flight crews and reduced the need for a costly invasion of the mainland of Japan. I'll give this tactic very serious consideration." Lemay got up looking somewhat relieved and went to Coltrane and put his hand on his shoulder and said, "Thanks again." Now what is the latest on 'The Gadget' and the temperament in Washington?"

Coltrane sat back down and started a detailed report. "Groves is driving everyone nuts as usual. Best guess is that they'll be able to test 'The Gadget' in late June or July. You know the problems from there. Is Paul Tibbets up and operational here yet?"

"Yes, security is still a problem with them," he replied. "Everyone wonders why they're not flying strike missions with the others. It does look suspicious, but it can't be helped. Anything new on separating the Army Air Force from the ground pounders?"

"Sure. Roosevelt is for it, but not until after the war. He sees the need but the Army and Navy don't see it that way as usual. I think it will work out in time. Personally, I see a threat developing in the post-war situation with Russia. The Bear is getting healthy and cocky these days now that Hitler is gone and we've pumped money, supplies, money, raw materials and more money into their economy. I see them as a future threat to our security. We must capitalize on that threat to get Congressional support to develop a strategic air capability to keep Russia at bay," Bart recounted.

"What about the Convair B-36 development?" Lemay asked.

"I spoke to Ted Hull recently. It's going to become a reality for us, but not in time to use against Japan. But it will be a fully intercontinental bomber that's nuclear capable. It will be our vehicle to create a separate air force to defend the U.S. against the Russians."

"Very well put, Bart," a smiling Lemay said. "Any problems with the bird itself?"

"Yeah! They've a series of design problems involving the hydraulic and fuel tanks that must be fixed, otherwise it's going to be leaving a trail flying hydraulic and fuel leak across the world." It still can't be refueled in the air like we had hoped. It's slower than constipation, and uses way too much fuel for a 6,000 mile range. If it wasn't for the four jets they added, it wouldn't get off the ground fully combat loaded," he said in despair. "Curt, we must think of the B-36 as an interim strike platform. Pray that George Schairer and the Boeing boys can make that model 424 idea fly. We need a pure jet bomber to provide us with the true deterrent that we'll need in the future. The jet bomber is the future for the U.S. strategic air capability and the new separate air force branch."

"Well, Bart, you've said a hell of a lot in the past thirty-five minutes, and I appreciate it. Are you going to see Hap soon?" Lemay asked.

"Yes Sir, he and I are meeting up in Washington early next week. He has to brief the President and he wants input on the same matters that we've discussed and to know how you're going to pull a rabbit out of the hat out here in your Pacific paradise," Coltrane said.

"When are you leaving?" Lemay asked.

"Tomorrow or the next day, depending on what space is available on an eastbound aircraft," he said.

"Don't worry, I'll get you out of here early tomorrow. Now let's go get a drink and something to eat. I feel like eating for a change," Lemay said as he headed for the door.

Helen tells me that you're going to be a father soon," Lemay said in a warm tone of voice.

"Yes, we were surprised to find that out last month. It should be out of the hanger and on the ramp by early August," Bart said proudly.

The Acacia C-47 circled just above the rugged hills surrounding the rough dirt landing strip near the Vietnam village of Cao Bang. Colin Majumder carefully landed the aircraft on the rough strip. There was no wind to help him on the short strip and the rain-drenched runway had many potholes, which added to the difficult landing. He taxied the aircraft to a secluded area where the trees had been cut back, so an aircraft could be parked out of sight of the Japanese recon planes. After he shut down the engines, he made his way past the cargo to the rear cargo door. As he got to the door he saw Ho Chi Minh, Vo Nguyen Giap and Phan Van Dong walking up along with a dozen others.

Bart Coltrane sends you his best and has a present for you. There are forty cases of new automatic rifles, fifty thousand rounds of ammo, four Hallicrafter radios and a ton of rice in here for you. Can your men unload it for me?"

Giap smiled and turned to the men around and said, "Our new friend has kept his promise. Unload the cargo quickly before the Japs discover the aircraft." The men quickly unloaded the valuable cargo with smiles on their faces.

Ho Chi Minh was the first to speak. "I felt sure that he would keep his promise and but I did not expect him to deliver this much so quickly. He's a man of honor."

"Well," Majumder said as he climbed down from the aircraft, "I have found that if he makes a business deal or promise he delivers everything and on time. He's the type of bloke that you can bet your life on. You don't see many of them anymore."

"Giap nodded as he waved to some of his men back in the shadows of the trees. They started to bring out four men on stretchers and a couple of men helping each other walk towards the aircraft. Giap then turned to Majumder and said, "We keep our word as well. Here are some of your American pilots shot down by the Japanese. Take them back to General Coltrane with our thanks. Also tell him that all of our wounded that he took back to Kunming for medical treatment are back to duty. If it was not for him, they would have died."

Majumder smiled and reached out to shake the hand of the three Viet Minh leaders. "All the best in your war efforts against the bloody Japs. We'll be back soon with more supplies." Majumder then climbed back into the aircraft and departed.

CHAPTER 73

Like most "temporary" buildings during the war, the headquarters of the XXI Bomber Command was a Quonset hut. It was March 6, 1945, and rain drizzled down on the Headquarters Quonset Hut. Lemay was seated in the dimly lighted war room, hunched forward slightly in a meditative posture, an unlighted cigar in his mouth. He flipped the pages of a voluminous data file, one of many such files and photographs on the large map type table before him. Presently the door opened and Colonel J. B. Montgomery started to enter on a routine matter before recognizing the General seated in the room.

"Sorry, General," Colonel Montgomery said, apologetically.

Lemay broke his train of thought and said, "It's alright, Colonel," as he slowly rose up to address the Colonel. "Matter of fact, I'm glad you're here." Lemay crossed the room, clasped his hands behind his back momentarily and then turned to Colonel Montgomery. Lemay continued, "I want to talk a little." Lemay began pacing back and forth – slowly – methodically. "You know, for years we've argued that our strategic air arms should be under the direction of field commanders who understand the technology and scientific application of air power." He paused momentarily – gesturing to emphasize his remarks before continuing to pace. Then he said, "Give 'em the authority to make decisions in the field and we'll win the nations' wars…without surface invasions that cost us the blood of our youth…with our Navy's isolation and our ground troops occupying. For the first time in the history of our air arm, we have all of that out here." Lemay stopped, looked at Montgomery momentarily then continued. "Trouble is, we've been getting a lot of publicity without having really accomplished a hell of a lot of bombing results!" Lemay walked to the table of data, picked up the related objects abstractly.

"Strike photos…mission reports….we've gone over 'em a dozen times in staff meetings. Sixteen missions…flown over the Japanese home islands since B-29 operations began out here…five thousand tons of high explosives…all without significantly affecting her WILL or ABILITY to wage war!" Colonel Montgomery stood there listening, not really sure what response to expect.

Lemay continued, "Well, the jet stream up there at 25,000 feet and above is killing us. Granted, we didn't know anything about that when we came over here. The wind velocities reaching two hundred miles an hour up there where our bombers fly. The Norden bombsight simply can't compensate for it and the damned weather too!" We've been lucky to get seven days a month of visual bombing. Of course, if the Russians had let us set up weather stations of there in Siberia, it might have been different. Excuses are pretty easy to come by, J.B. I can find excuses for everything that's happened… except one."

Colonel Montgomery asked politely, "What's that, General?"

Lemay said "I've failed to get results!" Lemay began pacing again. "If we've reached any significant conclusion from all our staff meetings, it's that pinpoint bombing with high explosive, general purpose bombs isn't working." Lemay crossed back to the data table, reached for a strike photo, handed it to Colonel Montgomery. "Eight missions against the Musashino plant up in Nakajima…last one was yesterday. Still operational! But…take a look at this," handing Montgomery a second photo. "Incendiaries…dropped from twenty-five thousand feet! A visual mission that turned into a radar mission. It was part of an idea that we tested on Hanchow at the suggestion of Bart Coltrane." Lemay gestured to the photo. "The mission commander reported such poor visibility that they had to climb above the cloud layer to keep from running into each other!"

Colonel Montgomery nodded, grinning wryly. "I remember! Everything went wrong on that one. The incendiaries fell everywhere but the aiming point."

Lemay then pointed to the specific areas in the photo. But look at that blackened square…stands out like a sore thumb because of the snow cover. Lemay looked at Montgomery now. "That represents one square mile of burned-out buildings! Enough incendiaries fell in concentration in that area to start a fire. He was tapping the photo with his finger again. "That's the results!' Coltrane was right. Lemay crossed to a large chart at the front of the room that had obviously been prepared for use in previous staff discussions on the Japanese urban areas. It depicted a circle of household-based machine tools supplying a feeder plant that in turn supplied the factory. Lemay contemplated the chart momentarily, and then he continued. "All available intelligence still supports our theories of the Japanese industrial complex... 'mom and pop' operations in the urban areas a drill press here...a lathe there... all of it supplying the feeder plants that feed the main assembly points here"... tapping the center of the hub with his finger.

"The factories themselves that's so hard to hit from high altitude!" Turning to Montgomery, Lemay continued. "That entire urban industrial complex is highly susceptible to fire!" Lemay went back to the table, thoughtfully, his hands behind his back, then said to Colonel Montgomery who by this time was totally entranced with what Lemay was showing him, Lemay's voice becoming hard, "A lower bombing altitude would increase bombing accuracy and concentrate the effects of the incendiary munitions. It would extend the life of our B-29s."

Colonel Montgomery pulled his head back slightly as he was growing wary of the low altitude tactic. "It might also increase losses to a prohibitive rate!"

Lemay quickly retorted, "We haven't found anything to support that assumption. In fact, the conclusions we've reached are just the opposite. He gestured to the table with the mass of data before continuing. "Japanese gun radar is inefficient." Only <u>two</u> Superforts have been lost to flak so far. Furthermore, the 88s they use up there are ineffective at lower altitudes. He began pacing again as he spoke, "and...current intelligence indicates only two units of night fighters in all of the home islands...and their radar equipment isn't effective. Our heaviest losses were twenty-nine Superforts! All of them lost to Japanese fighters during our daylight missions up there. Lemay took a long, thoughtful pause, then said in his customary voice of authority, "I've made a decision, J.B. - the staff meetings...the reports and data we've studied...they all point to one conclusion."

Colonel Montgomery quickly interrupted, "Are you thinking about a night mission?"

Lemay smiled at Montgomery and commanded, "I want you to begin profiling a mission that will use three hundred Superforts. Load 'em with M46 and M69 clusters." As he crossed to the wall map he said, "From a point east of the bay entrance here, they're to go in <u>singly</u>... at altitudes ranging from five to nine thousand feet!"

Colonel Montgomery's expression was one of total incredulity now, "But, General!"

Lemay was oblivious to the astonished response. His decision had been made. "Our radar veterans will act as the pathfinders. They'll use intervalometer settings of one hundred feet...the others at fifty feet! Or... one aircraft per sixteen acres of the Tokyo urban area – the target! The aircraft are to be stripped of ALL defensive armament! Saves weight for higher bomb loading...and...they won't be shooting at each other up there!"

Colonel Montgomery was totally dumbstruck. He looked at Lemay as if he were gazing at a lunatic. "General...I...."

Lemay again was oblivious to the response from Montgomery. "All bomb bay tanks are to be removed!" The gunners will be left behind except the tail gunner. He'll act as an observer only."

Colonel Montgomery was momentarily convinced that Lemay had gone mad.

Lemay continued, unaware of the devastated Montgomery. "Get the graphics on crew experience to help determine the gas load for each ship... then make up the difference with bomb loading. You'll need to load a few of those planes with high explosive general purpose bombs in order to keep the fire fighters from going out to fight the fires. Tommy Power is probably a good bet to lead the mission. "I...I think we can count on one hundred and fifty B-29s from the Seventy Third Wing...a hundred from the Three Thirteenth and fifty from the Three Fourteenth. This is TOP SECRET. Inform only those members of the staff who need to be informed. Get it done! I repeat, Colonel, get it done...Now!" Lemay turned to exit.

The stricken Colonel finally managed to speak. Colonel Montgomery said in a broken voice, "Curt…" Lemay turned back, frowned and said, "Yeah?" Colonel Montgomery said "You've always allowed us to..uh…speak our piece…at least until a final decision's been made."

Lemay nodded, "That's right."

Colonel Montgomery still numb with disbelief at what he's heard, "I…I just wanna tell you, in my opinion, you run the risk of losing all three hundred Super Fortresses up there…the crews…everything! It could turn into a slaughter!"

Lemay's voice was low and steel edged, "When all the information… and intelligence…available to a field commander points to a certain course of action…and that commander fails to make a decision simply because it involves a radical departure from all the theories he's been taught…then that field commander should be relieved and replaced. Hell yes, there's a risk involved! But I didn't arrive at this decision just last night you know. I've weighed it for weeks! Bart Coltrane has a brilliant military mind. He's in total agreement. It's lucky for Bart that he doesn't have to answer for any failure."

Lemay emerged from the War room, leaving Colonel Montgomery still standing in shock and awe of what had just happened.

Colonel Kissner quickly walked up to the General and said, "General…"

Lemay spoke with a trace of anger still evident, "Yes?" Colonel Kissner said "General Arnold's Chief of Staff's stopping by on his way back to Washington. Just got a teletype. Be in day after tomorrow..the eighth."

Lemay, beginning to grin, "Larry Norstad…" as he turned to walk to his office, "That's timely."

Colonel Kissner looked after him baffled.

CHAPTER 74

A four-engine military executive transport touched down at the Guam airport on 8 March 1945. Lemay stood bedside his staff car, waiting. The transport pulled up, turning broadside. The steps were pushed up to the hatch and General Norstad emerged, followed by two military aides who carried briefcases. General Rawlins was a part of the entourage. Lemay greeted Norstad at the foot of the steps.

Norstad smiled and said, "Curt."

Lemay smiled with his cigar still in his mouth. He shook their hands warmly. "Larry…good to see you." He said to General Rollins, "Ed."

"General Arnold sends his best, Curt," Norstad said perfunctorily. They crossed to the waiting staff car and drove off.

Lemay nodded, then, grinning wryly said, "Never have quite forgiven you for that North Africa debacle."

Norstad asked, "How's that?"

Lemay said in an almost sarcastic manner, "Hell, Larry…you left us high and dry out there at Telergma. Wasn't a damned thing there when we got down there from Regensberg, but empty buildings. Spaatz had promised your help you know."

"I had to go fight Eisenhower's war, Curt!" Norstad said in retort.

Lemay said "Well, that shuttle mission business...wouldn't have worked anyway," looking over to General Rawlins. "You're giving Ed the Pacific Tour?"

Norstad was grinning, "Yeah. Hear you've got something pretty big on the drawing board." Lemay nodded, as they pulled up to Lemay's headquarters. The three generals were in the war room of the Bomber

Command. Lemay, Norstad, Rawlins and Kissner stood before the maps in the war room. Lemay had obviously concluded briefing Norstad on the low altitude mission. Norstad was obviously awed by the mission ramifications.

"What do the crews think about it?"

Lemay calmly said, "Haven't been told yet!"

Colonel Montgomery entered the war room. Colonel Montgomery stood erect in a professional manner and said, "General…we've got to have a decision on the field order."

Norstad said softly to Lemay, "You going to clear it with Arnold?"

Lemay didn't answer immediately, then said, "No. I don't want him held responsible if it goes wrong," he said looking at Norstad.

"You think he's against taking a little risk now and then?" Norstad said firmly, "It's your decision, Curt."

Lemay gazed abstractly for a long moment, then turned back to Montgomery. "Cut the field order, Colonel, "Lemay ordered.

Montgomery and Norstad emerged from the war room, Montgomery hurrying off to set the field order preparations in motion. Norstad went over to a bank of teletypes and spoke quietly with the communication colonel at an adjacent desk. The colonel rose as Norstad brusquely approached his area. Norstad said "Colonel…I want to send a message to Lieutenant Colonel Hartzell, PR – Twenty-First Bomber Command, Washington." The Colonel sat back down, wrote out the message when it was given to him by General Norstad. Norstad smiled and said, "Just tell 'em to stand by for what may be an outstanding show!"

It was the early morning of March 9, 1945 at the sprawling XXI Bomber Command hardstand in the Marianas. The crews are quietly removing the ammo belts. Another group of men trundled M-69 incendiaries up to the gaping bomb bay doors. Still another crew removed the machine guns from the bottom turret. Colonel Agather, General Rawlins and Colonel Nelson arrived on the scene in a jeep, Agather at the wheel. They paused, observed the removal of defensive weaponry from a B-29. Nelson, Agather and Rawlins were shocked at what they're witnessing.

General Rawlins said reflectively, "Kinda scary…guns and ammo coming out before a mission."

Colonel Nelson stood quietly, then gestured toward the crews at work, "Never seem 'em like this, either. Thought they were going to mutiny when the briefing officer laid out the low level target approach. Now…nothing. It's downright eerie."

A USAAF priest was administering the communion sacrament, continuously, just before the men went to their aircraft. Some men were kneeling, others in the Communion queue. In the communion line, the priest said as he placed the wafer in the mouths of the communicants, "Hoc est Corpus Meum."

Almost without any fanfare or urging, the men went aboard the aircraft, started their engines and then, like ants, went single file to the runway and took off into history. The Air Mission Commander was Brigadier General Tommy Powers. He was at the controls of the lead B-29. The Mission Commander was a critical position and it carried the tremendous responsibility on this mission of great magnitude. Powers knew that this mission would be historic no matter how it turned out. He just wasn't sure if history would record it as a major success or a catastrophic disaster. The pressure weighed heavily on him as he completed his pre-flight check list.

His co-pilot looked at him as he took the left side earphone from his ear and reported, "Sir, all aircraft are ready to go….its time."

Powers looked over to him and smiled. Then he turned slightly towards the flight engineer and said, "OK, give me takeoff power!"

The flight engineer made adjustments to the controls at the base of the engineer's panel. Once he was satisfied, he turned to General Powers and said, "She's on 'the step' General Powers." The co-pilot glanced at Powers who gazed ahead, preoccupied. His stare was without focus, only ahead into the vast airspace ahead of them. The co-pilot said, "It's going to be a long night, General."

Powers only nodded.

Back in the operations center of the XXI Bomber Command at Guam, a long, mission progress board stretched from the Marianas to Japan. The Marianas were depicted on its surface on the left side and the Japanese home islands on its surface near the opposite end. The big wall map had a piece of red twine stretched from the Marianas to Tokyo with model pieces deployed along the routing depicting the unit and the size of the B-29 force en route and its progress to the target. Mission control personnel were positioned at telephone studded desks around the area, each the source of related information that's being processed and transferred to the various data boards along the wall by additional mission control personnel. General Lemay and General Norstad watched the progress intently from the command desk which was placed on a two foot platform. This gave the General a clear view of all operations. Presently, Colonel Kissner tore a sheet from one of the teletypes along a large bank of such machines, perused it momentarily before he took it to Lemay.

Colonel Kissner stated, "We've got three hundred and thirty-four aircraft up, General." It was two parallel streams of B-29s, four hundred miles long, headed north.

Just before midnight, Lemay glanced at his watch, saying "That puts the pathfinders over the target a few minutes after midnight on 10 March 1945," he said as a point of historical reference. Colonel Kissner said, "That's right, General!" as he looked at the operations room clock. It read 2015 hours...about four hours from now. I think I'll grab a short nap," he said to General Norstad and Colonel Kissner.

Lemay entered the operations center a few minutes before midnight and walked directly to a Silex coffee maker, poured himself a cup of coffee. While stirring his coffee, he turned to Kissner and Norstad who had entered behind him. Lemay said to them, "If this raid works the way I think it will, it'll shorten the war."

Kissner poured himself some coffee, and then reflectively said "You know, Curt, history will have something to say about what happens up there in Tokyo tonight."

Lemay was momentarily stung by Kissner's observation. Lemay looked at Kissner intently and said, "The more the better!" He moved over a couple of feet to lean back against a map table. "War's no longer an effective means of resolving man's conflicts of interest," Lemay said in a reflective pause, then added, "Never has been for that matter. But...we sure as hell can't beat our swords into plowshares until everybody else does the same thing!" Lemay was looking at Kissner intently. "My duty is to defeat the enemy! I'll feel dishonor only if I fail!"

Kissner quickly responded, "I…I wasn't questioning your moral integrity, Curt."

"You want to know what my solution to peace on earth is," Lemay said as he sat his cup down and lit his pipe. Through a cloud of smoke, he said, "Maintain an air arm so powerful…so professional…that no nation on earth would ever dare attack us! If we'd had a sufficient number of B-17s in the Philippines, and on patrol duty out of Pearl Harbor, the Japs would never have dared attack us in the first place, not with aircraft carriers and battleships anyway. As it was, we left our entire Pacific defense to a bunch of antiquated battleships! And they're still fishing 'em out of the bottom of Pearl Harbor!"

Kissner said shaking his head, "Tough philosophy to sell in peace time…particularly if you're talking about heavy bombers. But then, I don't have to tell you that!"

High over the vast Pacific Ocean just southeast of Tokyo Bay, General Powers' B-29 flew towards its target. The navigator plotted his dead reckoning course to the turning point just off Tokyo Bay. The navigator said in a professional tone, "Navigator to pilot, one minute to the turning point, General Powers."

General Powers depressed his intercom button and commanded, "Give me climb power." The flight engineer immediately sat the controls accordingly.

The flight engineer reported, "Throttles set for climb power." It was clearly evident to the flight crew as they watched General Powers' turn toward Tokyo, climbing slightly in the turn. The pilot and co-pilot prepared to assume control of their aircraft manually as it came off the autopilot. Powers was intent on the course line up to the target and leveling the ship at the proper altitude. General Powers said in the same tone that he would have ordered a hamburger and malt back home, "Powers to crew. We've leveled off at fifty-five hundred feet…two minutes to aiming point." The bombardier activated the bomb bay door switch.

The co-pilot was focused ahead and downward, "There goes the first pathfinder's load!"

The bombardier reported, "The target is marked! Bomb bay doors coming open!" The bombardier started dropped the first closer of incendiaries. They began tumbling from the bomb bay door at fifty-foot intervals.

General Powers said to the flight engineer, "Let's get upstairs." The flight engineer began engine adjustments for climb power.

General Power said in an intercom transmission to the crew, "This is General Powers. We're going up over the target for observation and photographs as briefed. Keep your eyes open." The heavy anti aircraft battery fires upward incessantly.

The rear gunner, now the bombing observer, could see the red balls of napalm boil upward through the houses and buildings. The massive devastation could be seen in the glare of the fire. The fires were beginning to spread through the houses and buildings themselves. He reported his observations to the pilot. Just then a search light probed the sky, its finger searching for the B-29s above.

The co-pilot was blinking his eyes against the blinding light, "Damn!" The pilot was bewildered, "Where's the ack-ack?"

The co-pilot said "Dunno. I saw muzzle flashes all over the place down there!"

The pilot responded in amazement "Must be over shooting us! Let's get the hell outta here." The pilot began a turn that took it out of the light beam and the safety of the darkness.

Back at the Guam operations center, the mission controllers were busy at their station board and telephones. J. B. Montgomery, Kissner, Sullivan and Norstad all sat quietly as Lemay paced, slowing, methodically, his pipe setting between his teeth.

Norstad glanced at his watch and said, "We should be hearing something by now, shouldn't we?

Lemay looked at Norstad and said, "I told Powers to stay up there over the target as long as he could and make sketches of the fire pattern just in case our photos don't turn out." Lemay continued his pacing.

Powers was almost over the fires gazing at the inferno. The B-29s were surrounded by a dense layer of smoke as they continued dropping bombs that spread the fire over great areas of Tokyo. The pilots were desperately trying to control their ships which were severely buffeted by the updraft form the massive fire below.

Powers muttered to his co-pilot as he struggled with the control yoke, "What the hell?"

The co-pilot replied "Updraft! Must be an inferno down there! There's hell on earth!"

Powers had placed a small sketch pad by his seat. He had drawn the pattern and effects of the fire as directed by Lemay. General Powers said to the radio operator, "Let's get a message off to Guam. Bombing target visually. Large fires observed. Flak is moderate and ineffective. Fighter opposition nil. Damage is massive and widespread."

When General Powers report was handed to Lemay, he smiled and went over to his chair and sat down, visibly relieved. He knew he had been right and there was a way to bring this war to an end, perhaps without an invasion. He looked up at the ceiling and remembered that he might have a viable back up just in case the firebombing didn't bring the Japanese to the peace table. It would be a gift from on high if "The Gadget" worked and could be delivered on target before the massive loss of life took place going ashore and through the fields and cities of Japan. He shook his head in an attempt to clear the mental picture of the carnage that would be inevitable if there was to be an invasion of the mainland of Japan. He got up and slowly walked along the mission status boards, getting a feel for the actual mission results and what could be changed to make these raids more effective and safer for the aircrews.

CHAPTER 75

Several days later at the presentation room at Joint Chiefs of Staff building in Washington, D.C., a 16mm motion picture screen displayed black and white motion picture cuts of aerial photo reconnaissance footage of a fire ravaged Tokyo, a section of the city that had literally been leveled by the incendiary raid. A USAAF Colonel briefed the Generals in narrative style enumerating the effective results of the destruction on the screen. The assembled Joint Chiefs and aides watched the footage intently. Marshall, King, Leahy and Arnold were visibly impressed with the magnitude of the damage. The Colonel said, "This concludes the footage of the March nine Tokyo strike. In summary, fifteen point eight square miles or eighteen percent of Tokyo's industrial area was leveled. Twenty-two numbered strategic targets and industrial plants that had been given special designation in the joint target group folder were bombed and have been struck from the joint target group list. More industrial targets were destroyed than by any other single mission in Air Force history," the footage concluded.

The Colonel moved smartly to the front of the room to face the assembled staff. The Colonel continued, "In fact, no other attack in the history of warfare has been so destructive to life and property. Tail gunners reported seeing the glow from the Tokyo fires for one hundred fifty miles" The colonel now began pointing out large aerial photographs that have been appended to the presentation board at the head of the room…gesturing to each photo as appropriate.

The Colonel continued, "On March eleventh, just twenty-nine hours after the crews landed from the Tokyo strike, Lemay sent three hundred and thirteen of the same crews…and aircraft…against Nagoyo. That resulted in two point five square miles burned out. Eighteen numbered targets struck from the target list! Again, the Colonel continues, "Thirteen March: Three hundred and one B-29s struck Osaka. With an eight-tenths cloud cover our bomber force using only radar destroyed another eight point one square miles of area with one hundred nineteen major factories located in the target area destroyed! Then, on Sixteen March…three hundred seven B-29s struck Kobe. Five hundred industrial buildings were destroyed, one hundred sixty-two damaged. Nineteen March – Three hundred thirteen B-29s returned to Nagoyo…leveling three square miles, wiping out the Nagoyo Arsenal, the freight yard and the Aichi Engine Works."

The Colonel began his summary, stepping away from the board to assume a more intimate position in front of the group. The Colonel looked at his audience, looking for possible questions before he continued. "By then, Lemay had used up his supply of incendiaries. In fact, every third plane participating in the second Nagoyo raid had to be loaded with general purpose, high explosives in lieu of incendiaries. In summary, gentlemen, one thousand five hundred and ninety-five sorties were flown between March nine and March nineteenth with a crew loss rate of NINE TENTHS OF ONE PERCENT! Less than ONE FIFTH THE AVERAGE LOSS RATE FOR PREVIOUS DAYLIGHT MISSIONS! And that's three-fourths as many sorties as have been flown in all previous B-29 missions. It's also three times the total bomb weight expended by all B-29 missions flown before March nine! A significant percent of Japan's total industrial capacity has been destroyed or damaged beyond operational capability. It would seem clear, as General Lemay had anticipated that the Japanese have no successful tactics for night interception. That concludes the report, General Arnold, do you've questions?"

General Arnold, still in a slightly stunned frame of mine, said "Thank you, Colonel." The Colonel got off the podium and left, along with the staff aides, leaving the Joint Chiefs by themselves. General Marshall looked at Arnold and said, "Seems we've a field commander equal to the task out there, Hap!"

Admiral King agreed, "Lemay surprised all of us with his B-29s, Hap, Admiral Nimitz included!"

General Arnold, trying not to smile or gloat said, "I believe he told Admiral Nimitz he was going to get eighty hours a month out of his crews..,and...if he ran out of incendiaries. Then that would be Nimitz' problem, not his!"

Admiral Leahy said calmly, "Surely Lemay will have an adequate supply of incendiary bombs as long as CINCPAC shipping can make it to the Marianas."

Admiral King added slightly sarcastically, "Lemay's problem is that he doesn't have enough hardstands out there to store those bombs on. You just can't stick 'em out in the cow pasture, you know!"

General Arnold injected as a jab at the Navy, "Since the Navy has insisted on maintaining control of the islands they've taken in the Pacific, they're responsible for construction the hardstands Lemay needs!"

Admiral King recoiled with his answer, "There are priorities, General. We just can't stop everything to go build hardstands for Lemay!"

General Arnold, trying to maintain control, said, "As it stands now, Ernest, the Navy has effective control of the amount of tonnage we're able to drop on the Japanese empire. Lemay has requested two hundred and ten thousand tons to be delivered to the Marianas on a well thought out and documented schedule. At this point, the Navy still hasn't indicated its willingness to comply with Lemay's request...or to deliver anywhere near that amount of tonnage to the twenty-first bomber command out there. How the hell can Lemay project his force if he doesn't know how much tonnage he's going to have on hand at any given time?

"Be reasonable, Admiral." General Marshall glanced at King ominously, "I think we'd better take a look at the Navy's construction priorities in the Pacific. In the meantime, Hap, you'd better take this up directly with Chester Nimitz. A trip out there for a personal conference might even be justified."

General Marshall continued the conference agenda. "Gentlemen, the Joint Target Group has concluded that Japan's industry, as a whole, is vulnerable to incendiary attacks on the principle urban areas. Therefore, they've designated thirty-two such areas as targets of sufficient importance to warrant inclusion in a comprehensive plan of attack."

General Marshall continued, "In addition, they've named certain priority industrial targets for precision attacks. These target lists – one for urban area bombardment, the other for daylight precision bombardment - will be given to Lemay to pursue at his discretion. If Lemay is successful in destroying those targets, Japan's industrial capability might very well be permanently paralyzed."

Leahy asked, "How about his force?" Does he have enough B-29s to keep up the pace?"

General Arnold answered the Admiral, "The 58th Bomb Wing has been redeployed from India to the Marianas. The 315th will be available to Lemay in early July." General Marshall said as he got up, "Well.. I guess that concludes our session, gentlemen." The chiefs rose to exit.

Leahy spoke with Arnold before doing so. Leahy said, "You know, Hap, I'm glad your B-29s finally came through for you." He paused, then added, "Couple of times there it looked like the saw was making the last cross-cut on the limb you were out on!"

Arnold only grinned as he shook hands with Leahy. Leahy smiled and said warmly, "Quite a show, Hap."

General Arnold replied, "Thank you, Bill."

Only Arnold and Marshall now stood in the room. Marshall took a document from a folder before him. General Marshall asked, "This letter from Lemay to your Chief of Staff…who has seen it, General Arnold?"

General Arnold replied, "Norstad, you and me."

General Marshall was reading from the letter, "This part where he says: I consider that, for the first time, strategic air bombardment faces a situation in which its strength is proportionate to the magnitude of its task. He glanced at Arnold, then continued, "I feel that the destruction of Japan's ability to wage war lies within the capacity of this command, provided its maximum capacity is exerted unstintingly during the next six months, which is considered to be the critical period." Marshall put the letter down and looked at Arnold. "Do you believe that's possible? Can we bring about a surrender of the Japanese government without an invasion?"

General Arnold replied, "Yes, Sir!"

Marshall pondered the letter for a moment or two, then placed it back in the folder, put the folder in his briefcase and exited the room.

Arnold gazed after him for a moment, then began placing his briefing papers in the briefcase, closed it and also left the room.

CHAPTER 76

It was slightly after 4 p.m. on a beautiful April afternoon in Washington, when three secret service agents entered the room. The lead agent said in a strong and urgent tone, "Mr. Vice President, please come with us to the White House. This is a national emergency. An agent lead the way to the waiting limousine with the other two on each arm of the Vice President. There was nothing but silence as they drove a short distance to the White House. They silently took Truman up the elevator to the Presidential residence. When the door opened, Truman saw Eleanor Roosevelt and Harry Hopkins standing along with six or eight military and government officials and the Chief Justice of the Supreme Court. Eleanor came over to Truman extended her hand and said, "Harry, so good of you to come over so quickly. We've lost Franklin. He died about an hour ago in Warm Springs. It's now up to you to lead our country. What can we do to help you?"

Eleanor, I'm so sorry. What can we do for you?" a shocked Truman said as tears started forming in his eyes.

Harry Hopkins gently grabbed his elbow and led him to the Chief Justice with Eleanor following him, and stood next to him.

The Chief Justice looked at Truman and asked, "Harry Steppe Truman, are you prepared to take the oath of office for the Presidency of the United States of America?" Truman responded in a heavy voice, "I am, and may God help us all."

After the formal swearing in and signing of the order assuming the Presidency and Commander-in-Chief of the military, Harry Hopkins pulled him over to a tight gathering of officials and generals. "Mr. President, there's a lot to do and little time. I'll collect the cabinet and other resignations and…"

"STOP!" Truman commanded. "No resignations from anyone. Everyone stays where they're. Nobody gets out of work…and that especially goes for you, Mr. Hopkins."

"Very well, Sir. We need to brief you on the situation diplomatically and militarily... the war plans and other domestic issues," Harry Hopkins said as they walked into the cabinet room where there were a dozen people standing along the walls with charts in hand.

The President looked at Hopkins and said with a smile, "This is going to take longer than an hour, isn't it, Harry?"

The heavy rains of the monsoon season had just started in northern Vietnam when Coltrane and Majumder landed the Acacia Air Freight C-47 on the road that served as a landing strip for the Viet Minh. Colin Majumder taxied the aircraft to the north end of the road and into Happy Valley. Before Colin shut down the engines, Coltrane got up from the co-pilot seat and went back to get off and meet Ho Chi Minh, General Giap and Phan Van Dong.

It had been eight months since Bart had been here. All the reports that he had received from Ho through Colin had been favorable. Supplies had been flowing from Major Patti's operation as planned. Today, Coltrane would get a first-hand report on the situation, and he would formally introduce Major Patti to the Viet Minh leadership.

The greeting between Coltrane and Ho was genuinely warm and friendly. Giap had his usual broad smile. As usual, Dong was friendly, but quiet and emotionless.

Bart noticed that Ho's hair and goatee had more gray hair than the last time. The pressures of war-time leadership were taking its toll on the fifty-five year old national hero.

"Sir," Bart said, addressing Ho, "I would like for you to meet the man who is responsible for the supplies and support that you've received from America. This is Major Archimedes Patti."

The Major came to attention and saluted the venerable leaders then extended his hand to shake their hands. "It's an honor to finally meet you after all these years," he said.

Ho shook his hand with a courteous slight head blow. "It's a pleasure to make your acquaintance. You've been most supportive in our fight against the Japanese. We're grateful for your kind support. Come, let's have some refreshments." Ho took the Major's arm and led him to a table under the trees.

Giap walked over to Coltrane and said, "It's good to see you again. We know that it was your report to the American President that got us the steady stream of supplies, especially the rice and medicine. It's kept a bad famine from becoming a catastrophe. We're very grateful. However, it does seem that the amount of new weapons and ammunition has not been in as big of volume as we had expected," Giap said as he carefully watched Coltrane's reaction and answer.

Bart spotted the loaded comment and thought for a moment then replied, "General, you know those C-47's can only hold so much, and the rice and medicine had to be the priority in these shipments. Besides, you did get thousands of grenades, rifles, and machine guns, and you've been extremely effective against the Japanese."

Giap smiled and uttered a slight laugh, "Well, General, I have the feeling that you may see the Viet Minh as a potential future threat to the French and British. Perhaps even America." Bart put his hand on Giap's shoulder and said, "I can only hope that such a tragedy never happens between friends."

The two Generals walked into the shadows, arm in arm.

CHAPTER 77

There was the usual afternoon rain in progress when General Arnold's Argonaut IV touched down at Harmon Field on Guam. General Lemay, General Giles, General Harmon, General O'Donnell were all standing by a staff car, obviously waiting for the Argonaut IV to park. The steps were pushed up to the aircraft as the engines stopped. General Arnold emerged, along with several aides and Lowell Thomas. Lemay crossed to shake hands with the General, followed by the others.

Lemay said smiling, "General Arnold…"

General Arnold shook Lemay's hand and slapped him on the back with his left hand. "Well, Curt…When I sent you out here last year, I wasn't sure the B-29 operation could be turned around. Now, you've got the whole world convinced it's the most powerfully efficient and destructive weapon ever developed."

Lemay grinned and said "Well, Sir, I believe we've just about convinced the Japanese it is anyway."

Arnold shook hands with the others as they all proceeded to the waiting staff cars which will take them to the operations center. They immediately went into the war room.

Colonel Kissner tore a page from a telex machine and quickly took it to the war room. Two MPs stood guard on either side of the door and opened the door. Kissner entered, the MPs closing the door behind him. Colonel Kissner entered and paused for the appropriate moment to approach General Arnold. Colonel Garcia was at the front of the room making a staff presentation of area operations to General Arnold and his group. General Lemay and his staff were seated in the group to the rear of the generals being briefed. A large "flip chart," made from butcher's paper rested on an artist's easel at Garcia's side, and he referred to it as he continued the presentation.

The printout on the Chart read as follows:

TARGET NO.	TARGET AREA FIRST PHASE	RATING
90.17-3600	Tokyo UA/1 (i.e., Urban area No. 1)	A
90.17-3604	Kawasaki UA/1	A
90.17-3609	Nagoya UA/1	A
90.17-3617	Osaka UA/1	A
90.17-3601	Tokyo UA/2	A
90.17-3618	Osaka UA/2	A
90.17-3618	Osaka UA/3	A
90.17-3611	Nagoya UA/3	A
90.17-3610	Nagoya UA/2	A
90.17-3630	Yamata UA/1	A

Garcia's pointer was on the Osaka UA/3 target read-out as he continued: "The June fifteenth 'mop-up' raid on Osaka completed phase one of the urban area attacks." Garcia flipped the chart.

Kissner used the interruption to approach Arnold with a message. Colonel Kissner said "Excuse me, Sir. This just came in from General Marshall."

General Arnold said, "Thank you." Arnold read the message then motioned for Garcia to continue. The date on the second flip Chart read as follows:

CITY	TOTAL URBAN AREA SQUARE MILES	PLANNED TARGET AREA SQUARE MILES	AREA DESTROYED SQUARE MILES
Tokyo	110.8	55	56.3
Nagoya	39.7	16	12.4
Kobe	15.7	7	8.8
Osaka	59.8	20	15.6
Yokohama	20.2	8	8.9
Kawasaki	11.0	6.7	3.6
	257.2	112.7	105.6

Colonel Garcia continued pointing to the appropriate totals on the chart.

"Those planned target areas total one-hundred twelve point seven square miles of which one-hundred five point six have been destroyed." Garcia stepped away from the chart, addressing the group directly. "The factories there have been destroyed or damaged beyond operational capability. Thousands of household and feeder industrial units have gone up in smoke. The evacuation of survivors has made it difficult to secure labor for the few factories that remain operational. The only foreseeable problem in carrying out the 'Empire Plan' would be a shortage of bomb tonnage. Since the Navy must approve and transport our bomb tonnage requisitions, they, in effect, control the tonnage we're able to drop on empire targets! I believe that concludes the presentation, General Lemay."

Garcia stepped aside. Arnold indicated the message he had just received. General Arnold said to Lemay, "This is from General Marshall, Curt." The Joint Chiefs are preparing a briefing for the President before he leaves for Potsdam. "He wants to know, 'Can we win the war by bombing?'

Lemay didn't answer immediately, rising instead and walking to the series of war maps of Asia and Japan that hung on the front wall. Lemay said in a firm voice, "In my opinion, General, the war against Japan has already been won!" He picked up the points, "She's no longer capable of supplying a war effort of ANY kind!" Lemay pointed to the land masses as appropriate as he continued. "It's become increasingly difficult for her to maintain simple communications with her forces on the Asian mainland, much less supply them! Her industrial capability is virtually paralyzed. As we've indicated, the 'empire plan' will finish it off completely. She's effectively blockaded from receiving imports of any kind…from anywhere!" Lemay turned from the maps to address General Arnold straight on, "But…even more conclusive, she's making overtures to the Russians…attempting to get them involved in helping her make surrender proposals to the Allies. Of course, we can't say anything about that publicly. Can't let the Japanese know we've broken their code just yet."

General Arnold pondered the information for a moment, then said, "You know, Curt, I've been asking everybody out here this question. Maybe it's the appropriate time to ask you. When do you think the war will be over?"

Lemay said "Well…give me thirty minutes and I'll tell you." He turned to Garcia and said, "Find out when we'll run out of targets on the joint target group's list, Colonel." Garcia then exited the war room.

Lemay reseated himself as General Arnold continued, "Admiral Nimitz has assured us you'll have all the bomb tonnage you've requisitioned…delivered according to your scheduled requirements. He's highly complimentary about the results you've been able to achieve out here with our strategic air arm. But, it's no secret; they'd still like to keep it a Navy war here in the Pacific. Been that way all along, I guess."

Lemay looked at Arnold and said to him in a jovial tone, "They've still go the war department convinced they're the nation's first line of defense, I suppose, battleships and all!"

Garcia entered with a sheaf of papers in his hand and said, "General, we'll have run out of strategic targets around the first of September."

Lemay gave a long, thoughtful pause, then said, "Then I don't see the war lasting much longer than October first, General Arnold."

General Arnold meditatively thought then said, "The invasion...It's scheduled for November fifteenth. The decision has been made by Truman. Look, Curt, I…I'm in complete agreement with your assessment of the situation here. I think you ought to attend that meeting in Washington. Brief the President and the Joint Chiefs just as you've briefed me. You…you can get away?" Lemay puffed on his pipe and replied, "I think so."

General Arnold nodded his head and said, "Then, I'll notify Norstad accordingly. General Arnold rose, his aides preparing to leave with him along with the others in the room. "Well…I'll be with Nimitz most of the afternoon. You'll be up there for dinner?"

Lemay, not terribly enthusiastically ,said, "I'd planned on it."

General Arnold grinned broadly and said to Lemay, "Mind your manners with the Navy people, Curt. Can't afford to make them mad right now, you know."

Lemay said dryly, "I'll try, General."

Arnold prepared to leave, then had a second thought and said to his Aide, "I'll be along." Arnold then went back to Lemay and quietly said, "By the way, would it create a problem if I had Erik Nelson's group transferred out of the command?"

Lemay considered the question a few moments, then said, "No. Their job is pretty much done here. Matter of fact…we're approaching a hundred twenty hours a month operational time on our B-29s."

General Arnold paced a bit and said, "You know Senator Dickson's son was killed a few weeks ago in a B-29 training flight back home? Senate investigating committee may be appointed." Arnold paused, looked directly at Lemay and said "I…I think it's highly advisable to have Erik and his people review our training procedures back there."

Lemay scoffed and said, "That crash…we heard it was an open and shut case of pilot error!"

General Arnold shrugged his shoulders as he replied to Lemay, "Yes… but the boy had written his father the night before. Told him the B-29s were not safe airplanes! All hell could break loose up there with the politicians." General Arnold paced a few steps, meditated, then turned back to Lemay. He leaned back against a map table gestured as he continued. "I believe what we're doing out here in the Pacific will go down in history as the classic example of the doctrine of strategic bombardment! Just as Mitchell and Douhet envisioned it long ago. I'm also convinced that President Truman and the Congress will soon insist on a separation of the Air Force from the Army. I'd hate to see some politically motivated Senate investigating committee jeopardize it all at this late date. Your buddy Coltrane was cornered by the President last week, who asked for his thoughts on the separation of the two forces. Truman probably wished that he hadn't asked the question. Coltrane hit him with both barrels with facts, numbers and threat assessment. He was extremely concise and to the point. I know Truman favors the separation, but he's to fight political battles over the issue. That damned Coltrane is smart and one hell of a pilot. He really knows how to get to the root of the problem and find a workable solution."

Lemay smiled, "That's why I got you and Dalton to bring him on board back in 1939."

"Well, I've brought along some decorations for Erik and his men. I'd like to present them at one of the awards ceremonies tomorrow," Arnold said.

Lemay nodded and said, "I'll have them assemble with the 58th Bomb Wing."

General Arnold said, "Good."

An aide stuck his head in the door anxiously and said, "General, you're due at Admiral Nimitz's Headquarters in ten minutes!"

General Arnold shook hands with Lemay and said "Until this evening."

Admiral Nimitz's quarters on Guam was a seaside residence, once the home of an island plantation type. The house had a veranda overlooking the Pacific. Lemay, Arnold, Giles, Arnold's two aides and two naval officers in dress whites were all standing on the veranda, with cocktails in hand. Lowell Thomas was talking with the officers as two Philippine houseboys attend to the group.

Presently, Admiral Nimitz emerged from the interior and spoke to the group casually as he took a cocktail from a tray proffered by a houseboy. Admiral Nimitz told the group, "Joe Stilwell's coming up in a few minutes, gentlemen. Seems he was half way across the Pacific when Washington got the word about General Buckner being killed in combat. They radioed Joe...Told 'em to turn back…he was taking command of the invasion of Japan!"

General Giles said sadly, "Too bad about Buckner."

General Arnold turned to Lowell Thomas and asked, "Lowell, weren't you up there in Okinawa with the General just a couple of days ago?"

Lowell Thomas replied, "Matter of fact, I was scheduled to go out to the battlefront with him! It so happened that I was late getting off Admiral Durgin's carrier. The General went on without me."

A Naval aide offered, "He was killed by a single mortar round...the only one fired into that position I understand."

Lowell Thomas continued, "If I hadn't been late, I'd have been right there at his side!"

General Stilwell emerged out on to the veranda.

Admiral Nimitz proudly said, "Here's the General now!" as he went to greet Stilwell. "Joe, how are you?"

"You know all these fellows don't you?" General Arnold could not resist the opportunity to kid the venerable General, "Well, Joe you might as well get on your airplane and go on to the States! The war's over out here, you know!"

General Stilwell smiled and said, "You'd have a helluva time selling that bill of goods to MacArthur!"

Admiral Nimitz added, "He feels an invasion will be necessary?"

General Stilwell jokingly said, "Says our doughboys will have to march in to Tokyo right to the Imperial Palace!"

Admiral Nimitz said in a more serious tone, "What do you think, Joe?"

General Stilwell answered in a concerned tone, "I'm in complete agreement. The Japs are a fanatical bunch of bastards! They'll fight to the last man!"

Lemay gazed at Stilwell for a moment, then Lemay stated pointedly, "The only reason our doughboys will march into Tokyo is to occupy the place! If the Japanese elect to die to 'the last man,' then it will be by starvation. They sure as hell won't be able to fight 'to the last man' because they won't have anything to fight with!"

Lemay's remarks cast fire in Stilwell's eyes.

Admiral Nimitz, sensing imminent confrontation, changed the tone of the conversation. "Well…I…I uh think it's pretty certain that Truman, Churchill and Chiang are going to demand "unconditional surrender."

The Naval aide added, "The Russians aren't going to help. With the war in Europe over with, they're going to declare war on Japan themselves in order to get in on the spoils of victory." One of the house boys nodded to Nimitz, gestured toward the dining room.

CHAPTER 78

A military air transport aircraft pulled up, turning broadside as its engines were cut. The Boling Field in Washington was a good sight to Lemay as he got off that beautiful day of June 1945. A staff officer waited by a V.I.P. staff car with the appropriate bumper flags. Lemay walked down the stairs from the aircraft with his briefcase in hand, followed by Colonels Sullivan, Blanchard and Garcia. Lemay's personal aide, a young captain followed, closely. The staff officer crossed to greet the Lemay party.

The staff officer said, "General Lemay…welcome to Washington." They shook hands then went to the staff car. "We talked with Mrs. Lemay this morning, Sir. She was terribly disappointed that she and your daughter weren't going to get to see you. But…there just weren't any rooms to be had on such short notice….anywhere in the city. General...There's been some confusion."

Lemay said, "Confusion?" The staff officer said "The International Date Line. General Marshall thought you were due in yesterday."

Chagrined, Lemay said, "But I…I was scheduled for the twenty-fourth!"

The USAAF staff officer said, "I know...Marianas time or Washington time though?" The Joint Chiefs went ahead and briefed the President yesterday. General Arnold wants to make your presentation to the Joint Chiefs anyway." They entered the car and drove off.

The Joint Chief's presentation room in the Pentagon was almost full. General Lemay carefully briefed the Joint Chiefs Marshall King and Leahy. Colonels Garcia and Sullivan sat in the back along with the aide. Lemay used appropriate charts and maps to illustrate his points. General Marshall appeared tired…and drowsy. Lemay said in a strong professional manner, "Therefore, when radar weather is predicted, my command will run incendiary missions against secondary industrial cities hitting several cities at one time with smaller forces. When visible conditions are predicted, we'll run daylight precision missions against priority targets." Lemay turned from the charts and addressed the Chiefs full on. "I believe this system of multiple targets which we call 'the empire plan' will allow us to complete our target list in minimum time…and bring the Japanese to their knees…even as early as the middle of September. There just isn't any way they can hold out much longer than that."

Admiral King said, "Lemay, let me ask you, have you checked out the proficiency of the 509th Composite Group…Colonel Tibbett's outfit?" Lemay, understanding the subtle thrust of the question said "Every unit that comes into the Twenty-first Bomber Command is thoroughly checked for proficiency, Admiral. The 509th was no exception. They're flying special types of training missions."

Admiral King pondered Lemay's response momentarily, then, in a tone which indicated the session was ended said, "Thank you, General Lemay."

General Marshall, who has been nodding off to sleep, was alerted by Admiral King's voice tone.

General Marshall quickly said, "Yes...yes, thank you, General." Lemay and his party then exited. The Chiefs glanced at one another then, there being nothing further, they prepared to leave. Lemay walked out first, in a hurry to head back to the Pacific. His train of thought was not on the mistake on the briefing date and his less than excited reception but what was the next step in the destruction of Japan's will to fight.

CHAPTER 79

Lemay was of mixed emotions as he left the conference room. He felt good about the bomb damage report he had given the group. He also felt very uneasy as to how the war would be ended. His bombing had essentially reduced the enemy's capability of making war, but it had not brought about surrender. The Japanese were a tenacious and committed populace that was far from being defeated. There was little doubt that an invasion would be necessary if the as-yet unproven atomic bomb didn't convince them of the futility of continued war. The General came to the realization that he had to use his remaining bomber resources wisely so as to destroy the Japanese remaining military capability and, more importantly, their will to fight. Down deep he knew that he couldn't do it with conventional weapons. He would have to send Paul Tibbett's 509th Group to deliver the massive blows that might end the war without the massive bloodshed involved with an invasion. He was shaking his down-turned head when he heard his name called.

"General Lemay," the voice of a tall man in a poorly fitting gray business suit said. "Sir, the President would like for you to join him for supper downstairs in the flag officer mess."

This caught Lemay completely by surprise. "The President! Here? Of course, please lead the way."

As he got off the elevator and turned towards the usually crowded private dining facility for generals and admirals, he saw Bart Coltrane standing just outside the door. The two old friends shook hands and gave each other a perfunctory hug of friendship.

Bart asked, "You here to see the President too?"

Lemay nodded as he looked around to see if there were others waiting. The secret service man came out of the mess, and motioned for them to go in. Being senior, Lemay went in first with Coltrane closely behind him. They saw that there was nobody but President Truman in the room.

The President quickly got up and greeted the two generals warmly. “Gentlemen, thank you for joining me tonight. I’m sure that you’ve a lot on your schedule and don’t need the loss of time to a crusty old civilian.” He motioned them to take chairs. “I thought that this place would be appropriate to our discussions out of sight of so many others and perhaps a little nostalgic as well. It was here that I first meet you under much different circumstances. Both of you were honest and straight forward with your opinions and assessment of the global situation. Nowadays, it’s somewhat difficult to get clear and honest answers to my questions.” Truman said as he looked the two warriors in the eyes. Both generals were fixed on every word the President said. Without taking his eyes of the two men Truman pushed two coffee cups towards them and pointed to the large silver coffee pot. I’m here to get that hard-to-find advice from you tonight,” he said as he stirred his coffee and put the spoon in the saucer.

The President became serious in his tone as he continued. “Both of you’re fully aware of the Manhattan Project and the atomic bomb that we hope to develop through that project. We’re very close, as you know, to achieving that goal. You would think that it would be a simple matter. You build a bomb then you drop it. Well it’s not simple. The devastating power of this bomb and its probable death and casualties inflicted has aroused the moral concerns of many in and out of uniform.” The President got up slowly to stretch before he continued his train of thought. “Albert Einstein sent me a letter back in March introducing one of his colleagues a Dr. Szilard who had serious concerns about using the bomb on Japan. He fears that death and destruction will go far beyond the military objective. There has been considerable debate among the members of the interim committee as well. Even today I had sixty-seven of our best scientists who helped develop the bomb sign a letter wanting me to demonstrate the bomb to the Japs before we dropped one on one of their cities. I asked their spokesman which one of them would be willing to fly in the plane that did the demonstration. It seems they had second thoughts when the subject of Jap fighters was addressed,” he said in an attempt to bring some humor to a serious subject. He sat back down and sipped from his coffee cup.

"Now the time for discussion and debate is almost over, and that means that I have to make a very important decision. Before I make that decision, I would like to ask the two of you some questions and get your opinions on the matter," he said in a tone of stress and concern.

"General Lemay," said the President "what have you accomplished to date with your bombing and what do you expect to achieve in the next forty-five to sixty days? Also, do you think that your bombing will eliminate the need to invade the Japanese mainland to secure victory?"

Lemay was awe struck by the questions and the tremendous importance of his answer. He leaned back in his chair staring at the ceiling momentarily then leaned back forward on the table and looked at the President and said in soft commanding tone, "Sir, we've destroyed over forty-percent of the Japanese cities where the military equipment and supplies are generated. By the end of September, the balance will be eliminated. We'll have bombed them back to sticks and swords. They'll not have the military capability to wage full scale war. But the bitter truth is that they'll take the remaining weapons along with anything else that they can use to fight to the death once we invade. The military is currently training all of the men, women and children above twelve to shoot and defend the Emperor to the death. Children younger than twelve are being trained to carry explosives under their clothes and detonate the explosive charges in groups of Americans or under our tanks. They've been nicknamed by our intel boys as 'Sherman Carpets.' The country may be obliterated by bombings in September, but their will to fight will remain extremely strong. The Japanese are far from being a defeated people. Our only choices rest in the devastating shock that only the atomic bomb can deliver. Even that may not be enough to achieve surrender. In my opinion, the only hope for a Japanese surrender rests with the effective and decisive employment of the initial three atomic bombs that we expect delivery of soon. Of course that's subject to the Trinity Test in New Mexico. Otherwise, it will take a very bloody invasion that could cost approximately 100,000 or more U.S. casualties, and many times that number of Japanese military and civilians. Admiral Leahy estimates that at very minimum over 250,000 American soldiers would be killed as a result of an invasion of the Japanese islands."

Truman sat motionless as he thought about what he had been told by this very accomplished military leader, who was on the front line of the war. "General, there are some military and civilian experts who would say that your casualty estimate was low. Others, who are against the dropping of the bomb, tell me that the loss of innocent civilians would be over a million if we dropped the bomb. Some say that we could be fighting on Japanese soil for months or even years should we not drop the bomb and proceed with the invasion. The cost in American lives could exceed a million men before the war ended. The loss of life will be staggering regardless of either course taken. Where do we as a civilized nation draw the line? How do we justify this magnitude of Japanese and American casualties?" asked the President as he looked at Coltrane.

Coltrane felt a cold chill come over his body as he heard the question poised to him by the Commander-in-Chief. He thought for what seemed minutes as he considered his reply. He looked at the President and swallowed hard as he started he reply. "Sir, I could give you many other factors to consider not mentioned by General Lemay but they all boil down to the fact that it's your obligation and responsibility as President to end this war with whatever means that you've available. The American people expect you to take the best course of military action that concludes the war and limits the loss of American and Japanese lives. The use of the atomic bomb represents the best chance to achieve surrender without massive and unavoidable loss of life on both sides. Given the fanatical mind set of the Japanese population, and especially the military high command, even this may not bring about surrender. But at least you've done all in your power to avoid a catastrophic situation that will be certain if we must invade. I strongly recommend that you use the atomic bomb as soon as it becomes available."

"It's decisions like this that make me miss selling suits back in Independence," the President said as he weighed the opinions of these two men. He looked up at the two generals and sighed before saying, "That's pretty much what I had come up with. I'm glad that you share my views on this matter. Don't say anything to the others but I have made the decision to go with the atomic option and for the same reasons that you've advanced. First, we must see if the damned thing will work. If it does we'll use it. I can just see Joe Stalin's face when I tell him about the bomb in Potsdam. He'll be demanding that we share the design with him." He looked at Coltrane and asked, "Do you think it will work as well as Oppenheimer and Groves claim it will?"

"Sir, I don't know Dr. Oppenheimer, but I do know General Groves. If it doesn't work he'll personally detonate and that will be a bigger explosion than the bomb," Coltrane said in attempt at humor in an ominous and serious atmosphere.

Truman broke out in laughter and said, "You're right about that. He'll be absolutely impossible to be around if it's a dud." The President stood and extended his hand to the two generals and said, "I appreciate your honest input into this matter. Lemay, you get back out there and bomb the hell out of them until I can get the big bombs to you. Then drop them on the best targets that will get their attention. Perhaps we can save some lives with it." Then the President left the room in his customary brisk walk.

Coltrane looked at Lemay and said, "I can't believe that we just had this conversation."

"It does stagger the imagination and puts a lot of pressure on me to end this war before Old Vinegar Joe has to come ashore," Lemay said in a subdued tone as he gently slapped Coltrane on the shoulder as they left.

The staff car bearing the Lemay party arrived beside the military air transport aircraft at Boling Field, Washington. Lemay and the others got out. Lemay shook hands with the USAAF airfield duty officer, prepared to board the aircraft…the pilot already beginning to start the engines. The Lemay party boarded the aircraft. The passenger platform was pulled away. The aircraft began moving out. The Lemay group settled in.

Colonel Garcia offered his opinion to Lemay. "I believe the Joint Chiefs are still convinced the invasion of the mainland is the only way to victory, General."

Lemay answered, "Yes, looks like they're misreading the intelligence data, alright."

Colonel Blanchard said, "Might have been different if the President had been there. Truman is on our side."

Lemay nodded and retorted, “Well, I spoke to him off the record downstairs and I know where he stands on the matter.”

CHAPTER 80

On August 6, 1945 – three lone B-29s from the 393rd Bombardment Squadron of the 509th Composite Bomb Group took off from Tinian, headed towards Hiroshima. The *Necessary Evil* was along to be a photographic aircraft for this special mission. Flying in the flight of three was *The Great Artiste* which carried a group of scientific observers who were going to measure the effects of the new weapon to be delivered that morning on the Japanese city of Hiroshima. A little after 8:00 in the morning Colonel Paul A. Tibbets, the air mission commander, and the pilot in command of the *Enola Gay,* told the bombardier, Major Thomas Ferebee to release, "The Special Weapon" or "The Gadget" as it had become known. Minutes later, the equivalent of twenty thousand tons of TNT was released by one bomb. A second mission piloted by Major Charles W. Sweeney was sent to drop another Gadget. This device was dropped from *Boch's Car* on the 9th of August, totally destroying Nagasaki. The devastation was so extensive the Emperor of Japan directed his government to surrender, without condition. **World War Two was over.**

CHAPTER 81

General Stilwell peered out the transport window intently. He looked over the vast devastation of the once mighty industrial city. Stilwell turned from the window, pondering the scene below. Yokohama Airport was alive with foreign correspondents and radio newscasters. Many newsmen were on hand for this monumental occasion. Some with newsreel cameras, hand held and on tripods, atop a specially constructed media stand. The stand was located a long distance from the airplane arrival position. One of the radio broadcasters with microphone in hand was telling people around the world listening, "And…we continue our live broadcast form the Yokohama Airport here where military commanders from all over the Pacific continue arriving to attend the formal signing of the peace treaty. The ceremony is scheduled to take place on board the U.S.S. Missouri, now lying at anchor, in Tokyo Bay itself!"

One of the camera crew directors on the stand above the broadcaster yelled out, "There's General Lemay!"

Lemay departed from his four engine transport, followed only by his aide. They crossed to a waiting vehicle, a rickety Japanese auto, got in and drove off.

Describing the arrival of Lemay, the broadcaster said, "Just walking down the stairs from his plane now, ladies and gentlemen, is Major General Curtis Emerson Lemay…old "Iron Ass" himself! Lemay's relentless B-29 foray against the Japanese home islands was the overwhelming force that finally brought the Japs to their knees, without the long-planned surface invasion of the Japanese homeland itself…an invasion that some say would surely have cost the lives of four to five million Allied troops!" Stilwell departed from his airplane. "The broadcaster continued, "There's Vinegar Joe! It's 'Vinegar' Joe Stilwell. General Stilwell was to command the invasion of Japan, an invasion that will thankfully never be."

Lemay's car pulled up to the Yokohama jetty on September 1945, where a Navy barge was waiting to take Lemay and his aide out to the Missouri. Lemay and the aide got out of the car and crossed toward the jetty. Suddenl,y Lemay stopped before boarding the barge, ostensibly gazing at the fleet anchored in the bay itself. "That's impressive, Captain," Lemay said to his aide. "Even if it is Navy…" Lemay's features were set darkly, gazed at the fleet as he walked a few steps away from the jetty.

The aide, sensing Lemay's reluctance to board the barge, attempted to soothe the situation. "You'll only have to be on board for an hour or so, General," the aide said reassuringly.

"Dammit!" Lemay exclaimed. "It's still a BATTLESHIP, Captain!" Presently, Lemay braced himself and they entered the barge which got under way immediately. Lemay went to be seated down below and found Bart Coltrane, Colonel Wild Bill Donovan and Sir Hugh Dalton also on board. "What a pleasant surprise," Lemay said as he extended his hand to the three gentlemen. "To what do I owe the honor to have Bart Coltrane and the world's top spies on my barge?"

Bart went closer to Lemay and said "Curt, of course we're here for the big surrender, but I wanted to personally tell you of my decision to get out of active duty and go on the ready reserves list."

Lemay was stunned, but kept his composure. Coltrane continued, "I had a personal talk a couple of weeks ago with the President. He told me that he would agree to a separate Air Force. It may take a year or two to go through the political wars, but it will happen. With that task being *fait accompli*, I've accomplished the most critical part of the objectives that you and Hap gave me. Now, I plan to become a civilian and join my wife in the development of an international air freight company. It's something that she and I can do together. Granted, we don't need the money, but this is a labor of love. We can have fun building something together. I really do love her, Curt."

Bart started to continue when Donavan interrupted, "Curt, it's not like he's totally out of the picture. Truman has me developing a more modern and extensive intelligence operation out of the existing OSS. He doesn't want the U.S. to ever be attacked without warning. Bart and his lovely bride have agreed to accept a lucrative contract with our group and with Dalton's spooks to fly our personnel and cargo under strict secrecy. Truman personally gave this his blessing. It's an important piece of our country's future clandestine intelligence gathering program."

Bart then continued, "I'll always be available to help you and the Army Air Force but I'll be in a business suit instead."

Lemay sat down without comment. He carefully thought about what he had just been told. Then he smiled and said, "That ragtag air freight operation in India that you set up was the beginning of your operation, wasn't it?"

"Yes, Sir. It's now owned and operated by Acacia Air Freight, Limited of London. "

Lemay slapped his knees with both hands as he got up smiling. "I'm proud of what you've done for me, our country and strategic bombardment. You've done more than your share. Now, you're going to continue your service to our great country from a little different approach. Congratulations, you and Annabel will do fine. I wish you two all the luck in the venture. I especially appreciate the job that you'll be doing for these two renegade spies. They deserve a good man like you."

Lemay had just finished as the barge bumped against the USS Missouri. The group climbed the stairway to the main deck and the surrender ceremony. The Japanese delegation formally signed the surrender documents. Hundreds of military personnel, soldiers and sailors witnessed the event from various vantage points. The USS Missouri band played "STARS AND STRIPES FOREVER."

Lemay stood along with Coltrane and Donavan and Dalton amidst the American delegation watching the ceremony. When the signing was completed, the distant roar of B-29 engines is heard, attracting everyone's attention. Lemay's aide glanced at the General, who was grinning from ear to ear. Hundreds of B-29s flew overhead in salute. Lemay had his eyes fixed on the mass of B-29s overhead. He thought to himself, "This makes all the headaches worth it! I hope these battleship lovers understand they're watching the beginning of America's first line of defense."

Two days later, General Stilwell's four-engine transport pulled in to park at Lemay's headquarters on Guam. General Stilwell gazed out the window as the aircraft maneuvered to its parking position. Lemay stood at his desk putting personal papers in a briefcase. Kissner entered, opened the door, peered in…astonished, he said, "Its General Stilwell, Sir!"

Surprised, Lemay said "Stilwell! You've to be kidding?" Colonel Kissner opened the door wider and General Stilwell strode into the room, crossed to shake hands with Lemay. Lemay said with respect, "General Stilwell." The General simply shook hands, still not speaking.

Lemay was disconcerted and gestured to the briefcase, "I…I was just getting a few things together. Rosie and I are flying a B-29 back to Washington...Non-stop."

"Yeah, I heard," Stilwell said grinning. "Still bucking for good press!"

Lemay nodded, smiled and indicated a chair and sat himself down as General Stilwell settled himself into a chair.

Stilwell got to the point. "Lemay…I saw Yokohama. Spent some time there in my youth…remember what it was like. It's been leveled you know… the entire industrial area…all of it. Your B-29s, they did that."

Lemay said cautiously, "We hit it once or twice alright."

General Stilwell was beginning to grin, "I made a special trip up here on my way home...made it just to tell you something. I was too damned myopic to understand what you were trying to tell me out there in the Changtu Valley last year…and later here on Guam. Lemay, I've been wrong about strategic bombardment! I was wrong about the whole concept Billy Mitchell had laid out years ago."

Lemay was moved by Stilwell's candor. "Well, you weren't traveling in the military minority, General."

General Stilwell responded quietly, "I know. You people had a helluva rough road to hoe in getting across the concepts you knew would work in this man's war! But…you did. And I guess that's what important…important to the whole damned free world as a matter of fact!" As he searched his tunic pockets, he continued, "I had dinner with some of your big-wigs up there in Tokyo. General Spaatz told us he'd sent a communiqué to Norstad after he had inspected your operation out here. I copied it down in long hand. Ah…here it's."

Stilwell began to read from the crudely scrawled note, "Lemay's Baker Two Nine operation, the best organized and most technically and tactically proficient military organization that the world has seen to date." Stilwell gazed at Lemay for a moment, then said, "Guess that just about says it all. Then Stilwell rose, a resigned weariness crept into his tone, ""I'm going home. I failed in China, you know. Couldn't get along with that Chink son-of-a-bitch out there! The surface invasion I might have commanded against the Japanese home land..well…your B-29s took care of that! The show's all over for me, Lemay, but…I have a feeling it's just beginning for you airplane folks, he said and extended his hand. "I couldn't be more sincere when I wish you the best of luck, son." Stilwell simply turned and exited, leaving Lemay gazing after him totally speechless.

CHAPTER 82

Monday, December 3, 1945 was an unusually beautiful sunny day in London. Bart Coltrane was at the pilot's controls of a new Douglas DC-4 going through the pre takeoff checklist with his co-pilot. Annabel Beddows Coltrane was strapped into the jump seat just behind the two pilots. She was smiling from ear to ear and had trouble keeping her excitement from being too obvious. After all, she was a Duchess. Today this Duchess was dressed in a baggy flight suit with several grease stains visible.

Coltrane looked down the Acacia Air Freight ramp at Heathrow airport outside London. He could see the five other DC-4s and fourteen Douglas DC-3s lined up on the ramp going through the takeoff checks. Today was the day Acacia Air Freight would deploy its first aircraft to its new operating bases. The DC-4s were bound to their new homes in Gibraltar, Kinshasa, Shanghai, Hong Kong, Bangkok and Jessove, India. The DC-3s were bound for the same destinations with the addition of Manila and Genoa, Italy. As agreed, two days after the Japanese surrendered, Acacia exercised its option and purchased the operation in India. The entire Acacia operation, including the old JU52s and DC-2 aircraft,had been moved to the new and recently modernized operating base at Jessore, India. The dream was coming true for Annabel and Bart.

Bart looked out of the cockpit window at Royston who had driven up the flight line verifying that the aircraft were ready to depart on their individual flight plans to various destinations. Royston looked up at Bart with a broad smile and gave him a thumbs up and a traditional salute Bart returned the salute and closed the side window. He depressed the transmit button on the control yoke and said, "Heathrow Tower, Acacia Air Freight, a flight of twenty aircraft is ready for takeoff."

"Roger, Acacia Air, you're cleared to taxi to Runway 27 for immediate takeoff!

Bart took his right hand off the four throttles and reached back and grabbed Annabel's leg and gave it a gentle loving squeeze before he reached back up and advanced the throttles to takeoff power. Bart smiled, as he realized that "The Coltranes" were starting to live their dream on Heathrow Runway 27.

For sales, editorial information, subsidiary rights information
or a catalog, please write or phone or e-mail
iPicturebooks
1230 Park Avenue, 9a
New York, NY 10128, US
Sales: 1-800-68-BRICK
Tel: 212-427-7139
www.BrickTowerPress.com
email: bricktower@aol.com.

For sales in the UK and Europe please contact our distributor,
Gazelle Book Services
Falcon House, Queens Square
Lancaster, LA1 1RN, UK
Tel: (01524) 68765 Fax: (01524) 63232
email: gazelle4go@aol.com.